The Prisoners of Niagara

or

Errors of Education

A New Novel Founded on Fact

Jesse L. Holman

Edited and with an Introduction by
Abigail Davis

FIRESIDE FICTION
2006

FIRESIDE FICTION
AN IMPRINT OF HERITAGE BOOKS, INC.

Books, CDs, and more—Worldwide

For our listing of thousands of titles see our website
at
www.HeritageBooks.com

Published 2006 by
HERITAGE BOOKS, INC.
Publishing Division
65 East Main Street
Westminster, Maryland 21157-5026

Other Books by the Author:

Hanging Katherine Garrett:
A Novel Based on the 1737 Trial of a Pequot Woman

International Standard Book Number: 978-0-7884-4068-3

Jesse Lynch Holman

Evermont

31 Whitford – farmer who saves him

32 Wilson – his eldest son
              + Evermont's enemy
   Pen   his dog
   Thomas Eagleton – merchant
                        of Baltimore

35 Zerelda his daughter
   Major Halyard – says he'll
              be Evermont's father

36 Emerine Halyard's daughter

40 Mrs Willford – he boards w/ her
       when he goes to Richmond
              our school

41 Armilda – child of Willford "

44 has sex w/ her

45 Emerald L

48 William Etherford – to go to prison
       Susan "

50 Amarette

74 Lafayette! He commandeers
              his horse!

80 Susan makes out

128 – William – the illicit
           offspring of Valindor
              + Miss Bradford
                 (Willford)

131 Carmont – Evermont saves
           from Indians

134 Alea of Bradford – disguise
           as Indian

TABLE OF CONTENTS

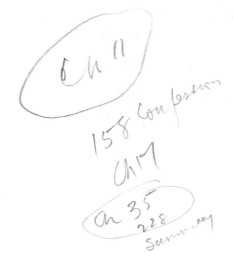

137 nape scene
153 9 days w/ no food!
157 Finally washes face!

iii

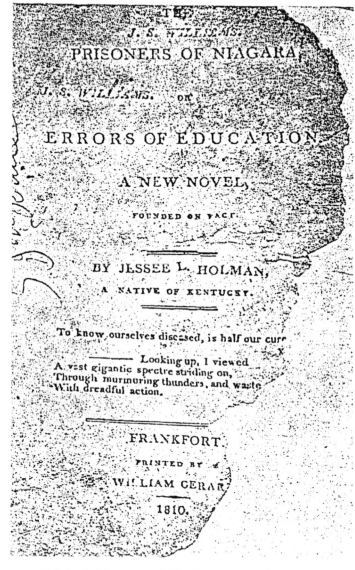

Original title page of *The Prisoners of Niagara*

Reprinted from *The Holmans of Veraestau* by Israel Blake
(Oxford: Mississippi Valley Press, 1943).

Jesse L. Holman home about 1890

Reprinted from *The Holmans of Veraestau* by Israel Blake (Oxford: Mississippi Valley Press, 1943).

Veraestau, the Indiana homestead of the Holman family, in 1943

Reprinted from *The Holmans of Veraestau* by Israel Blake (Oxford: Mississippi Valley Press, 1943).

INTRODUCTION

The Prisoners of Niagara, Or, Errors of Education, Jesse L.
Holman's only novel, was published in 1810 when Holman (1784-
1842) was twenty-six years old.[1] It is unknown how many copies
were printed in the first and only run. The book was reported to
have "gained a wide circulation for those days" although what
constituted a wide circulation in frontier Kentucky can only be
surmised.[2] I have been able to locate only two extant copies, one
in the Howard-Tilton Memorial Library, Tulane University, and
the other in the Alderman Library, University of Virginia.
Reference has been made to a third original located in the Bittle
Memorial Library, Roanoke College, but I have been unable to
confirm its existence. One copy is described as 357 pages, size 4
X 6 ½ inches, "and bound in worn boards and leather. It looks
more like a Bible than a novel."[3] Apparently the book went to
press before Holman had the opportunity to proofread and
contained so many errors that the author inserted an apology to the
reader at the end. There is a 1973 limited edition (500 copies)
which is a compilation of the three originals, none of which is
complete.[4] The reason for the near-destruction of the book, at least
in part, is owing to the author's attempt, "later in life [. . .] to buy
up and destroy the entire edition." The family biography, *The
Holmans of Veraestau,* credits Holman as saying that "the morals
of the book were not suitable for the minds of young people."[5]

The Prisoners of Niagara is strikingly different from the other
works of fiction printed in America between 1799 and 1850. The
staid subtitle might encourage readers to believe that the book is a
cautionary tale but that suggestion is misleading in the extreme.
Prisoners might even be called salacious: It features sexually
active young teenagers, incest, prostitution and rape, along with

the standard fare of Indian captivity, and, almost as an afterthought to justify the sanitary subtitle, some lines about the dangers of a liberal education. Much of the plot revolves around the fact that Evermont, *Prisoners'* protagonist, does not know who his parents are. Compared to earlier novels such as *The Power of Sympathy* (1789), *Charlotte* (1794), *The Coquette* (1797), *Wieland* (1798), *Edgar Huntly* (1799) and *Female Quixotism* (1801), and later works such as *Kelroy* (1812), *Hobomok* (1824), *The Last of the Mohicans* (1826), *Hope Leslie* (1827), and most of Hawthorne, in which sexual mishaps are either assiduously avoided or committed at a terrible price, the largely carefree antics of Evermont satirize drawing-room sensibilities and Puritan morals. Indeed, Evermont bears a closer resemblance to his English counterpart, Henry Fielding's Tom Jones (1749), than to any contemporary American character. Evermont's rather earnest morality in the later part of the novel is more cute than meaningful.

Two basic structures are at work in the novel. First, it is a picaresque, "the loosest of narrative forms [that] conveniently allows a central character (or characters) to wander the margins of an emerging American landscape, to survey it in all its incipient diversity, to sound out its different constituents from the most lowly, uneducated yeoman to those of high birth and great learning [. . .]."[6] The episodic structure allows Evermont to emerge as an engaging rascal, rambling between good deeds and mishaps from which he narrowly escapes. A later example in the genre is Mark Twain's *The Adventures of Huckleberry Finn* (1844). Second, Evermont is an unreliable narrator with profoundly poor judgment when it comes to women; he never meets one he doesn't like, at least initially. "It was dark and we were alone–she was in my power–lovely and desirable in the extreme–I was but man," he confesses.[7] The reader knows his trysts will get him into trouble long before he does; when he thoughtfully explains the reason for his next ill-advised assignation, we are well ahead of him. His narrative position is an internal feature of the work and creates a structural irony that is well adapted to the picaresque form.

There can be little doubt that the novel was perceived as scandalous by some (and perhaps was quite popular with others) in early nineteenth-century Frankfort, Kentucky, where it first appeared. Holman's later embarrassment over his early foray into fiction can be partly understood in terms of his distinguished life as an Indiana Territorial Legislator, a Territorial, State and Federal Judge, and a Baptist elder and minister.[8] There are sections of the novel which, compared with incidents in Holman's life, can be interpreted as highly autobiographical.[9] From a twenty-first century perspective, Holman has no reason to apologize for his work. He is a virtuoso of plot twists and character development, and he dips into nearly every genre employed by eighteenth- and nineteenth-century novelists, as if the writing of the text was a personal challenge to see if he could utilize them all. The style is described by Blake, Holman's biographer, as alternately "sentimental," "romantic," and "Byronic," but those terms do not begin to describe the range and variety of plot construction.[10] In addition to its function as a picaresque, the book is an historical romance and a mystery; it uses the captivity tradition, the theme of seduction and abandonment, multiple disguises, forged letters, cross dressing, deathbed confessions, and even briefly features a panther (which a reader of Charles Brockden Brown's *Edgar Huntly* would immediately recognize as a plot device). Holman creates parodies of several of these generic forms, which gives the work the aspect of a well-structured comedy.

Clearly, Holman was well read in topics other than law. Blake tells us that "he wrote many short poems which were published in his lifetime" and "two lengthy poems which were legends of Indian life"; the longer poems are collected in the Holman family papers.[11] In spite of the author's choice of weighty subjects such as orphanhood, child abuse, Indian captivity, and war, the book is lighthearted and often hilarious; no permanent damage is done to anyone as a result of youthful indiscretions. The good characters are blatantly good, the evil ones clearly evil; and, in a burst of plot finesse in the final chapters, loving marriages and wealth are the rewards given to Evermont and those he cares for. If the neat wrap-up seems unrealistic, so does the whole novel. One suspects that it was meant to entertain more than instruct, and perhaps it is that aspect that became problematic for the author.

In a preface, Holman declares that the novel was intended for "public amusement" but then goes on to "justify the moral intention of the work": "What are termed *natural dispositions, intuitive principles,* or *inherent propensities* are nothing but the habits of earliest existence, which are formed by the education of the infant, from the moment its vehicles of sensation, exert their powers with the influence of external objects. [. . .] The first years of [a] child's existence, are infinitely more important for the formation of its principles that [*sic*] any other period of its education; and to display the force of this theory [. . .] was the principle design of the following pages."[12] This is a description of John Locke's *tabula rasa*: the unformed mind before it receives the impressions gained from experience. Lockean psychological theory remained dominant throughout the eighteenth and well into the nineteenth centuries. It is a lofty philosophy to be sure but difficult to apply in a comprehensible manner to the plot of the story. Given Holman's Lockean assertion, it seems that poor Evermont, a white hostage who is stolen *from* Indians at the age of eighteen months and then endures a hellish first five years with a brutal foster family, should have been ruined. In fact, nothing could be further from the truth. Evermont is kind, intellectually curious, and open-minded—qualities that represent the antithesis of his early influences. This contradiction leads one to conclude that the preface was an afterthought, an attempt to raise the novel to a morally instructive level that the text itself could not support.

The author's early life as a child on the frontier undoubtedly made him familiar with the wilderness which he describes so vividly in his novel. Jesse Lynch Holman was one of fourteen children, the son of Henry Holman, a Virginian who came to Kentucky in 1776. The family had first-hand experience of Indian warfare. Henry is said to have been killed by Indians during a siege at his homestead in 1789 when Jesse was five years old. Henry's wife and children had been sequestered in a blockhouse while Henry, the father, attempted to run supplies.[13] At another time, Jesse's cousin, George Holman, was an Indian captive who was taken as a child and not returned until he was grown.[14] He unwillingly returned to his white family and was so anxious to return to the Indians that a constant watch had to be kept over him.[15] In still another anecdote, Jesse and his brother, Henry, were surrounded by Indians in the fort at Bullitt's Lick. Bardstown, fifty miles away, was the nearest station to which they could appeal for help. Henry snuck out at night past the Indians, got to Bardstown, found it similarly surrounded, and once again slipped through Indian lines only to be told by the frontiersmen that they could not spare any riflemen. Henry turned around, repeated his covert maneuvers on the trip home, and arrived back at the fort in a little more than two days from the time he started, having covered one hundred miles on foot through hostile territory.[16] It is not surprising that having grown up during a violent period in the Kentucky River Valley, and having had personal experience with Indian captivity, that Holman would use captivity and Indian raids as plot devices numerous times in his novel.

In spite of the family hardship caused by his father's death, Holman managed to get an education, studying law under Henry Clay in Lexington around 1800. Admitted to the Kentucky bar on September 2, 1805, Holman practiced at New Castle, Port William (now Carrollton) and later at Frankfort. He married Elizabeth Masterson, daughter of Judge Richard M. Masterson, in 1810.[17] *The Prisoners of Niagara* was published the same year.

One can only imagine the motives that compelled the young barrister and husband to bring forth a novel that reads in places like Puritan pornography, and to go so far as to name one of his daughters Emerine, after the heroine.[18] It is unknown when the book became an embarrassment and Holman undertook to destroy the entire edition. It is interesting to speculate how and why his perspective on the moral suitability of his subject changed between the age of approximately thirty and "later"; specifically, one wonders how his character Evermont could have metamorphosed in Holman's judgment from a randy, good-hearted, and thoroughly likable hero into a character whose exploits were unfit for consumption by "young people." That young people would have been openly reading a novel of this type is somewhat unlikely; if they did, it would have been acquired as contraband and concealed in a fashion similar to that in which teenagers conceal internet pornography sites from parents today. One possible explanation is that *Prisoners* was wildly popular among adults (and also widely circulated, as Blake suggests) and consequently difficult to keep out of immature hands. Perhaps Evermont was the Tom Jones or Holden Caulfield of his day and the mature, dignified Holman felt compelled to kill his darling. It is difficult to imagine that he would have felt the need to take such a drastic step if no one was reading the book.

The Holmans relocated to Indiana in 1811 and began building Veraestau. In a move that is duplicated in the novel, Holman freed the family slaves: "They took Elizabeth's slaves with them but when they arrived at the new home site the slaves were freed in accordance with Holman's conviction that the somewhat ambiguous phraseology of the Ordinance of 1787 did actually prohibit slavery already in existence: a conviction on which, as judge, Holman later helped to pass conclusive judgment from the bench, in the case of Col. Hyacinth Lasselle's mulatto wench, Polly."[19] In the final pages of *Prisoners,* when Evermont is married to his childhood love, adoptive sister, and newly-discovered cousin Zerelda, and the happy couple have acquired two enormous inheritances, he tells us, "I assembled all the salves of the Engleton and Valindon estates, and with the smiling approbation of Zerelda, declared that the *Bill of Rights,* drawn up by the immortal Jefferson, and sanctioned by the united wisdom of congress, was a sacred truth, that *all men were born free* [. . .]."[20] Evermont goes one step further and ensures the livelihood of all whom he frees by distributing "livings" in money and small farms and offering "a reasonable hire" for those who wished to continue serving at the mansion. It is clear that Holman drew upon autobiographical experience to forge his plot but Evermont's abolitionist stance and humanistic behavior did not precisely reflect the views of the older Holman, who "felt that colonization [in Africa] was the only salvation for blacks" and that they "could never become a real part of American civilization" because they are innately inferior.[21] In a handwritten, undated manuscript entitled "The Negro Question," which is now in the Wagenhals Collection,[22] Holman wrote that "a population so shiftless & consequently so illiterate and immoral will have a pernicious effect upon the whole community. . . . Wherever man degrades his own brother, the pestilential broth of his degradation will infuse its poison through his own character & enjoyments. . . . We are therefore vitally interested in . . . removing the degraded so far that we shall be less affected by their degradation."[23] In 1829, Holman was an active member of the American Colonization Society, a group which helped blacks resettle in Africa.[24] Between the writing of *Prisoners* between 1805-1810 and the idealistic good will expressed therein, and Holman's later (undated) treatise on "The Negro Question," the author had clearly modified his views on the subject. Holman remained in favor of emancipation as a first step; removal of blacks from America was the second phase. Perhaps Holman's fictional character Evermont more closely resembled the young, unmarried Holman, both in his generosity of spirit and his proclivity for sexual shenanigans, than the mature judge wanted to recall, at least in print. One wonders if Evermont's abolitionist position got the book into trouble, and if Holman's later political views were behind its retraction.

The Prisoners of Niagara opens in the later years of the Revolutionary War. Evermont, then twenty-one years of age, wakes up with amnesia in a dark dungeon surrounded by dead and dying men. Slowly his memory returns as he recognizes some of his fellow soldiers and concludes that they are prisoners of the British in Fort Niagara (now in New York State). It is a powerful opening scene. Conditions in the prison are hideous; the wounded are left without medical attention on filthy straw soaked with the blood of others. The stench is unbearable. At midnight, into this vividly described hellhole comes a heavily veiled woman with an attendant, bringing food and wine. She dresses wounds, eventually brings a doctor, and appears to recognize Evermont although he cannot see her face; he is so grateful for the respite that he half imagines that she is an angel. The pattern continues for many nights; the mystery woman engages in some very odd behavior while Evermont feigns unconsciousness so he can watch her through squinted eyelids. She comes to him, touches his face, his hands, his chest, and finally kisses his lips. He can't open his eyes but is in a state of excitement that he fears will end in a heart attack because of his weakened condition: "I could not believe my exhausted frame possessed such a flow of excitability, as was stimulated into action by this unknown hand."[25] This candidly described physical contact, and the many episodes which occur throughout to drive the plot, make *Prisoners* a parody of the seduction narrative. In other contemporaneous works, lovers don't actually *kiss* unless they are on the path to perdition, and even then the reader does not see it happen—all indiscretions are accomplished off stage, as it were. Evermont's flaw is that he is a fool for women—"I would have given half my existence for a single glance at her face and person," he says, careless of the fact that he might be executed at any moment—and that consistent weakness makes him a highly entertaining, if unreliable, narrator.[26]

Evermont is the male hero of a coming-of-age story while many protagonists of the early novels now known to historians and increasingly read as classroom texts are young women. As a young man, Evermont enjoys freedom of action that women, young or older, can only long for. The aging Dorcasina in *Female Quixotism* acts as her own decision-maker and makes a pathetic fool of herself. In *Charlotte Temple,* Charlotte dies a terrible death as the price for her elopement and affair. Multiple deaths result from the birth of an illegitimate child in *The Power of Sympathy. The Coquette's* Eliza Wharton, while refusing to marry a bore, has an affair with a clever cad. She becomes pregnant, the affair is discovered, and Eliza, exiling herself from her family, dies a lonely death. The male characters in these novels are rarely three-dimensional and range from the stereotypical sexual philanderer and fortune-hunter to the brooding presence of Kelroy. In contrast, Evermont cheerfully carries on without consequences for his energetic sexuality for much of the novel; his only punishment is an occasionally pained conscience. Even more surprising, the double standard does not apply in *The Prisoners of Niagara*. Nasty Armilda and depraved Emerald both survive, undamaged (and unchanged) by their indiscretions. Wicked Mrs. Willford is morally redeemed, after a fashion, at the end of the tale. Evermont and his supporting cast of characters do not have parallels in the novels of the early republic.

Back in prison at Fort Niagara, the veiled woman is eventually forbidden to visit. During her last appearance, she asks Evermont to write for her the story of his life. She produces pen and paper; the doctor will smuggle out the finished document. Chapter III begins a flashback in the form of Evermont's memoir that continues for most of the remainder of the novel, bringing the story full circle.

The "errors of education" to which Holman unconvincingly refers are introduced in the novel when Evermont is thirteen. At age five he had been rescued from his dismal foster home by Major Haylard and made part of a wealthy, enlightened family. He was educated by a country tutor in the neighborhood of Haylard Village. "My progress," he declares, "had been so extremely rapid in every branch of learning I had undertaken, that my father resolved I should be a master of a liberal education, and sent me to the academy at Richmond, at the age of thirteen."[27] Evermont had not lived away from home before and did not want to leave. Arriving in Richmond as naive and emotionally vulnerable as any character ever created, he boards with Mrs. Willford, a widow of forty, and her eleven-year-old daughter, Armilda. The only literary counterpart for Mrs. Willford in early American literature is the unscrupulous matriarch Mrs. Hammond in Rebecca Rush's *Kelroy* (1812) who seems harmless by comparison. Evermont is soon flattered and petted by Willford, who "possessed the true bewitching smile of a sycophant."[28] She believes Evermont to be the heir to a large fortune and wants him to marry Armilda. Evermont is taught to dance and indulges "in a profuse round of balls, assemblies, and amusement." He falls in with an "immoral and licentious" crowd, and being of an "ardent" disposition, becomes the darling of Richmond,[29] ready to "lead a dissipated life of fashionable coquetry and intemperance."[30]

Another parody that weaves through the novel is that of the "fashionable life" and the type of woman who pursues it.[31] In Willford, Holman has created a chic monster, so ruthless in her self-promotion and evil machinations that she becomes almost a stick figure, an unbelievable embodiment of moral decay who is too awful to be quite taken seriously. Armilda, encouraged by her mother, attaches herself to Evermont and soon their "innocent" caresses evolve into embraces. A sexual liaison ensues. "My expenses became excessive," Evermont moans, "and, unwilling that my father should become acquainted with my extravagance, had recourse to gambling, to supply the deficiencies of his liberal donations."[32] Evermont, analyzing Major Hayland's generosity from the perspective of a twenty-one-year-old prisoner of war, deemed his father's benevolence an "error of education," presumably because it allowed him to run amok. If Evermont's story ended badly, the reader could reasonably make the moral connection between too much freedom and money, and self-destruction. However, Evermont prevails nicely throughout the novel, becoming a liberal, generous man like his father; he suffers no permanent consequences for his teenage party ethic although he might have worn out a dozen guardian angels in the process. The happy conclusion does not support the author's insisted-upon theme of stern morality.

Evermont flees Richmond, having been led to believe by Willford that she is his biological mother and that he has committed incest with Armilda. His adoptive family has disowned him, thanks to a series of letters forged by Willford (in another parallel to Mrs. Hammond, who loved to write other people's correspondence) containing slanderous information about his character. He procures a "hunting dress, such as is worn by back wood peasants," and heads for the frontiers of Virginia to kill some Indians and let off a little steam.[33] His old home of Haylard Village is on the way and in a series of dizzying plot twists, he assumes the name of Holbert and meets Zerelda, who doesn't recognize him, and who spends a lot of time sighing about her lost Evermont and reciting poetry. Predictably, she falls in love with Holbert who seems a lot *like* Evermont, and she prays that when Evermont returns that "he may be the image of Holbert."[34] True to the form of the picaresque, Evermont decides to leave.

Wilderness bound once again, this time he assumes "Indian dress and paint," the new name of Bridford, and joins with fifteen other men to pursue Indians who have been raiding some back settlements of Pennsylvania.[35] In a hilarious satire of Indian captivity, Evermont/Bridford saves Zerelda (who doesn't recognize him as either Holbert *or* Bridford) from being sold by her captors to a lecherous British Canadian.[36] This is the third incarnation of Evermont Zerelda has fallen in love with, and even though he is much changed and wearing Natty Bumpo-like attire, it strikes the readers as comically impossible that she continues to fail to know him. Evermont rescues her and they experience six days of starving together in increasingly intimate but chaste fashion in the woods. Finally, Zerelda is at death's door, and in a fit of desperation, Evermont runs through the woods in search of wild fruit. Our woodsman hero gets *lost* but in the process discovers water–the Allegheny River–and finally finds his way back to the campsite. He picks Zerelda up in his arms and runs with her to the river, arriving in time, of course, to save her life, but not in time to make a full confession about his identity; she faints dead away the moment he speaks. In a manna-from-heaven spoof, Evermont, at the point of starvation, looks up and sees clusters of grapes hanging above his head. The next moment a wild turkey, possibly the most elusive of all forest creatures, nearly flies into his arms.[37] These few examples of the many generic forms employed by the author, and the intricately plotted story laced with parody and satire, are evidence of a gifted writer at work.

Although *The Prisoners of Niagara* failed to meet the author's later expectations, that does not reduce its importance for readers today. It is unique for the period because of its candor, and it is a skillfully executed, picaresque romp that bridges many genres with ease. If there is one criticism to be made, it would be the author's florid prose style which is often overdone. One example from the first edition will suffice: Zerelda effuses, "Departed hope awakened into living raptures; the morning sun of joy bursted over the dark horison [*sic*] of woe; my heart bounded from the deadly grasp of benumbing sorrow, to the happy freedom of enlivening extacy [*sic*]; my bosom hurled the fierce tyrant despair from his throne, and swelled into a wide, unconquerable disire [*sic*] for illimitiable [*sic*] enjoyment; my soul, shaking off the shackles of a dreadful destiny, rose from beneath the intolerable weight of calamity, caught on fire by the enkindling spirit of Evermont's attachment, and unfolding the pinions of affection, winged from misery to elysium."[38] Given the many strengths of this novel, perhaps a bit of purple prose deserves only a small objection.

NOTES

1 R. E. Banta, *Indiana Authors and their Books* (Crawfordsville: Wabash College P, 1949) 151. Holman's date of birth is given by Banta as 1784; *Prisoners* appeared in 1810 which made Holman twenty-six years of age at the time of publication. However, Israel George Blake in *The Holmans of Veraestau* states that Holman wrote the book before his twenty-first birthday (5). One assumes that Holman waited five years to bring the book to print and that these ages are not contradictory.

2 Israel George Blake, *The Holmans of Veraestau* (Oxford: Mississippi Valley P, 1943) 5.

3 Blake 5.

4 Will Friday, ed. *The Prisoners of Niagara, or, Errors of Education,* by Jesse L. Holman (Berea, KY: Kentucke Imprints, 1973).

5 Banta 151.

6 Cathy N. Davidson, *Revolution and the Word: The Rise of the Novel in America* (New York: Oxford UP, 1986) 152.

7 Jesse L. Holman, *The Prisoners of Niagara, or, Errors of Education* (Frankfort, 1810) 110.

8 Banta 151.

9 The autobiographical events I used as a basis for comparison were taken from the family biography of Jesse L. Holman and his son, William Steele Holman, *The Holmans of Veraestau by Israel George Blake.*

10 Blake 5-6.

11 Blake 6.

12 Holman 3-4.

13 Banta 151.

14 Banta 151. George Holman's captivity is described by Sanford Cox in his *Recollections of the Early Settlements of the Wabash Valley.*

15 Blake 3.

16 Blake 3-4.

17 Banta 151.

18 Banta 151.

19 Banta 152.

20 Holman 354.

21 Blake 29.

22 The Wagenhals Collection referred to by Blake in his Notes for *The Holmans of Veraestau* was, at the time the biography was published in 1943, owned by Holman's great-granddaughters, Miss Margaret H. Wagenhals, New York City, and Miss Mildred H. Wagenhals, Calistoga, California. The collection contains correspondence, rough drafts of speeches, official documents, briefs or court cases in which Judge Holman was interested, and other items. Blake apparently had free access to these papers while writing the biography.

23 Blake 29.
24 Blake 28.
25 Holman 26.
26 Holman 26.
27 Holman 53.
28 Holman 55.
29 Holman 55.
30 Holman 54.
31 Holman 55.
32 Holman 61.
33 Holman 117-18.
34 Holman 145.
35 Holman 172.
36 Holman 186.
37 Holman 206
38 Holman 319.

PREFACE

"The following pages were never designed for the press," is an expression too much hackneyed for a modern apology, but even if it was not, it is not applicable in fact to this little attempt at public amusement. The foundation of this story was compiled in early infancy on the basis of historic certainty, but while it was confined in the narrow pale of truth, its incidents were too much circumscribed, and its characters too obscure, to please even the imagination of the author. And after the sheets had remained unnoticed for several years, his own inclination, not *the request of his friends*, induced him to offer it to the public in its present fictitious form.

For entering first on the romantic list of Western America, I have no apology. Without patronage or solicitation, I commit the first essay of my youthful fancy to the high tribunal of public scrutiny, with the plea of *guilty* to all the crimes I have perpetrated in so doing. But if arraigned before the great Sanhedrin of hyper criticism, I shall plead to its jurisdiction. If it still persists in passing sentence, I shall maintain that the decree is *coram non judice*.

To the candid reader I will justify the MORAL intention of the work by a reference to the volume of Nature, entitled "Man," under the head of *vicious principles* and *practices*. He will there find sufficient evidence to convince his mind that what are termed *natural dispositions, intuitive principles,* or *inherent propensities,* are nothing but the habits of earliest existence which are formed by the education of the infant, from the moment its vehicles of sensation exert their powers with the influence of external objects. The strong inclination, or leading features, of almost every mind are generally supposed to be the impressions of nature because

1

their origin is not so obvious as the various progress of regular
improvement, but upon a critical examination they will be found
to be the legitimate offspring of cradle education. If this theory is
correct, it will exhibit the necessity of a circumspect attention to
the first notices of every infant mind, and convince the parent that
the first years of his child's existence are infinitely more
important for the formation of its principles than any other period
of its education. To display this force of theory, when reduced
into practice, was the principal design of the following pages. In
defense of the manner in which this design is executed, I have
nothing to offer even to the candid. A youth whose unguided,
unguarded imagination was filled with the first flow of
spontaneous images; whose unpracticed bosom was throbbing
with the uncorrected impulses of visionary speculations; whose
mind was governed by un-education, wild as his own will and
romantic and exuberant as the western wilderness in which he was
born in penury and educated in orphanage, could not be expected
to confine the untutored ardor of his inclination with the dull rules
of formal composition, to bend the current of his youth-warm
enthusiasm within the narrow compass of practical philosophy, or
limit the excursions of his inexperienced fancy to the fertile fields
of probability or even to the more extensive regions of possibility.
And if I have transgressed, it is in those particulars, and confiding
in the indulgence of every warm imagination, I trust this little
story to the public "with all its imperfections on its head."

In this attempt I would fain awaken the slumbering genius of
the West to an exertion of its untried powers, either in the
philosophical fields of instruction, or in the flowery gardens of
amusement. To aid this feeble effort, to give a tedious hour "the
fleeting wings of airy transport," I invoke the Western spirit of
TASTE and GENIUS, and the unwooed Muses of our poetic
clime:

Ye boundless fields of rich luxuriant bloom,
Ye towering hills, broad waves, and gloom-hung rocks,
___Give Spirit to my theme.

THE PRISONERS OF NIAGARA

Ye naiads who have fled Thessalia's streams,
To lave beneath Ohio's purer fount;
And ye wing-footed Nymphs, and Dryad throng,
Who float on Zephyrs o'er the floral hills,
Strew o'er my page, the flow'ry wreaths you've cull'd
Along Kentucky's wildly-winding shores.

CHAPTER I

I awoke from a dream of horror! My former existence
resembled a half-remembered vision, floating on the fumes of a
disordered imagination. I had no recollection of where I was, or
by what means I had been conducted thither. I raised my head
from a pillow of straw and endeavored to acquire some idea of my
situation, but so thick was the veil of darkness that no object was
discernable. I extended my arm to ascertain whether I was in the
open air or in a habitation. My hand fell on a face, cold as the icy
features of death, and was in an instant withdrawn. A shivering
sensation flitted through my nerves at the idea of being in
company with the silent corpse of fellow being!

I sprang upright on my bed, which was composed of cold
damp earth, and was proceeding to call for a light when a long
quivering groan arrested my purpose, and suggest an idea that I
was on the field of battle! Startled at this intimation, I paused. A
second groan, more deep and languid, vibrated on my ear! I threw
my eyes around but derived not a glimmer of information. My
enquiring ear impatiently waited for another sound to direct me to
the wretched sufferer, but I could perceive nothing but a hard
drawn breathing that gave notice of a person laboring with the
latest agonies of time! I attempted to grope my way to his
assistance, but while feeling for the ground, I unfortunately placed
my hand upon the wound of a person who was asleep. A
tremulous groan succeeded which startled me back to my former
position for fear of inflicting a further pang.

While endeavoring to regain my bed, I perceived a faint gleam
of light that appeared to issue through a crevice in a wall. Never
before did the beams of morning inspire such heartfelt rapture–it
came like hope to the desperate with ineffable joy on its wings. I

arose on my feet to fly to the window from whence it proceeded, but the first inclination of my body threw me against a person who was also in a rising position. We were both overset by the encounter, and fell upon the bodies of our miserable fellow sufferers! "Oh God! Oh God!" shrieked a voice beneath me with a tone of anguish that penetrated through my soul! I arose with the utmost caution, hoping to allay the pain I had innocently occasioned.

The clattering of arms arrested my attention. The grating clangor of bars and locks resounded. A door opened which gave me a partial view of this mansion of death. It was a narrow dungeon which at any moment could have aroused a sensation of horror, but how much more horrible was it at this awful period, when the floor was covered with mangled, bleeding, and dying men, some of whom were almost swimming in blood! I heaved an inward groan at the ghastly sight, "Where death with frowning grin triumphant smil'd." A stern officer in British uniform entered with a guard. He cast an eye of unconcern on the dreadful spectacle before him, and ordered all who were able to walk to follow the guard while the dead bodies were removed from the prison.

When escorted by the guard into the open air, I beheld myself in the midst of Fort Niagara, a prisoner in the British garrison. I now, for the first time, perceived a severe bruise on my left temple, which I concluded had been the effect of a blow received on the field of battle, and which had occasioned my late insensibility of at least twelve hours. But, notwithstanding my wound, the light breezes of morning shed a delicious feeling over my awakening senses. Every aspiration teemed with the principle of life, every breath appeared to create a new soul in my bosom, which "Wak'd my heart in orisons to heaven." I cast around an eye of inquiring wonder, and felt as if just arisen from the dead and initiated into a new world. My imagination was yet bewildered, and I gazed on every object with a stupor of delight. Never had I beheld the sun shed such vivifying radiance. His beams of crystal gold illumined a thousand enchanting prospects, *major anderville*

and falling in trembling showers on the distant bosom of Ontario, lighted up the waves into an ocean of flaming silver.

But fancy was not long permitted to enjoy this pleasing delirium, for the shattered fragments of memory began to unite and lead my mind along a melancholy chain of past events. My heart freezes into a fearful shivering in a retrospect of the life I have lived. I will never dare to venture through its dreary scenes of vice and misery while rebel fancy bows to the scepter of reason.

I caught a view of Major Anderville among the prisoners. He was endeavoring to stop the blood which flowed from a wound in his arm. I was flying to his assistance when the command of the officer remanded us to our prison.

We were crowded to the number of twenty in a room which was scarcely twelve feet square, the floor of which was yet covered with blood. A little loose straw, wet and smoking with the crimson fluid of our departed brethren, was at once our only seat and bed. There was but one small window, and when the door was closed the air became stagnant and too loathsome for respiration.

The moment we entered the dungeon I flew to assist and comfort my dear, invaluable friend Major Anderville, but with his loss of blood from his wound, which had remained undressed throughout the preceding night, and with his late exertions to walk into the open air, he had exhausted his remaining vigor, and fainted on a bed of straw. I immediately bound up his arm, and procured him all the assistance which our prison afforded, but it was several hours before he again opened his eyes, and when he revived it was in the delirium of a fever.

The keeper entered with our allotted provisions, which consisted of coarse relics of moldy bread and putrid flesh, of which famishing nature could scarcely be induced to partake. Major Anderville was too weak to receive the smallest portion of it, and continued to grow worse every hour for the want of proper medical assistance.

But he was not the only sufferer in our prison. Disease and death were the inevitable consequences of the inhuman treatment we received. Our company sickened with putrid diseases which so contaminated our atmosphere that death was in every pulse of air we breathed.

During three days we had not received the slightest attention except a supply of unwholesome food; our situation became intolerable. The damp fumes of our dungeon were poisoned into a nauseous stench which appeared as if it would suffocate life at every respiration. We sank rapidly beneath its pestiferous influence, and death, whose aspect is so terrific to the pampered world, became to us a subject of animating conversation, and a welcome, desired friend. Existence was too intolerable to be borne, and "eternity," thought oft dreadful, became to us a pleasing thought. Rather than continue longer under the scourge of monster time, we were all willing, all anxious, all impatient, to venture into that "variety of untried being" which stretches in an endless chain from the grave throughout the long ages of duration. On the forth day of our confinement, eight of our number winged away from their narrow dungeon to the wide realms of eternity.

The strength of Major Anderville's constitution still bore him up against the ravage of disease, but he was now in the latest stage of mortality. He had never spoken intelligibly since the first attack of his disorder, but whether awake or asleep, the name of Emerine was continually on his lips, and in his heated paroxysms he would lament her sufferings, and reiterate denunciations of vengeance against her destroyers. His delirious expressions excited in me the most unconquerable anxiety to know the destiny of this amiable female, for whose protection I would have risked every consideration of danger and death. But I waited by his pillow until the following day, in vain expectation that reason would exert her province over his bewildered imagination, that I might learn what misfortune had befallen Emerine.

In the evening he awoke from a slumber, and his countenance appeared more composed than it had ever been since his confinement. He turned on me a look of the tenderest affection. His eyes spoke the language of his soul, and seemed to say he was about to bid his dearest friend a final adieu. He attempted to

7

speak. "Emerine," he feebly articulated. "Zerelda" died on his lips. Our eyes met in exquisite embrace; it was the last embrace of our souls. He pressed my hand to his heart—felt a violent convulsion within his bosom—his eyes fell from mine, and sat in darkness.

The keeper entered with a guard to remove the dead. Three of the prisoners had in reality expired during the day, and Anderville, who was dead to every appearance, was seized among the rest by the rude soldiers to be borne to the general tomb. Racked with poignant agony, I clung to the silent bosom of my friend, and, in a voice almost suspended with sorrow, demanded to know whither they were bearing him.

"To throw him in the lake," cried the keeper, "where every rebel dog ought to be."

"He is not dead," cried I, "he is asleep. Leave him with me until morning and I will restore him to life."

The ruffians paid no regard to my expostulations, but attempted to tear the body from my arms. I had forgotten that my former strength was exhausted, and only recollected the dauntless ardor by which I was ever actuated.

"Monsters," I replied, "he shall not go. I will detain him here in defiance of your barbarity."

"We'll see to that," cried the keeper, "and two rough soldiers seized my arms which were unnerved by fatigue and famine, and bursted them from around the lifeless Anderville, and dragged him from me. My eyes trembled on his faded features as he was passing from my sight. A heavy anguish weighed my heart into horror as the door was closed, and Anderville gone forever!

I threw myself on the bed where he had died, in a state of mind stupefied beyond the power of reflection. Twilight faded—night succeeded, but evening and morning were now alike to me. My cup of destiny was full to the brim, and running over with the gale of misfortune. Robbed of Anderville, lost to Zerelda and Emerine, nothing remained that could please in life, nothing that could create a pang in death. I had no wish to rise from the bed where my latest friend had breathed his last.

THE PRISONERS OF NIAGARA

The prison fever had already begun its attack on my constitution, and in a very few days I expected to be bound from confinement to everlasting freedom, where imagination pictured Zerelda, Anderville and Emerine, walking the bright fields of Elysium, and anxiously awaiting my arrival. My gloomy desponding sensations increased the rapid progress of my disorder, and I expected before the morrow's dawn that I should lose the power of reason and recollection, and become forever after insensible to pain.

About midnight, the door of the prison was opened. A female form, bearing a lantern, made her appearance. I caught a glimpse of this strange unexpected visitor, and started from a deep reverie in which my mind, losing its hold on time, had strayed through all the imaginary labyrinths of eternity. She was habited in black and almost entirely concealed by a dark veil, which, extending below her waist, completely shrouded her form and features from my sight. But notwithstanding, there was something beautifully expressive in her appearance. Her air was the sylph of imagination, dancing on the sunbeam of a vision; her light movements, the motion of a zephyr, flitting over the morning dew; and had her dress been light, my heated imagination could readily have mistaken her for one of the ethereal visions that bask in the unknown Utopia.

I was yet reclining on my straw in the farther part of the room when she began in a low voice to inquire into the wants of my fellow prisoners. I could neither distinguish her words nor the particular tone of her voice, but the gentle modulation of her accents vibrated with a trembling sweetness on my ear and softly melted a passage to my soul. There was a tender symphony of sensibility in all her conduct that enchantingly accorded with the idea I had formed of angels.

She carefully dressed the wounds of two who were slightly wounded, and administered the welcome draught of consolation with such a charm of pitying sympathy that all the prisoners forgot their sufferings to listen and to gaze.

9

THE PRISONERS OF NIAGARA

Her attendant entered with a delicious repast of table delicacies and several bottles of wine which she bountifully distributed among my companions, and while they partook of her liberality, she stood and gazed in an attitude of rapture. The feelings of a benevolent soul that has conferred a blessing are a miniature paradise, and sweeten the countenance into a resemblance of angelic loveliness. I would have given a world to have beheld the features of this generous visitor at this interesting moment. My imagination pictured her countenance arrayed in the glow of angels, rejoicing over a redeemed world. Methough I saw a tear of joy leap from the cell of sensibility and hang with a pleasing sparkle on the verge of her eye, and the shade of sorrow that hovered over her visage dissolve in an instant, and flit away like the thin clouds which veil the morning sun before the kindling brightness of her features beamed with one sweet blush of smiles.

She now, for the first moment, had leisure to approach the mattress where I lay, to extend to me those blessings she had conferred on my copartners in distress. Her lantern shone full on my face. At the sight of my meager emaciated features she startled—stopped—and seemed to fix her eyes upon me in an attitude of terror. Her frame became so violently agitated that her veil trembled around her. Ah! Noble lady, your gentle nature has never witnessed such a melancholy spectacle before. This dismal dungeon is a scene too shocking for the tender nature of your mind. Such, indeed, appeared to be the case. Her feet became riveted to the spot, and she appeared as if almost petrified with powerful emotion. Her servant took hold of the food and wine, which would otherwise have fallen from her hands, and presented them to me, while she, somewhat recovered from her alarm, leaned on his shoulder, and in a quivering and almost unintelligible accent, enquired if I was ill or wounded.

"Benevolent stranger," I replied, "I have no wound in the compass of human skill to cure, no illness but the harbinger of ethereal joy, and no thought but gratitude for this unexpected benefaction."

10

"What brought you here?" said she, and the words almost died as they were uttered.

"Misfortune and war," was my reply.

An inward groan burst from her bosom and made her whole body shiver. She cast her eyes around the room, fixed them again on me, and, leaning on her attendant, turned hastily away and walked to the door. Again she stopped and cast her eyes for a moment on my wasted features, and disappeared behind the closing door.

Amazement filled the minds and sat in wonder on the countenances of my companions that such unexampled generosity could actuate the heart of a British lady, and they soon became lost in inquiries and conjectures concerning whom she was, and what was the motive of her singular conduct. I had a strong predilection against the British nation and all who bowed to her perfidious power, but there was such a noble humanity, such a flow of feeling tenderness and sympathy in the transaction of this midnight visitor, that all national distinctions were swept from my mind like a forgotten dream, and I could have clasped her to my heart as a sister, and crowned her as a queen of mercy and benevolence.

Shortly after she left the prison, the keeper entered with a soldier to remove the wet and almost rotten straw which composed our bed, who furnished us with a quantity of dry straw which rendered our situation far less intolerable than before. This piece of humanity, we had no doubt, was bestowed at the intercession or command of our female visitor, of whom we could learn nothing of the keeper but that she came with the commandant's order for admission, and had paid the keeper an extraordinary premium for cleansing our prison and furnishing us with straw. An act of such heroic generosity, in a land where oppression stalked and scowled with the frown of threatened terror, could not fail to inspire each prisoner with the glowing soul of gratitude and amazement. Sunk as we were in this nauseous dungeon, this sickening vault, "when hope was lost, life faith, and death at hand," we never expected to feel the divine streams of

pity flowing from mortal bosoms. To receive from a stranger such
kind relief, such unaffected sympathy, disinterested as the mercy
of Heaven, what heart so cold but would kindle into admiration,
and burn and burst into a flame of admiration, too bright and high
for the narrow powers of human thought? My soul swelled with
the generous deed, reflection expanded its emotions to grasp its
capacious object, but its mightiest powers were inadequate to the
operation and sank, overwhelmed, in profound wonder. But the
draught of wine which I had drunk soon threw me into a slumber
where I forgot the grateful emotions I felt for this stranger's
generosity, and I enjoyed a few hours of the most untroubled
repose I had ever experienced in this dungeon.

But before the rising dawn, my sleep was broken by the
grating of prison bars. The door again murmured on its hinges.
Our benefactress entered more deeply veiled than before. She was
accompanied by her attendant, who was loaded with fresh
provisions and several bottles of cordial to arouse and quicken our
fainting spirits. She advanced immediately to my bed, but I
pretended to be asleep that I might have a better opportunity of
investigating the motives of her conduct. She stood over me for
some moments, during which I could plainly hear her heart beat
against her bosom as if it would burst the bounds of that sacred
sanctuary of benevolence. A heavy sigh succeeded which rolled in
the deep and trembling strains of keenest anguish. She turned
away to pour the balm of consolation in the bleeding minds of my
companions. My eyes followed her with a reverential adoration,
and while with airy step she passed around the prison, dressing the
wounds of my comrades, and infusing the heavenly streams of
pity and consolation in their hearts with a voice sweet and melting
as the sympathy of angels, I beheld her as one of the ministering
celestials, flown from the regions of light, to bestow the
dispensations of mercy on expiring man.

The contemplation of her generosity awakened all the fire of
my mind into a boundless flame, and while gazing upon her, the
powers of fancy in an active train of associations pictured her
personal and mental image in my imagination. Her benevolence

He Wordens

(Carmont

was the model of her portrait, and her charms of mind and person appeared as conspicuous to the glowing pencil of fancy as if they had been unveiled by a long and familiar acquaintance.

I conjectured her tall and slender person formed with the most refined delicacy. Her limbs assimilated with an enchanting symphony, and light and gentle in their motions as the painted images that dance on the verges of the rainbow, "Adorned with all the captivating ease/ That angel hands could draw." Her face was the smiling beauty of a lover's imagination. The intermingled glow of white and red, in all the tender variations of lights, was planted with such a gentle softness on her features that the slightest breath seemed capable of melting the coloring and dissolving the enchantment. Her eyes expressed a soul visible in the ethereal brightness of deep blue animation, and melted into angelic kindness at every glance. Her cheeks, her lips, her neck, her bosom. Oh! Blissful objects where language fails and fancy feels ineffable delight. Her mind was the lovely, visionary perfection; it had every excellency possible to a warm, adoring imagination, "Delightful as the image of a god." Such was the power of my fancy while gazing on this invisible fair, while thus engaged in acts of charity, that I had not a doubt but that she was in the blossom of youth, and one of the most beautiful and lovely females that ever my eyes beheld.

She appeared to be in haste to depart before morning, and having executed the commission of her heart with the other prisoners, returned to my bed, where I yet pretended to be asleep, leaned over me for a moment, and breathing a long, thrilling sigh, departed.

But notwithstanding the humane attention of this unknown female, my fever continued to increase, and early on the succeeding day, I was unable to rise from my bed. My companions, but especially the grateful Carmont, were assiduous in their attention to all my wants, and exerted the utmost of their endeavors to prevent me from becoming the victim of that destiny which had befallen twelve of our brethren. But they were not long permitted to enjoy the dreary consolation of administering to a brother in distress. The inspector entered our dungeon and, after examining my situation, ordered the rest of the prisoners to follow him.

"Whither are we to go?" inquired Carmont.

"Ask no questions, but obey," said the inspector.

"When am I to return to my friend? And what is to become of him in my absence?"

"Attend to my command," replied the inspector harshly.

"My friend is unable to help himself. He once saved my life. Let me continue with him, I entreat you, or let him also be removed."

"Sir," said the inspector with an air of importance, "I am not used to parley with rebels. Follow the guard or dread my indignation."

"I am a novice at supplication," said Carmont, "but I beg. I implore you in pity to let me remain. If I am ordered to death, here let me be shot. It is no common cause that moves me thus to sue for favor, and if one spark of compassion warms your bosom, I pray you, as you hope to obtain the mercy of the eternal Judge, to grant my supplication, and suffer me to live and die with my sick, expiring friend."

"Guards! Perform your duty!" cried the inspector. "Conduct the prisoners to their destination."

"I am sorry to disobey," replied Carmont, "but I cannot leave this prison. I am bound to protect my friend, by obligations superior to the petty considerations of life or death, and a power short of that which can tear the earth from its orbit shall not move me from this dungeon."

"We'll see to that!" cried the inspector. "Guards, bind that audacious traitor."

"Bind the rolling globe or yonder sun," replied Carmont with a voice and looked irrevocably fixed, and, snatching a sword from one of the soldiers, continued, "Who dares to bind me? The wretch who makes the attempt shall dine in eternity."

"Guards! Seize the villain!" roared the inspector.

14

THE PRISONERS OF NIAGARA

The soldiers attempted to seize the sword of Carmont, he thrust them back, and with a look of cool but desperate determination observed to the inspector, "I perceive, Sir, that you do not know me. Can you have forgotten Carmont? It would be prudent, Sir, to take the remainder of the prisoners and quietly suffer me to remain."

The inspector appeared thunderstruck at the name of Carmont, and after a few minutes of profound silence, directed the guard to conduct the other prisoners away, and suffer that unmanageable fellow to remain for another day. The soldiers obeyed their commander, and Carmont and myself were left alone together. I grasped his hand in a transport of rapture and poured out my soul in a grateful fervor for the distinguished marks of friendship he had exhibited, and for the dreadful risk he had encountered to serve a helpless sufferer.

"Name it not," replied Carmont. "Have you not dared the wildest deaths for my protection? While I acquainted with my enemy, I knew I had nothing to fear."

"What mysterious virtue is there in your name, Carmont, that produced so sudden a change in the inspector?" inquired I. "Have you known him before?"

"My dear Evermont," he replied, "let me entreat your silence on that subject. It is one which should not be explained in our present situation."

I pressed him no further, but endeavored to sleep my emotions into silence.

Night came on, and I sank into a deathlike slumber, or my brain became delirious with the burning heat of my fever. When I awoke in the morning, my mind was crowded with a long train of bewildering visions. Either in imagination or reality, the fair stranger had entered my prison, and after a series of the most affectionate attentions, she knelt by my side, and raising her hands to heaven, poured up her soul in a fervent prayer for my recovery. A physician also attended me in my vision, but this proved an undoubted reality, for I discovered where he had bled me in the arm, and applied several medical plasters to my body for the purpose of extracting, or changing, the seat of my fever.

But a far more alarming circumstance in my vision was that I beheld the inspector enter the dungeon with his soldiers, and fall upon the unarmed Carmont and murder him before he was able to defend himself. I saw him fall beneath their united fury, and then beheld them drag him from my dungeon while I vainly strove to fly to his assistance. And alas! When I awoke and cast my trembling eyes around my dungeon, I beheld it awfully realized. Carmont was gone, and a large quantity of blood, which was scarcely yet cold, was sprinkled over the floor and walls. Shocked at this evidence of midnight assassination, I had no hesitation in concluding that the noble Carmont was dead, and that his death had been the consequence of some fatal knowledge he had acquired of the inspector, and which had procured his release on yesterday, that he might fall a more certain victim in the silent hours of slumber. Thus, I beheld myself alone, at the mercy of merciless barbarity unless the power of my mysterious benefactress extended beyond all rational belief or expectation. But hope, the busy deceiver, still played around my heart in connection with this unknown fair, and while contemplating the possible exertions she might use for my liberation, I felt an indescribable sensation of something resembling pleasure; it was like the fragment feeling of a pleasing dream before the eager grasp of recollection.

I was very much recovered from my fever before evening, and having received a large bench from my keeper, I was able to place it by my window and climb upon it so as to breathe the uncontaminated air of the atmosphere. The town was remarkably silent, and I could distinctly hear the dashing waves of the falls of Niagara, rolling on the troubled air in successive volumes of distant thunder. The murmuring current of Niagara River was faintly visible extending into the bosom of Ontario, whose untroubled surface presented a wide horizon, leading the wandering eye over a mighty tract of waters which were gradually mingled with the blue expanse of the distant ethereal.

THE PRISONERS OF NIAGARA

He habitually contemplates the universe

When night again shut up the world in darkness, and withdrew the dazzling curtain of solar rays from the unnumerable suns and worlds which rode through the wide kingdoms of ether, my mind, which is ever lost in the deep profundity of wonder at the contemplation of the immensity of the universe, shrank from the glittering prospect of those bright legends of an omnipotent creator, and I retired from the window wrapped in the bewildering magnitude of my own conceptions.

The hour of midnight arrived in which I calculated on receiving a visit from my unknown benefactress, and while I was contemplating on the mysteriousness of her conduct, she made her *she appears* appearance at the door. I pretended to be asleep that possibly she might be induced to unmask herself and afford me an opportunity of discovering her person, and by possibility her name and rank. She tripped to me with the lightness of an April shadow, dancing pathless over the bosom of the rose, stood by my bed for a moment, and then seated herself by my side, with a deep swelling sigh which trembled on my face as it escaped from her breast. She leaned over me and her breath fell on my features; the airy touch darted an indescribable sensation of pleasure through every nerve of my frame, and whispered unutterable emotions to my listening bosom.

The idea I had formed of her excellence and beauty sweetened the breath that melted from her lips, and while its gentle undulations kissed my lips and cheeks, it was connected with the imagined purity of the bosom from whence it flowed, and the delicious softness of the rubies through which it breathed, and kindled all my feeling into animation.

She laid her hand on my cheek, my blood warmed in every vein at the touch, and flowed rapidly from my heart; but my emotions were increased when she laid my hand on hers, and folded it with a gentle pressure. I could not have believed my exhausted frame possessed such a flow of excitability as was *aroused* stimulated into action by this unknown hand. Disease and weakness gave place to a flow of indefinable feeling, and every pore of my body seemed alive and rejoicing. She laid her finger

17

The Kiss

on my pulse with a touch as soft as velvet down; my pulse quickened its vibrations; the blood hastened down the artery, and seemingly flew to embrace the finger that pressed upon my wrist; my heart danced with a light and hurried motion, and a thousand pulses panted in my body. I would have given half my existence for a single glance at her face and person, for I imagined her "Fair as the beams of light in form, / In mind as pure as Heaven." But I dared not open my eyes and acknowledge my deception, and, even if that was done, I knew not but that she was yet shrouded in her veil.

She leaned her face so near to mine that I could drink the air as it flowed in warm waves of odors from her lips. A pause ensued in which scarce a breath agitated her lips or bosom. My heart almost ceased to beat at the solemn stillness—sensation became dumb, "And every thought in silence hung, / And wondering expectation." She involuntarily terminated the pause with a fluttering sigh, and in an instant brought her lips so near to mine that I could almost feel their pressure. What at this moment would I not have given to have been allowed to move my lips toward hers, if only the breadth of a hair; so powerful, so enticing was the attraction, that all the energy of my nature was scarce able to resist its enchanting influence. I felt it impossible longer to conceal my hypocrisy in pretending to be asleep; but at the very instant when she had breathed on my lips until every desire of my heart was irresistibly fired, she gently pressed her lips to mine, with a kiss as soft as the caress of love in midnight slumber. Oh! How my heart danced with imaginary rapture! But ere her lips had melted their spicy odors on mine, she withdrew them in haste, as if conscious of some impropriety. I fancied I beheld her blush to the eyes at the idea of what she had done, although she thought no soul would ever know it. I half opened my eyes to observe her emotions, but she had precipitously risen on her feet and concealed herself within her veil.

The physician arrived, and feeling my pulse a little roughly, I thought it a proper time to awake, and so opened my eyes. The lady looked at me for a minute and then flitted away in a thought.

18

She is commandant's mistress

THE PRISONERS OF NIAGARA

At the doctor's solicitation I sat up and partook of a warm
beverage that the stranger had brought, which he said would be
more conducive to my health than all the medicine he could
administer. He then gave me a little phial of medicine which he
directed me to take in small portions, at stated periods, and was
about to withdraw, but I desired him to tarry and inform me who
the lady was that had just left the prison. He replied that she was a
stranger to him, that he had never seen her unveiled, but had
understood she was the commandant's mistress, and from every
circumstance he had no doubt it was the truth, but her humanity
and generosity were unbounded, and ought to mitigate the
criminality of her errors which were doubtless occasioned by the
warmth of her nature. After this statement, he hastily withdrew,
leaving me to contemplate the character he had given my
benefactress whom I had heretofore considered "Perfection's soul,
in woman's fairest form." Is it possible so benevolent, so noble a
woman, is the mistress of a libertine? The sainted form she had
assumed in my imagination replied in the negative, and I could but
believe that the physician had been misinformed as to her
character. The caresses she bestowed on me, while she imagined I
was asleep, seemed to intimate that her inclinations were
licentious, but I could not believe a mind like hers, glowing with
godlike munificence, could even bear a thought of deviating from
virtue, and still believed her the sweet image of those ethereal
spirits which sport in the bright sunshine of Elysium.

The room adjoining my dungeon had also been used as a
prison, from whence I frequently heard the "doleful groan" ride
slow and mournful on the sullen pinions of my heavy atmosphere.
But during the preceding day, the melancholy rumor of woe had
died in the unintelligible void of silence. Who the sufferers were,
or what had been their fate, was unknown to me. A short time
before sunset, a massy casement had been removed which opened
a grated window that communicated with my apartment, to which
window I had frequently applied with the utmost stretch of sight
for information respecting the inhabitants within, but it wore the
blackest veil of midnight on its bosom, and repelled the sharpest

19

glance of vision. Shortly after I was left by the physician, a gentle sound of music stole through this window, and awakened me from a partial slumber. The sound was new. It poured a sweet cadence of living melody along the silent gloom, which gradually died, in lingering modulations, on the eager, wondering ear. To a bosom long accustomed to the harsh murmurs of despair, groaning and reverberating through all its secret cells, it was not difficult for a transient flash of bewildered fancy to suggest that those melting accents "rowed from heaven." I sat and leaned my ear to catch the succeeding notes—a full swell of harmony burst in trembling vibrations on my ravished senses. It played through my bosom like the visions of celestial choristers, and wrapped my soul into the fragrant arcanum of its sweetness. It spoke "all heaven in harmony" to my feelings, and I fancied it the divine symphony of angels, opening the ethereal gates of glory to a departing soul. The air appeared to breathe Elysian odors around my prison, and I felt as if in the immediate presence of a divinity.

The music was silent, but rapture appeared to breathe his smiling numbers along the air, and whisper the soul of melodious sweetness around my heart. I approached the enchanted window with reverential awe. The room within was instantly illuminated, and a full countenance, blazing with the majesty of sun-bright brilliance, flashed with inimitable brilliancy on my astonished sight. I shrank from the adorable apparition in amazement and delightful wonder. Again the melody swelled in the warbling softness of heaven-toned ecstasy, but I had no power to move toward the window. I continued to listen in impassioned devotion with full belief that the swelling rhapsody had borrowed its sweetness from the throne of deity.

The cadence fell. The sound died by degrees on the air, and softly glided from my ear into my breast and attuned my bosom to solemn, indescribable joy. My eyes turned to the window, but I dared not arise to look within. The music had wafted my sound from a discordant world to the flowery fields of everlasting harmony, but turning my eyes, as if in an instant, the lady was by my side with her lantern. I sprang back in affright, imagining her

THE PRISONERS OF NIAGARA

the heavenly musician whose notes I had just heard, and who had that instant alighted in my prison in a human form. But she held out her hand, and in a tone gently familiar observed, "Be not afraid. I will protect, not injure, you. I have brought you a cordial and some biscuit." I was not yet convinced that she was a being of mortality, but took the welcome present with a thankful yet palpitating, heart, and trembling hand. She perceived my tremor, and took my hand and led me to my bed of straw, but so wild was the infatuation of my fancy, that I could yet scarcely believe the hand that pressed on mine was not celestial. She gave my hand a fervent pressure, heaved a heavy sigh which dissolved in fragrance on my face, and lisped, with a voice musical as the tuneful solemnity of transport, "Hope in heaven, and be comforted!" Her light disappeared in an instant, and I was alone. Still more alarmed at her sudden departure, I dropped the cordial and biscuit, and became dumb with astonishment. But while all my faculties were thus stunned by the benumbing powers of superstitious awe, the transition was easy, and I fell asleep.

When morning had removed the shadowy phantoms of midnight, this mysterious woman and the more mysterious music, and the countenance I had seen in the adjoining apartment, were still enveloped in impenetrable darkness, and reason having no clue to unravel the enigma, I was compelled to leave it in the same obscurity.

The ensuing evening, the lady again returned. I again acted hypocritically, pretending to be asleep. She sat down by my bed, and gazed on my face for at least half an hour. She then took my hand and pressed it in hers with extraordinary warmth, and was placing it either on her lips or her bosom, but, as if startled by the idea of imprudence, she instantly relinquished it—then snatched it up again, and kissed it with a fervor that made my blood boil around my heart.

She then rose hastily on her feet, and I concluded that she had flown away as before, but, looking from under the corner of my eye, I perceived her yet standing over me. She again seated herself by my side, and began to play with the locks on my forehead, and

21

smooth my whiskers with her polished fingers. An unknown soul expanded its fluttering feelings in my bosom. She laid the ends of her fingers on my lips. Oh! How I longed, but dare not, kiss them. She placed her hand on my heart–the astonished, delighted trembler panted with a new delirium of emotions. She then, to complete the swelling climax of my fevered imagination, laid both her hands gently on my cheeks, and pressed her lips softly to mine until their melting nectar stole through the dilated avenues of my body, and told the inspiring tale to my soul. My heart danced joyfully, as if it had received the smiling impression of the sweetening rubies. Her embrace was long, but downy as a zephyr's kiss on the rose's bosom. My soul leaped to my lips, and tasted the fragrant spices, which melted from hers. My blood heated around my heart. A new world of enjoyment seemed to burst upon my imagination; a host of young desires arose in restless effervescence and wantoned in my bosom. My situation became intolerable; both body and soul appeared rushing to her lips, and it was impossible to continue motionless any longer. But as quick as I attempted to change my position, the light died, and she was gone in a breath. I looked round, but she was invisible–I searched the room, but she was not to be found. My astonishment was without form or bound, and left me a petrified statue of paralyzed wonder.

I attempted to sleep, but in vain. I sought composure from gazing through my window on the fields of night where a few lone stars were streaming their brilliancy through a wilderness of clouds, but the late impressions on my mind, enfeebled by disease and confinement, repelled both calmness and reason until almost break of day.

The sober sovereignty of reason at last enabled me to expel the idea that my visitor was superhuman, but was not able to explain the mysterious causes and motives of her conduct. I was left wrapped in conjecture and astonishment whither to attribute her embraces to the libidinous desires of a wanton, or the innocent warmth of bashful love. But whence could arise an innocent passion for a stranger whom she had never seen but in the gloomy

He speaks to her

regions of a dungeon? The improbability of this occasioned my faith to waver and a fear to rise, that her heart was stained with illicit emotions. I resolved to investigate her conduct further and awaited with anxiety for her return.

When another midnight had rolled its black shroud of vapors over the world, this incomprehensible woman again unbolted my dungeon. Her appearance, as she advanced, was the divine movement of an angel, flying on wings of compassion to execute the commission of mercy on the forlorn and miserable. Had I believed her the veriest strumpet on earth, conviction itself would have dissipated at her appearance, and I should have beheld her with trembling and superstitious adoration.

She advanced to where I was sitting on my bed of straw, and seated herself on a bench, observing that she had brought me something to eat. I almost imagined that I had heard her voice before, but it was evidently disguised so that I could not determine with certainty whether the fancied familiarity of her tones was real or imaginary. I resolved, if possible, to draw her into a conversation, whereby I might obtain some intelligence to satisfy the bursting anxiety of my mind, to unravel the mystery by which she was surrounded.

"Madam," I replied, "you have taken extraordinary pains to create unbounded obligations in my bosom, which has long since become bankrupt in gratitude. How much am I indebted to your generosity—what a despicable return I can make."

"If you ever performed a generous action yourself," said she, "you performed it as a duty. Suffer me to be actuated by the same motives. It is I that am in debt, for I have received the greatest blessing. Have you entirely recovered from your fever?"

"Entirely, Madam, and offer up my grateful thanks to you, my best physician."

She appeared cautious of speaking, as if afraid her voice would be recognized, and only bowed an acceptance of my proffered gratitude, and observed, "This prison is a wretched habitation. Would you do me a kindness, and beguile the tedious hours of confinement, by throwing together the most impressive occurrences of your history? I would accept it as a memorable favor."

"Most willingly," I replied, "had I the materials for writing."

"I have them with me," said she, and presented me with an earthen lamp, pen, ink and paper.

As she handed me the last article, I took the hand that held it. It was the first time I had ever beheld it without a glove. It was white and smooth as polished marble, and her long slender fingers, formed with a bewitching delicacy, were as soft to the touch as the bosom of the cygnet.

What a soul there is in the simple sense of feeling. The pressure of my fingers on hers spoke an intelligible language of pleasure to every part of my body, and stole into my heart, "and 'woke the tones of joy that slumbered there." I gave her hand a slight pressure in mine, and cast up a look of the profoundest gratitude. Her eyes were veiled, but she seemed to feel the spirit of the glance. A pause ensued—her hand began to tremble—she vainly endeavored to suppress the waves of emotion which were swelling in her bosom—they burst in sighs from the sacred chambers of sensibility, and told what sorrowing sympathy sanctified the vibrations of her heart.

"Why, noble lady," cried I, "am I thought unworthy to see and know my benefactress, the amiable preserver of my existence?" She sighed, turned her face away, and I imagined burst into tears.

I was deeply affected at her emotions, and pressed her hand to my lips with a kiss as fervent as the thankfulness of my soul, and if ever an ardent prayer was breathed for the happiness of a mortal, it was then breathed upon the hand of this mysterious woman. The fingers quivered on my lips as I embraced them, and were not withdrawn until they became as warm as the lip that pressed them, and blushed an acknowledgment of the ardor of my caress as she drew the hand under her veil.

She turned to depart. The door rung violently on its hinges, and the inspector rushed into the room, followed by a soldier. The lady screamed and was sinking to the ground. I caught her in my arms, and felt a pitying sensation of pleasure, even thus to be

24

enabled to press her slender waist. I felt for her alarm, but had never known the feeling of fear, or it would now have overwhelmed every emotion of delight.

"Fine doings, truly," roared the inspector. "Midnight revels and debaucheries in a prison."

"Debaucheries!" faintly echoed the recovering lady.

"Repeat that expression again," cried I, "and if your heart was clad in steel I'd spill its blood."

"Seize that strumpet," exclaimed the inspector to the soldier, "and conduct her to the pillory."

"Let any dare touch her," continued I, "and if he had a thousand lives, I'd send him to perdition."

The soldier drew his sword and advanced. I seated the lady on my bed of straw, and seized my bench with both hands. The soldier drew back. The inspector was about to call for more assistance.

I raised the bench, and observed with a voice which spoke a furious determination, "Speak not a word, or I will shiver you to atoms at a blow."

He stood against the wall, petrified with terror.

"Sheath that sword," cried I to the soldier.

He trembled and obeyed.

Then turning to the inspector, I instantly recognized the features of Whitford. "Mercy defend me," exclaimed I. "Whitford, is it you that's become this mighty officer? You threaten a woman with the pillory? Oh! Justice! Oh! Vengeance! Remember Richmond—remember Amacette, and stand and quake beneath my indignation till this lady retires to her dwelling. Then dare, presumptuous wretch, to utter one syllable about her being here, and I'll rend heaven and earth to avenge her wrongs. Her soul will emblazon the brightest of heaven, on the humanity of a world; whilst thou, despicable reptile of baseness, shalt crawl with toads and vipers. Lady, you can retire at pleasure. You have nothing to fear."

She appeared terrified, and could scarcely move. I took her hand and let her to the door, observing, as I perceived her yet in a tremor, "Do not be alarmed, these gentlemen will tarry with me till you reach your home; and dread no evil consequences from this affair, for if one expression ever falls from these miscreants on this subject, I'll burst the strongest dungeon in the universe to punish their perfidy. Even in death, I would be tremendous to them. But if it will be a greater security, they shall swear to secrecy." Then turning to them, I ordered them to raise their hands, and swear by everything sacred never to divulge what they had there beheld, nor attempt to disturb the peace of that benevolent lady.

They hesitated, and I again raised the massy bench over their heads, and they shakily granted the oath I required. The lady, then pressing my hand in her trembling grasp, departed.

I again turned to the inspector, and commanded him to swear that this adventure should in no manner affect either my captivity or punishment. This oath he granted as readily as the other, for he felt himself in my power, and had heretofore learned to shudder at the effects of my anger. When I concluded the lady had reached her habitation, I dismissed the dastardly inspector and his guard. As soon as they were gone, I began to consider the probable consequences of this intrusive visit, and of my roughness to the inspector, and immediately concluded I should be consigned to the same doom which befell the noble, unfortunate Carmont, but resolved to meet my fate with the same undaunted firmness with which I had ever encountered the terrors of misfortune.

The inspector had not long retired when the physician entered with some medical potions and powders, which he said were the last he should ever be able to bring.

"The inspector," said he, "has discovered my visits, and I must discontinue them or we both perish."

"Have you learned," inquired I, "that any unhappy consequence has befallen my benefactress on account of her generosity?"

"She, sir," said he, "is in no danger. She is indubitably the mistress of the commandant. She is very beautiful and accomplished, and can procure the utmost power of the commandant against the rage of the inspector, but I am undone if discovered."

"Is it possible," cried I, "that benevolent angel is a mistress—a prostitute—it cannot be!"

"It is most certain," he replied. "She lives with the commandant, and he has neither wife nor relation. I have several nights traced her to his palace, and discovered her enter his chamber and close the door, and have in vain waited for hours to see if she came out during the night. She is very carefully concealed during the day, but I have twice beheld her at his window, and a more beautiful form and face was never seen. She appeared as young and innocent as if the first ripe blossoms of conscious virginity had never been gathered from her lips or bosom, but her servant, who appears to interest himself warmly in her favor, says she has lived with the commandant for two years. I must away, but I will send her servant to your prison, that you may inquire more particularly."

"You need not be at pains," said I, "vexed at the confirmation of my fears. "Appearances are false, virtue is a toy to gull the prudent, and amuse the libertine! Youth and beauty are bartered for splendid infamy! The modest virgin is coy to the generous advances of merit, but seeks the rank bed of the debauchee, and sinks of her own accord into his wanton arms. The brightest image of Heaven is polluted–Satan is transformed into an angel of light!"

As I finished this exclamation the physician departed, and I threw myself on my straw, resolving never to trust human appearance again.

27

CHAPTER II

Motives for writing

I awoke in the morning with my mind crowded with melancholy reflections, at the thought that the fair unknown had proved to be a libel on the external image of virtue and benevolence. I felt as if robbed of a precious treasure at finding the apparent representative of Heaven developed into a hypocritical demon of depravity.

I had promised to furnish her with the particulars of my life. What! Shall I spend my time in writing for the amusement of a libertine? Shall I endeavor to draw the path of virtue, to feed the sarcasms of one who has rendered virtue a toy? Shall I picture the sacred precepts of morality to excite the burst of ridicule in she who has shattered one of its brightest mirrors?

Yes, I will write—gratitude alone is a sufficient excitative, but I will write of the dangerous allurements of pleasure and dissipation, and the dreadful punishment that hovers over their votaries, that the portrait may possibly deter her from a farther progress in licentiousness. I will also picture the sainted charms of morality, virtue, and love, that they may inspire her with those sentiments she has abandoned, those affections she has debased, and that soul of loveliness, that miniature of Heaven, which she has polluted.

But if this benign intention fails, I will write—that by possibility the scroll may light on the germ of budding vice and crush it in its birth; that it may arrest the dissipated youth in his career of ruin, may clip the wings of folly, and emulate the votaries of fashion and frivolity with an idea of happiness superior to the vapid scenes of pride and vanity.

I will write—that the social feelings of sensibility may have utterance in my lines that perchance the manuscript may beguile a

28 *Sensibility*

THE PRISONERS OF NIAGARA

weary mind of a melancholy hour; that it may infuse a sentiment of morality in the opening bosom, and teach one "young idea how to shoot"—that the tender virgin when she reads the blotted page may smile at the effusions of affectionate joy and look with the eye of pity, "When sorrow wrapt in midnight wings, / Tells the cold moon her fate."

I will write—that my sufferings may be known and claim a tear from the soul of humanity.

If all these objects fail, I will write—that by possibility the purity of my intentions may be seen and felt, and emulated.

What am I to write? A thousand matchless scenes appear—a life unparalleled awakes at once; a throng of forgotten visions burst from oblivion and hover round my memory. The meager shades of long departed hours rise from the tomb of slumber and stalk wildly through my imagination. A countless host of past emotions, bound upon the wings of recollection from a long tract of one and twenty seasons, swarm around this dreadful point of time. Wherever fancy turns, a shoreless ocean of dear and dreadful moments swells its rising billows: wave on wave, the tumult heaves it threatening surges, all rolling, all converging to the trembling throb that quivers in my bosom. This weakened form, this fainting pulse of being, must bear the might load that crushed and wasted out a life. Spirits of my noble countrymen, assist me; thou burning blaze of Columbian liberty, inspire me; tremendous genius of America, who from the high cordillera's top displayed the wide page of nature, and to the wondering eye of antiquity unrolled the mighty volume of another world; and thou, bright phalanx of celestials, who hailed the towering soul of seventy-six, whose voice of thunder roused a world to freedom—invigorate my mind to bear a dreadful weight of crowding evils, and give to erring man an awful lesson.

I stand on the quicksand brink of duration's lineless gulf. Imagination soars over the cloudy ocean of the past, but I must plunge into its dreary bosom and seek my floating cradle. Alas! My cradle was the rocky summit of the Allegheny, the fierce

21 yrs old

Calls to American Spirit

scowl of savage eyes my maternal benediction, the terrific war-whoop my lullaby.

I had, at different times, thrown together small fragments of my history, and collecting as many of those as I had with me at present, I began.

His life story

CHAPTER III

Stolen from Indians in PA

As far in the dim page of infancy as memory can pierce, I
knew from information that when I was about eighteen months of
age, I had been stolen from Indians on the Allegheny ridge by a
young man of Virginia by the name of William Evermont, who,
after giving me his own name and leaving me in the care of a poor
farmer of the name of Whitford, engaged in an expedition against
the Indians and had never since been heard of.

Thinks himself an orphan

Early as the dawn of ideas was my mind embittered by the
reflection that I was an orphan. My spirits were sensibly
depressed at the thought of living only for myself, and I felt as if
something was wanting to render my existence necessary.

Whitford and his wife lived very unhappily together, and were
incapable of exciting a genuine affection even in the hearts of
their own children, much less in mine, when I could plainly
discover that they considered me as a burden on their family. With
their children, their own examples of strife and discord prevailed
over the ties of nature, and as they had learned from their parents
to consider me as an outcast intruder, they treated me as a
dependant, and make me feel the humility of my situation. Scarce
a symptom of fraternal love existed among us, yet my heart
anxiously beat with an ardent wish for parents, brothers, and
sisters. The idea of father and mother had something so fond, so
endearing connected with it, that I seemed bereft of half my
existence at the melancholy reflection that there were no persons
in existence to whom I could lisp the tender appellations.

Age 5

When I was in the close of my fifth year, I had so long been
the pointed victim of all the broils in the family, whether of
parents or children, that my mind began to lose its natural vivacity
and sink under the weight of my forlorn situation. I was possessed

Depression

31

Virtue Power of sympathy

of a sprightly, affectionate disposition which would have inspired
my heart with an ardent fondness, either in filial or fraternal love,
if there had been anyone being to teach its young sensations the
sweets of mutual attachment.

Reciprocal affection is the angel mother of a thousand
generous virtues. It leads the tender mind, by the fascinating ties
of sympathy, into the exercise of every towering sentiment and
noble action, and blooms in the infant bosom with the glowing
blossoms of friendship, love and philanthropy. But I, alas, was
destined a stranger to its charms.

I had never received a single mark of affection except,
through the caprice of one, to irritate some other member of the
family who was offended with me. The wife, to vex her angry
husband, would treat me with unbounded caresses and, in the next
moment, expose me to his rage, or treat me with excess of cruelty
herself.

My heart was warm and tender, and I had performed many
services for the village children that were termed benevolent,
which excited the envy of Mrs. Whitford and her children, and
subjected me to the utmost of their severity. Wilson, the eldest
son, was several years older than I, but of a low, plodding
disposition, and the activity of my exertions always rendered me
his superior in every thing we undertook, and made me his
inveterate enemy. His brothers and sisters, and even his parents,
uniformly joined against me. So certain as I ever performed a
praiseworthy action, so certain was I to be punished in some shape
or other.

I had procured a little dog of one of the village boys, and as
my affections longed to be connected with something, they were
all bestowed upon my faithful Pen. He appeared sensible of my
kindness, and regarded me in return with a grateful, undeviating
attachment. But this faithful animal, in consequence of his
affection for me, was doomed to meet the resentment of the
family, and Wilson determined to kill him. He caught him for this
purpose, and aided by his brothers and sisters, they began to tie
him, that they might butcher him at their leisure. Poor Pen yelped,

gentleman finds him

MAN OF FEELING

and looked wishfully at me. My passions were rash and fiery—I seized a club and rescued the dog by violence. Sensible of the punishment that awaited my temerity, I retreated to the woods, and lamented in solitude that I had no relation or friend except my faithful Pen.

I sat down by a little rivulet "that tittered down the vale," and sighed to myself, "I have no father or mother." Pen lay at my feet. He saw that I was distressed, and looked up in my face with the most sympathetic tenderness. I took him on my knees and thought, "How happy I should be if thus caressed by a parent." My eyes run over with tears at the thought.

The sound of horses attracted my attention. I looked up—a gentleman on horseback had stopped in the path and was intently gazing on me.

"My good lad," inquired he, "what has made you cry?"

"I have no father or mother," sighed I.

The simplicity with which I spoke affected him. He alighted from his horse, and with a pleasing expression of pity in his countenance, took my hand, and asked, "Who was your father and mother?"

I sighed, "I do not know. They left me with Indians, and now I am left by myself."

"Where do you live?" inquired he.

"With father Whitford," I replied, "but he is not my father. I want a better father. Will you be my father?"

"You are the child that was rescued by Mr. Evermont!" continued he.

"Yes, sir," said I, "but he is gone. He was a good man, and would have been my father, but the Indians have killed him too."

"You want a father, my dear boy?" continued he, with the fondest look that I have ever seen. "Will you have me for a father?"

"Oh yes," said I, with rapture, kissing his hand.

He pressed me warmly in his arms, and sighed, "I sympathize with you. I will be your father, and you shall have a mother also."

"And shall I have sisters and brothers?"

33

"You shall have sisters," replied he. "Go quietly home, and I will come tomorrow and take you to see them."

"Yes, but they will kill poor little Pen," continued I. "Why do they want to kill him? He has done no wrong."

"They shall not kill him," said he. "I will take Pen with you."

"Will you? Oh, then I will love you more than ever, and Pen will love you too. He is the fondest creature in the world."

He seemed pleased with my innocent expressions, and embraced me with all the ardor of a parent, adding, "Farewell, my sweet child. I will come and see you tomorrow," and mounting his horse, rode off.

My eyes followed him with hopes and wishes until he was out of sight.

Filled with an overflow of rapture at the idea of having this good man for my father, I returned to the house, where I expected to be punished for my conduct to my foster brothers and sisters, but luckily, Whitford and his wife were from home that evening. Their children knew from experience that I was a full match for them all when I grew determined, and so made no attempt at retaliation, but threatened me with the vengeance of their parents the next day. But on that account I relied on the stranger's promises to ward off the approaching evil, and slept quietly till morning.

I was awakened by the cry of Pen, and hastily flew to learn the occasion of it. Wilson had arisen before me, and seizing that opportunity, had split the innocent animal's head with an ax. He lay bleeding and quivering on the ground when I reached the door! My anger was unbounded. I seized Wilson by the throat, threw him on the ground, and beat him severely. His brothers and sisters ran to his assistance. I knocked two of them down with a stick, and turning around to vent my indignation to its utmost on Wilson, discovered Whitford and his wife, running to protect their screaming children.

Alarmed at their impending severity, I retreated toward the woods. The father followed, but I outran him among the bushes, and continued my flight until out of breath. I was attentive only to

IN WOODS – FINDS PLANTATION – SAVES GIRL

the distance I ran from my persecutors, and when I stopped I was surrounded by a wood I had never seen. The idea of being lost in a wilderness was more dreadful than the punishment that awaited me at home, and I anxiously sought to find the way back to Whitford's again, but I rambled through the woods for several hours, still more and more bewildered.

I beheld, at a distance, the dark, cloudy hills of the Potomac, and hastening on toward the river, discovered an extensive plantation, which cheered me with a certainty of meeting some person who could direct me to the road to Whitford's. As I drew near, I heard a loud scream a little to my left, which was instantly followed by an exclamation of "Help! Help!"

Young as I was, the hope of assisting a suffering being overcame the idea of danger so natural to an infant mind, and I flew in an instant to the place from whence the noise proceeded.

Two servant girls were standing on the brink of a large pool, gazing in a state of distraction on an infant that was struggling in the waves. The child disappeared the moment I arrived. The water appeared deep, and I had but latterly learned to swim, but without hesitation I plunged into the pool. The child arose again to the surface, and I caught it with one hand and endeavored to swim with the other, but found myself unable for the enterprise, and sank with the child to the bottom. With a vigorous exertion I arose again considerably nearer the shore, and caught hold of a long cypress bough that hung over the pool which assisted me to bear the child triumphant to the shore.

It was a blooming girl about two years old, the daughter of Thomas Engleton, a wealthy merchant of Baltimore. His wife died when their little Zerelda was six months of age, since which her father had left her in the care of his sister, the wife of Major Haylard, who lived in retirement of the banks of the Potomac, in Hampshire County, Virginia.

Zerelda had been brought to the pool by the rambling inclination of her nurse, and suffered by carelessness to play unheeded on the brink until she fell into the water, where she would have drowned in a few minutes, had it not been for my

Major Hayland the man who said he'd be the father

opportune arrival. Major Haylard was walking at no great distance when he heard the outcry of the servants, and ran to their assistance at the instant when I arose on the shore with the smiling cherub in my arms. He was astonished at this remarkable exploit, of my youthful heroism, and clasped Zerelda and myself to his bosom in silent transport. Never did knight of the chivalric age rejoice with more exultation, when he had rescued the darling of his love from the grasp of a tyrant, than I, at this endearing moment, when I pressed the little Zerelda to my heart, and was myself pressed to the heart of Major Haylard.

I looked up in his face, and recognized the man who said he would be my father. He recollected me in an instant, and inquired by what means I came there.

Without attending to the question, I observed, "They have killed poor Pen, but I gave Wilson a whipping for it, and they intended to whip me, but I ran away and got lost. At last I came here and pulled this little sister out of the water. Will you not be my father now?"

Overjoyed at my artless statement, he clasped me again and again in his embraces, and replied, "Yes, my noble son. I will be your father."

He conducted me to his house, and related my story to Mrs. Haylard, who appeared more rejoiced than her husband. She embraced me with a shower of kisses, and asked with the kindest voice, "My sweet boy, will you have me for a mother?"

"Oh yes," replied I, "I have no mother, and will have you for a mother. And shall these be my sisters?" pointing to Zerelda, and Emerine, the only daughter of Major Haylard, about the same age as Zerelda.

"Yes," said she, "they will be your sisters."

I clasped the children, alternately, to my breast, and kissed them with the ardent joy of fraternal tenderness.

Major Haylard waited on Whitford immediately, and without difficulty procured his consent for me to live, for the future, in the Haylard family, of which I was now considered a member and treated by the generous parents as if one of their own children.

36

THE PRISONERS OF NIAGARA

BENEVOLENCE

The endearing kindness I received from my foster parents soon
gave scope to the fervor of my affections, and erased from my
mind the cruelty of the Whitfords, and the loss of my natural
relations.

For Zerelda and Emerine I contracted a fondness which could
never have been warmer for sisters, but for Zerelda my attachment
was increased by the circumstance of her being the object of my
first favorite act of heroic generosity. This is one of the most
exquisite consequences of benevolence, which not only renders us
better pleased with ourselves, but, at the same time, sanctifies the
object of our bounty with new and sympathetic qualities of
delight, and like the dispensations of mercy, "in blessing most, is
most supremely blest."

For four years I lived under the immediate care of those
worthy parents. From their affectionate regard for me, the names
of father and mother, and the tender endearment connected with
those delightful names, became so deeply impressed on my heart,
in the glowing colors of filial love, that no circumstance could
blot, or time erase, the lovely image. Nor could I ever afterward
distinguish those more than parents by a colder appellation than
father and mother.

With Zerelda and Emerine I lived as with sisters. Our
amusements were those which are first suggested to children of
lively imaginations. When I look back on this period of my
existence, my fancy burns into a flame of dear and innocent
delights.

I was now put under the care of a country tutor, in the
neighborhood of Hayland Village, where I continued four years,
during which I frequently visited my father's, and often remained
there for several months at a time. But this period of absence
never, in the smallest degree, diminished my attachment for my
parents and sisters. Whenever permitted, I flew to their embraces
with all the eagerness of a son and brother.

For Zerelda my affection still continued more fond and
delightful than for any other being, but it was not that passion,
drawn by some female novel writers when they make their hero

Female
novels

Revolutionary War

and heroine, in consequence of a matrimonial engagement, fall desperately in love with each other from the cradle. Although we had strayed together a thousand times through the romantic scenes of Hayland Village, feasted together on all the wild blooming beauties of nature, and together smiled and wept and wondered at the same pleasing, leery or stupendous prospects; although we had a thousand times thought and acted and enjoyed in unison, a thousand times felt the same pulses, throbs and tremors quiver in our hearts; and a thousand times, wrapped in each other's arms, experienced the same sensations, passions, and affections in floods of mingling emotion swell our mutual bosoms, yet we had never felt the power of sexual love, nor dreamed of matrimony, in application to ourselves.

My progress had been so extremely rapid in every branch of learning I had undertaken, that my father resolved I should be a master of a liberal education, and sent me to the academy at Richmond at the age of thirteen.

War had sounded his bloody tocsin in repeated thunders. The plains of Lexington and the heights of Charlestown had drunk the first streams of patriotic ardor, which were to burst and blaze from their sleepless tombs, and kindle all Columbia into inextinguishable flames. America had risen in her might and assumed her proper magnitude. Her chains burst and shivered into atoms, inadequate to confine a power so gigantic. Her united wisdom proclaimed, in a voice terrible to oppression, "Columbia is free." A dreadful gulf was opened between Great Britain and her colonies which can never be filled.

Major Hayland had long been distinguished in the service of his country, but the evident decline of his health prevented him from now engaging in this new and tremendous drama, which held the eyes of the world in wonder. But he employed his talents to equal advantage in defending the frontiers of Virginia from the depredations of Indians.

I was yet too young to perform a part in this momentous struggle for national liberty, and followed the plan of my father, who intended to form my mind for the service of my country in

13

Leaves for academy & Richmond

some future period. My separation from my family was truly affecting to my tender mind. We all shed mutual tears of sorrow, but my grief was more exquisite at leaving Zerelda. Our last embrace was bestowed with a fervor uncommon in children. We were pressed in each other's arms, our hearts panted together till they seemed that they would never separate; our lips pressed long on each other in our farewell kiss, and when I was forced to leave her, she lisped amid her tears, "Evermont, don't forget your Zerelda." My sensibility was too much excited for reply, and being hurried into the carriage, I was soon borne to Richmond.

"Evermont, don't forget your Zerelda."

39

CHAPTER IV

Boards w/ Mrs. Willford
a widow of 40 - coquette
ARMILDA - her child

By the arrangement of Major Haylard, I boarded with Mrs. Willford, a widow of forty who, with the small remains of a former beauty, a tolerably elegant person, and a large fund of vivacity and intrigue, led a dissipated life of fashionable coquetry and intemperance. Armilda, her only child, was about eleven, who with a lively, insinuating disposition was learning to trace the steps of her mother in all the insignificant routine of vanity and customary frivolity.

As soon as I entered this family, I was considered as the heir of Major Haylard's extensive fortune, and caressed and flattered into the most excessive vanity, and insensibly led into the dangerous school of amusement and dissipation. They, together with a number of their minions, persuaded me into a belief that I was extremely handsome, which idea rendered me excessively vain, and gradually drew me into the utmost extravagance in dress and company.

VAIN

The mother, who possessed the true bewitching smile of a sycophant, had concluded that I would be a hopeful match for her daughter, and spared no pains to draw me into the vortex of that life which she admired, and in which she was forming the mind of Armilda to act a distinguished character.

DANCE

I learned to dance very rapidly, and the insinuating mother led me to believe I was the most graceful and accomplished youth in Richmond. This induced me to put on the insignificant air of a coxcomb, and follow Mrs. Willford and her daughter in a profuse round of balls, assemblies, and gallantries, in the enjoyment of which I shortly became intoxicated with play and amusement. My studies were not yet neglected, but I was so far infatuated with the

enchanting frivolities of a fashionable life, that they were not
pursued with the same alacrity and energy as heretofore.

Almost every youth of my acquaintance was immoral and
licentious in his conversation and practice, which imperceptibly
corrupted the purity of those sentiments and principles I had
imbibed from my family. My disposition was ardent and
impetuous, and consequently the more capable of being hurried
into any channel by the force of examples and allurement. No
sooner were the sublime precepts of morality, inculcated by my
father, contaminated by the vicious pursuits of my companions
and the enticing blandishments of Willford and Armilda, than the
inherent fire of my passions predominated over the feeble barriers
of a youthful reason, and precipitated me into a dangerous career
of unwarrantable practices.

Ladies of the first rank in the fashionable circles were
delighted with me as an agreeable favorite and a hopeful minion.
They lavished on me those caresses which propriety prevented
them from bestowing on their gallants of riper years. I was
considered as a child, and the doting maiden, whose heart was
overflowing with effervescent fondness for her chosen suitor,
would receive me to her arms, and transport me with those
embraces which she dare not bestow on the object of her heart.
Thus I have hung on the bosoms, and drunk the ripe nectar from
the lips of the most beautiful and timid damsels, who would not
suffer the hand of a man to touch their sanctified persons.

With these powerful allurements, was it possible for a youth
of thirteen, possessed of a fond, susceptible heart and strong
romantic passions, to fail being carried down the destructive
current of folly and intemperance? Had I been educated in a
village, remote from the schools of fashion, dissipation and
luxury, the heated temperament of my disposition would have
been active and energetic in promoting the grand design of
nature—the happiness of man—but situated as I was, in the midst
of a volatile crowd of the votaries of pleasure, it was almost
impossible but that I should imbibe the poisonous contagion.

THE PRISONERS OF NIAGARA

A populous city is not the school for the unformed mind. There, the examples of vice are far more numerous and bewitching than those of virtue, and more easily imbibed and imitated by the thoughtless probationer. It is scarcely in the power of the most wary parent to prevent the most phlegmatic child from desiring and pursuing those fascinating amusements that lead into dissipation, and end in disgrace or ruin. Think of this, ye parents, to whom the dispensations of providence have allotted the superintendence of education, and while the blossom of your fondest expectation still hangs on your bosom for instruction, trust not the darling cherub of your hopes to the dangerous scenes of a town education, and more especially, if you are not present to guide the helm of his thought with hand of parental circumspection. Let my example be a warning to the indulgent father, and a dreadful memento to the doting mother.

The vivacity of my temper rendered me fond of society. The ardor of my passions inspired my friendships with enthusiastic warmth, and the impetuous flow of my feelings gave way to appearances, and opened my bosom to every agreeable and insinuating companion. Unknown to the calm, unfeeling medium of indifference, I was either the friend of the enemy of all my acquaintances. That broad basis of careless respect on which so many millions rest their affections was too narrow for the social energies of my nature. With a soul glowing with the effusions of sensibility, uncorrected by the cold speculations of philosophy, I could clasp every human being to my heart until some part of their conduct rebelled against the romantic theory of my caprices, and then I discarded them from my bosom forever. This enthusiastic impetuosity of my disposition has often led me into animosities, errors and views, and involved my life in the bitterest scenes of grief and repentance. But I lament not that nature endowed me with an ardent, susceptible nature, since it has rendered my friendships warm, vivid and endearing, and bound my heart to the human family, ties more affectionate and indissoluble than fancy ever presented to the benevolent soul of philanthropy. But I sadly lament that those glowing propensities of my mind did not remain

42

under the guardian tuition of my amiable parents, where they would have been taught to flow in the generous channel of virtue and affection, and not permitted, as they were in Richmond, to shoot forth in all the wild exuberant ebullitions of which they were capable. They soon outran the slow but steady paces of reason and judgment, and often hurried me inconsiderately into all the dangerous extravagancies of vice and folly, from which it was impossible that I could be extricated without the severest pangs of contrition and repentance, all which might have been prevented by a single expression from a friend, or a chiding glance from a parental eye.

Virtue and morality were taught in the academy, but it was with a cool formality which was below the reach of my aspiring inclination. I could have caught and drunk the precepts of virtue and religion, warm from the lips of a parent or a friend, but from my phlegmatic tutor they came with such an unwelcome insensibility that "they froze as they fell."

But it was from the intrigues of Mrs. Willford, and the playful blandishments of her daughter, that I was prompted to overleap the great boundary between innocence and criminality. From the commencement of our acquaintance, Armilda was fond of me to an extreme affection in a child, and exerted every infantile effort to render our attachment mutual. The mother displayed the utmost of her art to accomplish the desired union of our affections. Armilda was remarkably handsome and sprightly, and the natural fervor of my heart was not averse to her enticing caresses, but met them, and encouraged them with an affection equal to the warmth of her wishes, and the license of my desires. The infatuated mother appeared to consider us as children, and permitted us to enjoy the utmost liberty of intercourse for the purpose of uniting our hearts by an early passion.

Armilda's heart, like mine, was capable of a premature attachment, and being inflamed by the encouragements of her mother, began to beat with all the bewitching sexual allurements before the voice of reason or instruction had taught it the precepts of virtue. She experienced the emotions of joys while reclining in

43

my arms before the imbecility of her judgment suggested the impropriety of her conduct. Her passions were her sole director, and they threw her on my bosom without once reflecting on the dangerous consequences.

The dissipated mother not only permitted, but witnessed and applauded, our frequent interchange of caresses, and often exerted her cunning to keep us together in private or engage us in warm and animating embraces. Our evening rambles were not interrupted, and we were indulged in straying, arm in arm, through the winding labyrinths of an extensive garden, or sitting beneath the inviting shades of groves and flowers.

These rambles were at first as innocent as the blossoms we plucked and placed on each other's bosoms, but they became too frequent, and too long. We too often sat under the heavy shade of a tall Lombardy poplar where we were shut out from every eye by a thick hedge of quickset and raspberries. There was the place of our evenings' resort, and there we often remained until the budding blush on the little cheek of Armilda was hid by the smoky wings of twilight. Virgin modesty had not yet tempered her heart with bashful coyness that "shuns the embrace it loves," and she yielded to the caress of my arms with juvenile delight.

My sensations were those of riper years, and the little girl, in unsuspecting innocence, lay yielding and delighted on my bosom.

But let the eye of censure glance swiftly over the irregularities of affection while the corrective powers of reason and virtue still slumbered in the cradle of juvenileness—but let it light, with all its fire and energy, on the heedless mother by whom they were permitted and encouraged.

Armilda and I knew not how far we had deviated from the irradiating path of virtue. The ardor of our affections continued and increased as the tender fibers of feeling strengthened in our bosoms, and our correspondence in infantile embraces accumulated warmth and attachments with our riper years. We felt not but that our delightful emotions were the pure emanations of innocent affection, and while the voluptuous mother was perversely blind to the dawning beauties of her daughter's

44

disposition, they were insensibly losing their sweet ermine of innocence beneath the baleful shade of all contaminating vice.

But alas! This connection with Armilda was far from terminating my career of licentiousness. It threw the doors of dissipation wide open. Balls and assemblies became my principal delight. My increasing boldness and vivacity made me more caressed by the ladies, and the principal young men being absent in war, I became engaged in a ceaseless round of gallantries. My expenses became excessive, and, unwilling that my father should become acquainted with my extravagance, had recourse to gambling to supply the deficiencies of his liberal donations.

But those *errors of education* were not confined to Armilda *Title* and me. I could picture a similar progress of vice in a thousand instances, but must not deviate from my purpose to give the portrait of any except those whose history is inseparably connected with mine.

In the beginning of my fifteenth year, I attended Emerald L_____ from Mrs. Willford's to her father's. Emerald was the only daughter of a reputable merchant of Richmond, who, by industry and economy, had amassed a considerable fortune. He had reared his daughter with paternal tenderness, and cultivated her mind with a tolerable education, but being more intent on accumulating wealth than realizing the happiness of his child, he had left her entirely to the direction of her mother for the forming of her manners and the regulation of her conduct.

Mrs. L_____ was a votary of high life, the general consequence of which was that she was incapable of teaching her child the true principles of virtuous loveliness. She taught her to dress, and wheel around the giddy whirl of fashion, with dexterity and applause. At the age of twelve, Emerald fully understood that she was born heir to a considerable fortune, and a numerous train of admirers, and by the address of her mother, she was surrounded by a crowd of flatterers before she was thirteen. Thus, before she had acquired one sentimental accomplishment, the beauties of her mind were blasted by the pageant infection of vanity, and lost in the bewildering labyrinths of coquetry. After giving this

45

Coquette

dangerous inclination to her principles and practice, the mother died, leaving her at the age of fourteen exposed to all the alluring blandishments of dissipation and consequent voluptuousness. Her father was too deeply infatuated with the speculations of the counting house to trouble his mind with the conduct of his daughter. She, left entirely to the guidance of her own propensities, rapidly pursued the road pointed out by her vain and inconsiderate mother, and at the age of fifteen became that most insignificant of all females, a fashionable coquette.

Her person and features appeared as if they had been copied from her mind. Her figure was engaging, but seemed rather formed to excite the irregular fire of passion than to inspire the glowing soul of affection. Her features were turned with a lively, pleasing smile, expressive of the amorous inclination of her heart, and of a fond inviting welcome to the embraces of every lover. With these allurements, embellished with fascinating manners, she was continually surrounded by a throng of flattering admirers, and engaged in a wild dissipation of gallantry and conquests.

I had been for a considerable time acquainted with Emerald, and from the satisfaction she expressed in my company, and the pleasing embraces she frequently lavished on me, I was generally in the throng of her devotees. The practice of coquetry has an evident tendency to inflame those natural propensities which exist in every youthful heart. These propensities possessed a powerful predominance in the bosom of Emerald, and her incessant gallantries awakened them into their utmost warmth and activity, and as she could afford them a partial gratification by toying and caressing with me, without a supposed deviation from the customary rules of propriety, I consequently became her principal favorite. She was ever charmed and delighted in my company, not only for the gratification of her voluptuous inclinations, but also, that by bestowing her caresses on me, she could more easily arouse the desires of her surrounding suitors.

These considerations readily induced me to wait upon her with the most assiduous attention. When I accompanied her to her father's on this evening, we were entirely alone, and she, without

46

the least reserve, conducted me into her dressing room, and began with unwarrantable warmth to flatter my person and address, and lavish on me an enchanting profusion of embraces. Emerald, like all other accomplished coquettes, was deficient in the vital spirit of virtue. Notwithstanding that her conduct was not reprehensible in the eyes of society, her mind was devoid of that internal spring of propriety which presses all licentious desires into perpetual silence. The thousand-tongued thunder of fame awed her into apparent virtue, and the fear of dreadful consequences prevented her from indulging her voluptuous propensities with a lover of the years of maturity, but with a boy of fourteen she had nothing to fear.

Thus allured by the fascinations of Armilda and Emerald, I no longer hesitated at the commission of any immoralities or illicit gallantries. As in every laudable undertaking, so in my unwarrantable pursuits, by ardent and unconquerable ambition, could not brook an inferior grade, but hurried me precipitately into the highest and most conspicuous rank.

I frequently received letters from my family replete with ardent affection and the most fervent prayers for my prosperity. Those from my father abounded with moral instruction which would have formed my mind of the most exalted virtue had not the vices and allurements of society destroyed their generous efficacy. Zerelda's glowed with the pure effusions of her sublime attachments, and would have smiled any soul into the practice of every noble and benevolent action, if my mind had not already been ensnared from the melting softness of their sentiments by the bewitching sirens of licentiousness.

But the caresses of Armilda, the intrigues of Mrs. Willford, and the excessive blandishments of Emerald, could not entirely erase Zerelda's image or affection from my bosom. I still doted upon her memory with romantic ardor, uncorrupted and unequaled, by the bewildering pleasures I enjoyed in the bed of voluptuousness. She still existed in a sacred recess of my heart, where vice and intemperance had never dared to penetrate.

Nor could the infatuations of folly and dissipation, nor all the
hydra forms of licentious desires and pursuits, destroy the power
which sensibility and benevolence swayed over the tender
susceptibilities of my nature. For the proof of this statement I
could introduce many instances of my disinterested generosity,
but, as they have no particular influence on the succeeding
transactions of my life, their insertion would be superfluous and
justly branded with egotism. But the following is too intimately
connected with my history to be omitted. It delineates the
irresistible influence which the holy precepts of mercy still
exercised over my slumbering sympathies, even when in
opposition to the most powerful temptations to vicious enjoyment.

 The evening was exceedingly fine. Emerald and I were
walking together to enjoy it enlivening beauties in a spacious and
unfrequented forest which lay in a delightful valley behind the
city. To this retreat we had often strayed, where, secluded from
the scrutinizing eye of curiosity by fragrant groves of spruce and
myrtle, we had regaled ourselves on beds of delicious bloom in
the mutual indulgence of our transported appetence.

A little girl in a simple habit rushed into our path, and in a
tone of the deepest distress exclaimed, "Dear, gentle folks, have
mercy on my poor father–he is dragged to jail. Oh, save him! For
God's sake, save him!"

Affected at the piteous appearance and complaint of the little
girl, I was stopping to inquire the cause of her father's
imprisonment, but Emerald, impatient for the fulfillment of her
desires, urged me on, saying, "We can inquire into this affair
another time."

The little girl threw herself on her knees before me, and
raising up her eyes, which were streaming with tears, cried in a
pathetic sobbing voice, "Dear sir, you are a good gentleman. You
will help my father. Do let him out of jail—he will die if he stays
there."

"Rise, my sweet girl," said I. "I will assist him. Who is your
father?"

"William Etherford," replied the little girl.

48

THE PRISONERS OF NIAGARA

"And for what have they put him in jail?"

"For debt," said she.

"Do you know how much he owes?"

"No, sir," replied she, "I do not, but it cannot be much, for he was always very poor, and very good. Do, sir, assist him, and God will assist you."

She yet continued on her knees, weeping in the most piteous sincerity. My heart felt the full measure of her grief. My anticipated ecstasies with Emerald vanished from my imagination, my arm dropped from around her, and I clasped the little girl, exclaiming, "Yes, I will assist your father. I will follow you to the jail immediately."

"What! And leave me here?" cried the indignant Emerald. "Is this the way you requite my favors?"

"Oh, Emerald," said I, "a worthy man is in prison. Let us give him liberty, and then our happiness will be more exquisite."

"I discard you from my company forever," she replied. "If you do not come this instant, leave my presence, and never see me more."

Little Susan Etherford fixed her eyes on me with an anxious, imploring hope. My soul, bleeding with sympathy, hesitated not a moment, but replied, "If I lose every friend I have on earth, I will obey the impulse of my heart, and give freedom to the father, and joy to the daughter. Go, Emerald, and go forever, if your heart has no compassion for the unfortunate." Little Susan was frantic with rapture at my assurances of relief to her father. Emerald, seeing my determination immovable, altered hers, and agreed to accompany me.

On entering the prison, I discovered that the sum for which Etherford was confined was only twenty dollars. I gave him the amount, and unable to suppress his effusions of gratitude, was about to leave the room, when, in a corner of the prison, I recognized my later foster-brother, Wilson Whitford. Our joy was not great at meeting, nor our salutations ardent, for I could never learn dissimulation; but finding, on inquiry, that he had been arrested for a breach of peace and fined fifteen dollars, and being

49

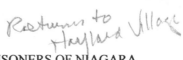
then unable to discharge the sum, was committed to jail, I presented him the money. Unwilling to see him embarrassed in expressing those emotions of thankfulness to which his heart was a stranger, I left him involved in wonder at the return of his former malignity, and taking the hand of Emerald, conducted her out of the prison amid the exulting prayers and blessings of Etherford and his transported daughter.

The afternoon was too far advanced for our intended amusements among the embalming zephyrs of the spicy groves, and we returned to Emerald's dressing room, where, in the course of the evening, I kissed away the sullen displeasure from her lips, and smoothed the indignant throb of her bosom.

Disgusted, in my sober moments, with the insipid scenes of volatility and vice, I frequently sighed for the calm and peaceful shores of the Potomac, and petitioned my father for liberty to return to the bosom of the family. At the expiration of two years absence, he granted my request and permitted me to return and spend two months of the vernal season in the delightful retirement of Haylard Village. Enraptured at the idea of flying into the warm and innocent embraces of the impatient, expecting Zerelda, I abandoned the now hateful caresses of Emerald and Armilda, and began my journey on the buoyant wings of anticipated rapture.

The early sunbeams were playing above the loftiest heights of Richmond and dancing in glittering gaiety on the dewy verdure which lined the road, and shed the sweet breath of morning in harmonious odors. My horse started at the sight of a beautiful little girl entering from the bushes into the road. She stopped at the sight of me and was turning into the bushes again. Then, as if recollecting herself, turned again, and stepped into the road, and with a fine blue and languid eye fixed on mine, inquired, "Dear sir, have you a mother?"

"Why this singular question, my charming Miss?" replied I. "Suppose I have a mother."

"If that mother, the dear author and nurse of your tender existence, was perishing through want and disease, and was to forbid you to ask relief of any being, would you feel yourself

50

bound to obey so severe a command, and see her perish in your arms?" The precious brilliants of affectionate sensibility trickled from her eyes as she spoke, and explained the purport of her question.

A tear, unexpectedly, fell on my cheek. "Where, and who, is your mother, my lovely girl?" I inquired, without replying to her question.

"Oh, sir," said she, "she has forbidden me to let any human being know her name, or place of retirement. But alas! She is at the point of death, and has nothing to eat!"

"She must not die," I replied. "Take this," giving her a ten dollar note, the last I had, "and hasten to procure her food and medicine."

"Indeed, sir, I am afraid to—to take this," said she, with a hesitating sigh. "My mother will be angry."

"Tell her a stranger compelled you to receive it. But what is your name, my darling cherub?"

"Amacette," said she. "But ah! Generous stranger, I must not, cannot receive so much money. Here, take it back. I will work day and night to obtain bread for my mother."

"I will not have it," replied I, "It is yours, and if you will not keep it, you may throw it away, for I am gone." I bowed to her, and gave my horse the rein.

"Oh, sir—if you knew," cried she, but my distance prevented me from hearing any more so that I was unacquainted with when then was to know, or what would the consequence be *if I knew*.

I had not ridden far before my reflections on the singular beauty of Amacette, and her unfinished expression, made me extremely anxious *to know*. Her interesting appearance and manners heightened my curiosity until I stopped my horse and breathed to myself, *Oh, if I knew*. I turned my horse to ride back and inquire of Amacette what it was she intended to relate, but the belief that she had left the road to return to her mother prevented the attempt, and I again started on my way, musing to myself, *If I knew, what would I know?* Only what I was doomed to learn at a later period of life.

CHAPTER V

Neither the intertwining streams of James River and the Rappahanock, nor the proud ramparts of the Blue Ridge, towering amidst the expansive drapery of ethereal wonder, could retard my hasty journey until I was happy in the arms of my parents, and transported on the bosoms of Zerelda and Emerine. The warm, sprightly imagination requires no description to know and feel the joy of our meeting, and the cold, formal soul could never experience its emotions if pictured in the glowing blaze of sunshine. The meridian of the day flew swiftly by on the pinions of delightful conversation, in which our hearts, warmed into rapture by the endearing sensations of such a meeting, spoke the undisguised feelings of social affection.

The evening was indescribably charming. A cloudless sun beamed through a clear ethereal on the romantic prospects of Haylard Village, where, in front, the broad stream of the south Potomac rolled majestically at the foot of a long, winding range of hills and broken precipices, and in the rear, a wide landscape of fields and forests terminated by the dark blue summits of the north and Jackson's mountains, rendered the scenery picturesque and interesting beyond the language of pen or pencil. Such elegant imagery, so fine an evening, invited Zerelda, Emerine, and me to ramble through the adjacent groves, and heighten the exquisite pleasure of our meeting by enjoying the beauties of nature in mutual emotion.

With those delighted sisters, each blooming with the bashful beauties of twelve, I strayed along the bending shores of the river, and traced the adjoining fields of cypress, with glowing sensations of transport, and a heart high bounding in joyful exultation. Enraptured with each other's company and

52

arrive at
Spot where
he saved
Z

conversation—enraptured with the distant prospects, the flowers that blushed as we passed them, and the birds that gave melody to the zephyrs—enraptured with all we saw or heard or felt, we arrived at the brink of the pool where Zerelda's infancy had once acknowledged me for its preserver. A long train of ideas awoke in our minds as we stood and gazed on that memorable spot. Each of my hands pressed the hand of a sister, and our enkindled bosoms swelled into that wide expansion of emotion, that boundless flow of unsettled, infective feeling, which can only be expressed, where the vivid mind runs into an immensity of expectation, by silence. Zerelda pressed my hand to her heart. The new sensation drew my eyes in that direction, and I beheld two Indians, at no great distance, stealing between us and the mansion.

d
Indians

My alarm was immediately visible. Zerelda and Emerine beheld the fearful cause, and shrank to my arms in speechless terror. We were not yet seen by the Indians, but, as the pool lay on the rear of the mansion, and the Indians were before us, it was impossible that we could regain the mansion without being discovered. At a small distance beyond us there was a little grotto, formed in a cragged bank of rocks, where we might lie concealed from the piercing eye of the enemy. Thither I led my trembling sisters, and in utmost anxiety for their safety, carefully watched the motions of the Indians.

They crept cautiously through the wood until they came in full view of the mansion and then concealed themselves in a close thicket of bushes. Terrified at the impending danger, I knew not what plan to pursue to ensure our safety. If we remained there till night, the attempt to escape would be dangerous, and in the meantime, I knew not but there were other Indians who, in concert with these, would attack the mansion while they were unprepared for defense. If we endeavored to all fly together and were discovered, Zerelda and Emerine would certainly be taken, for I had no weapon for defense except a small dirk which I wore while traveling from Richmond. My only hope was in leaving them concealed while I could hasten to the mansion and call my father and his servants to our assistance. Even should the Indians

Del-
emma

His
dirk

discover me, I trusted my speed would bid defiance to pursuit. But it was with difficulty that I persuaded the girls to agree to this proposal. They trembled for themselves. They trembled more for me. I measurably calmed their terrors, but left them shivering with dreadful apprehension.

I crept along the margin of the pool until about a hundred paces from the grotto, and looking round beheld two other Indians, gliding toward the door of the cavern. Defenseless as I was, I flew back in an instant, resolving to save, or die with, my sisters. Those Indians had discovered us when we retreated to our concealment, but fearing some danger if they rushed upon us while together, they waited at hand for a more favorable opportunity. As soon as I left the rocks, two of them resolved to secure the girls while two others passed around to intercept my flight. When I turned toward the grotto, those latter threw their tomahawks at me as I ran. The weapons whistled by my ears but impeded not my rapidity.

I was at the grotto the moment one of the Indians had entered and the other was ascending the rocky steps. The girls uttered a fearful scream which gave me tenfold energy and resolution. I plunged my dirk to the hilt in the back of the hindmost. The other turned round to learn what had happened to his brother, and I buried the bleeding weapon in his heart. They both fell down the rocks. I seized their guns and sprang into the grotto as a shower of balls rained on the rocks around me.

Zerelda and Emerine had become almost insensible with affright, yet they soon recovered sufficient sensation to understand the increasing danger, and to know that I was present, and clung to me, the speaking images of terror, in tremulous expectation.

The pursuing Indians were at hand, but the entrance of the grotto was narrow and directly fronting the pool so that they must come immediately before the door before they could do us any injury. I now had two well-charged rifles to guard us against their attack. They were apprehensive of our situation and approached our concealment with caution. One of them leaned his head round

54

Girls are terrified

the corner of the rocks to examine our covert, but seeing my rifle pointed in that direction, drew it back in an instant, and all was silent.

Panting, breathless, and afraid to move or breathe, the girls sat one on either side of me, quivering in an agony of terror and expecting every pulse of life to be the last. I was a novice in such terrific scenes, but the contest had already been so warm that every idea of personal fear was lost amid the fiercer sentiments of indignation and revenge. While the preservation of my dear and darling sisters was to be the prize of my valor, every power of my mind was collected into dauntless determination. I waited for some time, expecting the moment when the Indians would all spring to the entrance of the grotto together, but all continued dreadfully still.

At the first discharge of guns by the Indians, they had been discovered by the servants, and they spread the alarm to my father and the tenants of the village, who, apprehending that we were all murdered or taken captives, aroused in a moment and rushed to the pool. Their opportune arrival emboldened us to leave our cavern with transport, and fly to our father, who was no less transported at finding us in safety.

serv ants call father + villagers

We now perceived that the Indians, finding they could not accomplish their purpose by surprise, had silently retreated. It was resolved to pursue them immediately to prevent them from committing any outrages during the night. As the number of the assembled tenantry already exceeded the supposed number of the Indians, they would not permit Major Haylard to accompany them in the enterprise, but prevailed on him to return with his daughters and take care of his family, and theirs, in their absence. They also insisted that I, on account of my tender years, should remain with my father, but I was too much elated with my recent intrepidity to think of continuing inactive in so glorious an opportunity of signalizing myself as a youth of valor. Notwithstanding the persuasions of the peasants, and the kind entreaties of Zerelda and Emerine, yet, as my father gave permission, I resolved to accompany them in the pursuit.

PRIDE

attack
indians

THE PRISONERS OF NIAGARA

The neighboring peasants were already aroused for the Indians had stolen a number of their horses and taken several prisoners. Reinforced by these, we set out about sunset, and traced the flight of the enemy by moonlight. They expected to be pursued, and flew like lightening to the western wilderness. We continued our march for several days with increasing rapidity, and at last beheld them crossing the Kanawha on a raft of logs. We rushed down upon them with impetuous fury. They were unprepared to repel our vigorous assault and fled in confusion across the river, leaving behind them the horses and prisoners they had taken. Two of their party were killed in crossing the river; the remainder, about fifteen, escaped to the hills. We immediately followed them over the river but they had scattered in different trains, and having gained the mountainous desert between the little Kanawha and the great Sandy River, we perceived that it would be dangerous and ineffective to pursue them further, and returned by the nearest route to the Potomac.

When I arrived at Hayland Village, my father was there alone. He became alarmed for the safety of his family, from their late imminent danger and almost miraculous escape, and finding the Indians had penetrated thus far into the settlements, he was apprehensive that there might be other parties lurking among the neighboring mountains who would fall upon the defenseless village while the peasants were in pursuit of those that had retreated. Not willing to expose the safety of those he held dear to a possibility of danger, he set out with them the evening the first alarm was given. He conducted them to Baltimore, where they could remain in the family of Engleton, his wife's brother, until the enemy was entirely expelled from the frontier of Virginia. He had just returned after leaving them in security, and received me with the most flattering plaudits of my bravery. But this could not compensate for the loss of Zerelda's expected society, and I would have flown to her in Baltimore had not my father urgently solicited me to return immediately to Richmond, and apply myself closely to the improvement of my mind, as the critical situation of our country and the great cause of liberty would require me, as soon as I was competent to bear arms, to leave the peaceful walls of the academy and join the embattled field against the predatory hosts of Britain. I reluctantly complied with his request, and in the mournful solitude of disappointment, returned to Richmond.

Republican vertue

*and he has twice
saved Zuelda's life*

CHAPTER VI

Armilda met me with joyful embraces, Emerine received me to her bosom, and my delighted companions enticed me into all their delusive pleasures. But the meeting, and unexpected parting, with Zerelda had left a chasm in my bosom which all the alluring amusements of Richmond were inadequate to fill until time had worn away the exquisiteness of my feelings.

Zerelda wrote me a letter stating that she and Emerine intended continuing in Baltimore at a boarding school. Her letter contained a lively, feeling description of her sorrow at being compelled to leave my society so suddenly, and a warm and grateful acknowledgment of my second preservation of her being. But for my infantile bravery in rescuing her from the pool, she yet appeared infinitely more thankful and affectionate, and sent me a golden medal with a beautiful design representing a seraph, bearing a little female child from the fury of the waves, with this inscription: "Sacred to the bosom of benevolence." But gratitude from Zerelda was cold and insipid and incompetent to fill the wide vacancy I had discovered in my mind ever since I had last beheld her. Her letters glowed with fraternal affection, warm as ever heart of sister felt, but their most enkindling expressions were senseless and vapid to my feelings, and seemed to freeze with insensibility, to what she had formerly written. Those I perused again, hoping to find that soft effusion of sentiment, that flowing fervency of affection, which would meet and fill the indefinable deficiency in my own emotions. But they were equally dull and spiritless, and I read them again and again, still more and more involved in wonder how they ever afforded one a moment's delight.

58

Sex won't do it.

Vice

When fancy flew into her presence, and beheld in her a
complete assemblage of every beauty and loveliness, it seemed
impossible that such dry and formal epistles could ever emanate
from a bosom so warmly affectionate, so fondly glowing with
every sweet enchanting sensation, that dances in the enthusiastic
bosom of female vivacity. Those reflections filled me with restless
inquietude, and I threw by the letters as unmeaning trifles that
could only amuse the heart of a child. My mind was in search of
something it had lost, with a faint impression that it could be
found. It would grasp, and grasp in vain, with its utmost stretch of
thought, for this imaginary something which was ever before my
fancy, yet ever beyond its reach. Like the faded image of almost
forgotten pleasures, it would now hover round my imagination as
if just ready to burst upon my mind, then flit away in a twinkling,
into the profound vacuum of oblivion, where intelligence can
never dart a ray, and leave me bewildered with my own
sensations, in a shoreless void where no object was discernable, to
satisfy the craving anxieties of a thought.

The embraces of Emerald and Armilda could not gratify this
boundless vacancy of desire. Balls, assemblies, cards, gallantries,
and the whole phalanx of licentious pleasures, could not satiate
this mighty void in my enjoyments. Time rolled his tedious wheels
over the broad surface of another year, and left its fleeting shadow
floating away on the dark ocean of forgotten eternity.
Intemperance and vice had gained ascendancy over my faculties
and practice, yet still was the image of the distant Zerelda the
acknowledged sample of loveliness, and still was my mind
longing to grasp the unformed, featureless object of my anxiety,
yet still it eluded the boldest efforts of my imagination. But this
unweary restlessness of desire grew every day more weak as the
second year was mingled with those "beyond the flood," and I
plunged deeper into the vortex of dissipation.

Armilda was now in the close of her fifteenth year, when the
tender, germinal virgin love begins to expand its earliest leaves,
and open the modest blossom of affection in all the delicious
sweets of mingled bloom and purity; when the snow white veil of

59

Armilda now 15

She is never troubled by modesty — she becomes a nympho maniac?

modesty trembles on the female bosom with a quickness of sensibility, which is kindled into the bashful blush by the slightest suggestion of impropriety; when like the sensitive plant, the dawning desires in the timid heart venture forth in all the loveliness of maiden delicacy to embalm themselves in the soft emotions of a sympathetic bosom while fanned by the fragrant breezes of innocence, but startle into alarm, and frighted, shrink from the rude embrace or the gentlest breath of danger. But those beauties, those emotions, were never suffered to bud in Armilda's mind.

Her bosom, their native garden, was overgrown with the poisonous hemlock of illicit desires. Those practices, which commenced in the age of thoughtless imbecility, had imperceptibly lost the frightful shape in which they are beheld by the eye of virtue, and maturing with the progress of her mind, had grown into inveterate habit, until they were almost constitutional. Had her happiness occupied the smallest portion of her mother's serious thoughts, our unblushing correspondence would never have commenced, or would have been terminated in infancy, but she was hurled away in the wide whirlpool of fashion while her daughter's heart was permitted to fall before its bloom–a faded, blighted flower.

She had gained the dangerous reputation of a beauty, and being indulged by her mother in all the extravagance of dress and amusements, she was surrounded by a crowd of coxcomed admirers, whose attention and adulation poisoned her mind into the most consummate ambition and coquetry, which served to blight the last glow of hope that lingered in her bosom, and she was lost forever! But she, together with the numerous coquettish throng of Richmond, had power to plunge me, every day, still deeper in the gloomy gulf of vicious practices. The love and virtue of my distant relatives were too much weakened by absence to deter me. The natural propensities and principles of my mind were too far overpowered by the predominance of inflammable passions to restrain me, and at the close of another year I was still deeper involved in the dreadful sink of licentiousness.

coquetry

THE PRISONERS OF NIAGARA

At this period my father had promised that I should return to Haylard Village, but now he requested me to continue still another year in Richmond, at the end of which he had determined that I should enter the army. The enormities of my vices had not yet reached my family, for alas, they had so near a resemblance to the general practices of young men who are born to considerable expectations and raised in populous cities, that they were considered by more serious acquaintances as only the irregularities of youth, which would be corrected by maturer reason. But trust not indulgent parent, trust not mistaken youth to the efficacy of manhood and reason for the correction of the follies of a juvenile. Those follies too often become constitutional, even to the utter overthrow of manhood and reason themselves. While my vices were thus overlooked, my unexampled progress in science, and my friendly, benevolent disposition and practices, were the envy of many, and the admiration of all. While shamefully debased in folly, I was beheld by the world as a youth of the most brilliant expectations.

My life was regulated more by impulse than principle or inclination. I never intended to deviate from the strictest rules of virtue and morality, and ever resolved that the last act of intemperance I had committed should terminate my disgraceful career, but in the next moment, led blindfolded by the force of example or stimulated by ungoverned appetency, I would rush into the perpetration of a similar debauchery.

My connection with Armilda grew every day more alarming. Both she and her mother conducted themselves toward me as if they were confident that I intended to marry her, whereas nothing was more distant from my intention. I therefore resolved to break off our dangerous intercourse, and for that purpose was continually reserved in her company. This was no sooner discovered by the mother and daughter than they employed their utmost enticements to chain my affections in the power of Armilda's charms. So energetic was their influence that when I came completely within the sphere of their attraction, my resolutions vanished, and I was the abject slave of her will.

61

He will not marry Armilda but they respect him

THE PRISONERS OF NIAGARA

Several months passed away in determinations to oppose, and obedient submissions to her desires. In all our interviews, she appeared anxious to extort from me a promise of marriage, and at last grew so urgent that I resolved to abandon her forever. This resolution I had punctually adhered to for two months, when passing by the door of Mrs. Willford's chamber at a late hour of the night, I overheard the pronunciation of my own name, and, pausing a moment, was shocked into astonishment at the following shameless conversation:

Armilda: But I fear he will never be brought to consent.

Willford: You must not permit him to escape from your allurements, for if once the spell is entirely broken, it will be impossible to persuade or frighten him into a marriage.

Armilda: I am resolved, if he will not marry me, he shall never marry any other. I would ransack heaven and earth for vengeance, and if he will not love me, he shall learn to dread me.

Willford: We are not forced to that fatal extremity. Allure him into another interview and yield to his solicitations. I will come in and witness your interchange of caresses and terrify him into a promise of marriage. But if that should fail, I have an effective scheme which I will communicate hereafter.

Confounded at the matchless depravity which this dialogue evinced, I hastened to my room. It was now evident that the amour of Armilda was conducted by the advisement and machinations of the infamous mother, and with the express intention of compelling me into a detested marriage. I awoke like a knight of romance when a peal of thunder dissolves his enchantments, and castles, towers and cities fall in crashing ruins around him, and vanish in a horrible chaos of sound, leaving him alone in the midst of a wild and dreary waste. A too-well remembered dream displayed the dangerous windings of my past irregularities, and a quickened reflection beheld the perils of my present situation: Standing on a wasting quicksand, torn on either side by the swelling billows of danger and disgrace. I saw that by deserting Armilda I would be plunged into ignominy, pursued by the vengeance of two artful, ambitious and implacable women, and probably abandoned by my

family to the influence of poverty and merited contempt. But I had
no hesitation in choosing this dreadful alternative, for the idea of a
marriage with Armilda rung more dismally in my mind than the
doleful dirge of death, and like the features of an awakening
gorgon, froze me into horror.

It required a shock like this—a shock of startling thunder—to
arouse my slumbering reason into action. It now awoke
"Emerging from a sea of dreams, tumultuous—" but was involved
"In a black tempest, and a night of clouds," which its dawning
beams could scare illumine, but it assumed its prerogative and
swayed the long neglected scepter of my passions, and I resolved
to throw myself, a destitute penitent, into the inviting arms of
protecting virtue. I abandoned Armilda, Emerald, and all my
immoral companions at the same moment, and shut myself
entirely from society, under pretense of being unwell, for the
space of a month. I had not sufficient fortitude to inform my father
of my dilemma, but earnestly supplicated permission to leave the
academy, but received no immediate answer. My desires to see
Zerelda grew infinitely more strong than they had ever been. The
secret unconquerable longing for an unknown enjoyment which
had so racked my imagination for twelve months after I had left
Zerelda, but which had been latterly suppressed in a measure by a
ceaseless routine of bewitching amusements, now awoke in my
mind with new and restless anxiety. All the happiness of
expectation appeared to hang on the possession of this
unintelligible desire.

Nor did this letter from Zerelda allay this ferment of anxiety.
But, before I repeat Zerelda's letter, it may not be improper to
state that when she was first left by her uncle with Mrs. Haylard
and Emerine in Baltimore, both she and Emerine soon grew
dissatisfied with the new and fantastic frivolities of fashion. When
Mrs. Haylard, in about two months, returned to Hampshire, they
obtained her permission to accompany her, and flew with gay
delight to the romantic scenes of their former retirement.

Mrs. Haylard, although reared and educated in the first circles
of Baltimore, had seen and lamented the superficial and defective

manner pursued in the education of fashionable females, and gladly recalled her tender daughters from the first female academy in Maryland, that she might have a complete opportunity of forming their minds by the fairest model of sentimental virtue and uncorrupted intelligence. This was a task which accorded with the warmest desires and highest ambition of Mrs. Haylard, and for which few women were better calculated. She immediately commenced the plan of their education, and, understanding the whole texture of their minds, so happily adapted her instructions to their desires and capabilities that she rendered their severest studies a pleasing variety of gratifications, and the dullest fields of science a delightful garden, where they could stray with pleasure, and while contemplating the useful vegetable, amuse their fancies with the embryo blossom and the expanded bloom. With such an instructor, those sprightly girls displayed the opening genius of science, taste and sentiment. Their minds began to expand the young flower of hope, in all its infant beauties, to catch the cherishing rays of the morning sun of reason, and bid fair, ere long, to receive on their expanded bosoms the bright beams of meridian intelligence.

Zerelda had transmitted to me a regular account of her improvements, and so anxious was she to render one acquainted with every thing which was pleasing to her, or which she imagined would be amusing to me, that almost every post brought me a circumstantial account of her weekly readings and pastimes. Her letters not only afforded me a scale whereby to scan the rapid advances of her mind, inhaling the sweet day-beams of intelligence, but completely drew aside the shading curtain with which female reserve too often veils the brightest features of their dispositions, to the utter extermination of native simplicity and unsuspecting innocence. She threw off every mask, and, emboldened by conscious virtue, appeared before me without the faintest disguise. All her propensities, principles and sentiments, all her loves and hopes and wishes, all the panting desires of warm flushing youth, all the chimerical speculations of uncorrupted enthusiasm, and all the fond ardor, the soaring anticipations of romantic vivacity, were spread, in unreserved delicacy, to my admiring bosom. The most minute circumstances could not escape her, and she wrote me details of all her rambles, and pleasures, of every new enjoyment that nature opened to her imagination—of every new flower that bloomed in the village, and every sweet prospect of gratification that fancy anticipated in the ensuing season.

But, ah! Of what amount were those enchanting epistles to the wild voluptuary who whole mind was corrupted by the vapid mania of dissipation?

Zerelda had been nearly three years under the tuition of her aunt, but about two months before she wrote this letter, she, accompanied by Emerine, had visited her father, and spent the time until she wrote in the gayest circles of Baltimore. But I have already deviated much farther than I intended, and will proceed to the letter.

Baltimore

Dear Evermont,

For I cannot call you brother—that once delightful sound has become tasteless and insipid. I know not the cause, but a secret whispering of my heart revolts at the coldness of the tender name, yet shrinks, and trembles and blushes, at the strangeness of its desires.

I have long tried the efficacy of all the amusements of Baltimore: balls, theaters, card parties. Do not blush, my dear Evermont, I was never at a card party but once, and then only to gratify my female acquaintances, and will never be at another. There is something in gambling even for amusement which makes delicacy tremble. Did a modest woman ever play? Dancing, too, has occupied my attention, but I have sought diversion from it in vain. It might afford pastime for children, and children ought to dance, but how an intelligent, feeling mind can delight in such a volatile, unmeaning exercise, is to me a mystery. The warm,

[handwritten annotations: "Dancing is indelicate — she forswears — This is just going to turn him on"]

irregular propensities, which should be curbed in every mind, are stimulated into activity by dancing, but not one noble, generous, or affectionate impulse receives the slightest energy or operation in its bewildering labyrinths. It appears to have been originally suggested by unwarrantable feelings, and is indecent in its tendency and immodest in practice. I will dance no more. Dancing is laudable for the improvement of children, but is frivolous and insignificant in men, and indelicate in women.

I have also experienced the inefficacy of dress and company. I have been flattered and caressed. The wealth of my father has drawn around me a crowd of fawning females and buxom butterflies of men, but they are all strangers to my heart. Like swarms of insects in a summer evening's sun, they only infest and interrupt my enjoyments. I am everywhere surrounded by admirers, but the language of their admiration is unintelligible; it reaches not to the deep vacancy in my heart, nor fills, nor explains the wilderness of my desires.

[handwritten annotation in left margin: "free femme questions"]

The whole round of fashion is a class of frivolities and unsubstantial scenes which cannot supply nutriment for a single thought. I want—I know not what I want. I want something to make me happy and want to know what that something is. I ransack every new amusement with the eager hope that my desires will be gratified, but, instead of allaying, it increases my wants, and serves to show their insatiable nature. O Evermont, I want—I want to see you, but cannot help blushing while I express this wish. I sat down to petition uncle Haylard to request you to visit me here, but my feelings trembled, my heart panted strangely at the idea, as if I was doing wrong. My desire increased but my tremors became more exquisite, and I was compelled to relinquish my design. I communicated my wish to Emerine, but even this occasioned a new fluttering sensation in my bosom, and aroused a strange glow of color in my cheeks, and my voice faltered so that I could only express my request in broken syllables. Emerine laughed at my emotions, and wrote to her father as I desired, and then penned this paragraph for me.

[handwritten annotation in bottom left: "Emerine writes for her"]

Evermont, I am a strange girl. I leave Baltimore next week, disgusted with fashionable society. I return to Hayland Village but the cravings of my heart are not there. I look round the world and am vexed to see every thing so void and dreary. My heart was formerly as light as a feather playing along an April breeze, but it is so no longer. Come to Hayland Village and see what a restless, spiritless being I am become.

ZERELDA

This letter contained a train of feelings similar to my own, but it explained not their source. I sometimes imagined, from descriptions I had read in romances, that this feeling was occasioned by love, but this suggestion would not bear realizing for I fancied I had always loved Zerelda, and I had never experienced those sensations until latter years. But this letter increased my impatience to see Zerelda, and I wrote again to my father, urging my former request.

As I walked down the street to put this letter into the post office, I caught a glimpse of little Amacette, whom I had relieved on my journey to Hampshire. She was entering the door of Mr. L____, and notwithstanding my anxiety to learn what had become of her mother, yet I would not venture into the house for inquiry for fear of meeting too potent a temptation in the address of Emerald. On my return, I understood that Amacette had been for about two weeks in the service of Emerald as a chambermaid. This intelligence was extremely unpleasant, for the countenance of Amacette was expressive of innocent simplicity that had excited in me a strong interest for her happiness, which I knew would be destroyed in the service of the licentious Emerald. I resolved to draw her from the infectious influence of that voluptuary, and for this purpose very frequently passed the house that I might obtain an interview with her unknown to Emerald.

Not long after, Emerald visited Mrs. Willford in company with Wilson Whitford, and I, judging it a favorable opportunity to further my purpose, immediately repaired to Mr. L____'s to

67 *Benevolence!*

confer with Amacette. She was in evident confusion when I entered. She blushed, startled back, and trembled, so that she could scarce desire me to be seated, and was immediately retiring from the room.

"Madam," said I, "will you favor me with your company for a moment? I have something particular to communicate."

"I—I—sir, will return in a moment," she replied with a faltering utterance and a frightened countenance, which seemed to be unaccountable, and was hastening from the room, notwithstanding I repeated my request in more urgent expressions. Mr. L___ entered the room and entirely frustrated my design. After tarrying a few minutes, I returned to my habitation, endeavoring in vain to unravel the enigma of her conduct.

I supped that evening with a very lively company of young people at the family table, and could not with propriety retire to my room immediately as I had usually done to escape the allurements of Armilda. She was gay this evening to an extreme. The richness of her dress gave additional attractions to her person, which, together with the vivacity of her wit and conversation, rendered her one of the most desirable women the eye of the voluptuary ever beheld. She directed her attention principally to me, and before the company retired, I had been exposed to the most bewitching arrows of desire, and led thoughtlessly into slight caresses, by the sprightly playfulness of her conduct. She had engaged me in an interesting discourse as the company retired and I could not immediately withdraw. Mrs. Willford left the room, and the door was purposely closed as if by accident. This was the crisis I had dreaded. I had passions–they were now fired by inviting glances, warm and inflaming as ever lighted from the eye of woman. I knew the power I possessed over this woman. I knew the danger also, but I was—

The door flew open and Mrs. Willford entered. Armilda pretended to faint. As this was no more than I expected, I was carelessly passing out of the room, but Mrs. Willford, with the countenance of a fury, demanded what I had done.

68

Calls rape / He calls her a pimp —

Armilda

a prostitute

(wish)

"Nothing, Madam," said I, "but what you intended I should do."

"Monster! Have you not ruined my child?" continued she in a still more furious tone.

"You ruined her yourself," replied I, "but if you are prudent, you will moderate your voice, unless you with the world to witness her disgrace."

"Unfeeling wretch," she cried, "is it thus you mock the miseries you have brought on my family? Oh! My heart! My heart!" Saying which she sank down upon the bed by Armilda but took care not to become insensible, for when I was again retiring from the room, she sprang out of her trance and shut the door to prevent me, exclaiming with a menacing air, "You shall never leave this room until you atone for this injury. You have seduced my daughter and ruined her reputation, and shall never stir from hence until you retrieve her character by marriage."

"Mrs. Willford," said I, "a few words will settle this affair. I have become acquainted with all your arts to draw me into this dilemma. I was a witness to your conversation when you laid the plan for this interview more than two months ago. I have exerted all my power to preserve your daughter from infamy, but you were determined she should be prostituted to your ambition. But remain silent, and the world will know nothing of your degradation. But if you wish to divulge this affair, I have sufficient evidence to convince all mankind that Armilda is a confirmed libertine, and that you have acted in the honorable capacity of her procuress, So, Ma'am, this plan has failed, but you said you had an effective scheme that you are to *communicate hereafter*!" As I finished these expressions, I threw open the door and left the room before the storm that was gathering on her brow had time to burst.

I abandoned the house immediately, and retired to a public inn. My mind was now completely bewildered in forming the plan of my immediate conduct. I could not return to my father's without his consent, for my veneration of his authority was a cheerful and implicit obedience to his will. I could not inform him of my having left Mrs. Willford's without giving some reason for

His predicament

my conduct. I could not give the true cause without revealing not only my own disgrace, but also the disgrace of Willford and her daughter, which would be little short of villainy, and to relate a falsehood had made me shudder from childhood. At last I resolved to write to my father, in pathetic terms, the perils of my situation from the expected invasion of the perfidious Arnold at the head of the British army, and of the dissipation in Richmond. This letter I wrote immediately, in the most forcible and persuasive manner. I also wrote to my mother, urging the same request, in arguments tender and affectionate, and petitioned her to plead with my father on my behalf. I also wrote to Zerelda and Emerine, and engaged them to join in my solicitations, and felt somewhat calmed in mind with an almost certain expectation of obtaining the desired favor.

CHAPTER VII

The sun that shed the blaze of another day was lingering on the flaming bosom of the western clouds. I left the city to enjoy a solitary ramble where the rapid waves of the James River were tumbling among the rocks of the falls in a waste of murmurs. I was scarcely beyond the suburbs of the city when I beheld *Amacette* walking slowly along the road, a great distance before. Prompted by a desire to warn her of the danger she incurred in the service of Emerine, and also by a curiosity to learn the cause of her agitation and embarrassment when I visited her at Mrs. L____'s, I increased my pace with the hope of overtaking her. The sun had set, and the heavy forests which stretched along the river shed a solemn twilight. A close carriage drove by me. It arrived opposite Amacette and stopped. Two men sprang out and seized the defenseless girl. She could but scream, but her scream rang through the listening courts of Heaven. I outflew the tempests to her assistance, but in an instant she was in the carriage and the horses in full speed.

They were already a great distance before me, but I ran, I flew to overtake them. The windings of the road soon placed them beyond my sight, and I knew not that I ever should be able to behold them again. Two strange officers advanced down the road on horseback. I seized the bridle of the foremost. My mind was in tumultuous agitation, and my words and actions accorded with its boisterous feelings.

"I must have your horse," cried I. "Dismount in an instant, or she will be lost." The stranger stared at me in astonishment. His companion seized a pistol, thinking me a highwayman. "Almighty God!" continued I, seeing him hesitate. "Have you no heart? Will you not lend me your horse to wrest her from destruction?"

71

THE PRISONERS OF NIAGARA

"Where—what! Who is she?" demanded the stranger.

"An angel," replied I, almost distracted with delay, "in carriage! By a villain! Oh! For God's sake! Here is my purse—my notes—my watch—everything—oh, pity! Oh!"

Tears flowed in a shower. The stranger dismounted, I sprang on his horse, leaned forward, gave him the whip and darted like an arrow. His companion followed at full speed, but I had bounded far beyond his sight. From the summit of a hill I beheld the waves of the James River, glittering with the broad beams of a rising moon, and the carriage standing on the brink. I flew thither like lightening. The miscreants had left the carriage to the driver, and held Amacette in a boat halfway across the stream. Amacette beheld me on shore. Her mouth was confined—she was unable to call. She raised her hands and face to heaven. The ethereal appeared to burst into a new blaze of brilliance. She strained her extended arms toward me—I know not my emotions. I grasped the pistols from the holsters and plunged into the stream. The waters foamed around my horse as he beat the billows with impatient fury. The boat was rowed with violence. Amacette fell on her knees and stretched her arms to God, and to me. She tore the bandage from her mouth and exclaimed, "Oh, God! Assist him!" My horse seemed invigorated with the same spirited resolution with which I was inspired, and dashed through the current with vigorous impetuosity. I was soon near the boat. One of the villains sprang from his oar and discharged a pistol at my head, but Amacette, with the courage of an Amazon, threw him overboard at the same instant, and the ball whizzed through the air innocuous.

We were near the land, and my horse struck the shore some distance below the boat. I leaped from him, and beheld the other wretch, who was none other than Whitford, spring out of the boat. I discharged one of my pistols at him, but he rushed so suddenly into a grove of willows that he escaped unhurt, and I was too far exhausted to pursue him. I ran to the relief of Amacette, who extended her arms, and fell in mine, in a joyful silence. The man she had thrown overboard reached the shore and fled after his companion. I led my horse onto the boat, and Amacette held him

Amacette throws the kidnapper overboard!

She saves him!
he saves her! Her story

Noble youth!

THE PRISONERS OF NIAGARA

while I rowed the boat to the other shore where the stranger who
had followed me awaited my arrival in profound astonishment. He
grasped my hand and Amacette's with rapture.

"Noble youth," said he, "you are generous and invincible. Oh,
that I had such a friend!"

"You may have such a one, sir," said I, "if you will receive
him. My heart is open to all in the human family, and panting to
fly into every congenial bosom."

oh, good grief!

"Yes, you shall be my friend," cried he, still holding my hand.
"I will cultivate my present impulses until they strengthen into the
generous ties of friendship. And you, dear Madam," addressing
Amacette, "you have a worthy protector, and are doubtless worthy
of his courage and intrepidity."

"My heart feels the merit of his generosity," said Amacette, "it
glows with gratitude and admiration, but his actions are superior
to my praise, my thankfulness, or any power of making
compensation."

"You have overpaid me already," said I, and led her to the
carriage which yet remained on the bank of the river. Ordering the
driver to proceed to Richmond, I mounted my horse and followed
after, accompanied by the officer. As I proceeded slowly by the
side of the carriage, Amacette informed me that Whitford had long
endeavored to gain her hand to no purpose, and, finding all his
attempts unsuccessful, had once before resorted to force, but was
prevented by the assistance of a generous man whose name she
concealed. Afterward, her mother, fearing a second attempt, kept
her constantly under her care until, finding herself in straightened
circumstances, she permitted her to enter the services of Emerald
L____. She had been there discovered by Whitford the evening
before, and resolved to return immediately to her mother. She
obtained the consent of Emerald and set out for home, but on her
way was overtaken and seized by Whitford in the manner already
stated.

The secret protector

When she concluded, I inquired, "Who, my dear Amacette, is
your mother? And what are these new distresses you mentioned?"

73

THE PRISONERS OF NIAGARA

Amacette shook her head. "I know you are generous and compassionate," said she, "and I can be grateful, but cannot be disobedient—pray inquire no further."

I thus made several attempts to learn something further of herself and her mother, but she evaded all my inquiries and persevered in mysterious concealment.

We drew near the city and found the officer whose horse I borrowed amusing himself with gazing on the sheets of foam that whirled along the breaking billows of the falls, and in listening to the lonesome melancholy roar of the agitated waters.

"Well, have you saved her?" cried he, transported at seeing us return.

"Saved her!" cried my companion. "It was impossible but he must save her, and yet it appeared impossible that he could do it. I never saw determination personified before. My Lord Marquis, I would that you had seen him darting over the hills like a shooting comet! Seen him buffet the current of the river into a bed of foam, to bear him victory and glory."

He thus proceeded, with ardent animation, and related the particulars of my success. His embellishments and energy of description charmed the admiring Marquis, for I now discovered the officer who lent me his horse was the noble Marquis de La F____. He clasped me to his heart, exclaiming, "Oh! My valiant youth! How my soul dotes on such generous heroism! We must be friends."

"Noble Marquis," replied I, "you confided in me while an entire unknown; for that I admire you. You lent me your horse to save me from despair; for that I esteem you. You heart bled for the misfortunes of an unknown woman; for that I revere, I love you, and would die to befriend you."

"But where is this fortunate lady," said the Marquis, "who has so brave a champion to protect her? I long to congratulate her on her good fortune in finding such a friend." We opened the carriage, but looked in vain for Amacette. She was flown. My companions look at me in astonishment, but I was not much

Where is Amacette?
She's vanished!

surprised. "My God, she is gone," said the Marquis, "or have you been fighting for a spirit?"

"Yes," said I, "a spirit pure as the breath of chastity, or I am much deceived. I expect she is not with her mother who lives somewhere among these hills. Her flight is not surprising, though I neither knew nor expected it."

"Who, and what, is she?" exclaimed the Marquis, still more confounded.

"All I know," said I, "her name is Amacette. I know not her other name, nor will she communicate it. Her mother is poor and concealed from the world. I have been in the girl's company twice before, and then not twenty minutes, but she is—I know she is innocent and amiable."

"And have you performed this for a stranger?" inquired the Marquis.

"Certainly," said I, "would you not have done the same? Did you not do more in lending me your horse?"

"Dear amiable youth," cried he, and warmly pressed my hand. We discovered a paper lying on the seat which Amacette had left, and some others near the door. We took them up, and hastened to town for a light to read them.

When at the inn, we found the one on the seat written with a pencil and directed to me.

Inimitable Evermont,

My heart beats with high gratitude, but the commands of a mother will excuse my reserve. I leave you this to account for my flight, and assure you that before you read it, I will be on my mother's bosom.

AMACETTE

The others were mostly fragments of verses, and descriptions of her own imagination, which she had dropped by accident, among which was an unsealed letter to her mother and a poem on love, concluding with these ecstatic lines: "Of earth no more, I'm

75

born of heaven:/ I love, and am beloved." The letter to her mother contained this enigmatical expression:

Evermont lives in this place. You commanded me to shun him but you do not know him. His appearance is noble and dignified, but he has such a mild, benevolent aspect that it teaches all who seem him how to love. His person is tall, his features are bold and commanding, yet open and generous. His dark eyes are quick, piercing and determined, yet at the same time as gentle and smiling as the lighted dew drop on the morning lily. He may be the son of my cruel father, but even if he is, I know he is a good man.

This letter contained a mystery which my companions were as capable of explaining as myself! But we all gave curiosity th reins of imagination in vain, for we knew not when our conjectures were in the right. My companions became interesting in conversation, and before the hour of separation, I became warmly attached to them both. The Marquis de La F____ was affable, open, and intelligent, and dissipation the prepossession I had imbibed against all foreign nobility. In him I beheld all those attributes concentrated which constitute the man, the friend, and the philosopher, and I could not only allow him the title of Marquis with pleasure, but gave him a throne in my heart. His companion was of the name of Anderville, a captain in the army of the United States. He was a man whose appearance and demeanor could bear a comparison with the Marquis without disparagement. He was sedate and contemplative, but at the same time unreserved and cheerful in conversation. He spoke on any subject without reflection, yet spoke as if he had reflected on the subject all his life. In short, he was calculated to prepossess a generous mind into respect and friendship, and to secure it in his favor by the ties of pleasure and approbation.

We conversed, with mutual satisfaction, on the state of the war, and the different interests and powers of the French, British, and American governments, and in the close of the evening they made me very advantageous proposals to join the army, and urged

He's offered a commission

Haylard killed by Indians?

me by the strongest entreaties to accept a commission in the American service. I could not be prevailed upon to act without the authority or permission of my father, yet promised them if I could procure his consent, I would join them with pleasure. On those terms we parted, for their duty required them to leave Richmond by break of day.

Soon after I had been separated from those noble officers, a traveler reported at the inn that Major Haylard had been slain by a party of Indians on the headwaters of the James River. Alarmed and affected at this report, I endeavored to believe it without foundation, yet feared and trembled lest it should be true. But alas! This melancholy account was indubitably established in a few hours by the arrival of a man who had been with Major Haylard when he fell.

"I accompanied Major Haylard," said he, "with several farmers of Hampshire to a large purchase of land they had made on Jackson's River. The land lay a considerable distance beyond the settlement, but as there had been no Indians in that part of the country for several months, we traveled over it without a thought of danger and began to survey it. But early one morning, when our party had all gone hunting, except Major Haylard and me, about twenty Indians discovered our camp. I was accidentally about a hundred paces from camp when I saw them rush Major Haylard. He was unprepared for resistance, and was immediately cleft to the earth by the nearest Indian. I saw him fall, saw the blood gush in a torrent from his head, and his murderer spring upon him with his fearful scalping knife. It was impractical for me to render him any assistance, and fearing a similar fate, I fled immediately to the settlements. The rest of my company also escaped unhurt, but we found the peasantry too weak to resist the Indians, and it was three days before we assembled a sufficient force to venture to the place where Major Haylard was slain. When we arrived there, the Indians had retreated, but we found no relict of Major Haylard—not even the stain of his blood was to be seen, and we concluded he had met with the fate so dreadful yet so common to those who fall by the savages at a distance from the settlements,

He's gone

that of being left a prey to the ravenous beasts of the desert. It was too late to pursue the Indians with effect, and we returned again to the settlements."

What child of sensibility, who has witnessed the death of a parent, but can feel and bleed with the sorrows which preyed in a sudden torrent upon my heart when I thus learned that my father—my more than father—was torn from my heart without one parting blessing, one farewell sigh or look. When I could not even pour out my soul in his fainting bosom nor close the eye which had so often smiled upon me with ineffable tenderness—no—nor embalm his endeared remains with one filial tear, warm with the vital ardor of my heart. A void opened in my bosom. It was the sacred recess once filled with the idea of a living father, but it was now dreary and wild. A damp chillness crept, shivering, through my feelings. A lonely, melancholy rumor mourned in my bosom! My soul sank in a sigh, and I sat the model of vacancy while my eyes streamed uninterrupted tears.

It was long before my reflective faculties could glance over my loss or contemplate the virtue of my venerable departed parent whose life had been advantageous to his country, honorable to himself and memorable to his friends. He was esteemed in public, and revered in private life. His country, his neighborhood, will feel and lament his loss, but to his family, where he was the prudent head, the generous guardian, the affectionate husband, and tender father, his fall will be wept and commemorated with tears more pure and sacred than ever decked the death of monarchs or the fall of empires.

To me his death was a severe, irretrievable loss, which the feelings of my heart were unprepared to receive. Since my late reformation he had become peculiarly endeared to my bosom, and I looked up to him as the guardian genius who was to complete my progress in the paths of virtue. Though surrounded by the most imminent danger from the machinations of Willford and her daughter, and the displeasure of Emerald, who had attempted in vain to allure me back to her embraces, yet the sweet and solemn

78

The surprise letter (

sensations of filial love and filial sorrow were indulged without restraint to the warm excess of my affection.

I resolved to return to my family and participate in their grief, and, if possible, to lighten the exquisite weight of their sorrows by teaching them a doctrine I had not yet learnt myself—the doctrine of resignation.

While my mind dwelt mournfully on this melancholy subject, I received the following singular note:

Mr. Evermont,

Will confer a memorable obligation by repairing to Cherry Vale below the falls precisely at ten o'clock this evening, where he will be received by his much indebted friend

SUSAN ETHERFORD

N.B. Communicate this request to no person or the happiness of the subscriber is forever blasted.

S.E.

Surprised as I was at the reception of this note from a girl whom I beheld as a child of uncorrupted nature, I resolved to meet her agreeably to her request, although at an unseasonable hour and in a lonesome part of town, and learn the purport of her secret communication. I had once relieved her father from prison, and I knew not but her present object was to solicit my assistance for him or some other person in distress whose circumstances would not permit a public application to be made. With these reflections I was at Cherry Vale as the clock rung ten. Susan was already there, and notwithstanding that the moon was wrapped up in a thick atmosphere of clouds, yet she was entirely veiled as if in deep distress. She took my hand in silence and led me through a small gate into a little cluster of trees, formed into a kind of arbor, and seated me by her side on a settee of grass. Still more and more astonished at these enigmatical proceedings, I sat in listening anticipation until she pressed my hand more closely in hers, and

uttered a heavy sigh which seemed to rend her bosom with its swelling waves.

She then leaned her forehead on my hand, and after a long, solemn pause, observed in accents faltering and broken, "Mr. Evermont, you will be amazed at what I am about to declare, and probably shocked at my dereliction of the principles of my sex, but my heart is too full and it must have a vent or burst. You relieved my aged father from a hopeless imprisonment, I beheld you as the angel of humanity, your image took possession of my soul, I strove for months and years against the force of my attachment—" but her voice died. Her head fell on my shoulder, and she was compelled to wipe the effusions of strong sensibility from her eyes. I was deeply affected at her emotions and pressed my arm around her waist. This she received as a token of encouragement, and raising her eyes which were yet veiled, she said in a faint voice which shook and trembled amid her billowy sighs, "Oh! Speak Evermont. Ease my anxious, breaking heart—pronounce me wretched."

I pitied the poor unfortunate girl from my soul. I had seen her several times since I relieved her father, and although my pursuits had prevented me from becoming intimately acquainted with her, yet I always considered her as a picture of pristine beauty and innocent simplicity—a pure and blooming blossom amid a withering wilderness of dissipation. But her present inexcusable conduct overturned that opinion, and I concluded that she had heretofore banished the modest reserve of her sex, before the bashfulness of female timidity would have permitted her to have undertaken this unwarrantable step. My silence appeared to confirm her fears.

"Alas!" she cried, "I have trampled on the principles of my sex only to ensure certain misery. Ah! Unhappy Susan."

"Indeed, Madam," I replied, "at such a time and place, I know not what to say. At some other time—"

"You then condemn my imprudence," cried she. "Undone! Undone!" and seemed to faint in my arms.

THE PRISONERS OF NIAGARA

The ardor of my disposition ever acted most powerfully on its immediate object. It then clung with all its might, and lavished all its powers until some new object attracted its attention with sufficient force to draw it from its former operations, and then all its energy was bestowed upon its new pursuit. Thus it was that in one moment I could be swallowed up in dissipation, and in the next, be all benevolence and virtue, and thus could I bound in an instant from the extremes of love to those of hatred, or from the most poignant sorrow to unbounded rapture. And it was this singularity of temperament with which, a few hours since, I wept the loss of my father with all the sincerity of a heartbroken son, but now, having lost the immediate sight of my mournful subject, I felt the ardor of my passions burn in a new channel while this deluded girl lay motionless on my bosom. I plainly discovered that she had not fainted, and removing the veil from her face, I indulged my rising ardor in a shower of embraces. *His ardor rises.*

Although it was now too dark to behold her beauties, yet I knew she was a sweet, delicious girl. It was dark and we were alone. She was in my power—lovely and desirable in the extreme. I was but man—.

What is man? exclaimed a sublime moralist when he discovered the frailty of his nature. *What am I?* could I more justly exclaim at this moment of acknowledged imbecility, when all my virtuous determinations were swept from my mind by an impetuous torrent of passion. And I could not be induced to separate from Susan until, by long entreating, she consented to meet me at the same place and hour the ensuing evening.

I had determined to leave Richmond on this day for Hayland Village, but my engagement with Susan prevented me from putting my design in execution. My anxieties to meet and Zerelda were warm and enthusiastic; but my passion for Susan had its object more immediately in view. The attraction was stronger and my propensities irresistible. My journey was therefore delayed another day.

I again visited Susan, and again at parting forgot my former resolutions, forgot my virtuous sorrow for my father, forgot my

81

His rising ardor over-takes the veiled lady

return to Haylard Village, forgot Zerelda, forgot everything, and prevailed on Susan to admit another interview. Several days thus glided away in my forming the most powerful determinations to adhere to virtue and return to my family, and several nights were passed with Susan in breaking those solemn determinations and procrastinating my journey, during which time I had never seen the face of Susan unveiled, except when the night was too dark for me to distinguish her features. The true cause of the secrecy I was unable to learn, but supposed it was intended to conceal the blush which irritated Modesty had planted on her once unsullied cheeks when she fled in anger from her bosom, and withdrew her sacred insignia from those blooming beds of roses.

His ... ... actions

2d stroke of thunder!
(His mother + Zerelda
No money forthcoming)

CHAPTER VIII

But from this infatuated dereliction of every principle of duty and propriety, I was to be aroused by a second stroke of thunder, more terrible than had ever yet burst from the atmosphere of my expectations. It was the time when I expected my regular *money* remittances to defray my expenses, and I repaired to the agent of my father to receive them, but they had not arrived. In their stead I received the following letter from my mother:

SIR,

You request permission to return to your family. I am surprised that you should desire to see those persons you have abandoned and disgraced, but when you learn to treat the name and memory of your deceased patron with proper respect and veneration, and your own character, and the character of your disconsolate foster relatives with due deference and propriety, you will then, and not till then, be permitted to return.

"Discarded, abandoned, undone!" exclaimed I. The letter fell to the ground. A small slip of paper which had been enclosed lodged in my hand. It contained these words:

Mr. Evermont will please to return the medal he received from me, or strike my image from the face of it.

ZERELDA

Gracious God! What were the suggestions of this request? My mother's letter, the idea of being driven from my family in poverty and contempt were lost in the more violent tumult of my feelings, which were occasioned by this unexpected shock. It shivered every fiber of my bosom, it came home to my heart, and convinced me that the long, painful vacancy in my enjoyments could only be filled by Zerelda, and that, in losing her, the world to me had rushed into chaos. I now beheld her in imagination, traversing the flowery fields of virtue, shining as a glittering cherub, "With each perfection dawning in her mind, / All beauty's treasure opening on her cheek," while I was separated from her by the deep, impassable gulf of my own abandoned practices, doomed forever to gaze and admire, but never, never to obtain her charms. The dark enigma of my desires was explained, and all my fond delights, my longing anticipations, now centered in her smiles. But ah! Distressing thought, I was now adjudged unworthy to wear her image on my bosom.

The medal was resting on my heart, my only gem of joy, the sweet token of Zerelda's affection. It seemed that all my heart strings were severed when I tore it away. I laid it on my lips as the last relict of hope, the last prospect of bliss!

"Go, thou memento of forfeited esteem," cried I, "go to thy gentle giver, whose affections no longer fly on 'fancy's wing' to the melancholy abode of her deserted Evermont. Bid her also tear my image from her bosom. Oh! Ye powers of love and sympathy! Can she forget the myriad instances in which our infancy has known but one heart and one soul? Can she forget the tender infantile expression, "Evermont, don't forget your Zerelda.' No, O God! It was thine to plant those emotions in her bosom, and no daring hand shall pluck them away. Go then, endearing medal, recline on that breast whose earliest, sweetest throb was mine. Thy language will be felt, it will quiver to her heart and speak of me. Thy gentle accents will awaken all the past in fond remembrance, and call from oblivion a thousand forgotten incidents to play in pleading pity around her feelings, and list the sovereign voice of mercy and forgiveness. Go, golden emblem of unfading virtue, 'go on her purer bosom rest,' lead her to the brink of the pool. Heavens! What must be her sensations then? Will not the young effusions of warm yet timid affection rise in kindling fervor on the swelling sensibilities of her heart burst beyond the forbidding

Regrets his depravity — but excuses himself

bounds of her bosom, and pant in one throbbing flow of sympathy in every nerve of soul and body."

This request convinced me that Virtue was the divinity of her adorations, that on her glowing alter she had sacrificed the dearest anticipations of her heart—the sweet, unequaled emotions of a first, a virgin affection. I now felt my own unworthiness with the keenest sensibility—I sank in my own estimation to the lowest depth of humility and degradation. I lamented the loss of Zerelda's affections, but in more sharp and exquisite pangs, lamented the depravity of my conduct, which had been the fatal cause. I knew that my practices, base as they were, had been misrepresented by my enemies to produce this melancholy change, but I resolved never to see Zerelda more until I could render myself worthy of her esteem. Her love I knew was mine, a dear immortal passion, and although its sensations might be suppressed and forgotten, and a warm and lasting flame burn over its faded ruins, yet its germ would live, "a sleeping beauty" in deathless slumber, until the voice of reason would vibrate on its latent fibers, and awake its silent pulses into action. It then would burst in embryo from the cell of oblivion, expand the beauteous blossom of virgin fondness, and bloom delightful luxuriance over the flowery garden of her bosom. Hope painted not the time when I could rise to merit over the shattered ruins of my reputation, but aspiring love rendered everything practicable, and I felt a pleasing certainty of meeting Zerelda when the blush of shame would be overshadowed by the spreading wreath of virtue.

But my anxiety to retain this evidence of Zerelda's former affection induced me to practice an innocent deception. I procured an ingenious artist to copy the medal so exactly that the difference could never be detected, and while I apparently complied with her request, I retained the original on my bosom, and sent the copy, with this inscription in small letters: "Forfeited by the fascinations of vice."

I resolved to leave Richmond, and wander in search of virtue and honor. I sold my books to discharge my existing debts. Some few volumes remained at Mrs. Willford's. I sent for them and they

pracices

"innocent deception"

enemies

Resolved to wander in search of virtue + honor

were returned, but between the leaves of one of them I found this
alarming epistle:

Sir,

      I have discovered a secret in which you are intimately
concerned. I have found the son of your deceased brother who was
supposed to have perished by the Indians. I was his nurse, and
have abundant marks of his person to justify my belief. He is now
in Richmond, and fast approaching manhood, and is a youth
deserving of his father's fortune. You know his claims, and the
necessity of keeping them in oblivion. They are known to none but
yourself, but when you recollect the affinity we bear to each other,
and how far I have already been accessory to his wrongs, you will
expect that the feelings of a mother, and the claims of a son,
should supercede all other considerations. But you also know my
wants and may command my silence. I shall await your answer
before I form my determinations.

                        ANN WILLFORD

    This letter had not long been written, and was not directed. It
conveyed no intelligence on which my mind could rest, but great
God! What a labyrinth of suggestions it excited. I had no doubt, at
first, but that I was the person alluded to in the letter, and if so, I
was the son of Mrs. Willford, which was an idea that flashed with
petrifying horror to the bottom of my soul. But this dreadful
supposition was banished by reflecting, that had I been her son,
she would never have permitted my intercourse with her daughter.
Though I believed her capable of glaring crimes, yet I could not
imagine her as a monster of such hellish depravity as to connive at
a horrible incestuous connected between her own children. While
the dreadful images which this paper had created were flitting
darkly through my mind, a messenger from Mrs. Willford came to
inquire for it, saying it had been left in the book by accident a few
minutes before. I followed the messenger to Mrs. Willford's. She
received me with a haughty frown and demanded in what
character I dared intrude within her doors.

He faces mrs Willford
Her ultimatum Marry daughter or
be ruined.

"In the character of a suppliant," said I, "to request an explanation of this mysterious letter."

"First swear," said she, "never to divulge anything relative to that letter, or anything you have witnessed in my family." I gave the desired asseveration. "Now," continued she, assuming a tone of less severity, "your destiny is in my hands. Marry my daughter, and I will raise you to fortune and honor. Otherwise infamy and destruction will pursue you to the extremities of time."

"But is she not my sister?" inquired I.

Is she his sister?

"Suppose she is not. What will be your determination?" said she, with a look that seemed to hope a favorable answer.

"Indeed, Madam," replied I, "I cannot dissemble. My heart belongs to another."

"Then," said she, with an enigmatical frown, "your fate is decided," and whirled out of the room.

Thus ended all my hopes of information on the subject of my parentage, but I immediately concluded that this letter was only a pretense to further the scheme of Willford in Armilda's marriage, and entirely banished the frightful idea that I was her son.

Figures it's a trap

But before I left Richmond, I resolved to meet Susan again, and warn her of the dreadful danger of pursuing the paths of prostitution. I repaired to the Cherry Vale at the appointed hour, but some person had arrived before me, and was leading Susan through the garden. I attempted not to interrupt them, but returned to my room and wrote her a farewell note in which I reprobated her conduct in the severest terms, and enclosed in it a bill for ten dollars, which was the last money I possessed on earth.

Early the next morning, I disposed of all my clothes, which enabled me to procure a hunting dress, such as is worn by the backwoods peasants, and a rifle. Thus equipt, I bid farewell to Richmond and dissipation.

Gets hunting clothes

The field of carnage opened my only road to glory, yet I was averse to the abominable science that instructed in the extermination of man. I never possessed sufficient courage to butcher a brother, no matter by what name he might be distinguished, or in what uncultivated region his mind had been

Dresses like Daniel Boone

hampered by the shackles of ignorance or barbarity. My bosom swelled beyond the narrow bounds of party prejudices, and the jarring distinctions of names, titles, and nations, and was sufficiently capacious to embrace the whole human family as a band of brothers. I beheld the conquerors of antiquity as a herd of mighty monsters, a black catalogue of abominable blots on the pages of nature. The war with the Indians who invaded the frontiers of the colonies was a war in which my antipathy to human massacres was measurably lost. By them my father fell, by them I imagined I had lost my natural relatives, and these considerations, together with the glowing hope of arresting the tomahawk which was uplifted to stain the mother's bosom with the blood of her suckling, determined me to repair to the frontiers of Virginia and render myself an abject terror to those midnight assassins.

I had proceeded but a few miles from town when I perceived a little path which led from the highway and wound around a low ridge of rocks, and it being not far distant from the place I had first discovered Amacette, I was induced by curiosity to pursue it in hopes of finding her mother, and unraveling the mystery which enveloped her and her daughter. I had not walked far before I came into a low valley, entirely covered with a heavy grove of cypress, which intercepted the light of a meridian sun. A short distance in the valley I beheld a small log cabin built under a jutting rock, and almost hid from view by the surrounding shade. I drew near, and was surprised at seeing several men at the door, and among the rest the detested Whitford. When I came near the door, I beheld a middle-aged woman in the custody of the sheriff, and the beautiful Amacette leaning on her shoulder, almost senseless with grief. She seemed wholly lost in tears and abstraction until I darkened the light of the door. She then raised her eyes, and on seeing me became frantic with joy. She sprang up, throwing her arms around my neck, and exclaimed, "Oh, you will save my mother—you are an angel—you will not let us go to jail. Dear Mother, this is Mr. Evermont."

THE PRISONERS OF NIAGARA

Her mother raised her eyes, and feebly pronounced, "Ah," and seemed violently agitated by some internal commotion. I turned to the officer and demanded by what authority he interrupted the peace of that lady.

"By authority of my office," said he, "she is taken in execution."

"At whose suit?" I inquired.

He replied, "at the suit of Mr. Whitford."

"Whitford," repeated I, and turning around seized Whitford fiercely by the throat, and continued, "wretch! This is thy doing! Release her instantly, return the execution satisfied, and fly from my presence, or you will lament that nature was ever disgraced by your existence. You know me. Shall I be obeyed?"

"Y–c–s s–i–r," stammered he, affrighted, and ordering the officer to desist, slunk away in silence.

This man had been reared in a family where broils and discord were constitutional. He imbibed the contagion, and had become heartless, cruel and crafty. From his earliest infancy he had been accustomed to drinking hatred and revenge from the eyes of his father, and with the milk of his mother, and this, too, at a time when the mind is soft and tender as the undimpled pool which receives impressions from the lightest atoms, and tenacious as the lime twig which clings to every impression. Thus educated, it was almost impossible but that he would become hardened in vice by the frequent reception of punishment, crafty and hypocritical in endeavoring to evade them, and cruel and revengeful to those in his power by way of retaliation. This might be expected from his education, and this was his character—an awful example to parents to beware of the early education of their infant children.

When Whitford was eighteen, he joined in the practice of stealing horses from the Indians and selling them in Richmond, and being extremely crafty in his depredations, he soon accumulated a considerable property, and deserting his family, endeavored to cut a figure in Richmond by speculation. While thus engaged, he became acquainted with Amacette, and after using every possible effort to gain her within his power without

89

effect, he had forged a bond and procured a judgment against her mother, which he had put in execution, until he had taken every article of furniture from their hut, even the bed on which they slept, and now intended to drag them to prison. The mother and daughter had resigned to this as the last calamity they ever were to suffer, but when I terrified Whitford into a relinquishment of the claim, and the officers had departed, the mother became somewhat calmed, and raising her eyes, inquired what had become of the sheriff.

"He is gone," said I. "Be composed, Madam, the debt is discharged."

"Discharged!" cried she in astonishment. "Is there so much generosity in the world? Ah! Evermont, you have a fatal name but your goodness is unprecedented. I owe my life to your first benefaction, when I was dying of disease and hunger. I owe the life and honor of my daughter to your noble interposition. Now this donation. My heart is grateful but my gratitude is too narrow for such boundless generosity. But tell me—who—where is your father?"

"I am an orphan, Madam. My father and mother are unknown."

"Your name?"

"I inherit it from a stranger who rescued me from the Indians."

"Where is he?"

"He has never been heard of since that period."

"Oh, then he may be true," exclaimed she, in apparent rapture. And after the indulgence of her feelings, proceeded to inform me the cause of her inquiries and exultation. Her narrative, though truly affecting when minutely related, must be abridged in this statement. It amounted to this.

In her youth she was loved by a young man of the name of Evermont, who I doubt not was my preserver. She returned his passion and their hearts were united, but there was no person in the neighborhood, in the county of Amherst, to perform the marriage ceremony, and they agreed, as many others in the country, to live together as man and wife. Of this union Amacette

She had loved Evermont (his benefactor) They did not marry but had a child Amacett. Indian attack. She escaped to Richmond.

was born, but shortly after her birth, Evermont had left her one morning and never more returned, nor could she ever learn the cause of his absence or what had become of him. Shortly afterwards, the Indians attacked her house, from which she escaped with her infant daughter, and beheld her little possessions entirely destroyed by the enemy. She then removed to a poor relation's near Richmond, where she lived until a few years past, when her relation died and left her friendless, at which time the persecution of Whitford began, and to secure her daughter from his outrages, she had procured this solitary hut where she had expected to spend her days uninterruptedly, but the inveterate Whitford had pursued her, even here, and she must seek some other dwelling.

"That shall be my care," replied I as she concluded her history. "I have friends and will procure you a comfortable subsistence through life." And after laying my purpose before her, she forgot her antipathy to my name, which had been occasioned by supposing that I was the son of her treacherous husband, and consented to accompany me to Hampshire. Amacette, whose mysterious conduct had proceeded from the same source, became entirely cheerful, and almost enraptured with my proposals. There being nothing in the cottage worth our attention, we set out on foot immediately.

Mrs. Evermont, after the desertion of her husband, had adopted her maiden name of Holbert, and I prevailed upon her to *His alias* always mention me as her son, for I was resolved to remain unknown while I continued in Hampshire. I conducted my new mother and sister to the house of Mr. Shenstone, my father's steward, to whose humanity I trusted for their supper and protection. They were hospitably received, and when I had taken Shenstone apart, and painted their sufferings in a pathetic description, I interested his feelings in their behalf, and he immediately provided them with a cottage, and a small farm already furnished, and a couple of servants to attend then, and promised that they should want for nothing until I returned from

the man of feeling again   Mr. Shenstone

the wars, which I informed him would be in the course of the ensuing winter.

CHAPTER IX

While thus at Haylard Village, I visited those scenes which were peculiarly dear to my infancy. I stopped at the memorable pool. The surrounding groves of cypress, and a profuse undergrowth of flowers, were dressed in the rich drapery of nature's vernal holiday, and awakened a thousand tones of memory to rise and throb with the delicious fervor of past delights. All my little rambles with my tender sisters, all the playful, joyful emotions of infant years, all the endearing expressions and caresses of Zerelda's innocent affection, started again into being, and wantoned with delicious poison on the woe-worn strings of my sensibility. They played on my narrowed feelings like the busy images of an enraptured vision, that flutter in airy gaiety in the imagination that awakes to wretchedness, shedding on the mind the melancholy reflection of what was once the fond anticipations of hope, but now the visionary forms that vanish at the approach of reality.

It was you, ye dear, desirable scenes, that warmed the dawning buds of artless pleasure to shoot forth in my bosom, and enkindle, by a lively succession of fond amusements, into that delightful glow of innocence which blushes on the bashful blossom of love. It was amid your shades that my heart was first taught to beat with joy—a joy of unsuspecting simplicity, which happy in its present gratifications, felt not the trembling pang of anticipated pain.

Can I look around and forget Zerelda? No. My soul will retain her name engraved in the legible characters of love to the latest ages. Even when its earthly form shall dissolve into its kindred ether, on its susceptible essence, her image will still be chronicled in a blaze of sunshine, "—And live down time/ Into the bosom of eternity."

A faint glimmer of the Haylard mansion is discovered through the lightly skirted forest. Ye powers of sympathy and association, how subtle and penetrating are your energies, either in the invention of bliss or of woe. An infinitude of silent emotions slumber on the same chord of memory, "Awake but one, and lo! what myriads rise." Thus, by the sight of the habitation of my infancy, all my former existence was revived in a nocturnal throng of exquisite sensations.

I repaired toward our little grotto, which commanded a beautiful prospect of the pool, reflecting from its mirror surface the overshadowing cypresses, in the pleasing enchantment of an inverted forest, and gave the eye a long tract of sublime imagery in a gradual mountain, rising in a variety of undulations, until its summit rode on the clouds into the ethereal bosom of the distant heavens. How shall I speak my astonishment and delight when I drew near the well-remembered cell? A thousand various odors sported on the air, and seemed to breathe the divine essence of celestial incense. My delighted soul seemed bathed in balmy breezes, and all my senses perfumed into rapture, by the living fragrance. But these exhilarating gales of ambrosia were but the commencement of those enchanted scenes, and my wonder was swelled to its highest key when the blushing fountain, from whence their sweetness was distilled, burst upon my sight in an endless diversity of bloom. It appeared as if all the border of the pool, where Zerelda had once fallen in, and all the rocky grotto, had flushed at once into a wide effusion of flower.

The laurels planted by Zerelda and me appeared to be one sweet blossom of woodbine, and the space between them and the grotto was variegated by wild roses and a number of other flowery shrubs, scattered in undulating walks and circular arbors. But the decorations of the grotto exceeded all the descriptive images which fancy can mold to the compass of language. The rocks rose over each other in the form of an amphitheater on both sides of the grotto. Each of the ascending seats was almost lost in the flowers which were planted upon it. Those flowers all arose in regular gradations, and changed their now separate, now mingling, hues in every ascending grade until all their thousand tinted graces appeared to concenter in the sober majesty of a spiral cedar, which grew immediately on the brink of the rock above the grotto.

The entrance of the grotto was shaded by a curtain of woodbines, which were planted in flower pots above, and streamed down to the bottom of the rocks in all the profusion of fantastic pageantry. These gay streamers, with all their variety of leaves and blossoms, had been interwoven together with exquisite skill and inimitable taste. The flowers were taught to bloom in unison in the forms of wreaths, garlands, or chaplets, or to shed their solitary blushes among clusters of vines and leaves, in all the regularity of embroidery, yet in all the living sweetness of wild, unrestrained nature.

This inimitable curtain was formed to veil the whole entrance of the grotto, but parted in the middle, and could be gently drawn aside to admit the wandering visitor to the arena of sweets within. But the most elegant design, the most ravishing scene of beauty and wonder, consisted in a bright rainbow of flowers curiously arched above the door. Here both nature and art appeared outdone. The blossoms were planted so as to bend in regular rising over each other, and harmoniously mingled their various dyes, from the full crimson of the red carnation, gently shading into the paler rose, and gradually dying in the fainting violet. Wrapt in amazement and ecstatic imagination, I stood and gazed in unutterable transport until the tears of emotion flowed from my eyes. I entered the grotto. All the walls were flowers flinging forth myriad changes of bloom and fragrance. I was no longer myself—no longer a being of time. All around me appeared enchantment. I felt as if in a celestial region. Each flower seemed an ethereal spirit breathing heavenly incense to the divinity. I had no heart, no soul, but for love, and joy, and pleasing wonder.

What a scene to enkindle the flame of love into enthusiastic adoration! The being I worshiped was the divinity of my fancy. It was a heaven to breathe the atmosphere of her smiles. Here she seemed the present presiding deity of this consecrated temple—I was entranced into an imaginary region at the thought. I felt as if her invisible spirit was breathing the zephyrs of love through my breast. I almost imagined that I should see the light glow that dropped in odors from the flowers receive the impulse of divine radiation, and expand its fragrant smiles into the image of Zerelda.

While I was thus transported from all terrestrial things, and riding on the "soul of roses" to worlds of visionary bliss, a soft note of music stole along the air, and swept all my sweet delirium of newborn emotions into another channel. I at first supposed it a new illusion of my bewildered senses, and my glowing fancy could have readily believed it breathed from the invisible genius of the grotto, but as the sound was dying on the ear, a higher string was touched, and a still higher immediately vibrated, until a full strain of melody floated around the grotto. I flew to the door to discover the musician, and was about to withdraw the yielding curtain when I perceived by the sound that the music was immediately over my head. Unwilling to interrupt so sweet an enjoyment, I drew back from the door, and listened to the finest air I had ever heard. It came with a soul that glided into mine, and embraced, inspired, and sublimed all as conceptions, until they swelled, and panted, and vibrated, and became lost in a delicious vision of aerial melody. Every tone appeared new and more than human, and every falling note appeared not to die away, but only to slumber on the "blossoms' downy bosoms," again to awaken into raptures at the call of the enchantress.

I hung upon the sounds as upon the breath of inspiration, and when they died away in a long, slow, and lingering cadence, they still appeared to live in the grotto, and whisper their soothing accents to my bosom.

No sooner had the sound of the guitar lulled its last echo into silence than a female voice swelled its symphonious numbers, and heightened all my thrilling faculties with a new and sweeter delight. She sang the following stanzas, and the interest they awakened in my agitated, trembling, bursting bosom so deeply impressed them on my memory that they can never be forgotten:

THE PRISONERS OF NIAGARA

Rise swelling heart, and fondly beat,
    Those tones to memory clear,
Whose pulses most divinely sweet,
    Were first excited here.

Thrill the soft notes of happiness,
    That o'er my feelings stole,
When the young throb of hope and bliss,
    First trembled in my soul.

When rapture's earliest blushes smil'd
    That pure, delightful morn,
When symphony's bewitching child,
    Was in my bosom born.

The warmth that o'er my feelings rush'd,
    My fears and fondness prove
I on the darling smil'd and blush'd,
    And kissed, and call'd it love.

Oh! Love within my bosom rest;
    My soul thy sway will own–
While truth shall reign in William's breast,
    My heart shall be thy throne.

Those tender infusions of sensibility were inspired by the adorable spirit of almighty love, and I doubted not had flowed from the bosom of Zerelda before she had learned the profligate life of her Evermont. But the following, though sung in the same air, I concluded she had added when she was compelled by the command of virtue to exile him from her heart:

But ah! Fond heart, thy dreams are past,
    Thy sun has set in gloom;
Hope in my bosom breathes its last,
    No more to bud or bloom.

Love lingers there forlorn and wild,
 Outcast from every joy,
A wandering, weeping, hopeless child,
 And yet forbid to die.

Oh! William, had thy bosom known,
 The fondness here for you,
How warm a heart was all your own,
 You ne'er had proved untrue.

  The music ceased, but the lines had drawn my mind from all the speculative raptures, to the cause which had excited those feelings in the musician. The pathetic concluding apostrophe taught me the feelings of Zerelda, and I felt her sorrows more poignantly than I could have done in any other situation. My sensations could not be restrained. Nature–venerable nature!–will assume her sovereignty over man, and I would not banish that susceptibility, which gives her access to my soul, for the boasted firmness of a Cato, or the daring intrepidity of a Caesar. No, gentle divinity—a tear is the offering thou requirest, and at thy alter I bow, with penitential fervor, and gratefully present the acceptable oblation.

  I was all anxiety to see the musician, but on approaching the door, I heard her voice in a distant part of the wood, and while my heart was warm with the air, I copied her verses with my pencil, to which I subjoined the following unconnected stanzas, and hid them in a corner of the grotto under a cluster of blossoms:

But love thus wounded cannot die,
 He yet with joy may live,
Bliss may awake the pleasing sigh,
 And hope again revive.

Thy fluttering heart supremely blest,
 May former raptures prove,
And every chord that tunes thy breast,

Vibrate with earliest love.

They grief has pierced thy William's soul,
 His heart has felt thy pain,
And while the wheels of time shall roll,
 He'll ne'er offend again.

Lost to thy heart, his only prize,
 He yields to misery,
And with a solemn farewell, flies
 Far from the world and thee.

Far, where no heart shall with him weep,
 But those that weep in blood,
Where he will sink to endless sleep
 In death's forgotten flood—

My attention was called from the completion of my verses by
a gentle sound. I turned my eyes and beheld the object of my
Parnassian attempt. She was again passing toward the grotto, and
with an unsuspecting air was carelessly touching on the notes of a
tune. I was as yet undiscovered, and might continue so if she did
not visit the grotto. But, as if was impossible to depart without
being perceived, I determined to remain, and meet the enchantress
in her temple.

She was dressed in the sable weeds of sorrow for her deceased
uncle. "Born to each grace, with every virtue blest," she appeared
by the fascinating symmetry of her form, and the easy elegance
and natural harmony of its motions, to tell "the divinity that dwelt
within her." Her amiable spirit communicated itself to her person,
and every step, every movement, and every gesture conveyed
information of the winning sweetness, the superior endowments,
and enlightened discretion of the pure intelligence by which they
were actuated.

She advanced to that part of the pool where she had fallen in,
where our infant laurels, by being frequently entwined round each

other, had almost grown together, and were now in appearance but one flourishing tree—a beautiful emblem of our early minds. She played for some time with their branches, winding them round each other, and weaving them into fanciful wreaths and crowns, threw her voice into a plaintive air, then skipped with sylphlike lightness to where a wild rose tree, in full blossom, flung a thousand luxuriant delicacies on the view. There she played with and caressed the flowers, strung her voice to a hundred different tones, and indulged in every sportive gambol of her native gaiety, without the ceremony of attention or the disguise of thought. Stripped to nature's self, divested of the restraint of company or the gloss of unmeaning civilities, her vivacious disposition displayed its delightful variety of animation in an infinite succession of airy amusements. Heavens! What an Elysium for the imagination of a lover! I had rather see her thus, thoughtlessly curvetting among the flowers, and flitting over the lawn with a step that scarce disturbed the slumbering dew drop, than to enjoy her company an age among a mingled crowd. All around me were bewitching, sylphlike fairy images, and she appeared the bright queen from whom their magic beauties emanated, and from whom they borrowed their painted drapery. She sprang from the rose tree with her bonnet in her hand and her hair floating in light curls on her neck and forehead, and seemed with a single bound to be again at the laurels. In a moment she became thoughtful. Her vivacity fled, and she solemnly walked toward the grotto with her bonnet resting on her arm. "Heavens! What a form/ Of pensive majesty—" Gracious powers! What was I as she advanced? "—Every sense/ Revolted from its office; my rapt soul/ Fled at my eyes—" and sank prostrate at her feet to sigh for pity, pardon, and love. She reached the rocky steps, drew aside the curtain, and, without casting up her eyes, sprang lightly into the grotto.

I arose in confusion and attempted to speak, but "—My heart, as with a sudden leap,/ Sprang to my trembling lips, and stopt my tongue." She was not less confused, but, deeming me a stranger, her agitation subsided with the first impression. I began to stammer an apology for my intrusion, but she gave me a smiling look of dignified familiarity, which would have composed any man but myself, and observed, with a sprightly modulation of voice adapted to the dissipation of my uneasiness, that it was her duty to apologize, and hoped I would excuse her for interrupting my meditations, and requested me to resume them.

"No, Madam," said I, a little recovered, "they are now consummated. Accident threw me into this temple of elegance and beauty, and I could but pause and wonder. But my astonishment has changed its object since the mistress has appeared."

"I am glad," said she, "that you have been pleased with my flowers."

"I was not admiring the flowers, Madam," replied I, "as much as the elegance of the concert—that taste divine which planted such a happy selection of imagery in such graceful variety, such pleasing irregularity, and in such a lovely enchantment of confusion."

"Your partiality for my plan," said she, with a significant smile, "induces me to think there was some merit in the invention."

"This little paradise of beauties," I replied, "speaks its amiable queen more intelligibly than the descriptive energy of any human language, for it speaks the language of nature and imagination. But Madam, to what divinity of fancy is this delightful temple consecrated?"

"To the divinity of Retirement," answered she, with a blush that spoke a softer term, and would have said *to the divinity of love*.

"Then am I committing sacrilege," said I, "by violating her unsullied altar? I will retire."

"You were certainly paying her your devotions when you were led to this solitary retreat," said she, with a seeming wish that I should continue.

"A lonely wanderer," continued I, "finds her in every scene in life, but here I should become an enthusiastic devotee, and pour out my soul in a continual strain of adoration. But indeed, Madam, I never knew that Retirement arrayed herself in such splendid

101

habiliments, such surpassing gaiety. Those gaudy decoration, those flowing robes of richest bloom, and this profusion of a thousand spangled drapery, would more become a gay and sprightly goddess than the serene equanimity of her pensive majesty."

"Is not Retirement," said she, "the daughter of Nature? And as such entitled to all the ornaments and jewelry of her mother?"

"But Retirement," I replied, "is not the only daughter of Nature. She has other children to whose youth and beauty those lavish brilliants are better adapted. The three blooming sisters, Pleasure, Joy, and Rapture, who inherit so large a portion of their mother's coquettish graces and laughter-loving propensities, are certainly entitled to a proportionate share of her gayest apparel. But I should imagine Love, her bosom's darling, on whom she had beamed her sweetest smiles and loveliest features, has the superior claim to these, her best robes, and this, her brightest temple.

"Is not this the darling urchin nursed on the lap of Retirement? Do not those sprightly sisters receive their highest zest in her sober temple? Every mortal worships at her altar; every heart beats fondly in her presence. When thus adorned, how sweet to ramble in her sacred shades, and feel we have a soul.

"Selkirk thought differently," I continued, "when he exclaimed, 'Oh solitude! Where are the charms,/ That sages have seen in thy face.'

"Every child of affliction thinks differently when he beholds nothing but the insignia of despair on her bosom. The hapless orphan against whom the door of hospitality is shut, and the gates of society perpetually barred, looks round on the solitary fields of nature, but all is a chaos, where he can find no resting place for one rising throb of his heart. Even the blossom's dewy bosom, which drinks the risen morning and gives the eye a reflected sun in a thousand varying spangles, conveys no idea to his heart but the somber image of pale, fainting melancholy. The child of penury, to whom nature has given a warm susceptible soul, but who is cast by wayward fortune in the proud fields of avarice and ambition where the flower of sympathy never blew—whose heart beams with fond anticipations, but can find no genial bosom whose kind embrace will nurse the embryo raptures into life, and they are left to perish in abortion—where are the charms of Retirement to him? Sometimes a transient flash of deluding fancy will bear him from the dreary scenes and waft him beyond the regions of possibility to a momentary Eden in a transporting futurity, but the pleasing vision, like the midnight meteor, glows but for a moment to discover how dark are all the realities around him. But Nature has not annexed those hard conditions to your being, and you only behold them as the chimeras of romance. And may they never approach so near as to convince you that they have a substantial existence. May they never hang their images around your beloved temple."

But her countenance during these observations plainly discovered that she was not a stranger to a part of my description. The color flashed in her cheeks, then fled, then gently rose in fleeting, varying blushes, "shooting less and less, the live carnation round." Her eyes sparkled, languished, sank, and dropped a tear upon the fold of her drapery. Silence reigned a moment. She then raised her eyes and fixed them on mine. Their former sprightliness was but in its twilight, but its solemn, dewy mildness was more fascinating than all its former radiance.

"I thought," said she, with an attempt a vivacity, "I should admire the pleasures of Retirement as long as I could enjoy her presence in this little cavern. But you have flung so many gloomy sprites on her brow, that I fear I shall never be able to brush them away."

"Forgive me, Madam," replied I. "I would not cloud your enjoyment by a single vapor for the world. I spoke without reflection, but the full heart will too often vent its murmurs and scatter unintended pain in the purest bosoms."

"The *full heart*!" repeated she. "Surely the picture you have given me is not drawn from experience?"

"Madam," answered I, "you are here remote from the frequent walks of misery, and should live as happy as you are innocent. Such a bosom I could never pain by unavailing complaints. I have already offended your trembling sensibility, and would not increase my crime."

"*Offended,*" repeated she. "Not at all. I have been entertained, delighted—" A faint blush concluded the sentence, and silence again presided. Her fingers passed involuntarily over a small guitar she held in her hand. She started at the unexpected sound, and observed, "I have overstayed my hour. I wish you pleasant meditations."

I stood, irresolute whether to accompany her or not, until she had glided entirely within the wood. I sank upon a settee of grass with my eyes fixed on the path she had gone, and lost all power of reflection in the wild labyrinth of my thoughts. When I awoke from my vacant position, a heavy shade seemed to be flung upon the flowery radiance. I would have followed Zerelda, and I would not. I got up vexed with myself—vexed with the profusion of flowers for not affording more gratification. A linnet began to sing on a neighboring bough. I picked up a pebble and drove it away. Ashamed of the deed, I threw myself again on the settee in sullen disorder. My thoughts turned on leaving Zerelda, and I involuntarily exclaimed, "No! Never! Never!" Restless, agitated and undetermined, I started up and rambled to Mr. Shenstone's.

I knew the rudeness of my dress, and the circumstance of my being considered the son of Mrs. Holbert, would conceal me from suspicion, and I resolved to continue in the village, not only for the purpose of establishing Mrs. Holbert in her new residence, but also to sound the feelings of Zerelda. And what then? That, I was unable to determine. Futurity was so bewildering that I scarcely had a settled thought of purpose beyond the present moment. I appeared to forget myself in a soothing slumber, and two weeks rolled away in a dream. I was never in a state of mind during that period to keep a regular account of my emotions, thoughts or actions, and will fill the chasm by an extract from the journal of Zerelda, which fell into my hands one morning at the grotto.

It was the repository of all the thoughts and secrets of Zerelda from the time I entered the village and inspired her by my presence at the grotto. After giving our conversation verbatim, she proceeded:

THE JOURNAL   *Zerelda's*

This conversation touched upon so many of my heart's most exquisite strings that I could support it no longer. But when I retired, my thoughts still lingered behind. My curiosity was not satisfied, and I condemned myself for having left the stranger so abruptly. I dared not return—I dared not even look round, but hurried with irregular steps to the house. I threw myself on a chair with a restless sensation of wildness. Emerine saw that I was agitated and inquired the cause.

"Oh! Emerine," cried I, springing up and throwing my arms round her neck, "I have seen a new being—a prodigy—a wonder."

"Girl, are you crazy?" replied Emerine. "What have you seen? You are all in a tremor—your cheeks vary like the hues of the rainbow."

"Oh! Such sentiments," exclaimed I, "such expressions! His words flowed like the music of inspiration. Then his countenance—his eyes. Oh, what a soul—what sweetness—what harmony!"

"What, was it a man," cried Emerine, "that had occasioned all this flurry of spirits?"

"*A man*," retorted I, piqued at her manner, "to be sure it was a man. What else should it be?"

"I suppose it could not possibly be anything else," replied Emerine with a burst of laughter.   Vexed at her raillery, I threw myself peevishly in my seat and leaned my head on my arm, which lay across the back of my chair.

"Do not be offended," said Emerine in a soothing tone. "I could not help indulging my humor to see you in such unaccountable earnestness. Come, let me see if you can smile. But who is this wonderful stranger? I am all curiosity and impatience."

My inclination to talk of the stranger was too strong for me long to remain in an ill humor, and I immediately communicated all I knew.

"This is really an adventure," cried Emerine.

"But, oh think, Emerine, that such a man as this should be in distress. I wonder if I could not relieve him?"

"I expect," said Emerine, "he belongs to the poor family who has lately come to the village, and probably all his distress lies in pecuniary matters."

"If it does," I replied with joy, "I will make him happy. Such a man should never be poor."

A billet came to invite us to take tea with Mrs. Shenstone, which we gladly obeyed in expectation of again seeing the stranger. Mrs. Shenstone introduced us to Mrs. Holbert and her daughter, Amacette, but my eyes wandered in vain for the man I had seen at the grotto. Shortly after, Mr. Shenstone came in, but the stranger was not with him. My disappointment rendered me too much dissatisfied to support the conversation which was immediately entered into with considerable vivacity, but my attention was soon arrested by Mrs. Holbert inquiring of Shenstone when he had seen her son.

"I saw him an hour since," replied Shenstone, "rambling along the shore of the river."

"He appears more melancholy than usual this evening," said she. "I fear he is not satisfied with the idea of entering the army."

"Is he going to the war?" cried I, with an eagerness which so discomposed my spirits that I could pay no attention to the reply, and to heighten the embarrassment of my feeling, the young Apollo appeared at the door. Mr. Shenstone took his hand and introduced Emerine and myself to Mr. Holbert. He blushed as he bowed, and faintly pronounced my name, and appeared in a modest, graceful confusion, which rendered his countenance infinitely more interesting.

He immediately seated himself in a remote corner of the room, and remained for some time wrapped up in a pensiveness, until Shenstone inquired how he was pleased with Haylard Village.

"*Pleased*," replied he. "Oh, it is delightful!" Then sank again in his melancholy attitude.

"Have you seen Miss Zerelda's elegant grotto?" inquired Mrs. Shenstone.

"Yes," answered he, and I thought he sighed. "I have seen it." This was the only manner in which he conversed during the evening. I felt but little inclined to conversation myself, but Emerine was more lively than I had ever seen her, and became thoroughly intimate with Mrs. Holbert and Amacette.

The moon was fine, and we proposed returning, and nothing would satisfy Emerine but the company of Amacette. Amacette appeared unwilling.

"Oh, but," Emerine replied, "you positively must go," and taking her arm, hurried from the house without paying any attention to me. Mr. Holbert, seeing me left behind, stepped up and modestly inquired if he might have the honor of attending me. I bowed assent, and we walked on in silence. Neither of us appeared inclined to speak until our eyes were turned at once to where the moon flung her beams in a silvery shower on a wide site of hills that arose romantic on the opposite side of the river.

"What a sweet prospect," said I, as I saw him lost in contemplating it.

"Oh, it is transporting," replied he. "How fine the beams delineate the tops of the forest, while all below is diversified with different shades of vapors. And how sublimely the farther hills accumulate a deeper and still deeper curtain of ether until they disappear in the heavens. But nature enkindles the glow of enthusiasm in every scene. Although that distant prospect is better calculated to awake the faculties of the soul into joyful admiration, yet, to a heart at ease, those moonbeams silently slumbering on the gliding waters display a more enchanting scene, more emblematic of rural happiness, and more congenial to the sober raptures of social felicity. To those who can look upon nature through the clear prism of prosperous innocence, everything appears lovely and teeming with bliss. And that, I presume, is Miss Engleton's situation."

"Mine! Oh, no," cried I, without knowing what I said, but suddenly recollecting myself, I continued, "I certainly can enjoy the smiles of nature, and cannot imagine how any being can be so unhappy as not to feel a partial gratification when all creation is rejoicing around him."

"And yet there are beings," resumed he, "whose imaginations have been so often palled by disappointed hope that they view the fairest fields of bloom with the same cold languor with which they gaze on a waste of rocks."

"Such beings," said I, "cannot be numerous, for the active imagination is ever grasping for some new, and that hope 'which travels on, nor quits us when we die,' is ever willing to feed the mind with future prospects of happiness."

"So says the glowing fancy of unblasted expectation," replied he. "Hope is a darling cherub, whose ever-willing smile pours a welcome balsam into the bleeding heart until misfortune snatches the last wish from the unfortunate—and he can lost no more."

"But are not the inspirations of hope sufficiently alluring to repair the utmost losses," said I, and to entice even despair into new expectations?"

"There are losses, Madam," said he, and he sighed as he spoke, "losses which are irreparable—losses of that tender nature that they rend even the heartstrings. And to those, hope can apply no remedy. But those dreary speculations should never be wafted to your ear. Here, in this seat of domestic quiet, with nature all in blossom around you, the ardor of youth burning in your imagination, and sainted innocence smiling in your bosom, you can live a stranger to sorrow, and sail down a life of pleasure like the unruffled moonbeam, swimming on the balmy zephyr."

"Do you suppose then," replied I, "that I am callous to the miseries of others? That I can enjoy uninterrupted contentment while those around me are unhappy?"

"No, Madam," he answered, "I suppose you possessed of all that benevolence of which your countenance gives intelligence, but I do not expect you to feel for those distresses to which you are a stranger."

Shakespeare p 111
Milton 113
Man of Feeling 115

We were joined by Emerine and Amacette, whole sallies of
humor appeared not to accord with the feeling of Holbert, and he
continued almost silent until we reached the mansion. He took my
hand to assist me over the stile. His fingers scarcely touched on
mine, but I could feel that they trembled, and when I was over,
before I could turn around, he was gone.

I walked silently into the house. Emerine began immediately
to converse with Amacette about her brother. I listened with
avidity, but Amacette was extremely modest on so delicate a
subject, and seemed anxious to decline the conversation.

I shortly after retired to my pillow. My mind was uneasy, but I
could not define the cause. My thoughts ran over the whole
deportment of the stranger. "Oh! That Evermont was like him," I
sighed, without knowing the cause of such a wish. Evermont was
the fondest joy of my infancy. His image is too deeply engraved
on my heart to ever be erased. He cannot be as criminal as he is
represented. His heart is too pure—too noble. But I hope he will
soon return. My prayer is that he may be the image of Holbert: So
free—so graceful—so dignified, and yet, so modest. The features
of Holbert are very similar to what I imagined Evermont's would
be. If Evermont has but the mind, the countenance, the speaking
eye, the sprightly, yet pensive, air of Holbert, I shall love him
more than ever. Thus my reflections ran until the clock struck two.
I was surprised at the lateness of the hour, and endeavored to
sleep. But while I slept, I was still with the stranger in my
slumber.

Emerine and Amacette were in too sprightly a mood at
breakfast to interest my present feeling, and I left them to enjoy a
ramble. I went to the grotto—every scene was blooming—but I
was not satisfied. The stranger was not there, and I went back
again, musing on what method I should take to allay his distresses,
which appeared to weigh so heavily on his feelings.

Amacette and Emerine endeavored to rally me into spirits on
my return, and I at last became as sprightly as they, but it was
transient. I sighed involuntarily, and withdrawing from the room,

found myself returning to the grotto without have once thoughts of going there. I blushed to myself, and returned.

I was surprised on my entrance to find Holbert with the girls in the music room. He arose and bowed, but I was so confused that I could scarcely return the salutation, and he sat down apparently mortified.

Emerine observed, "Mr. Holbert has come to take his sister away, but I have determined to punish him for the intention by confining him also."

"You must," said he, "invent a punishment more terrific, or I shall never cease offending."

"I am extremely fond of a compliment," replied Emerine, "and in return for the one you have expressed, I feel inclined to make you do penance while here by playing us a tune. Amacette says you are a musician."

"If that is the decree of the company, I suppose there is no appeal," said he, turning his eyes on me.

"It has my sanction," I observed, "not as a decree, but as a request."

"Well, Miss Haylard, I submit," he replied, "but you must set me an example of what I am to suffer."

Emerine played an air on the piano. Holbert then turned to the harp, and swept over the strings with indescribable sweetness. The air was a composition of exquisite melody, and accompanied by a voice soft, trembling and animated. I gazed and listened in transport. My heart thrilled with every vibration, and every chord seemed as if it was singing in my bosom. His countenance glowed—his voice quivered—his fingers trembled on the wires, but the harmony seemed more delightful. My feelings were enraptured, and appeared to play unison with the notes. I scarcely knew when he ceased, for all within me was melody.

Emerine paid a high eulogy to his art, but I was far too bewildered to think or speak, and remained in silence, dissatisfied with not commending his performance, yet unable to find one expression of applause.

He took up a volume of Shakespeare and seemed to be reading attentively, but never moved his eyes.

"You are an admirer of Shakespeare?" inquired Emerine.

"*Shakespeare!*" repeated he, as if surprised at such a question. "No, Madam."

"He is generally approved," continued she, "by most critics as the poet of Nature."

"He is one of Nature's poets," said he, appearing to collect himself on the subject, "but he is like many of the fields of Nature, 'Where weeds and flowers, promiscuous shoot,' and on that account has gained the precedence of many more enchanting poets, in the same manner that we pass by the gay ornaments of the garden when all is blooming, yet hang with delight on the solitary rose that blushes in a wild of thistles."

"Then you suppose," said Emerine, "that his celebrity arises from the number of weeds that surround his flowers?"

"Measurably so, Madam," replied he. "He has many wild vagaries which excite the momentary smile by their oddity. A few scattered elegances of the sweetest fancy, and many bursts of blazing genius that wrap the soul into admiration, but all these are very much overrated because they were written by Shakespeare—Shakespeare, the author of so may pages of irregular, unmeaning, or uninteresting dullness. I am not an admirer of flowers where I must wound myself with thorns to obtain them, when there are others, equally sweet and beautiful, which may be gathered on the smiling lawn, or the verge of the unbillowed stream."

"Then you are not inclined to enhance the enjoyment of the possession," said Emerine, "by the difficulty of the pursuit? Or to labor for pleasures through the arduous fields of toil and danger?"

"Not if they can be obtained without," answered he. "But I am a devotee to exquisite enjoyment, and if there was but one flower in bloom," continued he, with rising animation, "I would ransack nature to breathe its fragrance. Toil and danger would never operate as an inducement to the pursuit, but their power should never deter me from seeking the possessions. Instead of

111

discouraging, they would invigorate my ardor, and the prize would blush new inspiration as the difficulties swarmed around me. There are flowers I would trample on worlds to enjoy."

His countenance beamed living eloquence as he spoke. The color rose in his cheeks, his eyes shed quick and vivid dashes, and every glance burnt with enkindling radiance. My bosom throbbed, my soul grasped to catch every expression, and I stared on him with immovable attention. While I was in this position, his eyes rolled on mine. My blood flew and glowed in my cheeks, and I turned hastily away fro the gaze that seemed to see my soul.

But his ardor appeared to have run its race and sank on a languid key. His energies seemed all collected with himself, and his countenance sat in modest, pensive retirement. We were summoned to dinner, and immediately after, Holbert, finding his sister would not leave the mansion that evening, took his leave.

The next day I was at the grotto with Emerine and saw Holbert approaching. He came to the laurels Evermont and I had planted. He appeared to be in deep contemplation, and agitated by his own reflections, and gazed on the laurels in apparent wonder and pleasure. We expected he would enter the grotto, and walked out, to prevent his being surprised by our sudden appearance.

He met us with a modest bow and observed, "Am I ever to be so unfortunate as to disturb the repose of this sacred retreat?"

"Do you account it a misfortune to meet with your friends?" cried Emerine.

"*Friends*," repeated he. "The term 'friend' is very significant," continued he, with a sigh, "but if I could complain of meeting Miss Haylard and Miss Engleton, I never ought to be blest with society. I should be unhappy to interrupt their pleasing retirement. Yet this scene so strongly awakens the remembrance of my infancy, when, like you, I lived in the innocent joys of nature, that I cannot abstain from visiting it."

"It is claimed entirely by Zerelda," said Emerine, "and if she permits you to ramble in it, it will be a privilege she has not rendered very extensive as yet, from a want of company who had the curiosity to admire it."

112

"Mr. Holbert," replied I, "need not doubt his visits meeting with my approbation, for I am so much delighted with the scenery myself that I wish all my acquaintances to partake of my enjoyments."

"But if you are so selfish as to wish to be here alone," resumed Emerine, "we will retire. If not, you must go into the grotto and play us a tune."

"The last injunction I will gladly comply with," said he, "if it will confer a pleasure."

He attended us to the grotto where he played a most delicious air on the lute, and accompanied it with his voice, and with the verses I can composed for Evermont, which he must have overheard at the grotto when he was there before. I trembled with the forcible sweetness of his music, and he appeared not less agitated. He then requested me to play. I felt myself too discomposed to perform to my own satisfaction, yet my anxiety to gratify him induced me to make the attempt, but my voice was faint and shook on every note. A tremor ran through my bosom, and communicated itself to the strings of the lute. The wires jarred, the tones were discordant, and my embarrassment increased so that I was scarce able to fly even irregularly over the air. I saw his eyes fixed on me with a gaze of the brightest luster, which I fancied was occasioned by his surprise at my deficiency in melody. I blushed and turned away in the highest possible mortification. He remained silent until Emerine observed, "Zerelda, you play badly today."

"*Badly*," repeated Holbert with a burst of animation. "My God! What music could warble sweeter?"

My pride rose over my confusion at the earnestness of his exclamation, and smile a consolation in my bosom. Emerine seemed now the only person inclined to talk, but she could draw nothing but monosyllables either from Holbert or myself. At last, growing uneasy at our pensiveness, she took up Milton from a little shelf which contained a few books, and observed to Holbert, "This temple is not dedicated to silence, and if you will not sing, you must wing your poetical fancy by the soaring flights of Milton."

"I am not pleased with the company of unknown, ungenial beings," replied he, "and for that reason I am seldom a guest in Milton's ethereal. I am more delighted with the imagery of those poets where I meet with feeling souls, enkindling fancies, and bosoms glowing with the ardor of nature, throbbing with the impulse of spontaneous rapture, or thrilling responsive to the young emotions of the sweet unknown delirium where the new sensations of earliest love begin to play, and smile, and tremble on the wondering fibers of unpracticed feeling. Where I can see the bounding heart, gently cherished into that state of blossoming maturity, when all its desires are alive to happiness, when it leaps out into a thousand involuntary caresses, smiles and weeps—it knows not why—looks round unknown to itself for a kindred bosom, blushes and trembles when it finds it, and is unblest when most wrapped up in bliss."

This description was not lost on Emerine. To me, it was so complete a transcript of my present condition, that I blushed with the thought that he had read the secrets of my feelings, and painted them precisely as they were. But this image of his fancy had a more visible effect on himself. His countenance bespoke confusion. He trembled as the arose to walk across the grotto, and stopped at the door where a bullet had scaled the rock when I was here preserved by Evermont. He gazed on the place a moment and heaved a sigh. I saw a tear fall from his eye and light on a rose that bloomed a little below the mark of the ball. His agitation increased, and he bowed, bid us good evening, and departed.

I flew to the rose that caught his tear. The little inestimable sparkler hung on its bosom with a smile. I raised it to my lips and drank it with rapture, then kissed the flower a thousand times, and, opening my handkerchief, pressed it to my bosom.

Emerine was astonished at my conduct, but was too much affected herself to give vent to her humor, and I escaped her expressions of censure. We returned with little conversation towards the house. On the way we were met by tenant Hudson, who inquired if we had seen Mr. Holbert.

"Why do you want Mr. Holbert?" requested I.

"Why, do you see Madam," replied he, "because he is the best man in the world. He is so good to everybody in the village, so familiar and so obliging. Why, Ma'am, he has been in the village but a little while and yet has done something for everyone in it. He works a little for everybody, but will have no pay, and yet he don't seem like he was raised at work. But he is too good for this world, and will always keep himself poor. For day before yesterday, the sheriff was about the drive away the last cow of neighbor Marfard ~~to~~ for a small debt, and leave his little children to cry for milk. Mr. Holbert came by the cottage, and saw the mother and children all crying at the thought of losing their cow, to which they were attached because she had been long in the family. He followed the officer when he drove her away, and having no money, sold his gun and paid the debt, and made the officer drive the cow back again. As soon as we neighbors heard of this kindness in Holbert, a number of us pitied him, for his gun was the only piece of property he had in the world, and we made up the money and repurchased the gun for him. It is now at my house, and I want to find him that I may return it to him."

I was charmed with this piece of Holbert's generosity, and highly commended Hudson for his conduct. I pulled out my purse and requested him to receive the amount he paid for the gun, but he would received nothing, and hurried off in search of Holbert.

"Emerine, we must relieve that man," said I. "His noble heart must not be restrained in the indulgence of its generous impulses."

"Take care how you attempt it," replied Emerine. "The delicate refinement of his sentiments is not to be tampered with without the utmost tenderness, for although he has a rustic appearance in his dress, I plainly perceive he has a cultivated mind, and a proud heart that would disdain the reception of a present."

We walked on, thus thinking of what method we should undertake to effect this object, but could come to no determination.

Three days passed away, in which I was frequently in the company of Amacette, and often talking of Holbert, but never saw him. The whole village rang with his praise, and recounted a thousand little acts of his generosity, which declared how charitable he would have been if he had had the means in his power. I was told that he had again sold his gun to relieve an unfortunate old man who had just escaped from the Indians. I immediately gave money to a trusty servant to repurchase the gun and return it to Holbert without permitting him to know I was concerned in the affair.

I was that evening rambling carelessly towards the grotto, thinking of the conduct and poverty of Holbert. I drew a comparison between him and what Evermont was reported to be, and sighed as I reflected on Holbert's superiority. Why was it not Holbert instead of Evermont to whom my gratitude is so much in arrears? Why was it not he that delighted my infant heart with so many instances of affection and tenderness? If Evermont had continued as he was, he would have been what Holbert now is. These reflections rendered my mind dreary and disconsolate, and I laid my hand on my bosom and sighed, "I am not happy." I raised my eyes and beheld Holbert approaching so near that he heard my last expression.

"Can Miss Engleton be unhappy?" cried he. "If so pure a being is not entitled to an exemption from pain, who need ever to expect it?"

"Exemption from pain," replied I, "should principally belong to those who delight in relieving the distress of others."

"Then," replied he, "Miss Engleton should be happy, for none ever possessed a more generous disposition at your years. You have not yet arrived at that blissful period when the divine benevolence of love awakens in the bosom, and attunes all the feelings to continual strains of generosity."

"Cannot a person be generous," inquired I, "without being in love?"

"Not in so high a degree," replied he. "No other passion can give full exercise to the sympathies of nature, or call forth all the consentaneous feelings into action. It belongs to love to mature the sublime desire of rendering other happy, and to draw the heart from itself, and all its own enjoyments, to rest for happiness on other bosoms."

We continued walking toward the grotto, and had now entered
its pale, and were at the laurel. He noticed the manner in which they
were entwined together, and observed, "Such is the early union of
two desiring, consenting hearts." I could make no reply, for I felt a
recollection of the emotions with which they were planted, when
the hearts of Evermont and myself knew no wish but what was
gratified in each other's company. Holbert continued, "Fair scions,
sweet emblems of mutual bliss, may you ever flourish in unfading
spring."

We entered the grotto in silence. He walked to the shelf and
looked over my books, and turning to me, where I was playing with
a blossom, observed, "You have selected very desirable company to
regale your fancy in retirement. One who chooses Thompson,
Akenside, Petrarch, and Goldsmith for the companions of her
private entertainment can never be unhappy."

I felt myself incapable of conversing, and desired him to choose
one of the authors, and read me some of his favorite passages. He
took up Thompson's *Spring*, and seating himself by my side, read
for some time with musical animation, making his own comments,
and pointing out with the most exquisite taste and judgment the
fairest beauties as he proceeded. His happy fancy discovered so
many new charms which I had passed unnoticed, and gave such an
air of sweetness and harmony to every expression, that the limes I
had read a thousand times appeared in such a soft, enchanting
elegance that I almost imagined it the first time I had ever heard
them.

He paused and shut the book. I observed, as I saw him silent,
"Poetry has a most happy tendency to awaken life in harmonious
numbers. It gives such elasticity to the imagination, such pleasing
imagery to the surrounding objects, and leads the various trains of
feeling to such lively, soothing channels, as to give new charms to
existence. I often wonder why it is not more generally admired and
cultivated."

"The reason is," replied he, "that few minds have the genuine
refinement and liberality of Miss Engleton's, and it is the practice
of man to condemn what he is incapable of imitating or enjoying.

117

Thus it is that the genuine works of taste are discarded by the dull sons of interest, and corrupted by the dissipated votaries of fashion. The fertile regions of fiction are the native fields of the warm imagination. There it delights to create new worlds, and glory in its own creation. It is there that the mind is purified from the vulgar errors of custom, enriched with the novel beauties of virtuous simplicity, and refined by the fancy into the purity of primeval innocence—the only source of sublime enjoyment. Oh, ye happy beings," continued he, laying his hand on mine, "whose imaginations possess sufficient energy and animation to soar beyond the regions of ambition and prejudice, and build the basis of your felicity upon the bosom of nature. It is for you that existence opens the purest fountains of untasted pleasures, and Love, in smiling rapture, weaves the rosy garland of affection to bloom forever, in joyful fragrance, around your feeling and sympathetic hearts."

His hand pressed on mine as he spoke, but I scarcely felt its pressure until he concluded. I then found his fingers wrapped around mine. A tremor flitted along my nerves, and my heart felt "unutterable things." I withdrew my hand in an instant, and a silence succeeded in which my sensations were so strange—so delicious, and yet so painful—that I longed for the silence to continue, yet felt unable to bear it longer. Holbert gazed on the outside of the book. I tore at elast twenty flowers to pieces.

Emerine and Amacette sprang into the grotto and awakened us from our reverie. They passed some lively remarks upon our situations, but I was unable to attend to them and walked to my shelf of books. Holbert made some reply to their observations, but I could not hear it distinctly, and after a few minutes he withdrew.

When we returned to the house, we received a number of letters from Richmond which proved that the charges against Evermont were forgeries of Mrs. Willford and her family. This made us sorely repent our cruelty, more especially as Evermont had left Richmond and no person knew whither he was gone. And to complete my mortification, I received the medal I had presented to Evermont with this inscription: "Forfeited by the fascinations of vice." His yielding it up so readily, and without one line, one word to either me or the family, induced me to believe that so long an absence had removed the fond impressions of our youth, and that all the interest I had ever had in his bosom was forgotten.

"I could have loved him," I sighed, "if I had seen him at a time when the heart pants for reciprocal enjoyment. But the love of our infancy was but the blossom of what the bosom desires. It was a fair and fragrant flower, but he permitted it to wither. I owe him everything, for my life I hold by his bounty, but he has deserted me now, when my heart had discovered that it wants him most. The heart when warm with the fervency of youth must have an object, and its desires cannot be held by one that is almost visionary and only retained by the memory of childhood. Am I then censurable if I do not love him? I cannot love an unknown being. Had I seen him in manhood—had he been what fancy has represented him, and had he been present of excite and gratify the desires which have been long budding in my bosom—to fix the wandering wishes of my heart, and to center the increasing ardor and fondness of my soul for him, I could then have repaid him for my life—repaid him for all the tender attentions of his infant affections. But now, where am I?" I sighed, and could reflect upon the subject no longer with any regularity. I could not think of forgetting the attachment I had formed for Evermont in my infancy, and I could find no place for him in the dearest throne of my bosom.

In this state of mind, I was perplexed for several days. I frequently met with Holbert, for Emerine would be continually with Amacette, and Holbert was often necessarily in their company. He strove to appear unconcerned and to pay a general attention to all around him, but I could plainly discover that I was an object of his peculiar regard. His partiality flattered my feelings but perplexed the desires of my heart. His reputation increased in the village, and every peasant's wife could give long lists of generous actions. He obtained a warm interest with Aunt Haylard and Emerine, but with me, he was more than my heart was willing to acknowledge. His sensible and animating conversation, his nice, discriminating judgment, his sentimental and judicious criticisms on the various

119

authors which he often read to us when together, so deeply interested my feelings that I involuntarily adopted all his sentiments, and felt delighted with no objects but those he admired. I was always anxious to be in his company, yet when he was present, I felt restless and dissatisfied, but the moment he was gone, it appeared that I had lost something that was wanting to render me happy. Emerine often rallied me about the state of my feelings, and would often attempt to convince me that I was in love, but this was a thought so new that I would not acknowledge it to my own bosom, and for the first time began to disguise my feelings from Emerine and my aunt. I became distant when in the company of Holbert, and learned, though it was grating to my heart, to speak of him without any particular respect or emotions. By this means I concealed my sensations from the eyes of others, but I felt them more severely in my own bosom, where their language would be heard. My reserve had a visible effect on Holbert. He appeared more unhappy, and my conscience condemned me for being the cause.

I met him unexpectedly at the grotto one morning. Her was remarkably pensive, and I endeavored by the utmost familiarity to render him cheerful, but produced no visible effect.

I inquired after the health of his mother, and he informed she was well, and added, "She possesses from the noble humanity of the village almost every wish of her heart. It is true she is poor, but I hope she will not long continue dependant after I can see her entirely settled to her mind, so that I can leave her without apprehension."

"And you will soon depart from the village—from your friends?" said I.

"I should have left it long ago," sighed he. "I should never have entered it. I was unhappy when I came here, but I shall depart." He stopped, attempted to suppress a sigh, and became silent. "I go," resumed he, "to purchase that oblivion of pain in the field of battle which I cannot find elsewhere. I can there obtain all the indispensibles of life, for agreeable to Goldsmith, 'Man wants but little here below,/ Nor wants that little long.'"

"The world thinks differently," said I, without reflecting.

"And Miss Engleton thinks with the world," replied he, and his countenance appeared to sink into immediate gloom.

"I have regulated my thoughts more by feeling than custom," replied I. "I behold happiness distributed to every station where innocence and contentment reside, and know not why any being should be unhappy for the want of possessions which he cannot enjoy."

"My heart feels that it wants far more than it can ever possess," replied he, "which is the broad base of every misery. My soul has dared to center all its wishes—all its happiness, where the child of penury should have stood aloof. But I fly from the illusion of my fancy; I fly and leave my heart behind, but I fly to prevent Miss Engleton from witnessing the misery she has innocently occasioned."

He turned to the door—stopped—seemed irresolute, and again returned to me, and took my hand in silence. O! How my bosom trembled, and my whole frame was agitated. He perceived my emotions and faintly articulated, "You have a heart that pities, but not a heart that can rise superior to the proud suggestions of fortune—and relieve."

"Ungenerous Holbert," cried I, "what part of my conduct has induced you to believe me the slave of pride or fortune?"

"Pardon me, madam," cried he, "my distress has distracted me. You are all the heart love can wish," and in speaking, he raised my hand to his lips. I had never permitted such a liberty to man before, and was not prepared for the sensations it would occasion. The fire of his lips appeared to run through all my frame, and center with a tremulous delight in my bosom.

At that moment, Emerine again entered the grotto. I turned hastily to a cluster of flowers, and Holbert received her with a confused salutation, and attempted to support a conversation, but found himself too much agitated, and departed. Emerine immediately perceived our mutual embarrassment and advanced to me, not in her humorous manner, but with a countenance of concern. She took my hand and read my looks in silence. I burst

121

into tears, threw my arms around her, and exclaimed, "Do not censure me."

"I have no thought of censure," she replied. "But Holbert? What have you done!"

"Nothing—what should I do? He loves me."

"So I suspected," replied she. "He is a stranger."

"He is no stranger to my bosom," sighed I.

"He is poor."

"O! He is rich in every virtue—every tenderness."

"He is obscure."

"His noble soul will rise to splendor when uncurbed by fortune."

"But Evermont—" said Emerine.

"He has deserted me."

"Did you not desert him first?"

"He should have been such a man as Holbert."

"You know not but he is such a man."

"Alas! He was not here when I was obliged to love."

"Then your father—? O, he will delight to own such a man as Holbert for his–son-in-law," added she, pressing her hands to my cheeks, which were all alive with blushes.

CHAPTER X

Here the manuscript broke off, but it was not until the ensuing morning that it fell into my hands. I was again drawn to the grotto with the hope of accomplishing the fondest wish of my heart, that of obtaining the loveliest of women by my personal merit. I found her writing in the grotto, and saw Emerine and Amacette at a distance. She attempted to conceal the manuscript, but in her confusion, let it fall behind one of the benches. She received me with an embarrassed yet gratified air.

"Miss Engleton," said I, and took her hand, "we are allowed but one moment, for your cousin is coming, but let that moment be decisive—dare I to hope?" She was silent, and I perceived her frame in a tremor. "Why this agitation?" continued I, laying my arm lightly around her waist. "Is it a sentence of banishment?" She tried to speak. Her lips quivered, but were void of moisture. Her color rose and fell in an instant, and at last she articulated a feeble, trembling "No." "On that word my life will rest," cried I, and clasped her in my arms. She had never known such emotions as that embrace inspired. All her frame shook in my arms—I felt her bosom throb.

We saw through the flowery curtain that the girls were at hand and withdrew from the embrace, and went out to meet them. After a short ramble, we all repaired to the mansion, but I could find no vent for my raptures in company, and retired to enjoy an uninterrupted flow of feeling. I was at the grotto before I had a thought whither I was going. I saw the manuscript Zerelda had dropped. I took it up—delicacy forbid that I should read it, but love that knows no concealment prompted my eyes over the pages, and I read the foregoing journal. I beheld the progress of Zerelda's affection with rapture—a rapture I should never have known if she

123

had loved me as Evermont, for her affection was entirely drawn out by the similarity of our sentiments, and not influenced by, but in opposition to, the gratitude she imagined she owed to Evermont.

Before I had fully indulged the new delight which this paper excited, I beheld the girls returning, as I expected, in search of it. I was not prepared for their company, and retired round a corner of the rocks. They entered the grotto and continued some time in conversation, until Zerelda, looking among the flowers, discovered the verses I had heretofore written. She snatched them from their concealment and read them with astonishment.

"This is Evermont," exclaimed she. "This is Holbert! Amacette, how is this? Who is your brother?"

Amacette was affrighted, and wildly replied, "He is my brother," for she was under the most sacred promise to use no expression that would discover my disguise. But her alarm served but to defeat its object, and excite a stronger suspicion. Zerelda and Emerine read the verses again.

"It is Evermont," exclaimed Emerine. "Amacette, acknowledge the truth. I know you cannot tell a positive falsehood. Say, is not this man Evermont?"

Amacette trembled, and was silent.

"Disguise is no longer necessary," said Zerelda. "His object is obtained, and I insist that you remove every doubt."

"I fear he will be angry," cried Amacette, bursting into tears, "and I am indebted to him for my life, my honor, my mother, my all."

"Then he is Evermont?"

"Yes," answered Amacette, "and the best and noblest man alive." And began to relate the manner in which I had assisted her and her mother.

But in an instant she was without an auditor, for Zerelda and Emerine, after embracing her with transport, were flying toward the mansion with a wildness of joy to communicate the happy tidings to Mrs. Haylard. Amacette followed them, and I was left to determine what method to pursue. I had not yet rendered myself sufficiently dear to Zerelda to banish the impression of my errors

124

from her memory, and resolved to withdraw from the village until I could determine whether she had the same affection for the guilty Evermont as for the innocent, but rustic, Holbert.

I had been anxious to visit the place where Major Haylard was slain, and to erect a monument to his memory. This purpose I now resolved to effect.

Mrs. Holbert and Amacette were sufficiently known in the village to meet with every assistance, and without waiting to see them again, I immediately started on my road toward the head of Jackson's River to perform a service which would gratefully be accepted by all my family, and render me more dear to the heart of Zerelda.

CHAPTER XI

While preparing for the execution of this design, I stopped at a village in Shenandoah. My host, who inhabited an old but elegant mansion, entertained me with genuine hospitality, and being remarkably loquacious, gave me a history of the surrounding country and all the remarkable transactions which had transpired within his recollection. And when I admired his farm and mansion, he gave me a history of its former proprietor, and the means by which he became possessed of it.

"It was erected," said he, "for Sir William Valindon, who although the son of Lord Willford of England, yet, being a younger brother, left his country and sailed to Maryland where he married a beautiful woman of great fortune. And, preferring a retired life, chose this seat as his residence. It was reported that he was principally actuated in this removal by the hope of eluding a subtle woman with whom he had been too intimate while in Baltimore. But he was not long permitted, even here, to enjoy the quiet sunshine of life, for when he had been here about six months, and became the father of a son, who bore his name, William Albertus, this young woman discovered his retreat and pursued him hither with a child about three months old, which was supposed and reported to be the son of Sir William. Finding he could not get rid of her, he settled her on a little farm, and provided her with everything necessary for living comfortably.

"Soon after the arrival of Miss Bridford, the name of the young woman, Lady Valindon feel sick and died, lamented by all the village to whom she had been an angel, and who wept for her as if they had lost a mother. It was supposed by some that her death was hastened by Miss Bridford, but no inquiry was ever made on the subject. After the death of his wife, Sir William became extremely

126

Miss Bridford's William + what happens to her [handwritten annotation]

subject. After the death of his wife, Sir William became extremely melancholy, for he was one of the best of men and tenderest husbands, and being compelled to go to Baltimore to arrange some business, he left his household, and his little William Albertus, in the care of Miss Bridford until he returned. But he never beheld his son again. He fell sick in his absence, and, notwithstanding all that Miss Bridford and the whole village could do, he died a few days before the arrival of his father. When he returned, he was so distressed at the loss of his wife and child that he resigned himself to continual sorrow, and it was believed he wept himself to death, for he died about a year afterwards of a consumption, and now sleeps by the side of his wife and son in the garden, where his friends have raised a monument to their memory.

"When he was dying, he was extremely fond of Miss Bridford's child, which was also named William, to whom he had paid no particular attention before. He kept him continually in his arms, acknowledged him for his own son, and said he was the only connection he had on earth. And when he made his will, he left this estate to Miss Bridford, and made William sole heir to all the rest of his fortune.

"After his decease, Miss Bridford became less circumspect in her conduct. She had been suspected for a connection with her servant of the name of Huron, but now she was possessed of an independent fortune, she openly avowed her attachment for Huron, and made no secret of their illicit intercourse. She soon after offered this estate for sale, and I became the purchaser." *Huron* [handwritten annotation]

He then proceeded to tell me all the particulars of his own settlement here, in which I felt no concern. But having become interested in the story of Miss Bridford, I inquired what became of her after she sold the estate.

"She removed to Pennsylvania," continued he, "but the Indians attacked them on the road and killed her little son. After which I heard nothing of her for many years, but have latterly learnt that she is living in Richmond, under the name of Mrs. Willford."

"*Willford!*" repeated I, in astonishment, and connecting this story with what I had read in Willford's enigmatical letter, beheld

She is mrs Willford! [handwritten annotation]

within the curtains a dreadful mystery. I rushed from the presence of my host to indulge a rising chaos of agitation.

It was evident that I was the William who was reported to be slain—the illicit offspring of Valindon and Miss Bridford—the wretched son of the abominable Willford—the incestuous monster of his own sister!

Great God! What a thought! It wheeled in a whirlwind of contending passions, through the elements of distraction—lashed every imaginary prospect of happiness to the ground in shattered confusion—played in frenzied wildness with the keen lightning of certain wretchedness, which pierced, and re-pierced, my soul, and with delicious pleasure, dandled despair on my bosom! I felt every string crack that held me to mankind. I felt myself wrenched out of the chain of society—all the humanity in my nature curdled into poison. It was a moment of frantic agitation, a moment awful to recollection. Deeds of honor danced in my imagination: "I could call down the blasting fire of heaven!/ Could alight the subterraneous mines!/ Explode the world, and crush the human race." I could hold the seven forked flame of ignited vengeance to consume even my own mother and sister—.

I required no confirmation of those fatal particulars. The mind transported to "Ride on the vollied lightning through the heavens," could not fail to rush precipitately into desperate conviction.

All powerful disposer! How was thy throne of vindication scaled by daring man, and thy clouds of sleeping bolts, "Hurled headlong down through seas of blazing air,/ In terrible explosion—"

This storm of furious desperation existed but in imagination, and was awed into murmuring silence by the reason of a moment, but left me rocking on the unallayed billows of passion, which it had thrown into maddening confusion. I felt, I knew I was wretched, and wretchedly criminal. The sins of my father were visited on my head in a voice of thunder that rived even the love of life. But I myself had provoked the latent shafts, and pulled them down with accumulated fury.

I had often longer to know my parents, but finding them thus was the commencement of endless agony.

It was impossible that I should become composed under the weight of this afflicting discovery, yet I was able to reflect and resolve, and I determined never to see my mother or sister more. All the dear and enthusiastic delights of nature's children to live under the benign influence of a parent's smile, all the sweet delirium of ecstatic emotions that leap into the filial heart at the name of mother, were swept with violence from my thoughts, and fancy dare not glance at my relations without an internal shivering.

From Zerelda I resolved to fly forever, for she was too pure to be connected, even in thought, with a wretch abandoned by hope—a wretch denounced of nature.

Here was a pang to which the sons of medium passions, who float carelessly down the surface of life, are, and ever must be, strangers—a pang of dissolving nature—a pang of expiring hope. Death may be terrible to some; to me it would have been Elysium.

I watered the grave of my father with the tears of penitential sorrow, and invoked, with fervent reverence, the hand of omnipotence to draw the veil of mercy over his offences, and my own.

My conduct must have astonished my host, but that gave me no concern. To a mind like mine, borne down by the heaviest calamities of being, what are the commonplace occurrences of like? What all the painted bubbles which excite such hurrying confusion in a bustling world but the quivering atoms of down, driven along by the convolving billows of the wind, and followed by a succession of others, which are equally light, and as suddenly whirled into oblivion?

I abandoned the thought of erecting a monument over Major Hayland. War was the only theater that accorded with the turbulence of my passions. I could have waged war with the universe, and dealt out, with tremendous fury, the awful magazines of omnipotent vengeance!

CHAPTER XII

With fifteen resolute companions, I immediately joined in the pursuit of a band of Indians who had committed some depredations on the back settlements of Pennsylvania. Our march was rapid, and we overtook them shortly after they had crossed the Allegheny. Their number far exceeded ours, but we attacked them at break of day. They had no expectation of our approach, and fled at the first encounter, leaving seven of their number dead in their camps, and their arms, horses, and two Pennsylvanian prisoners fell to the lot of their conquerors.

This exploit being accomplished, my companions appeared disposed to return, but my mind was desperately bent on dreadful scenes of carnage, and by long entreating, in such arguments as the violence of my emotions suggested, I prevailed upon nine to accompany me in carrying the war into the heart of Indian territory. The others returned to their country.

We equipped ourselves in Indian dress and paint, and mounting ten of the horses the Indians had deserted, proceeded in the most daring expedition ever yet undertaken. Several of our party were well acquainted with the country, and we hastened with rapid marches toward the Indian settlements on the Muskingum and Lake Erie.

We discovered a tract which had been recently traveled by some Indians, and pursuing it some distance, beheld them about a mile before us. The moment we were discovered to be enemies, they began, as was their custom, to tomahawk their prisoners. We no sooner perceived their purpose than we gave our horses the rein. My horse proved the fleetest and I was first among the Indians. They had murdered three prisoners, two men and a woman, and attempted to murder the last, but he being resolute, and seeing

130

4mos of the Indians raiding. Again - to the rescue!

THE PRISONERS OF NIAGARA

assistance at hand, broke from them and retreated in hopes of escape, but was overtaken and a tomahawk raised to cleave him to the earth. But I had arrived. I had discharged my gun and pistols as I drew near, and had no weapon wherewith to oppose a host of enemies, but disregarding the bullets that showered around my head, I leapt from my horse and attempted to seize the tomahawk which was raised over the trembling captive.

I effected my purpose, but only threw the tomahawk from the head of the prisoner, and the blow fell on my own breast. My companions now arrived, and the Indians being unaccustomed to such an impetuous attack, retreated in the utmost disorder. _CARMONT_

The young man I had relieved was of the name of Carmont. He expressed a frantic flow of gratitude for my timely interposition in saving his life, and ever afterwards displayed his thankfulness in a chain of noble actions, which endeared him to my heart.

My wound proved to be but slight, but left a scar on my breast, which Carmont said he should ever remember as the palladium of his existence.

We now considered ourselves almost invincible, and by the secrecy and fierceness of our attacks, and the frequent and rapid changes of positions, were enabled to penetrate the Indian villages and encampments, and defeat many of their bands of warriors, and release to the number of twenty prisoners who were destined to the most awful of deaths. Our determinations were executed with such resolution and impetuosity, our garb being the same with the Indians, and our retreats so rapid, that resistance was ineffectual, and pursuit unavailing. Thus, for four months, while the principal number of warriors were absent in the war between Britain and her colonies, we carried terror and devastation through all the eastern part of the territory west of the Allegheny.

It was now the latter end of September, when their soldiers were expected from their summer campaigns, and we concluded it most advisable to return nearer to the American settlements. But we had grown scarce of provisions, and several of us rode out in different directions, to kill some of the wild animals with which the country abounded. I had not proceeded far before I killed a large

131

deer, and threw it bleeding on my horse to bear it to camp. But my horse became frightened at some other object, and breaking from me, threw off the deer, and ran full speed back to camp. I heard a heavy firing shortly after, and hastening on, perceived a large body of Indians plundering our camp, but was unable to discover what had become of my companions. Meeting one of them about twelve months afterward he informed me that when my horse ran to the camp, covered with blood, they had no doubt but that I was slain. A party of Indians attacking them immediately afterwards confirmed their belief, so that they thought it a desperate undertaking to risk an engagement with a far superior force for the hopeless purpose of rendering me any service, and after discharging their pieces retreated without the loss of a man. But they had the utmost difficulty to prevail on Carmont to follow them, for he lingered behind with the hope of discovering what had become of me, until he was several times almost in the power of the enemy.

Finding myself alone, almost in contact with an irritated host of Indians, I was alarmed into a thought of seeking my own safety. For although I felt indifferent at the approach of death, I had no disposition to rush into it in the horrid form of the savage orgies, and turning the heels of my shoes before, to mock pursuit, I silently retreated to the shores of the Muskingum, and traveled down the beach, sometimes in, sometimes out of the water.

I was not pursued, and heard no more of this party of Indians. I now felt perfectly at ease, and having resolved to abandon every endearing object in human society, began to turn my researches for a solitary situation where I could live and dies unknown, and bury my crimes and miseries together in oblivion. But alas! I appeared the football of destiny, and was driven from even this dreary determination.

I beheld a party of Indians crossing the Muskingum with a number of prisoners, among whom was a female, and although a single individual, I formed the forlorn resolution of liberating the captives and defeating the Indians. My mind was gloomy and desperate, and I considered that if I saved the life of any human being, at the expense of my own, I should render the world an infinite service, and mitigate the injuries I had inflicted on society.

Thus resolved, I chose the hour of midnight. The moon was smothered under a western cloud, and the Indian fires shed a feeble and portentous luster on the gloom. The Indian reposed in unguarded security, and I entered their camp undiscovered.

This, though at present not very alarming, is in general a wretched mode of warfare. How shocking! How terrible it is to the imagination to steal upon the unthinking slumberer and hurl him out of existence, before he is aware of the necessity of self-defense! When sleep draws his downy umbrage over man, his protection should be a more inviolable sanctuary than the alter of refuge, or the sacred temple of divinity. But custom, blind offspring of hereditary error, has sanctioned the barbarous practice of midnight butchery, and irritated passion justified its continuance. This inhuman mode of assassination has entailed the name of savage on the unenlightened Indians, but man—civilized man!—who boasts the sublime illuminations of the all irradiating day-star of heaven, still pursues the same abominable barbarity, and would be thought just, humane, and benevolent. Gracious Father! What monsters are we rendered by the chimeras of ungovernable passions.

These suggestions deterred me from my first determination, of butchering the Indians while they slept, and I contented myself with releasing the prisoners. But even this I could not execute with safety, for when I had unbound their fetters, and all had withdrawn from camp except a female, she, in the dark, unfortunately struck her foot against the face of an Indian, who immediately awoke, and raised the alarm. The prisoners fled in disorder. The camp was in an uproar. The female whom I held by the hand sprang from me involuntarily when the Indian awoke, and endeavoring to recover her again, I seized hold of an Indian. He yelled the whar-whoop, and I was willing to relinquish my grasp and retreat. I retired to a secure covert in a thicket of sedge when grew in the edge of the Muskingum, and awaited the effect of my enterprise.

THE PRISONERS OF NIAGARA

In the morning, I perceived that all the prisoners had escaped, except the female, and although pursued by the Indians, they were never overtaken.

The Indians erected tents, as if they intended continuing on the banks of the Muskegum, which would give me an opportunity of liberating the captive lady.

About mid-day, a party of the Indians came to the river for water, and approached within a few paces of my concealment. Peace, trembling heart! What were thy feelings at that moment! Every nearer step appeared to shake an arrow through my body. I did not imagine that even death could have inspired such a tremor. Yet, notwithstanding all that heroes have evinced by their examples, and philosophers by their precepts, we are still the slaves to death. Go, daring warrior, after having rushed upon the blazing bolt of canon, and sported among the whistling torrents of leaden death, retire from the fury of slaughter, and if you do not find a secret something that is startling in death, when he unexpectedly approaches in some unknown but terrible form, I will again acknowledge myself a coward.

The Indians were retiring. I raised my eyes and beheld the female captive. Her face was towards me. Angels of mercy! It was Zerelda. My blood sprang from every extremity of my body to my heart. Every pulse burst into a throbbing delirium. "On every fevered sense, a storm arose,/ Sudden and wild—." It was scarce possible for a hundred uplifted tomahawks to chain me to my bed, for my soul was bursting f rom my bosom, and rushing to her assistance. But prudence bore rule for once, and I continued silent that I might relieve her more certainly at another period.

My God! What a dreadful destiny is hers. Torn from friends and family by the fearful, heart-chilling savages under the most alarming circumstances—what were her sensations when she first behold herself in their grasp? It was the grasp of a torpedo, and shot the benumbing effluvia of death through her soul. How did her tender heart, the seat of every generous virtue, toss itself in the bosom with a frightful quivering? Their painted visages, their eyes scowling the dark fire of revenge, their yell of hideous horror, were

134

Jealousy !

as tremendous to her shirking senses as the sight of death, stalking in grinning fury amidst the myriad trains of his ghastly apparitions. Then the foreboding apprehensions of meeting a fate, from which the lion-heart of valor shrinks back in trembling horror! The picture is too dark for the most daring imagination.

What a throng of writhing pangs must have wrung her delicate frame while traversing a long tract of uninhabited wilds—a frame which appears as soft and susceptible as the shadowy sylph that dances in dewy fragrance on the morning sunbeam, which bends the aspiration of a zephyr, and dissolves with the rough visits of the wind. Yet she was enfeebled by enervating fear, and possessed of all her trembling feminine tenderness, compelled to trace a pathless route of rugged rocks and briery wildernesses—melancholy reverse of the affectionate care she received from her family, who would not suffer the weight of a frown to light upon her.

And what shafts yet hand in fate's exhaustless quiver to be feathered at her heart! But she shall not fall beneath their threatening power—no. Oh God! If one drop of mercy remains in the treasury of heaven, it will be wafted down, by smiling angels, to bear Zerelda home.

I could discover all the movements in the Indian camp, and perceived that they were all engaged in different pursuits of business or pleasure, and that Zerelda was permitted to go unnoticed, except when one of the young men, who appeared to possess an American air and manner, compelled her to listen to some disagreeable solicitation. His attentions were frequently animated, and even rude, and excited in me a most dreadful jealousy that he was actuated by a barbarous passion of love. But is it possible for any human to look upon her sainted and countenance and feel the impulse of one impure desire? Her chasteness has a majesty of virtue, which would congeal the fire of a licentious thought, and awe the daring breath that would waft one soul expression to her ear.

But this ungovernable youth felt not the sacred influence of virtue, divinely beaming in her features with the lustered dignity of ethereal spirits. He dared to sail the commanding chastity of her person by the polluting touch of libertine caresses.

The camp was accidentally deserted by the Indians, and he availed himself of that opportunity to further his abominable purposes. She attempted to fly, but he grasped her hand, and growing violent by her resistance, attempted to thrust his hand into her bosom. My heart swelled with furious vengeance, and had not the Indians returned to her relief, I should in this moment have flown from my concealment, and risked every danger, to baffle the designs of the daring assassin. But when the Indians came into camp he desisted and made no further attempt during the evening.

At midnight all was silent. I stole into the camp, but their fires being nearly extinguished, I could not distinguish one person from another. I found a parcel of dried venison with which I filled my pockets, and renewed my search for Zerelda. I discovered the figure of a woman alying in the bosom of a man. Her form appeared to resemble Zerelda's. Startled at the thought, I was proceeding to examine them more closely when I perceived the glimpse of some person gliding from the other side of camp to a distant thicket, and fearing I was discovered, I cautiously retreated, and remained for a few moments in timid, trembling suspense.

A faint, distant scream issued from the direction in which I had observed the figure to move. It was shrill and tremulous, and smothered in an instant—it was the scream of Zerelda! With the wings of lightning I flew to her aid. It was dark, and no sound succeeded. I reached the place where I imagined the sound was heard, but all was silent. I paused in horrible anticipation. I knew Zerelda was in the grasp of a monster! The thought was barbed with distraction—it stilled the pulse of breath, the throb of life in listening agony! At that moment, tremendous to memory, a barbarous wretch was rifling the fairest flower that ever bloomed on nature's bosom.

Mighty God! Is this Thy sovereign will?

A feeble cry stole from a cluster of bushes—it came like the moaning sigh of departed hope. I reached the place in a thought. The moon burst from under a cloud and flung her full beams upon

136

Rope of Zerelda ; he
tomahawk,
the gu

the scene. The last tremor of invigorating virtue had expired. The last struggle of Zerelda was exhausted.

The heartless wretch had forced open her mouth with a rude piece of iron as she slept, and thereby restraining her voice, bore her to this retreat. In struggling, she was able to raise one feeble cry, but she was now entirely overcome, and fell without life into the destroyer's arms at the moment I arrived. He having thus, by brutal violence, subdued her opposition, was clasping her to his bosom with the exulting certainty of gratified desires.

It was not a crisis for deliberation. My mind was a chaos of avenging passions. Without a pause, I raised my tomahawk and sunk it deep in his head. He fell and expired in a gasp.

Zerelda lay insensible—a moment's delay would be ruin! I banished suggestions of ceremony, clasped her in my arms, and flew to the Muskingum, a short distance above the camp.

Zerelda recovered. "Oh God! Protect me!" she faintly articulated, and almost escaped my arms at a single exertion.

I caught her by the hand and observed, "Be under no apprehensions, madam, you are safe. Be silent, and there is no danger." My voice inspired the dying pulse of animation, and stopped her flying soul to listen, and to hope. I gave her to understand her situation. She recollected the first attack of the ruffian and her soul was alive with sensibility, to know what had transpired in the oblivion of memory which succeeded, but she was unable to express her anxiety. I understood her sensations and assured her that she was a pure from his villainous intentions as when the zephyr of Love first melted his ethereal spices on her lips. The fearful suggestions of trembling innocence subsided.

"You are my guardian genius," cried she. "May heaven reward you," and by an unsuspected reliance on my for protection, convinced me of the unbounded gratitude of her heart.

137

CHAPTER XIII

The moon smiled upon us from an ocean of azure, but the frowning Muskingum was to be passed. There was no boat and it must be swum. I threw away my gun, and confining my pistols and powder on my head to keep them dry, prevailed upon Zerelda to dismiss her maiden delicacy so far as to yield to necessity. At last with a panting heart she accorded to my request, and clasped her arm loosely around my neck, while I wrapped my left arm around her waist, and in this situation entered the river. I had never swum under the influence of such unconquerable palpitations—I had never swum with such an inestimable prize—but with determined exertions I reached the other shore.

After a short pause to rest, we began our journey, the distant termination of which was scarcely visible to hope. You who know the enthusiasm of my nature, and the ardor of my passion for Zerelda, can feel in imagination my boundless flow of emotions when I gave her my arm to lead her to her distant friends.

But here recollecting what I had not thought of before, that the Indians had horses, I left Zerelda, re-swam the Muskingum, and procuring the best one I could catch, returned, and seating her behind me, proceeded with the utmost speed.

In the morning, Zerelda was so far exhausted with fatigue and the loss of sleep that we were compelled to stop that she might enjoy a few hours repose. I was still in the habit of an Indian, with my complexion rendered rough and dark by a tincture of copper, and my features entirely disguised by various paints, so that it was impossible I could be recognized even by the scrutinizing eyes of love, and Zerelda, so that she considered me as an entire stranger, and in this belief I resolved she should continue, still firmly resolving to banish all thoughts of enjoying her love, and after I had

138

conducted her to her family, to bid her farewell forever without permitting her to know she owed her life, her honor, and her deliverance to the love of Evermont. I assumed the name of Bridford when I left Shenandoah, and by this name alone I determined that she should know me.

Zerelda had never before consented to resign the guard of watchful modesty in the presence of man, but nature wearied out, and she appeared to place such firm doubtless faith in my honor that she slumbered as securely as if surrounded by an army of virgins. I felt the force of this flattering confidence and would not have stained the ermine of her innocence with the impurity of a thought.

Never was imagery more exquisitely designed either by nature, art, or imagination to kindle all the fine, indescribable tones of which the soul is susceptible to swell with love and ecstacy than the form of Zerelda while she slept. A black silk dress dropped lightly over her limbs. A veil of dark gauze half shaded her bosom and waved with every vibration of her heart. A serene smile slumbered in sober majesty on her countenance. A gentle shade of clear transparent red was basking on her cheeks and lips; it seemed alive with sensibility, and appeared at intervals to steal gradually over a wider space, and mingle with its borders of ermined white, yet exhibited such a tenderness of susceptibility that it seemed that I could blow it away with the breath of a sigh.

O nature! How lovely is the simplicity of thy children! All the myriad universe of worlds that catch the glimmer of yonder sun could not inspire such an enthusiastic flow of living raptures as the benign aspect of sleeping Zerelda. Past time a futurity dissolves, and my eternity is the moment of her slumber.

Nature suggested—love smiled—chastity consented—and I touched her lips with the warm breath of mine. No impurity left a stain—no sensitive modesty was alarmed—and the stolen kiss was never revealed to warm the glow of her cheek.

When she awoke we renewed our journey, and as we rode she gratified my anxiety by unfolding the particulars of her captivity. Her statement, as she supposed it made to a stranger, contained *her captivity narrative*

many family descriptions, which are already known. I shall therefore abridge her relation to suit my own story.

Her father had left Baltimore and retired to a family seat in Bath, and was conducting Zerelda from Hayland village to take the charge of his domestic concerns. They had no company except a Mr. Barville, a young and wealthy acquaintance of her father's, and while passing through the mountainous country which lies between Hampshire and Bath, they were attacked by a party of Indians. At the discharge of their guns, their father's horse was frightened and bore him swiftly on his course. Her horse was killed, and Barville discovered her situation, and being a man of consummate prudence, and withall a votary of the principles of self-preservation, left Zerelda to the mercy of the Indians, and turning his horse, fled to secure his own safety. Thus, left without protection, she was taken by the Indians and conducted through the mountains to the Allegheny River where they were joined by many others, among whom was the ruffian who had assailed her virtue, who was a British Canadian. He became enamored of her beauty, and immediately purchased her of the Indians by whom she was taken. He treated her with great kindness, and gave her a horse to ride, while all the rest of the prisoners were compelled to walk on foot and carry heavy burdens.

sarcasm

This enabled her truly feminine constitution to support her rout to the Muskingum. But she had not traveled far before her master discovered his diabolical intentions by frequent solicitations and dreadful threats, and had even dared to exert force in several instances, but had been thwarted by the interposition of the Indians, who possess the virtue of chastity in a higher degree than any modern civilized nation.

When I effected her liberation with her fellow prisoners, she attempted to fly, but before she was out of camp she was retaken, and again consigned to the brutal attacks of her master, which was the most dreadful calamity she feared. But my opportune assistance had prevented this destiny, when it was brought to its most awful crisis.

Indian chastity

THE PRISONERS OF NIAGARA

At night we resolved to enjoy the benefit of uninterrupted slumber. It must have been painful to Zerelda, notwithstanding her apparent cheerfulness, to remain all night with an entire stranger, without a single curtain to separate them. Notwithstanding her firm belief of my honor, a thousand little indefinable fears would be naturally suggested by modesty, and create an uneasy restlessness in her mind, yet she slept with the slumber of a peaceful conscience.

flatters himself

Soon as the glittering harbinger of morning rode above the horizon, we renewed our journey, and traveled for several days without any inconvenience except a continued fear of the Indians who swarmed through the country, and from whose notice it was a miracle that we escaped.

Our horse became lame, and gradually grew worse, until with our utmost exertion we could force him no further, and were compelled to leave him and venture our solitary journey on foot. But this change had no effect upon the spirits of Zerelda, who had become sprightly and unreserved, and chatted and sung the dreary hours pleasantly away. But at night she slept more soundly than heretofore, on account of her greater exertions in traveling.

At break of day the wolves raised a hideous howling almost in our camp. The sound burst at once in a thousand different tones of shrill and fearful horror. Zerelda sprang to me for protection—I caught her in my arms, and delicacy terrified into silence suffered her to rest on my heart. The wolves were irritated by hunger, and approached within a few paces of our scent. I discharged a pistol at the foremost. They retreated a short distance but instantly returned with more tremendous yelling than before. I discharged my other pistol. One of them was wounded and fled with a dreadful yell. The rest followed, and Zerelda was relieved of her panting apprehensions.

CHAPTER XIV

Morning hung her smiling ensign over the eastern hills. We traveled on, and shortly entered a level waste parched by a burning sun, without the welcome appendage of one refreshing stream. We were almost exhausted by thirst at noon, but were compelled, weary and famishing, to wander on over unshaded plains, which appeared as if they had never drunk the weening fragrance of a dew. Every rising ground we ascended, hope anxiously anticipated the desirable cordial at the bottom of the descent, but we were again disappointed. We hoped again and again, but again disappointment came.

Night arrived with a sable vapor of scorching fevers on his wings. It was impossible for us to pause under the influence of a thirst, which fancy imagined could never be allayed, and with Mars, who shot his fiery arrows from the East for our guide, we rambled in a vain search of water until morning. The sun arose, but his beams fried in the air as they darted along a wide level of prairie. Zerelda became too weak to make our accustomed progress toward the still expected stream. The risen sun poured a baleful shower of heated radiance around us. We endeavored to console each other with prospects which neither of us believed; we avoided wounding each other by unavailing complaints, but mutually felt and lamented each other's sufferings.

We were descending a hill, at the bottom of which the prairie was terminated by a margin of woods, but nature was almost wearied out in Zerelda—she was scarcely able to move. I held one of her hands in mine, laid my other arm around her waist, and thus assisted her in a slow progress toward a distant hope. Oh! How I bled for her sufferings! My own pangs were unutterable. My blood ran like streams of burning sulphur; my heart throbbed with a fever

142

of fiery billows; the air I breathed was a crackling flame to my vitals, but the agonies of Zerelda added a tenfold poignancy to my tortures. Her hand burned in mine. Her face was inflamed in crimson, but not a drop of sweat moistened its heated surface. She could bear up but little longer. We had nearly reached the bottom, but she was exhausted! The last struggle of famishing nature was dying. She pressed my hand, looked up in my eyes, and fainted.

Heavens of mercy! What was to be done? I seated her on the parched grass and leaned over her in a state of stupefied distraction. To have saved her, I would have torn open my own bosom, and she should have drunk the blood of my heart.

Stay here, and she never opens the eye of light again! This dreadful certainty rendered me frantic. I caught her in my arms and ran at least a mile through the bottom. She had not revived, but I had reached the long sought blessing. The water was stagnant and impure, but I poured a plentiful draught in her lips, and threw it in showers over her face and person. Her pulse leapt from oblivion—I saw "the beam of her eye." She revived in a transport of smiles, but attempted not to express her gratitude in words. She pressed my hand, and gave me a look that led me into her soul.

I built up a fire, shot a brace of partridges, and rendered this a scene of joy and festivity, resolved to tarry here all evening.

Zerelda became every day more attached to me. A spirit of solicitous kindness had formed its residence in her bosom, and gratitude, sympathy, and the homogeneity of our sentiments interested her heart in a generous anxiety for my happiness. The similarity of our situations, our hopes and fears, our pleasures and pains, so often mingled our sensations, and our souls so often called every tone, every sentiment, and every emotion of our throbbing hearts into unison that it was impossible but that all the springs of nature should flow in the liveliest streams of friendship for each other, and the repeated evidences I received of her affection for Bridford often created a secret jealousy in the mind of Evermont.

She was extremely cheerful and even vivacious, and appeared to strain her volatility to the utmost stretch to designate the weary tedium of our journey. Our conversations were animated and

With an Indian?

THE PRISONERS OF NIAGARA

sentimental, and frequently interspersed with poetry, music, and
criticisms on the various works of taste which had fallen under our
observation, in all of which, it was evident, that nature had given
our souls the same organization, and tuned them with the same
strings of sensibility and affection. But hers was a pure as when the
inspiring breath of love first warmed it into being, while mine—O
horrible!—was so deeply stained with guilt of such awful dyes, that
could my eyes flow down in streams of contrition, it would be
inadequate to wash away the enormity of its crimes.

I was anxious to sound her heart to know the station Evermont,
the guilty Evermont, still held in that sacred arcanum, but the
subject was too delicate and dangerous to be attempted by a
stranger, and I always delayed it for a more seasonable occasion.
This evening offered the fairest opportunity I had yet received. We
were reading Thompson together. It was the only book with which I
had not parted when I left Richmond, and I had ever since kept it in
my bosom as the dearest friend in adversity. I turned to the close of
spring, where that inimitable painter of the human emotions gives
his most exquisite delineations to the passion of love.

Zerelda was all heart and animation, and evinced all that her
soul was love for some desirable object, and I imagined that object
was Evermont. But before I had completed my researches into her
affections, we were alarmed from our poetical entertainment.

A panther of enormous size had stolen close up to Zerelda, and
was in the act of springing upon her when she discovered it. She
screamed and fell in my arms. My pistols were by me, and I gave
him a random shot which had no visible effect but to frighten him
away. I dropped the pistol and pressed Zerelda. She seized the hand
that had shot the pistol, and in a transport, raised it to her lips
without a blush. It was the embrace of gratitude, and I would have
devoted my life to her service for the happy sensations that were
born of that embrace.

Night came on, but when we were preparing for sleep, we heard
the panther scream on the hill. Zerelda had laid down at a little
distance, but she arose in a tremor, and came and sat by me. I felt
the delicacy of the situation; propriety revolted at the idea of

144

PANTHER

sleeping too near me, and her terrors were too violent to be borne at a distance.

I took her hand and observed, "Miss Engleton, you will be in danger if you sleep apart from me. I know the feelings of a mind like yours at the idea of sleeping at my side, but banish them as unnecessary and improper at present. You have abundant evidence that I design you no injury. Otherwise, a thousand other opportunities have transpired to have furthered my purpose, and even here a few paces could not protect you. But woe betide the wretch who saves the drowning victim to butcher him on the shore! Even the dear partner of your heart would condemn you for objecting to this proposal."

"Who informed you," said she, with a sally of vivacity, "that my heart was in partnership?"

"Nature, madam," replied I. "That great teacher who taught you the worth of a congenial soul. Such feeling, such sympathy, such sentiment, could never have been born in a bosom which was a stranger to the darling relation of love—a kindred heart."

She appeared unwilling to enter again on a subject which excited so many powerful emotions, and evasively observed, "Nature has formed a great many apparent oddities, and amongst others organized such a being as myself, without deeming it necessary that there should be two such strange chimeras in existence. But if you waste your time in examining the nature of my composition, the Lethian deity will require you to perform penance at his alter, while the sun will blush at your devotion." *altar*

I obeyed her indirect request and abandoned the subject, but my observations produced their desired effect, and she, dismissing her apprehensions, lay down by my side.

I had not lost the fire of those passions which hurried me into all the wild reveling of licentiousness while in Richmond, nor had they dissipated a volatile particle of their excitability, but they were never aroused for the destruction of Zerelda. I felt as man must feel in my situation, but Zerelda was hallowed as the spirit of awe, and I would have sacrificed the hand that dared unbidden to assail the sanctity of her person—even if it had been my own. I would have spared no heart, not even the one which throbs in my own bosom, that could have meditated her dishonor.

CHAPTER XV

A few days passed away unnoticed in the annals of our calamities, but soon the fatal morning arrived which produced a new disaster. I had built a fire on the bank of a creek and was loading my pistols to shoot something for breakfast. I charged one and handed the powder to Zerelda, who was sitting by my side. I was at some difficulty to draw the rammer from the other, which fixed her attention, and she forgot the powder which lay loose on a paper, and being wholly engrossed with what I was doing, the paper fell from her hand into the water. We both endeavored to recover the powder, but it was scattered from the paper and washed down the stream. Zerelda was frightened and unable to speak. She took my hand and raised her eyes to mine. The timid trembling soul of entreaty was in the look and seemed to lisp "forgive." I would not have been angry for the world. I returned her a smile, the kindest my nature knew, and pressed both her hands in mine. It relieved her tremors, for she feared I would be angry, and a look, a word of displeasure would have sunk her to the earth.

"O Bridford, forgive my carelessness," said she. "I would rather have lost my own existence."

"You are not even censurable, Miss Engleton," replied I. "It was the effect of accident. But the powder may not be wanted, and if it should, we have both learned how to suffer."

"I should be contented," added she, "if I could bear our awaiting danger alone, but by palpable negligence to consign you to hunger, and probably to death, is unpardonable. It is a sad return for your kindness."

"You misconstrue a casualty into a fault," said I. "You are not in the slightest degree blameable, and could you be so selfish as to wish to deprive me of the pleasure of participating in your affections?"

"Bridford, I owe you everything," cried she, "and would sacrifice my soul rather than subject you to the horrors of famine, and one who could pain a heart like yours deserves to suffer alone and unpitied."

"Zerelda," and it was the first time I used that familiar and endearing name during our journey, "you know the pleasures and privileges of sympathy, and need not expect to pay your devotions in her temple without the mingling orisons of your friend."

Thus with cheerful sallies I dissipated her uneasiness, and as we were in no great need of our breakfast, we preserved our charge of powder for our last emergency, and continued traveling during the day. In the evening we came upon the route I had pursued when I left Virginia, and I was convinced that we were a long distance from the Pennsylvanian settlements, and must inevitably perish if we met with no miraculous supply, for the woods were too barren to afford us the least provision. But this melancholy discovery I concealed from Zerelda, who was just beginning to recover from her mortification at the loss of our powder. She was not born for sorrow, and amidst all our calamities her lively, flighty spirits remained unbroken. The exhilarating effusions of her vivacity were a refreshing cordial in the torrid zone of burning thirst—an invigorating spring of energy in the dreary region of fatigue. She had always been in a sprightly mood, surrounded by the dancing, laughing graces, and displayed such an enchanting variety of enlivening humor and sentiment that she bewitched the threats of danger into smiles, and made the "desert blossom." Her animation, which had been checked by this late disaster, now revived in her bosom, and she redoubled all her former efforts to give to time the fleeting wings of airy transport.

She perceived the heavy seriousness that was gathering a gloom on my brow, and opened her inexhaustible treasury of wit and cheerfulness to disperse its disagreeable shadows, and plant the bright halo of pleasure in its stead. I was ever the willing subject of her divine incantation. She could at pleasure take hold of my soul with a hand of irresistible magic, and mold and shape it as she pleased. Every faculty, every sense, and every tone awaited but the flying touch of her enchanted finger, to expand, and pant, and thrill with the emotions she intended. Her glance of sorrow benumbed every pulse of vivacity, withered every blossom of ecstasy, and burst every pathetic spring of my heart to flow with the tears of sensibility. But when the smiles of joy blossomed on her countenance, the folded flowers of delight blew open; the unstrung harp of rapture was attuned, and vibrated; the rifled wings of felicity were feathered and expanded; and my soul, wrapped in the bosom of a sweet fascination, was wafted into Heaven.

We were seated on the dry grass by a small fire. She had used a thousand little sorceries to divert my reflections from our melancholy situation; my mind was obsequious to her biddings. Unless by the interposition of providence, there was a certainty of death before us in the meager, emaciated garb of famine, but the inspirational emanations of sympathy stole all the powers of my fancy from the contemplation of the alarming prospect, folded them in the arms of airy gaiety, transported them with the embraces of delectable sensation, and dandled them with blissful animation of the lap of Elysium. I forgot that death was at hand, and had he then arrived, the moment of my dissolution would have been an age of rapture, for I should have died with the joyful Zerelda.

She sung an air, which had several times tuned the wilderness to harmony. The fine, delicate touches of her voice symphonized with such indescribable sweetness and melody that I was entranced from myself into the utopia of love. The world contracted to the space that contained Zerelda. An eternity hung upon the present moment, and I could have flown with her to the everlasting snows of Zembla, and lived possessed of every wish.

"O Zerelda," said I, and I took her hand as I said it, "what an Eden of bliss has nature treasured for the happy man who obtains this divinity of charms, which can rhapsodize a wilderness into paradise."

"He would soon find this divinity bereft of her spell," said she, smiling, "and in the midst of his vision awaken, still in a

149

wilderness. But it is now your turn to melodize this dreary wild, as you term it."

"I am not fond of singing men," I replied. "The sweet softness of the female voice is alone calculated for vocal melody. But if is a duty, it must be performed."

I was anxious to know with what tones the remembrance of Evermont would sweep the lyre of her bosom, and sang the same verses with which she had surprised me in the Hayland grotto. She could not discover that I knew their author or their subject, but I perceived in her the mingled emotions of surprise, pleasure, and anxiety. Her eyes unlocked the secret cabinet of her heart, and I beheld Evermont there.

Her countenance dropped into seriousness, which after a minute was half irradiated by a smile, with which she asked, "Pray, Bridford, from the lips of what muse did you sip that air?"

My look, had it been understood, would have answered, "Your own," but I observed, "I heard them sung by a particular friend."

"You are very tenacious, Mr. Bridford, of your particular friends," said she, "not to let me know the names of them. Names sometimes contain both music and sympathy, two of the divinities of your pantheon."

"The name of this friend," I replied, "is, or ought to be, both musical and sympathetic, for music and sympathy were the inmates of his bosom. However, you shall determine as to its poetical properties. It was Evermont."

Evermont! The sportive, gamboling playmates of her nature hushed at the sound, and all their air-dancing sisterhood could not conjure up another sprightly expression.

"*Evermont*," repeated she. "Where were you acquainted with him?"

"In Richmond."

"Excuse my curiosity," said she. "I knew him when a child and feel interested in his prosperity. Can you inform me whether he still continues in Richmond?"

THE PRISONERS OF NIAGARA

"No, madam. He left there in the spring, being necessitated, as he informed me, to discontinue his education on account of some secret disasters which had taken place in his affairs."

"Whither did he intend going?"

"I believe, madam, he was without an object. Some misfortune of the tenderest nature, which he closely locked in his own bosom, rendered him melancholy, and sometimes almost distracted. When he left Richmond, he informed me, with tears in his eyes, that he had lost all he held dear in time, and was a forlorn wanderer, to whom the whole world was an unpeopled wild."

She sighed, and continued, "While a child he had a charming disposition. His heart was a pure emanation of generosity and sensibility; his bosom was the glowing receptacle of honor, virtue, and friendship; the noble benevolence of his soul had all animated nature for its object. But alas, I have understood he became very dissipated in Richmond, and lost all the darling attributes of his infancy."

"He was very dissipated but never forgot the principles of his youth."

"Have you never heard of him since he left Richmond?"

"I saw him in Shenandoah a short time before I began this expedition, but he was then on the verge of desperation. He sang those verses repeatedly, with a melting air of sorrow, observing, 'they were composed by a young lady on whom the pendulum of my existence hung. She once presented me with her picture, and I fondly hoped I possessed her heart, but it was a dream. I was banished from her bosom on account of my profligacy. I awoke to despair. To complete my agony she demanded her picture.' His voice sank and he wept like an infant. 'I gave the picture,' continued he. 'Yes, if she had asked my life, I would have given it, but it rent my vital heartstrings to tear it away! O, she was a beaming spirit of light! She was an angel of humanity! But ah! She knew not the pangs she inflicted! She might have left me that dear memento of its bright original. It was my last hope—it would have cheered my dying moments with a kiss. It is gone, and I shall never smile again.'"

151

THE PRISONERS OF NIAGARA

[handwritten annotation: Deer / no food / no food for 9 days]

I had proceeded too far. Tears burst from Zerelda's eyes and rolled down her cheeks before she perceived, or was able, to check them. I lamented my rashness, and endeavored, by complimenting her sympathy, to atone for my violence on the tenderest susceptibilities of her heart, but the secret fountain of her sorrows was broken open, and they flowed in ceaseless waves from her bosom. It was long before I could divert her mind to any other object but the sorrows of Evermont, and it was only effected at last by the soothing sweetness of Thompson's fancy.

While she slept, her mind again reverted to the source of her grief, and twice in her troubled slumber I heard her exclaim, "O Evermont."

Next day I discovered a large deer at a distance. I crept through the bushes until within a few paces of him as he fed quietly through the grass. My heart beat high with anticipation—I made a certain aim and discharged my last prospect for provisions. The impetus of powder was insufficient; it gave him a slight wound and he bounded away, and with him flew our only hope.

My mind became gloomy under the ominous presages of starvation. Zerelda again endeavored to exhilarate my spirits, but her efforts were irregular and ineffectual, for while summoning her animation to chase away my uneasiness, her imagination would soar away to my other self, and drown her in the depths of melancholy abstraction.

This was the third day we had spent without food, and we continued traveling for six days more in this desolate condition.

Zerelda grew weaker every hour. Her frame and constitution were never calculated for traversing the wilderness, and were almost exhausted with fatigue. She now yielded to the mighty pressure of her calamities. She became faint and sickly, and was unable to travel but a small part of the day, and then only with the utmost of my assistance.

On the evening of the ninth day she had fasted, she was unable to stand. She took my hand and entreated me to fly to Virginia, and let her die alone.

152

"My God!" cried I. "Do you suppose me capable of such a deed? I would sooner feed you with my own flesh!"

"O Bridford," said she, "what a noble heart is yours! You have rendered yourself inestimably dear to my soul, and for God's sake, fly and preserve your life!"

"And what would be my life when thus preserved but one unchanging scene of horror? Could I forget this moment? Could I think of it without distraction? If I could, I would spurn myself as the veriest monster in being! You know not how closely I am riveted to your existence. I live but to die in you. Death with all his frowning legions cannot force me from your presence. Heaven and earth! To leave you to perish? No. No. Zerelda, your existence is the arbiter of my destiny!"

"Be cool and consider," said she. "You will render my death doubly painful. You——." Exertion to speak overcame her. She fainted in my arms and fell into a troubled slumber.

The moon rode over the night in a wide field of deep blue ether. I left Zerelda and ran through the woods in quest of some wild fruits of the desert, but every forest was as waste and barren as the tomb of famine. The wolves swelled their nocturnal yellings. I felt the fears and danger of Zerelda and hastened to return, but I had been indifferent to the direction of my ramble, and could not find my way back. Distracted at finding myself bewildered, I called with my loudest voice. The sound ran through the woods in vain. Echo awoke on the hills and murmured in reply. The owl screamed her piercing omen over my head. The wolves renewed their howlings in redoubled clangor. A heavy cloud rushed along the east and shut up the moon in darkness.

Spirits of horror! What tortures were then hurled in a whirlwind upon my soul! I called till the woods could no longer hear the hoarse clamor of my voice. I ran through the hills in every direction till my blood was on fire and bursting from every vein. Thus throughout the night I rambled in frantic agony. It was a night from which memory recoils with horror. It was an age to which all my former existence was but a moment. It seemed as if the wheels of time were stopped, "—And nature made a pause;/ An awful pause!

Prophetic of her end." But when the long, long desired light entered the vestibule of morning, it was as hopeless as the eternity of midnight, for horrible anticipation beheld Zerelda torn into a thousand pieces to feed the prowling monsters of the desert. And even now I knew not where I had left her, but from the hill where I stood I beheld the rolling Allegheny. This prospect last evening would have been lighted by the dayspring of hope, but it is now too late. The dreadful dye of fate is cast. Zerelda is no more! But I will seek her and die by her side. The same wide desert shall be our urn—the same dew shall embalm our bodies—the same wild winds, reverberate our requiems.

After two hours search, I found the place where I had left her. I flew to the place with the presages of a forlorn hope—she was not there. All the images of frenzied desperation rushed with wanton fury on my imagination. I saw her seized by monsters fiercely wrangling for her blood, and in an instant, mangled into direful carnage to feed their infuriated ravage. I was ready to let go the thread of life, and exclaim with Milton's Lucifer, "—Hail, horrors! Hail,/ Eternal worlds, and thou profoundest hell,/ Receive thy new possessor."

On examining, I discovered a track leading from the place, and pursuing it some distance, beheld her in the grass. She had wandered in search of water, but was unable to find it. Sudden as the lightning of transition, I was wracked from the extreme of desperation to a frenzy of joy. The look she gave me was the look of a dying saint; she was unable to speak, but gave me to understand her thirst. I instantly allayed it, and taking her in my arms, without a pause ran to the Allegheny.

She recovered her speech, and taking my hand, with a look mild and beneficent as the ardor or mercy, observed, "My dear Bridford, I am never to repay what you have done for me. I feel that I must die, but my soul will remember you in heaven." She paused for breath to proceed, and then continued, "I have a mountain of lead upon my bosom. It was I that drove Evermont to distraction. It was I that forced this picture from his heart. But it was not done to drive him to despair, but to reform him from vice, for I loved him. God

154

miraculous appearance of grapes + turkeys

knows how dearly I loved him! Bear him this medal, tell him it is
warm with the departing soul of Zerelda—tell him how I
loved—and how I died—tell him—."

Her voice sank. I could hold no longer, but straining her to my
heart exclaimed, "I am thy Evermont!" But she was insensible
before the accents reached her ear. "She will never revive," cried I,
and my pulse was the throe of death at the thought. "I will die with
her; in her arms it will be a blessing to die."

I gazed on the fields of nature. The sun, "shorne of his beams,"
rode slow and ominous, a globe of sullen fire in the smoky ocean of
Indian summer. A heavy cloud of vapors was rapidly increasing on
the solemn atmosphere. The Allegheny crept, a dull current through
a waste of mountains. Desolation sat in gloomy attitude on a
wilderness of rocks, which on every side was bounded by the blue
wonder. I appeared the only being the dreary world contained.
Darkness reigned in the heavens. Wildness presided over creation.
Zerelda lay in death before me. The peopled regions sank into
annihilation—the mountainous wild seemed brooding with the
genius of destruction. The universe was trembling with an awful
nonentity. I sank to the earth without thought or motion.

I recovered sufficient energy to recollect my situation, but I
could only breathe, "O! For a morsel of bread to save an angel!
Millions are reveling in luxury while Zerelda expires with famine.
Is the bounty of heaven exhausted? Is there no bright seraph around
the eternal throne to descend with a crumb of mercy to expiring
innocence?"

I raised my eyes and beheld a cluster of grapes, hanging in
mellow clusters from a bending bough above my head. I sprang
from the earth, gathered the blooming vintage—the most blissful
prospect I had ever beheld in the realms of vision. I flew with them
to Zerelda, and pressed the ripe juice in her lips. The mild taste of
the enlivening cordial revived her, and she drank it with uncommon
avidity, and immediately fell asleep.

A flock of wild turkeys flew from the other side of the river,
and I caught one of them before it could make its escape.

155

THE PRISONERS OF NIAGARA

"O God! Receive my thanks." I raised a fire and prepared some of the best of the flesh. Again awoke Zerelda with a draught of my new distilled wine, and so far refreshed her that she swallowed a sufficiency of the flesh to stop the progress of her hunger, and eat by slow degrees until she satisfied the cravings of nature. She again fell into a slumber, and with all my tender anxieties, I could not refrain from following her example. When I awoke, she was eating again. She gave me a smile from her soul, for she never trusted her gratitude to the faint description of any language: "It reigned in the throb of her heart;/ It beamed in the glance of her eye."

By evening she was much recruited, and we conversed on the past scenes with a solemn pleasure. When we touched on her dying hours, she blushed, and asked me for the medal. It was in my bosom; I gave it to her.

"How is this?" exclaimed she, with a modulation of wonder.

I had given her the original medal, to the back of which I had affixed her miniature, obtained from memory. I attempted to take it again, saying, "I have given you the wrong one," but she held it fast, alternately fixing her eyes on it and me, in astonishment and doubtful inquiry.

"How came you by this?"

My deception was at an end. Her eyes riveted on my soul in restless expectation. I dared not utter a falsehood, and cast down my eyes in confusion. Her anxiety increased, and with a voice tremulous with timid joyful hope, she exclaimed, "Bridford, remove this suspense. I dreamed last night that you were Evermont. Tell, oh, tell me!"

"What says your wishes?" replied I.

"O, my fond heart! It is!" exclaimed she, and sank in my arms.

What a blissful scene, had I been free from former crimes. What a heart here offered its love: A heart—but perish the hope of describing it. It was a heaven in miniature. But fate had dropped its curtain between it and mine. No, there was nothing between them; they had flown from our bosoms into each other, and mingling all their pulses, nerves, and tones, panted, throbbed, and thrilled in one. They were not to be severed; the attempt would rend in sunder

156

Now he washes off the paint

their whole organization, and burst the cells that held the "ethereal flame."

But such was the fiat of that destiny I had incurred, that they must be separated, although I felt that they would beat their latest throb in the operation.

She was in a sweet dream on my bosom, while my tears, the burning tears of anticipated anguish, laved the blossoms on her cheeks.

She awoke and looked up in my eyes. "I was mistaken," said she. "I thought this was Evermont," giving me a portrait from her bosom; but her pencil had caught the fire of her heart, and all its delineations were dipped in the magic ether of love, which without changing, sheds an indefinable luster on the features of its object.

"My present features are artificial," said I, and immediately washed the paint from my face.

"Now you are my Evermont," cried she, "but how could you practice this cruel deception, and that at Haylard Village? I would punish you severely, but you have stolen my affections while I imagined myself secure with my noble Bridford, and defrauded me of the secret weapons of female authority. But, hypocrite, how came you by this medal?"

"Zerelda gave it me, it grew to my heart, and can you find no excuse for my keeping it there?"

"Am I to find excuses for your mal-conduct?" replied she with a smile. "And when did you obtain this flattering image you have given me?"

"I copied it from my heart, where love had recorded its fair original."

My mind instantly reverted to my banishment. Zerelda's touched on the same subject. A languor overspread our countenances.

"It was produced by abominable falsehood," said she, rightly interpreting the subject of my feelings, "and we have bitterly repented of our cruelty. We received a number of letters under different signatures containing the blackest aspersions—we were offended at the moment and wrote—but the post was not out of

157

The poison-pen letters

Benevolence personified

sight before we lamented our rashness, and immediately wrote for you to return to Hayland Village, but you were gone. We inquired into the truth of the letters, and found them to be the base forgeries of Mrs. Willford, and ardently longed for your return, that we might supplicate your forgiveness for our inhuman treatment. O Evermont!" she continued, raising the animation of her voice, "you have heard my verses at the grotto, you have read my heart—can you pardon and forget the pangs I have inflicted on your generous, exalted feelings?"

"My heart never accused you of wrong," I replied. "I have been a wretch, but I ever loved, I ever adored you, and if there is anything to forget, I forget everything but your sweetness and love."

"O you are benevolence personified," cried she, "but what could have irritated Mrs. Willford and her daughter in such a manner as to produce this sad mistake?"

"They are women," exclaimed I, "whose arts have led me into crimes, the bare mention of which would make thy two eyes start from their spheres, and all thy bosom's blood to boil in frightful indignation, and abhor the man you love—crimes which hang with leaden vengeance on my soul, '—And gulph me down,/ Down to the abyss of the unbottomed deep' of human depravity."

His crime

Zerelda was alarmed at the vehemence of my exclamation—I had gone too far, for a disclosure of my crimes, at this moment of her debility, would have endangered, if it had not proved fatal, to her existence. I changed my tone and continued, "Zerelda, be not astonished. I am distracted. Think not of what I have rashly uttered, and when we arrive at your father's, you shall know all."

"You had really frightened me," said she, "but it is past. You are too noble for the commission of a crime. You may possibly have been irregular and unguarded, but I will not injure your generous nature by a thought that you could be a criminal."

Night had passed rapidly on, and we were startled from our conversation by a fierce yelling of wolves on the hill, which, together with the loud and shrill screams of the river birds, so frightened Zerelda that she trembled and learned in my arms for protection. She was weak and exhausted, and neither fear nor joy could long dispel the influence of slumber. She soon dropped to sleep on my bosom, and slept quietly in my arms till morning.

When I awoke, she was closely locked on my breast. Her arms were folded round my neck and her soft cheek rested on mine. Our bosoms beat, and our lips breathed together. I could not bear the thought that her tender feelings should suffer the mortification of finding herself in this condition, and gently withdrew without interrupting her slumber.

I formed a raft of some old dry timber, and when she had finished a breakfast out of the last of our turkey, I took Zerelda's hand, pressed it to my lips, lead her on my rudely constructed boat, and rowed her to the other shore.

CHAPTER XVI

Before evening, we reached the settlements in Westmoreland, where the kind Pennsylvanians received us with a generous hospitality peculiar to the peasantry of that benevolent people. There is a noble method of conferring benefices, only known to nature, which imperceptibly steals away the weight of the obligation, and while it increases the gratitude of the receiver, so refines and enlivens its emotions, that they pass with such easy transition through his bosom as to appear a part of his composition. He feels delighted with his benefactor without perceiving that his partiality arises from the favor he has received. Benevolence thus administered has the fascination of sympathy in it, and never fails to confer a blessing on the giver and receiver, and render them more pleased and charmed with each other. It was thus we were treated by the Pennsylvanians; their hearts beat true to the generosity of nature. They inquired not whether we were deserving of their bounty. They asked not if we were the pampered children of wealth who could requite their favors with gold, or with smiles. They saw that we were unfortunate; they required no more, but threw open their doors and their hearts to relieve the needy, and smile away the wrinkles of distress.

When we parted from them, they furnished us with horses to perform the remainder of our journey, but when we arrived in a few miles of Engleton seat, Zerelda became too ill to ride, and I left her in a friendly cottage while I bore the happy tidings of her return to her father, and procured a carriage to bear her home in safety.

As I rode to Engleton seat, my imagination was on the liveliest wing at the prospect of the raptures of Engleton when he heard of the return of his daughter. My fancy was transported at the expectation of beholding the flow of ecstasy which would lighten in his countenance and overwhelm and stun the energies of his mind for a moment. Then they would spring into action again, with the elasticity of hope, and swell with unbounded emotions of joy and exultation.

Thus elated, I arrived a the door of his mansion. I has thrown away my Indian garb and again adopted my hunting dress, which was considered by the votaries of fashion as evidence of rudeness and poverty. In this point of view I was considered by the servants, who came to conduct, or rather to prevent me from going, to their master.

I inquired of a waiter for Mr. Engleton.

"He is engaged," replied he.

"Can I not see him?"

"No, sir. If you have business you had better call on the steward."

"I wish to see Mr. Engleton himself."

The servant hesitated, muttered to himself half audibly, "I do not know, but I'll see," and went in. He returned. "My master is engaged and will not see company. You must go to the steward."

"Can he not spare a few minutes for business of importance?"

No, sir, he can't attend you now. He is at cards."

"At cards!" repeated I, with a tone of chagrin. "Then I will wait till his game is over."

"His game will not be over till night," replied the servant.

"Then tell him I must see him now," said I to the waiter with severity.

"He will be angry, sir," said the waiter, "if I return."

"He shall have no cause to be angry with you," I replied. "I will go myself and inquire if I may see him."

"He will be displeased if I let you in," said the servant.

"Do not be uneasy. I will put him in a good humor."

Engleton was sitting at the card table with Anderville and another companion. Anderville, I perceived, was advanced to the rank of Major, but he did not recognize me in my present dress. He appeared as much astonished at Engleton as I was myself, but Engleton sat with the countenance of apathy, unconcerned at what passed around him. I never felt more disposed to torment a man in my life.

"Well, sir," said he, with the air of a man whose importance is only known when he tells it himself, "what is your mighty business?"

"To inform you of the death of your daughter," said I.

"I knew that before," said he, with a careless air. "I do not wish to be distressed by a repetition of it," and was turning again to cards.

Has this man no sensibility? O nature! Where are your powers? Your magic chain that links the heart of the father to the child that is alive to the tenderest touch, thrills and trembles with the slightest vibration? Can this be Zerelda's father?

"But I suppose," continued I, "you would wish to hear how she died."

"I saw her fall myself," said he, "and do not wish to hear any more on the subject. I am engaged."

Spirits of scorn and indignation! What a being! Anderville was astonished. I was almost overcome by contemptuous anger, but was resolved to probe his soul for a single particle of feelings.

"I promised her to bear you a message," said I, "and a promise made to a dying woman I will perform, whether you will hear or not."

"Well, what was her message?" said he.

"It was in her last moments," said I, "when she had been with the Indians until emaciated to a skeleton. Meager and pale, they were leading her into a dreadful fire. She discovered me, who was also a prisoner, and with tears in her eyes made this solemn request, which I have walked five hundred miles to execute."

"Well, don't be so tedious," said he, impatient to be at his cards again. "What was the request?"

"'I have a dear and reverend father,' sighed she, 'who will weep when he hears of my death. My only torment is that I am never to see him more. I could die contented if he was here to embrace me, and shed one tear on my cheek. Bear him my love—tell him of my death.' She could say no more. Her eyes bled with sorrow. She was dragged into the fire—the flames blazed and fried around her. She stretched her hands to God, then turning her eyes on me, exclaimed, 'Remember me to my father,' and sank down in a billow of fire."

I spoke this with the tone and air of reality. Anderville wept and left the room. Engleton and his companion put on a solemn air, but the sufferings of Zerelda never reached their hearts. After a pause, the young man observed, "It is useless to weep for what is past and cannot be reacalled." Engleton was of the same opinion, and began to shuffle the cards.

The word "monster" unintentionally escaped my lips.

"What, sir?" said Engleton.

"I spoke not to you," replied I.

"Sir, I am—" cried he.

"I see what you are," answered I, "a rude mockery of a man!"

"Do you dare—" roared he. "Leave my house, or you shall repent your rashness.

"Poor pitiful worm," cried I. "I despise you. Great God! That such a reptile should have a daughter, and see her broil in Indian flames, and yet remain unconcerned, at a game of cards." I spoke this with the vehemence of indignation, and turned out of the room.

I met with Anderville in the passage. His eyes were wet with sorrow. I pitied and relieved his heart by informing him of the situation of Zerelda. He was transported! He clasped me in his arms and offered me his purse.

"Anderville," said I, with a full look in his eyes.

"Is it possible?" he exclaimed. "Evermont—O my friend!"

Our embrace was warm but hasty, for I was impatient to leave the house. He promised to order a carriage and conduct Zerelda home immediately, and we embraced again and parted.

I hesitated as I mounted my horse. Shall I see Zerelda? Her feelings will be wounded at our meeting, and every heart-string wrung at our parting, which must be forever—forever. No. I cannot bid adieu to that eye which is the only day beam of my soul, those sips whose smile is my only heaven. I must live in her bosom—O, the dear and precious mansion! Then with all the loves and virtues

163

for my companions, I shall hold the fairest while feeling's soul has memory.

Say, ye ministering spirits, on whose ethereal wings the invisible flame of love is wafted from heart to heart, was it not the most refined cruelty in fortune, after I had flown into the heart of danger to avoid Zerelda, to throw her into my protection under such a combination of circumstances as could not fail to call all the powers of love and sympathy into action, and render the possession of her heart an indispensable requisite to my existence? Had we not traversed the wilderness together, where I caught every principle of her soul, every emotion of her heart, and they became indelible in my bosom, time might have worn a part of her image from my memory, and permitted me to enjoy a negative contentment in some distant clime. That is now impossible. I have felt the full measure of the happiness I shall lose by the separation, and all other enjoyments have faded from my imagination. We cannot part. The loudest voice of fate commands it, but I shall obey no commands but the thunder of death.

Zerelda was surprised at seeing me return alone. I could not inform her of the reason, but stated that her father was preparing the carriage, and that it would be there in a few minutes. I then informed her of my intention of visiting her mother and sister immediately. She endeavored to prevail on me to return with her, to her father's, but I saw the carriage advancing, and no argument could have induced me to tarry a moment longer. I pressed her hand to my bosom, laid my lips on her cheeks, and was gone.

I assumed my proper dress before I arrived at Haylard Village. I stopped at the cottage of Mrs. Holbert, and was joyfully received by her and Amacette, who lived comfortably under the protection of the whole village, and particularly of my mother. I left them and hastened to embrace my mother and sister.

CHAPTER XVII

It is a cold imagination that cannot anticipate my reception; it is a lifeless heart that cannot feel it without a description; it is a daring pen that would attempt to describe it. I was in the arms of both mother and sister at once, and almost devoured by transports and embraces. But there was a delightful contrast in their emotions. Mrs. Hayland received me to her bosom with a full flow of sober ecstasy, which, like the mid-day beams, completely filled, enlightened, and surrounded my heart, while Emerine, like the morning bursting over the horizon, sported, danced, and gamboled around me till I was overwhelmed with a new birth of delight, and my soul became as joyful and sprightly as her own.

But their enjoyments were heightened when they heard of Zerelda's return. They loved her as a daughter and a sister, and like Engleton, believed her dead, but infinitely superior to him in soul and sentiment, they heard of her adventures as if she had arisen from the dead—with unexpected, unbounded rapture. Explanations of the past took place, and the whole evening flew away on pleasure's lightest wing.

When I retired to my chamber, I thought not of sleep—I thought of Zerelda. What must be the state of her mind in her present situation? Raised apart from her father, she has nothing to attach her to him but the name, and how weak that normal tie, when their dispositions are so variant, their souls so discordant. She will obey him, but it cannot be with that alacrity, that ingenuous delight, with which she would desire to obey a parent. She has been reared among kindred souls, and experienced with Major and Mrs. Hayland the sublime enjoyments of a reverential and mutual affection. But in Engleton she will in vain inquire for those tender parental solicitudes, which are the first touches on the wakeful strings of a daughter's heart. How often will her eye wander to his to catch the warm spark of a parent's soul, and return dissatisfied with an increasing weight in inquietude? With what inventive anxiety will she exert her liveliest caresses to awaken his mind into a train of feeling similar to her own, and to allure it into a participation in those sentimental enjoyments which her soul is enchantingly textured to feast on itself, and inspire in the bosom of others? But how often, with the sad sensations of disappointed pleasure, will she have to lament that the lifeless apathy of his nature is blind to all the endearing efforts of affectionate ingenuity? This restless anxiety for Zerelda's happiness, together with the emotions which the late events of my life had inspired, kept me from the mild lap of slumber until morning.

A hundred questions were panting for precedence on the lips of Emerine as she skipped into the hall with her morning salutation, and, as she was too animated to arrange them, her inquiries flowed from her lips as fast as they could give them utterance. I took out my pocketbook, and deliberately requested her to repeat them, and I would minute them down, for my memory was inadequate to retain the twentieth part.

"Well, Mr. Formality," said she, "take your notes at large. Did you fall in love with Zerelda?"

I pretended to write, and observed, "Well what else?"

"No, answer at once," said she.

"Do you always answer such questions so precipitately?" replied I.

"Pshaw! I was not speaking of myself, but indeed, brother, I am serious. I feel deeply concerned for both yours and Zerelda's happiness, and fear by your leaving her so suddenly, that you have not felt all that sympathetic delight in her society which I had anticipated."

"You expected, then," said I, "that because I rescued her from the Indians, I was obliged to love her? Do you suppose love such a rough and hard-favored being as to be engendered in the wilderness?"

Radcliff
reference

"He was formerly a very soft and tender companion for you both," replied Emerine, "for I believe you have loved each other since you were babies, and more particularly when you were here in disguise last spring—but that must all be over now, for I suppose she will be married in a few weeks."

"Good heavens! Zerelda to be married?" exclaimed I, with startled animation, in which my voice, my looks and emotions, convinced the flippant Emerine of what she was so anxious to learn.

"Aye," cried she, "I thought love could not be born in the wilderness? Come brother, you have entrapped yourself. Inform me how your heart stands with Zerelda's in the Ledger of Love."

"Such conversation, Emerine," replied I, "is too light on a subject of such interest."

"Give it then," said she, "as many sighs and scowls as Mrs. Radcliff gives the monks of her novels, if you please. Only conjugate the verb love through two persons; I love, she loves. Can you say that by heart?"

"Yes, from the bottom of my soul," answered I, "and if I do not very much mistake, I can proceed much farther, and say you love."

"That is not in my grammar," cried she, "but Evermont, can you keep a secret? Your wild sister has a spark, one much like yourself, who gives love such a sour, frightful fizz, that I often scamper away and leave him to enjoy his melancholy Cupid alone."

"Well, sister, be as generous as I have been. Who is this sighing lover? And what progress has he made in teaching you the willow-weaving science?"

"He is a Major Anderville, who belongs to the northern army. I saw him at uncle Engleton's in Baltimore last winter, and made a conquest at once. While I was there he told me all the sad tales of love he had learned from tragedies and novels, then conducted me home, sang the same doleful ditties over again, and left me as wild and light-hearted as he found me."

"An officer too? And raise the siege before he had reduced the fortress?"

Parody

167

Anderville and Emerine

"O sir, the fortress was like the enchanted castles of the fifteenth century, and could vanish from his power in a twinkling without suffering him to make the least impression on it. But you must have seen him. He wrote me from uncle Engleton's the morning before you arrived there."

"Alas! I fear it was the officer who met with the fatal accident—"

"What accident? O speak!" cried she in a voice of serious alarm.

"He was a tall, comely young man, elegantly shaped—"

"Do not torture me," cried she, "tell me what happened."

"Now sister, acknowledge the effect and success of your own stratagem," said I, with a voice that convinced her I was in jest. Her fears subsided as I spoke, but the thought that Anderville was in danger awakened all the emotions of a virgin affection into terror, and she yet trembled as she learned on my shoulder.

"O brother! You have convinced me how dearly I love. I will confide to you the secret of my heart. I am convinced of Major Anderville's affection, and he is the man I would choose from a work, but he knows not the interest he has in my bosom. Love is a dangerous science without a monitor, and I am happy that you are returned to guide the wayward hand of your wild, yet loving sister, while she throws the important die on which her all is at stake."

Tears ran down her cheeks. I pressed her in my arms and assured her that the heart of a brother never felt the interest of a sister more sincerely than I did hers. I gave her an account of my acquaintance with Major Anderville, and concluded with warmly approving the choice she had made.

Happy Emerine—her sorrows were as artless as her love, and as short-lived as those of the innocent on its mother's bosom whose tears were dried with a breath, for Mrs. Haylard coming in, she became as gay and sprightly as if she had never known a serious thought.

As Major Haylard died without a will, his whole fortune regularly descended to his daughter, but Mrs. Haylard possessed a separate property equal to his. Desirous to unite Emerine and myself in every tie of filial affection and interest, she communicated to us that she had made me her heir. Emerine was delighted. I was grateful.

This, with a thousand novel amusements, stole away the day in a lively routine of pleasurable enjoyments. Emerine was forever in her air-winged chariot of vivacity, and the flippant effluvia of her spirits communicated its light sparks of volatility to the elastic springs of my bosom, and my heart bounded with her in all her aerial excursions.

How happily adapted to each other is the different organization of the sexes. Man, whose duty requires the severe exercise of his powers, both body and mind, is provided with a constitution and energy of reflection, completely suited to the execution of his various occupations, but his serious tone of spirits, together with the unavoidable inquietudes of life, are calculated to render him morose and hypochondriac. To prevent which, nature constituted woman—sprightly, inventive, and susceptible of all the finer feelings, all the exhilarating sentiments of soul—with a person, the medium by which her soul is conveyed to her partner, adorned with all the soft and pleasing tenderness of grace, and beauty, to give those propensities of her soul a more easy and enchanting access to his bosom, which enliven his spirits, and dissipate the consequent languor of his pursuits.

Yes, it is woman—lovely, volatile, capricious woman—that feeds the mind with a never-failing feast of variety, cheers it with the sunbeams of vivacity, animates it with the glowing treasures of fancy, and transports it with the alluring fondness of affectionate caresses, and thus renders the cares, the storms and wilderness of life, a changeful diversity of delighting scenes.

In the evening, Emerine and I visited the grotto and the adjacent groves where our juvenile imaginations had pictured the liveliest images of delight.

Hail, ye enchanting scenes! When memory wafts me back to the halcyon hours of infancy, when every object starts the pulse of a forgotten being, and in an instant my present life is bewitched away, and I live again the golden age of youthful innocence. Live,

ye delighting transports of "other moments," live in the sorrowing
bosom of Evermont, and enkindle anew a lasting flame of infantile
simplicity and rapture. Give wings to the long suppressed emotions
of thoughtless transport, and an eternity of existence to the playful
effusions of artless joy.

From the grotto, where winter had nipped the latest flowers, we
repaired to the dwelling of Mrs. Holbert, for Emerine considered
her a second mother, and her daughter Amacette as a warm and
affectionate sister. Amacette accompanied us home, and the
evening was spent with mutual enjoyment. A packet arrived from
Zerelda. I read her letter to me with avidity:

"You concealed the cause of your sudden departure from me
for fear of giving pain, but too soon was I destined to learn it from
others. Ah! My dear friend, your noble feelings were severely
pained, but recollect it was Zerelda's father—he has severely
repented, and I conjure you by the tenderness with which you
conducted me through the wilderness to forget the rashness of his
conduct. You know the feelings of a daughter's heart when the man
she loves is exasperated against her father, and you know how to
forgive.

"I am much recovered since my return. O Evermont! What a
source of felicity will our journey be until the latest hours of our
lives. It has opened innumerable springs of unknown feelings,
which would otherwise have rested in oblivion in our bosoms, and
sublimed the penetrating soul of sympathy to search and find new
ties to connect our hearts in a more endearing union.

"I severely feel the loss of your society, for I have been spoiled
by the exquisite tenderness of your attention, until no company but
yours is agreeable. My father is too much engaged in his own
concerns to satisfy all those boundless sentimental anxieties which
you have excited in me, and which you must feel yourself
responsible to gratify, or you will have done me irreparable wrong.
For had you not inspired them, they never would have excited, but
you have given them a being that can never die, and you only are
capable of satisfying their capacious desires.

170

THE PRISONERS OF NIAGARA

"Major Anderville's attention and tenderness to me deserves commendation and gratitude. For other particulars respecting him, inquire of Emerine's bosom. The other gentleman you saw at my father's was Mr. Braville, whose company, you must know, is not calculated to fill the expectations of a wild girl who is buoyed up with your animated philosophy of the heart.

"He intends traveling with my father to Charlestown in a few days, and I shall spend a month of their absence at Haylard Village. But if they do not go, you must come with Emerine to Engleton seat. My father will be pleased at an opportunity of repairing the wrong he has done you.

"You must come a smooth my brow of vexation at not finding an Evermont in every person I have met. Come and cure the longings of a doting heart. Come to the open bosom of your"

ZERELDA
Direct

Let the sober prude, whose heart is shrouded in a cold, Lapland cloud, condemn the candor of Zerelda's letter. Zerelda can feel no disposition to deprive her of the moth-eaten pleasures of censure. *address* Live then, ye prudes, and when you see a warm ebullition of affection burst from and overflow the bosoms of Zerelda or Emerine, accept of your only boon, the pleasure of calling it immodest, indelicate, monstrous, or what you please.

I had just finished this letter when Emerine, who had been reading hers, exclaimed, "O you unaccountable piece of innocence. You never informed us of your treatment at uncle Engleton's."

"My son, you have been sadly used by my brother," said Mrs. Haylard, "but you must forgive him. He is the father of your Zerelda."

"He is already forgiven," said I.

"He is very different from the rest of his family," continued she, "owing to the nature of his education. My father had made his fortune by merchandise, and determining, as he was his only son, to bring him up to the same business, and kept him in the compting houses from his infancy. There are few employments so dangerous

171

Forgiveness + education

to the human heart as commerce. It opens a wide source of gain to
the merchant, but contracts the generous virtues of the man. It
enriches a country, but plants the seeds of its destruction.

"In the compting house, my brother imbibed a narrowness of
disposition and an inordinate love of wealth, even in his infancy,
which were sufficient to lock up his heart against every liberal
sentiment, and every genuine principle of a noble soul. My father
saw and repented of the manner in which he had reared him, but it
was too late. The texture of his mind was formed and unalterable.

"My father died shortly after my brother arrived to manhood,
and left his fortune equally divided among his three children. But
my brother, entering immediately into extensive speculations,
became completely ruined. But by the death of my sister and her
son, which took place about the same time, he was left heir to her
fortune, whereby he entered again into business, and by his industry
and economy has amassed an incalculable estate. He now conceives
that wealth is the only merit a man can possess. These principles,
together with the supposition that you were a child of poverty,
produced the harshness with which he treated you."

This was not a desirable character, but I was induced to believe
it had received all the flattery the natural feelings of a sister could
give it, and was convinced that Engleton was a more haughty,
unfeeling man than she supposed him.

A week—an age to a lover's heart—rolled away before we
heard anything further from Zerelda, at the termination of which I
received the following letter:

"My father has departed for Charleston, and I am permitted to
enjoy a month at Haylard Village, but I cannot fly to you with the
light heart of joy I expected. I have various sources of uneasiness.
Every movement at my father's is ominous of my future
unhappiness. My father, without preface, informed me a few days
since that Barville intended paying his addresses to me on the
subject of matrimony. You must feel how I shuddered at the idea of
marrying such a man. I have too long seen and enjoyed the dawn of
that infinitude of bliss which is stored in the treasure of Evermont's

172

Another Zerelda letter

BARVILLE Enters picture

heart for the woman he loves, to even think or dream of happiness elsewhere.

"I candidly confessed to my father my prepossession against Barville, and the impossibility of his obtaining my affections. He said he should not force my inclinations, but leave the matter wholly to Barville, whom he said I must receive as a suitor.

"What a wretched condition you have left me in to listen to his civilities. Yours is the only mode of wooing that could meet the welcome smile of my soul. You wooed my heart with an irresistible sweetness that compelled it to listen and consent, and spring with rapturous embrace into yours.

"But the same day was productive of a more alarming event: the arrival of Mrs. Willford and her daughter. O! Evermont, feel how I felt at the sight of your abandoned persecutors, but how much more was I shocked when I understood Mrs. Willford was to have charge of my father's family under the name of housekeeper. And when, on expostulating with my father on the subject, I related her conduct to you, I was imperatively commanded to mention the subject no more, but consider her as a mother. I cannot divine the issue of this mysterious proceeding, but find my father completely under the influence of this hated woman. She is the sole manager of everything, and affects to consider me as a forward child, with the stern authority of a stepmother.

"Miss Willford is a true flirt of fashion, pert, vain, and haughty, and plays off her airs upon me as she would to a rude country girl. But I could behold her only with eyes of internal horror when I recollected your emphatic expression on the banks of the Allegheny. Yet I can but wonder how she had power over a heart like yours, even for a moment.

"Mr. Barville has paid me several visits with formal politeness, but has never afforded me an opportunity of acquainting him with the state of my mind. He has gone with my father.

"The post will bear you this tomorrow. I set out immediately, and will be with you the ensuing evening."

This letter excited a most serious apprehension. A lover's fears, though mighty, are hung on slender threads. Barville's fruitless

Mrs Willford as to be Zerelda's father's house-keeper!

the arranged marriage plot + step-mother plot

rivalry created a dreadful jealousy, for the slightest breath that there was a possibility of losing Zerelda swelled all my feelings with the deep murmurs of alarm. Monster as I was, I could not think of resigning her to another.

But the conduct of Engleton to Willford and her daughter was portentous of a more than trivial danger, and bespoke some dark secret which time had yet to unwind.

But the composing affability of Mrs. Haylard, and the exhilarating sprightliness of Emerine, afforded me a degree of cheerfulness and hilarity until the succeeding evening, when, with Emerine, I rode to meet Zerelda.

Our eyes were continually on the road to catch the glimmer of her carriage. Every passenger excited the palpitation of hope, but left us disappointed. The sun poured his last tipping tints of gold on the tops of the loftiest hills. Suspense grew painful. Twilight yielded to moonbeams, and the leaden load of doubt threw down the scale of fear. Emerine suggested a wish to return, but I was alive with the circumstances in Zerelda's letter, and objects as important as life and death appeared to hang on the thread of every instant, and I could not listen to her request. Time wore slowly on his sullen wheels. My soul was hovering on the wing of tremor, and would have flown the lightening to have met Zerelda. Would Emerine have consented, I would have rode even to Engleton seat, but she, though somewhat alarmed, strove to quell my apprehensions, and at last prevailed upon me to return, and wait another day. But during that night, I neither ate nor slept. It was a night of dreary solitude of soul, when every unformed fear was floating half-shaped in my imagination. Give me all the terrors of certain dissolution in preference to such sensations, when I may strive, but strive in vain, to catch the frightening shadow at which I shudder.

Another painful day of disappointed hope was closing, and yet the joint entreaties of Mrs. Haylard and Emerine dissuaded me from flying to Engleton seat until morning to learn the cause of Zerelda's delay, and fruitlessly strove to divert my mind from its sad forebodings. But like a shooting star in a sea of darkness, their

Another Captivity — by Wilford letter from Zerelda

efforts were faint and unimpressive, and left my mind an accumulated gloom.

Midnight found me gazing on the light clouds that wheeled around the moor. The winged army of shadows that sailed over the woods and hills in a variety of procession could not divert a thought from Zerelda. My soul was wound up to a key of suspense, little short of frenzy.

A horseman alighted in haste at the style, and in an instant I was at the door. He presented me a letter, and Mrs. Haylard and Emerine, discovering his arrival, were with me in the hall as I tore it open. It was from Zerelda.

"I have disappointed the expectations I excited, but the cause must be my apology.

"I had ordered my carriage without informing Mrs. Willford of my intention, and was with my woman at the door. She discovered me, and with an imperious frown, demanded, 'What's all this for?' I ordered the carriage near the door and cooly told her where I was going. 'I think, miss, you have great assurance to act without my orders,' cried she.

'I obey the orders of my father, madam.'

'You shall obey mine,' said she, with scornful severity, 'so trudge back to your room. March. And you, sir,' to the driver, 'return the carriage to the stable and wait my commands.'

"I disregarded her threats, made no reply, but sprang into the carriage and ordered the driver to proceed. Willford flew into a rage, threw back my woman with violence, and vociferated to the servants. They were all bribed in her service and sprang at her command. And while the driver was reigning up the horses, he was knocked from his seat.

"The Willfords burst open the carriage door and dragged me furiously into the house. I was choked and overwhelmed with a torrent of chagrin and vexation. O! Evermont! Feel for me—I am closely watched and have no possibility of escaping. I have twice attempted it in vain. Once I had the carriage prepared and was caught at the door. Willford saw my purpose, caught me by the hair, and dragged me again to my room.

Emerine & Evermont
to the
rescue

I am most eminently wretched in my present situation. Can you again encounter dangers for your"

ZERELDA?

Yes, if they come in the whirlwinds of infuriated vengeance! In the red torrents of exploding volcanoes! I would encounter all the demons of envy and malice, writhing their gorgon features with all the venom of infernals. My blood was in a boiling ferment, my teeth grated together, my sinews were nerved and contracted. I would have felt supreme delight in daring. I ordered my horse immediately.

"Brother," said Emerine, "take the carriage and let me go with you."

I consented. She flew to her room to prepare, and we were on the road in a few minutes. We drove with such rapidity that we were at Engleton seat the ensuing day.

Zerelda beheld us from her window and was in Emerine's arms as I handed her from the carriage. The meeting of these affectionate sisters was as warm as their hearts, but amid her transports at meeting Emerine, Zerelda remembered and welcomed her Evermont. After the first flood of rapture subsided we beheld the Willfords staring at us from the door with all the snarling venom of rage.

The sight of those monsters of inequity, connected with the idea of them being my mother and sister, filled me with the most agonizing sensations of horror, contrition, and indignation. My soul sank and sickened as I reflected, "this is the mother that bore me."

I took a hand of each of the girls and led them to the door.

"Who gave you authority to enter here?" cried Mrs. Willford.

"The extreme good nature of Mrs. Willford," said I, "never failed to welcome a guest."

She saw that I determined to come in, and drew back into the hall.

Zerelda conducted us to her chamber where we were immediately followed by the Willfords. I advised them to withdraw, or they would hear some disagreeable truths. Mrs. Willford replied that the house was her own and she would stay where she pleased.

"Well, stay," said I, "and writhe under the rehearsal of your detestable deeds. Zerelda, inform us what prevented you from coming to Hayland Village as promised."

"Nothing but the pure tenderness of my would-be mama and her gentle daughter, who out of extreme kindness dragged me out of my carriage."

"You impudent—!" cried Mrs. Willford.

"Silence," said I, with a voice stern and commanding.

"I will not be abused in my own house," said she, "by a lying—"

"Stop, madam," cried I, "and you and your envious urchin sit as mute as death or I will unfold a tale which will overwhelm you with shame and trembling."

"I defy your threats. I am mistress here, and will exercise my authority."

"Yes, and I am master of a secret that twines around your heart with a lash of scorpions."

"Out with all the secrets you know," muttered she. "I know a secret, too, which shall make you repent for this in tears of blood."

"You know nothing, madam," said I, with a significant smile, "but that Armilda and myself—in Richmond—by your consent—were—"

"Dare you to insinuate," exclaimed Willford, with a blush of confusion. But Armilda wore the brazen look of audacity itself.

"I have insinuated nothing," replied I, "unless it is aided by a guilty conscience. But I will now insinuate that a certain woman, after destroying the happiness and lives of a worthy family, sold her own son to the Indians to be massacred."

"O God!" exclaimed Zerelda and Emerine. Willford gave an inward groan.

"Go to your room, madam," continued I. "I have unraveled the fatal web of your abominations. I have pursued you from Baltimore to Shenandoah, and from thence to Philadelphia, and will shortly trace you to the end of your schemes."

177

Willford shuddered, but in a moment renewed her imperiousness, and finding we could not remain in quiet, we left the mansion.

When we were seated in the carriage, Zerelda and Emerine requested an explanation of my discourse with Willford.

"Pardon me, my dear sisters, but that subject is involved in darkness and danger, and should not have been whispered even to the statue of silence. I have no substantial evidence of the facts I rashly stated. Time will mature them. Until then, will my sisters excuse me when I inform them that their brother's fate depends upon his caution."

"Certainly," replied Zerelda. "We could require nothing that would occasion you danger or uneasiness. I feel interested, but my curiosity is not so feminine as to desire a gratification which you judge improper."

"Indeed, brother," said Emerine, "you must have been a vile sinner while in Richmond, you are so anxious to conceal the particulars of your conduct."

"Have I a sister who would require the particulars of a brother's conduct whom she already knows has been a monster in every vice? I have already informed you that there is scarcely a crime in the dark catalogue of human depravity of which I have not been guilty, and for which my soul has not been wrung with contrition until it has almost bled away its vital fluid."

"Evermont," said Zerelda, with one of those looks which glided into my soul and hushed the tumult of emotions into the calm of pleasure, "whenever you speak of Richmond, you make me tremble. But neither Emerine nor myself have a wish to renew those moments of inadvertent sorrow, but will exert our lives to blot them from your memory."

Emerine forgot her remarks, and with her usual elasticity of spirits, called our attention to a prospect where a succession of white-edged clouds were lightly skimming over the blue summit of a distant hill.

"If I was on that hill," cried she, "I could woo the Muses, and poetize your slumbering faculties into animation."

178

"You possess that power in a superior degree," replied Zerelda, "but I doubt whether your Muse would have sufficient wing to bear up the weight of my apprehensions."

"With the aid of your own musical inclination," replied Emerine, "I would give one half of them to that light vapor which undulates from the valley of the sun, and the balance I would lull on the edge of your cloud, among the 'sleeping sun-beams.'"

"But what would you do with mine?" said I. "They would be so dark and heavy, your Pegasus would shudder under their pressure."

"They are truly boisterous and unmanageable," she answered, with a smile, "but with a few flashes of *your* poetical lightning, I could conjure up a whirlwind to bear them to the bosom of that dark cloud which is trembling down behind the hill. But if I had the enchanting numbers of Zerelda, I could steal you from yourself, mount you on the wings of affection's melody, and waft you to Elysium."

"You have a flattering opinion of my prowess," said Zerelda.

"It is evident to demonstration," retorted Emerine, with archness. "There is poetry in your look, for when you fix a glance upon his eyes, I see it glide into his bosom, and tune a soothing ditty to his feelings."

I smiled at the truth of this observation, and Zerelda—whether to make the experiment, or knowing she possessed the power, resolved to exert it—fixed her eyes on mine with a look of melodious smiles. The effect had been delineated by Emerine. It awoke my heart to harmony. My hand involuntarily pressed hers. Her eyes fell, and mine followed their example, for those feelings are excited which can only be conveyed in that expressive silence in which sympathy steals her kindred souls into each other.

Emerine knew the exquisite enjoyments of those silent moments, and permitted our hearts to repose in a delightful slumber on the downy pillows of each other's bosoms.

But these ecstatic emotions were not long to be enjoyed by the profligate of Richmond. The carriage was stopped by a man who demanded if Evermont was within. I opened the door.

"Have I found you!" exclaimed a man I had never seen before. "Villain! Monster! Debauchee! Come out and receive the deserts of your crimes."

"What have I done?" exclaimed I.

"Wretch! Have you not polluted the marriage bed? Ravished the wife from her husband, and prostituted her to your hellish passions?"

I shuddered with serious alarm, but continued silent while he proceeded in frantic exclamations until I learned his name was Dawson, and that he had married Susan Etherford shortly before our intimacy in Richmond. He had learned of our criminality by receiving the letter I had written to Susan when I left her, and had abandoned her immediately. He concluded his observations by presenting me with a pistol, and commanding me to die like a man.

The girls screamed and clung to me. I could not deny the charges, and endured the horrors of eternal perdition. I was ever too cowardly to fight a duel. I could undauntedly meet the thunder of an irritated army when my passions were aroused by some inspiring motive, but dared not rush against offended omnipotence. Nor could I raise my hand against a man I had basely, though unintentionally, injured, but pitying the distress of the girls, requested him to meet me some other time.

"Now, sir, is the time!" cried he. "Take the weapon or I will blow a ball through your head."

Distracted with the tortures of my crimes, I tore myself from the carriage, seized the pistol, and commanded him to fire. He shot without effect. I discharged my pistol in the air, threw it down, leapt into the carriage, drove off at full speed, and saw the frantic Dawson no more. Zerelda and Emerine were recovered, but were tormented with shuddering sensations at the charges against me, and the danger I had incurred. They fixed their eyes wildly upon me. I told them I was the wretch I had been represented as, but explained the nature of my offense, which lightened the weight of horror that pressed upon their trembling bosoms. They, perceiving the agony I endured, appeared to forgive and forget my crime, and sought to erase its deep impression from my memory. Their efforts long contended with my gloomy reflections, but at last succeeded.

Many will wonder how it was possible for my mind to bear the load of life with such a tremendous weight of guilt upon my conscience. I will once and for all inform them that my constitution was bold and vigorous, and could bear unbroken an awful succession of misery. My spirits were sprightly and elastic, and might be dreadfully depressed without being crushed or unnerved. But yet my constitution and spirits were fainting and would have broken and decayed had I not met Zerelda among the Indians, imbibed an unconquerable passion, witnessed the ardor of her lover, and returning to my foster family, experienced the additional affection of Mrs. Haylard and Emerine. To the ardent fondness and incessant attention of those three females I owe my being, and the checkered scene of pleasure and awful sensations I have since felt and endured.

They now with united exertions calmed the wild anguish of my heart, and buoyed it up to participate in their favorite enjoyments.

A few days after our arrival our minds became mutually and sympathetically cheerful. Zerelda had forgotten her apprehensions from Barville and the Willfords. Her spirits could sink with ease into the fountains of sorrow, and weep with all the sincerity of affliction—then rise, like the morning sun through dewy ether, and beam forth all their beauties in a shower of gladdening smiles. I was entranced away from the black account of my guilt to the charming fields of fancy, and led Zerelda to the piano with the genuine raptures of a lover.

Her elegance of person was enriched with the heightening graces of art. She was dressed in all the gaiety of the prevailing mode, and ornamented with every species of fashionable jewelry, except earrings. She was fond of a modest elegance in apparel, but was incapable of embellishing her native charms by an ornament which could not be adopted without the mutilating cruelty necessary for wearing this savage gewgaw.

You, whose cold hearts are only capable of loving to a certain degree, may censure my attachment as insincere for fixing my

181

address to reader

attention for a moment on the dress of Zerelda. But tell me, ye formal lovers, what injury the most beautiful picture will receive from being enclosed in a frame of diamonds? And you, ye visionary etherealists, who would rivet the affections on the mind alone, and condemn my attachment to the person of Zerelda, are not the beauties of nature more enchanting when beheld through a transparent prism? Is not the sun more bright and enlivening when beheld through the dewy medium of morning? And are not the enlightened endowments of a woman's mind more sweet, more impressive, more fascinating, when beheld through a person—all expression, all action, all loveliness?

Zerelda's face was one of those that cannot be copied. It, alone, could intelligibly speak its thousand mingling graces, which could be caught and felt, but never delineated.

Her spirits were in their sprightliest elements, and while she rested on my arm, and moved lightly to the piano, it seemed that I could bear her upon a finger.

The piano of her mind was in its sweetest tune. She swept over the keys with a flying finger, and then touched on an air she had adapted to the lines I drew in the grotto, and accompanied it with the melody of her voice. When she concluded, I gave her an expressive look, with these words: "'Twas thus, the syren sang my soul away."

Her eyes met mine as the notes gradually melted into silence, and our hearts embraced in the glance. I laid her hand on my bosom—she felt the palpitations it inspired, and a tender solemnity threw her eyes to the floor.

Emerine tripped into the music room, and observing our silence, exclaimed, "You are the most unaccountable lovers I ever read of. I expected to find you smiling and caroling together, but behold! You are silent and sorrowful as if vexed at being in each other's company. If my swain was here, I should be so light and airy that I could dance tiptoe on a moonbeam."

"I doubt not," said Zerelda, "that his powers of transporting would wrap you to the sylphs of love, but I am much mistaken if

Thompson again.

they would not soon lull your flighty emotions in the delicious
bosom of a feeling silence."

Akenside

"You own, then, that you were enjoying this delicious silence?"

"Yes, and glory in it without a blush," replied Zerelda.

Young

"Indeed you are mistaken," cried the laughing Emerine, "or I
don't know how deep a glow of roses make a blush."

Watts

Zerelda had blushed to the eyes as she make the welcome
acknowledgment, but when it was followed by the arch expression
of Emerine, her heightened color spread over all her features, and
she lightly dropped her forehead on my shoulder.

Goldsmith

"Zerelda," said I to Emerine, "will have an opportunity of
punishing you for this when you are in company with Major
Anderville."

"I am anxious how soon she may have it in her power," said
Emerine, and left us again together.

Zerelda raised her eyes in all their sweetness. Her blushes were
yet in their twilight. I pressed her hands to my lips—it increased the
crimson of her cheeks, and continued our silence.

I lead her to the library where we charmed our fancies with the
flowing numbers and unexampled imagery of Thompson, imbibed
the energy and animation of Akenside, caught the bold fire and
solemn sublimity of Young, and sweetly soothed our feelings with
the soft melody of Watts and Goldsmith. Time, thus transported
with the Loves and Graces, and inspired by works of taste and
beauty, flew rapidly down the current of duration.

One evening Zerelda and I accompanied Amacette to her
mother's, and beheld her with a young infant in her arms. Zerelda
and Amacette eagerly inquired, whose was it?

"The child of a poor unfortunate creature," said Mrs. Holbert,
"who was sinking down at my door through cold, fatigue, and
sickness."

"Where is she?" we all inquired at once.

"In the other room," said Mrs. Holbert.

We all hastened to see her, but ah! The rising pang of guilt! It
was Susan—the wretched wife of Dawson! I started back in a
tremor! She was in a high fever, and spoke for some time

183

Susan returns! with a baby! oh, guess whose?

[handwritten margin notes: "Charlotte Cogette or" / "Evermont the father of Susan's baby." / "Feeling Benevolence" / "No Kidding"]

unintelligibly, and concluded, "O, Evermont! O! The father of my child!" and sank into a slumber.

The ladies looked at me with astonishment. My feelings were agony. It had been twelve months since I parted with Susan, and the child appeared about three months old, which, together with the wild expressions of the mother, convinced me beyond a doubt that the child was mine. I rushed out of the room, and clasped it to my bosom with frantic emotions. Zerelda followed soon after. Her countenance sickened when she beheld the child. She took it in her arms, and I saw her eyes fixed upon it, to discover the infant features of Evermont.

Mrs. Holbert and Amacette came in, but were silent and gloomy. I could bear it no longer, but took the arm of Zerelda to go.

"I will take it home," said Zerelda. "Its mother is too ill to attend to it."

Seeing her determination, I took it from her and bore it on my arm, and we walked slow and sorrowful toward the mansion.

Zerelda stole frequent glances at the child—her hand trembled on my arm. I saw she had attempted an act of heroism to which her powers were inadequate in endeavoring to rise superior to those feelings, which are naturally excited by such a circumstance, to a mind situated as hers was with mine. She was unable to support the resolution she had assumed—her tremor every moment increased, and she was sinking down through weakness. I caught her, and seated her on the trunk of a fallen tree. She leaned her forehead on my shoulder while my arm sustained her from falling.

O! How keenly did I feel my crimes, like ravenous vultures gnawing my vitals! I abhorred myself as an assassin that had stabbed the happiness of that bosom in which the ministering spirits of love had blushed with the radiant smiles of celestial innocence.

Zerelda, without raising her eyes, inquired with a deep sigh, "This child—whose is it?" I could not have spoken for both the Indies. She continued with a voice more tremulous, "Evermont, I am miserable under this suspense. Tell me—tell me—is it yours?"

"Alas, I know not," cried I. "Its mother is the wife of Dawson!—You have heard!—What a wretch am I!"

184

THE PRISONERS OF NIAGARA

"O God! How dreadful I feel!" she sighed half audibly. "Evermont, you have undone me—"

Her words quivered as she spoke, and darted with the stings of scorpions to my heart, while her tears streamed on the child.

I wept the tears of blood from my heart. It would have been a light stroke to this that would have burst the cordage of my nature, and set my suffering soul at liberty.

My abandoned mother! My abominations with Armilda, with Emerald, the dying Susan, the frantic Dawson, all rushed at once upon my mind! "Merciful Omnipotence!" exclaimed I, "is this the visitation of my crimes? O! Monster! Ingrate! I have burst the bonds of nature—I have planted agony in the bosom of Zerelda! Spurn me, ye frowning woods, as a wretch accurst! Why am I permitted to exist one moment?"

Frantic with the rending throes of burning anguish, I threw myself at Zerelda's feet, clasped both her hands with violence in mine, and exclaimed with a voice that shuddered at its own expression, "Behold a miscreant of every murderous depravity! A fit associate for savage monsters! Load me with your execrations—drive me to the beasts of the desert—spurn me from you, and end my miseries. Denounce me, and let me die."

The violence of my emotions alarmed Zerelda, and she forgot the excess of her affliction in the vehemence of mine.

"O Evermont!" cried she, "my dear Evermont! Do not use such horrible expressions—recover yourself from this alarming frenzy. I am not distressed. I am quite well. For the sake of this dear innocent, be composed, I beg, I entreat you." In saying which she had raised my hand to her lips.

Emerine, who was coming to meet us, arrived at this moment. My anguish raged afresh. I arose and gave the child to her as she stood in petrified astonishment, and then rushed from their presence. The entreating voice of Zerelda followed me, but I hurried beyond the torture of its echo.

In addition to the accumulated weight of my crimes, I felt the miseries I had occasioned my adopted relations. The pangs of the

Regret

distracted husband, and dying mother, were a diminutive part of my sufferings.

I found myself at the grotto. How pure, how noble were my thoughts, my deeds, and my emotions when first I visited this place! Ah! Miserable me! What are they now? The contrast distracted me. I threw myself on a rock almost stupefied with horror. The poignancy of my sensations wore away by their fierce attrition, and I wept, but my tears burnt on my cheeks. Terrified, lest the family would be alarmed with a fear that I would commit some desperate action, I returned slowly to the mansion.

Zerelda, with the infant on her bosom, and her arm interlocked in Emerine's, was waiting with a mournful pace in the garden. I passed on the other side as if I had not discovered them. Once inside, I threw myself on my bed in a state of quickened reflection.

Zerelda and Emerine returned to the house, and as they entered the passage, I overheard Emerine observe, not in a voice of anger, but pity, "Poor William is an unfortunate brother," which was followed by an expression from Zerelda, "Its features are not the features of Evermont."

I heard the child cry. Its voice seemed to weep the villainies of its father. A wild sweep of irregular fingers rang over the piano, but their tones died in murmurs, and the house became as silent as the overwhelm of woe.

Sleep is ever fearful of the sternness of a guilty conscience. He fled far from me and I continued in a restless gaze, on a black cloud which rode up the west, in an atmosphere of heavy gloom, while the wind groaned on the hills, and sang mournfully around my windows.

In the morning I saw Zerelda with the infant at the door. Her countenance was unusually solemn, but I thought it beamed forgiveness and love. "What a wretch am I," I thought, "to wound a heart like hers."

I heard Emerine attempt to waken the melody of the harp, but it baffled her exertions, and only struck with the grating tones of discordant melancholy.

I entered the library to dissipate, if possible, a grief that was corroding my vitals, but I threw every book from me with chagrin.

Emerine came in with a cheerful air, and observed, "Brother, you are distressed. Let me remove or share your sorrow. Tell me," laying her hand on my shoulder, "but do not be uneasy. Is this little cherub yours?"

"Emerine," cried I, "you increase a wound you cannot cure. Leave me, I beseech you."

"Evermont, I would not give you a pain for the world. I sympathize, I bleed with you, and let me know if this sweet babe is my niece, and I will clasp it to my bosom with the love I feel for my Evermont."

"Emerine, can you love a monster like me? O! It is profaning the sacred name."

"Yes, if your irregularities counted a thousandfold, I would love you. They have ceased in a life of repentance and endearing virtue. Angels love the penitent, and so will I. Come, dispense with what delicacy is now superfluous—is this babe yours?"

"That is only known to its mother," I replied.

Emerine sighed, "It is a sad affair, but may be bettered. The child I expect is yours, and if so, you will never deny your own precious offspring, no matter under what dark circumstances it had its birth. I will bring it to your arms."

She tripped away, and left me astonished at the liberality of her sentiments, which had not tarnished feminine delicacy, but ennobled in a manner inimitable by the squeamish prudes of fashion. And I have ever remarked that genuine virtue is anxious to draw a veil over the errors of others, and gently lead them to repentance, while the formal hypocrites discard them at once, and suffer the frowns of adversity to drive them still deeper into guilt.

In a moment, not Emerine, but Zerelda, entered with the child. "Evermont, I bring you a blessing," said she, "the smile of an innocent babe."

"Ah! Zerelda," stammered I, in confusion, "how can you look upon me without abhorrence? This cheerful countenance is a dagger."

"Talk not thus, Evermont," she replied. "With all your past imperfections around you, I love you as my own soul. I cannot lose you, and would not give you pain, so let us forget the past, and seek a happy futurity."

"You have given me life," cried I. "Your love would absolve the blackest sinner from guilt."

She held me the babe. I hugged it to my lips. She looked delighted. I clasped her to my bosom. Our hearts leaped to the embrace and panted against each other. Our cheeks met and our mingling tears cemented them. Their blood warmed in their union, and they kissed each other with a hundred pulses.

"This is a sight of rapture, the union of penitence and forgiveness," cried Mrs. Haylard, entering, and throwing her arms around us both at once. "May the purest blessing of heaven smile upon my affectionate children."

Zerelda withdrew from my arms and threw herself upon the bosom of Mrs. Haylard, with tears of delight still glistening in her eyes.

Emerine came in, and a cordial reconciliation took place which removed a weight of affliction from my heart, and gave partial cheerfulness to every bosom.

I went with the girls to Mrs. Holbert's. Susan was much recovered by the attention of her kind hostess. Zerelda and Emerine entered her room. She extended her arms for her child, and clasped it with the fondest caress.

"Where is the father of this sweet babe?" inquired Zerelda.

Susan wept. Mrs. Holbert observed to her, "This is the lady I mentioned to you this morning."

"Yes, you are under a dreadful mistake," said Susan. "You suppose this child is Evermont's. If you were not a stranger, I should disdain to answer such an ungenerous supposition. Know, that if I was the guilty creature you imagine, I would scorn to live. This is the child of my husband."

Zerelda was transported. She waited to hear no more, but sprang into the room where I had remained. With a countenance arrayed in the sunrise of joy, in all its brilliant bursts of blushes, beaming through the ethereal odors of morning, she laid her hands on my shoulders, and with the look of a rejoicing angel, observed, "It is not yours. It is her husband's."

I clasped my arms around her, and she sank upon my bosom, but suddenly withdrew, with a majesty of rapture, and returned to Susan, and embraced her with the fondness of a sister, for the information she had given.

Susan, discovering I was in the house, was impatient to see me, and I entered her room.

"Ungenerous man," cried she. "How could you destroy a woman who owned her own happiness, and the happiness of her father, to your bounty? How could you write that false, abominable letter?"

"Madam, this is not a time for explanations of this kind," replied I, extremely embarrassed by her question.

"It is, sir," cried she, "a time for explanations of this kind. That tremendous letter has deprived me of a husband, my babe of a father, and consigned me to disgrace, misery, and death." *Forged letter*

"Did you not give the occasion?"

"What occasion?"

"Is not this your writing?" handing her the note I had received from her.

"My God! What is here—my name? How came you by this? It is a villainous forgery."

"Did you not send it?"

"As God is in heaven! I never beheld it before!"

"Do you not remember Cherry Vale?"

"I was never there."

"Then you have been basely abused," replied I, and proceeded to explain my motives for writing to her, and was convinced by her surprise, and unaffected ignorance of all the circumstances I related, that some other person had assumed her name, and had veiled herself on that occasion to prevent detection. Her conduct soon removed every shadow of doubt, and we all became thoroughly satisfied of her innocence. But the sad mistake had produced a long series of evils.

Her father had died about six months before her marriage, and when she was deserted by her husband, she was bereft of every friend, and had been a homeless wanderer ever since. Nor were her calamities now at an end, for her husband still believed her guilty—we knew not where to find him to convince him of his error. But she was now received into the family of Mrs. Haylard, and cheered with the hope of again meeting her husband, and living in that union of unsuspecting tenderness and humble happiness which she formerly enjoyed, and beyond which she nor her husband had ever aspired.

This explanation removed my recent distresses, and enabled me to enjoy the happiness which again became a lively guest in the Haylard family.

CHAPTER XVIII

Near two months had glided swiftly down the smiling lawn of pleasure since the arrival of Zerelda, when a shade of gloom was cast over our prospects by the following note:

" It is the will of Zerelda's father that she return home immediately, and without company."

ANN WILLFORD

"Yes," replied Emerine, "and it is a will that will not be obeyed while it comes in that style, and under the authority of that signature."

Zerelda grew pale.

"Do not be uneasy, my dear Zerelda," said Mrs. Haylard. "I have been your mother, and did not raise you to receive such messages as this, and will protect you in paying no attention to such harsh, unnatural mandates."

"He is my father," sighed Zerelda.

"It was not your father gave this command," replied Mrs. Haylard. "He has resigned his authority to an abandoned woman. Would he bear rule himself, and as a father, you would be all obedience, but while he is the dupe of an intriguing hypocrite, my house shall be your home."

"O my dear, dear father! What shall I do?" She turned her eyes as if to inquire of me.

"It requires no deliberation," said I. "Willford's designs are the destruction of your happiness. She has gained ascendancy over your father, and you will be exposed to her power, and suffer under her unparalleled malignity. I know that woman, and would sooner see you sleep in your coffin than within the circle of her machinations."

191

Our arguments at last prevailed, and Zerelda, with the mournful feelings of a discarded daughter, consented to disobey, not the will of her father, but the base inclinations of Willford.

She wrote her father a melancholy account of what she had suffered in his absence, and the impossibility of her remaining in his family while Willford was in authority. This letter, teeming with all the affection of a weeping, but a tenderly obedient daughter, was accompanied with this from Mrs. Haylard:

"I am no less afflicted than surprised at the manner in which you permit your daughter to be abused. She was raised with a delicate tenderness, and from what I have received from undoubted authority, Mrs. Willford and her daughter are characters too base for her to associate with, and much less should she be subjected to their envious spleen, and insulting control.

"Recollect, that your dying wife gave her Zerelda to my arms, and implored me, in the name of that heaven to which she was hastening, to raise and educate her as my own daughter. Recollect, that at that moment you consented to her request that Zerelda should remain in my family, and never be subject to the authority of a housekeeper or stepmother. If you have forgotten this promise to an expiring wife, I have not forgotten it to a sainted sister, but shall now remember that the time is come when the necessity for such a promise, and for its faithful performance, is undeniably evinced.

"When you retired from business, I consented for Zerelda to live with you as the mistress of your household. But now you have discarded her from that honorable station, and placed her under the command of a base wretch, which I blush to name. I do not hesitate to retain her in obedience to the last injunction of her mother, and if you will reflect on the sacred oath you made to your dying wife, you will abandon the thought of removing her from my family.

"Her heart is all affection for her father, and she reluctantly consents to remain here by my command, a command she has held sacred from her infancy."

THE PRISONERS OF NIAGARA

These letters were dispatched with the carriage which was sent for Zerelda, but they could not calm the perturbations of a daughter's heart.

She knew not her father by any endearing attention to her happiness, by the fulfillment of any one parental duty, but she knew and felt the sacred obligation that existed between parent and child, and longed to comply with those filial duties which were an inseparable condition of her existence. She anxiously longed to be acknowledged in her father's bosom as a dutiful daughter, whose prompt obedience and tender attachment had amply rewarded the parent that gave her being.

Spring was beginning to blossom from the bed of winter, but the increasing beauties of nature could not restore contentment to the mind of Zerelda. Her love for me continued pure and unbounded, but I was convinced from various conversations that it would be almost impossible to procure her hand contrary to the will of her father, which I never hoped to obtain.

This rendered the state of my mind as gloomy as hers, but the dark pressure of my crimes, more than the fear of not succeeding, prevented me from pressing the ardent desire of my heart. I knew Zerelda would be superlatively miserable if we were finally separated, and I dreadfully feared she could not bear a disclosure of my disgraceful origin and unnatural crimes, yet I never could bear a thought of entering with her into a union of heart and soul while one secret circumstance or crime was locked in my own breast. I resolved to unfold my soul in all its blackness and infamy, and trust the event to her decision. I awfully feared it would plant the eradicable seeds of death in her bosom, and consummate the dreadful drama of my existence. But a fearful shock of misery was to be our portion in some shape or other, and my mind desperately longed to know its issue.

I made repeated determinations to execute this design, but always shuddered and shrank from the performance. I became melancholy under the burden of my resolution, but was unable to put it into execution. My spirits became depressed to their lowest ebb, and I felt that the moment I was thoroughly know to Zerelda,

typo

known

193

her love would be turned into indignation. The family discovered my increasing uneasiness, and added to its weight by anxiously endeavoring to discover its source. A month passed away, and still left my mind in this dreary situation.

The wife of Dawson had heard nothing from her husband, Zerelda had heard nothing from her father, and an unusual sadness began to prevail over the whole family. Nor could the gay vivacity of Emerine, or the serene equanimity of Mrs. Haylard, secure them from the solemn contagion, but when they perceived that my mind grew more and more gloomy, they assumed a temporary cheerfulness, and united their exertions to restore me to my accustomed serenity. Zerelda, too, affected an unreal sprightliness to inspire me with animation.

We were seated together in the grotto, which was again taught to bloom with all the flowers of this enchanting season. She was uncommonly assiduous to please and charm me, and finding her efforts unavailing, inquired with a tender solicitude for the cause of my unhappiness.

"Can I be otherwise, Zerelda," replied I, "when I see that I am soon to lose you forever?"

"What could have put that into your mind? Do you doubt my heart?"

"No, Zerelda, your heart has the perfection of an angel, and only differs from celestial spirits by being surrounded by imperfect scenes, but it is from its purity, from its exalted love, that I dread my sentence—my execration. When you know that I was born in infamy and nurtured in guilt, you will spurn me from you as an object of detestation and horror."

"Evermont," cried she, "you have often mentioned this dreadful subject, and filled me with trembling agitation. Let me now request you to unfold it. I am anxious to know from whence your uneasiness proceeds, yet I am confident it cannot be so dreadful as your suggestions have represented it."

"It is more shocking," I replied, "than can be conceived by the darkest imagination—but I can conceal it no longer. Prepare, then,

194

He is going to confess to Zerelda but a letter from her father interviews. He repents maybe

to hear a tale of unparalleled atrocity—a tale which will make your blood run in horror."

Zerelda grew pale as I spoke, and listened with agonizing suspense. I summoned all my courage—and was commencing. A servant came running with a letter. His agitation startled us into a conjecture of some sad disaster. Zerelda broke open the letter. It was from her father.

"I know not by what title to address you, for I have disgraced the name of father, but O Zerelda! If you can forget what has passed, and think of me with tenderness, you will hasten to receive the last blessing of your only parent.

"I am very ill, and calculate but a few more days to live, and my greatest fear is that I shall die before I receive the forgiveness of my daughter—before I fold you to my heart, and hear your lips pronounce a solemn farewell.

"You need apprehend nothing from any person in my family. You shall receive the kindest attentions of a repenting father.

"My days are numbered—they are rolling swiftly from me—sickness overpowers me—fly to your dying father."

Zerelda sank pale and trembling in my arms, but the ardent love of a daughter for an expiring father soon baffled her debility. She arose, forgot the alarming narrative I was commencing, and we hastened to the mansion.

She was resolved to fly immediately to her father's embraces, to cheer his latest anguish, and receive his dying benedictions. No one attempted to dissuade her, and she was prepared in a few minutes.

Mrs. Haylard was in a delicate state of health and Emerine could not leave her, or else she would have accompanied her weeping cousin. I had long been anxious to revisit Richmond, and repair as far as lay in my power the injuries inflicted by my vices, and particularly to return the money of which I had defrauded my companions by the *honorable* robbery of gambling. I chose this as the most suitable opportunity, when, after conducting Zerelda to her father's, I should be deprived of her society. I gave my horse to my servant, and took a seat in the carriage with Zerelda.

They return to Richmond. He will make amends

the Big Kiss

THE PRISONERS OF NIAGARA

Her agitation at the sudden illness of her father, her fears lest he should expire before she arrived, engrossed every faculty of her mind, and she was unable to feast on the exquisite waste of beauty and sublimity which spread in profuse variety throughout this mountainous tract of country. Nor could my utmost efforts to afford consolation find a passage to her heart, through its crowding swarms of fearful presages, so as to make the slightest impression.

We arrived in sight of Engleton seat. I had no intention of seeing Engleton, and we both knew we were about to part. We had been a long time silent. Our eyes now met in a sorrowful, tender glance of love. No circumstances could weaken the strings that twined our hearts in one; we felt how dear we were to each other, and our looks expressed our feelings. Our bosoms enkindled from the soft animation of each other's eyes, and she welcomed the pressure of my arms, and leaned to my bosom. Our embrace was sweet and solemn—our hearts met in sober rapture—our sensibility was quickened—our tears started at once, and ran together. Her swimming eyes again looked up in mine. They smiled a positive delight. I drew her more closely to my breast. My wet cheek pressed more warmly to hers. Our eyes again embraced in glistening tears, and her lips, without recoiling, received the light pressure of mine. It was a liberty I had never taken except while she slept in the wilderness. It excited sensations unknown to her bosom. Her lips now shed their virgin odor on the lips of love. The blood ran swiftly into her face and covered her cheeks with the deepest blush they had ever worn. Her forehead dropped on my shoulder. It was a moment of the sweetest silence. The carriage reached the gate—we must part! I strained her to my bosom. She seemed to aid the pressure, as if anxious to be pressed into my heart, while her eyes were immovably fixed on mine in a look that expressed the desires of her soul. Her lips again consented to a warm and sweet embrace, which was our only adieu, for neither of us could utter a syllable. Our tears gushed anew. I burst from the carriage, mounted my horse, and immediately rode away, but my eyes wandered back to Zerelda until I saw her enter the door. A strong presentiment seized me that she was lost to me forever.

196

I had not thought of Engleton's illness, but my servant informed me he had inquired of the boy that opened the gate, and was told her was recovering.

The idea of Willford and her daughter rushed into my mind. It was sickening madness to my soul to reflect that they were the only relatives I had in existence. It was impossible that I could think of them with filial or paternal regard. Mother and sister were enthusiastic titles until I discovered the wretched being that bore me, but ever since I have discovered that those once enchanting names are interwoven with my crimes, I cannot pronounce them without reverting to Willford and her daughter, and shuddering with internal agony. These sensations compelled me to measurably disuse those endearing titles when in conversation with Mrs. Haylard and Emerine.

Fearing the sight of those detested women would swell my feelings into rage and abhorrence, I hastened beyond the view of the mansion.

CHAPTER XIX

I arrived at Richmond. It is painful to visit those scenes where every object presents a witness of guilt and deserved wretchedness. I took a survey of the grand scenery which surrounds the city before I entered it. It was arrayed in the liveliest apparel of nature. The rosy-bosomed daughters of spring appeared to vie with each other in beauty and elegance, which, together with the majesty of James River and its romantic shores, were calculated to expand and enliven the imagination into animated enjoyment and pleasurable expectation. But the wide area of my guilt was before me, and the vivacity of my fancy only served to augment the number, and magnify the atrocity, of my crimes. I knew no scene I could behold without anguish, no friend I could embrace without the pangs of melancholy recollection, and retired to an obscure part of the city.

I immediately visited the prisons, and the huts of the unfortunate, and relieved every object of pity whose sorrows could be alleviated with money. I received many thanks and excited smiles of joy, but none could communicate a smile to the heart of Evermont, for my spirits, harrowed and depressed, had wandered to the dark abyss of mournful forebodings, and could not be recalled.

I found many in distress of whom I had won money, and immediately repaid them, for man never acquired a right to property on account of having won it. Gambling is a species of swindling, and the pickpocket and gambler are equally entitled to their gains. They are instigated by the same passion of indolent avarice, and their only difference is that gambling is tolerated by custom, and practiced by the proud and powerful.

My former companions flocked around me, but as our friendship was the passion of dissipation, it now found no place in my heart, and I received their embraces with indifference.

Carmont

challenge
to a
duel

One evening, passing down a dark alley, I met an old man in a habit of distress. He fixed on me a pair of heavy eyes, muttered to himself with a voice of tremor, "Great God! It is he!" and hastily passed out of my sight.

Astonished at this unusual salutation, I endeavored to discover where he had disappeared, but it being dusk, my eyes were unable to follow him. I continued my walk, meditating on the singularity of his exclamation, when he again met me, walking in the same direction as before. His gaze was dark and ominous, but he passed in haste, and was out of sight in a moment.

Wondering at the mysteriousness of his conduct, I visited that place for several evenings, but he had discontinued his walk or purposely avoided me.

Returning one evening to my room after one of those rambles, I received this note:

"Sir,

I understand you are the villain who has ravished away the unfortunate Amacette Holbert. You will please to meet me at the foot of the rapids at six in the morning to answer this charge."

ELIJAH CARMONT

I was surprised at this until I recollected that Carmont only knew me by the name of Bridford, and returned an answer that he might expect me.

I repaired to the place. Carmont was there with his friend. His eyes darted fire, his bosom was agitated with passion, for he had no recollection of the features he had seen, only when disguised with Indian paint.

"Where is your friend?" said Carmont.

"I have no friend," I replied. "My dearest friends have deserted me."

"Where is Amacette?"

"I have no answer," said I, "for a peremptory demand."

"Altercation then is useless," resumed he. "You do not deny the charge. Choose your weapons."

199

THE PRISONERS OF NIAGARA

The preliminaries were adjusted. We took our positions and unlocked our pistols.

"Do you not tremble," said I, with cool deliberation, "at the deed you are perpetrating?"

"This is no time for reflection. Prepare," said he.

"This is the last time you may have to reflect," continued I. "In another moment you may be in eternity to answer for this transaction. Do you not shudder at meeting your God thus unwarrantably?"

"This is the pretense of a coward," cried he. "I will hear no longer."

"Well then," said I, opening my bosom, "discharge your pistol here."

Carmont beheld—he beheld the scar that had saved his life. The pistol fell. He raised his hands and eyes in a momentary stupor of astonishment, then rushed to my arms, exclaiming, "My friend! My savior!" and embraced me with trembling ardor, shuddering at the crime he was about to commit.

When his transports had subsided he pressed my hand, and supplicated a thousand pardons for his sacrilegious rashness, but urged his ignorance for my person, and fondness for Amacette, as an alleviation of his offence.

He informed me in a few words of the reason for his singular conduct.

"I was deprived of my last parent," said he, "at the age of eighteen. I had received a tolerable education, but had no fortune to support me, and shortly after the declaration of independence, I enrolled in the American service, and aided in several expeditions in the northern states. But not being entirely satisfied with my situation, I procured my discharge, and returned to my former residence in the vicinity of Richmond.

"I was fond of romantic scenery, and often rambled along the wildest shores of James River.

"In one of those solitary excursion I had proceeded far beyond my accustomed haunts, and discovered a female witting under a fragment of rock, sketching a prospect of the scenes before her,

200

which were striking a picturesque. Her dress was rustic, but her person and features appeared to me the idea of perfection, for they filled my mind with the highest degree of pleasure I had ever known.

"I attempted not to interrupt her, but gazed on her until she had finished her drawing. And when she retired, I attempted to follow her, that I might discover where she lived. But she had not proceeded far before she disappeared in the windings of a field of broom, and I could trace her no farther. I visited that place for several days in hopes this rural beauty would renew her rambles, but my wishes were left ungratified.

"One evening I was sitting under the same rock where I had beheld her, drawing the same prospect which had engaged her fancy. A slight rustling occasioned me to cast up my eyes, and I beheld the pleasing stranger standing near me. I had not moved my head, so she knew not that I had seen her. She was in the attitude of turning away, but the position of her face seemed to express a wish to remain a little longer. I appeared to be intently engaged on my drawing, but narrowly observed her from under the lids of my eyes. She retired step by step, turning at every step to cast a glance at my features. When she had withdrawn to some distance, she entered a little grove of underwood, and I imagined she continued there—but when I arose and walked that way, as if by chance, I could see nothing of her, and felt severely mortified that I had not saluted her when she was near me. On a sudden she shrieked and sprang into my arms from a covert of rocks and bushes, and pointed to something that had frightened her. I examined, and beheld a huge rattlesnake, coiled in a posture for striking, with his yellow spotted skin glittering with rage, his eyes glaring a flame of yellow poison, and darting his red forked tongue from his mouth in keen, terrible menace. I never beheld a more striking object of terror. I immediately killed the snake, and turned to the lady who expressed her gratitude in a smiling blush of modest confusion. I never felt so far from myself in my life—I knew nothing to say or do. With any other lady I could have expiated on her alarm with an ebullition of hyperboles, but with her I could say nothing. But when I saw that she was leaving me, I requested permission to accompany her home. She bowed an assent, and we walked together with but little conversation, and that on the scenery around us, until we reached the field of broom where I had lost her before.

"She now made a stop, and with a deep blush observed, 'Sir, you will have to excuse me. I am now out of any danger, and particular circumstances require that I perform the rest of my ramble alone. I would feel highly gratified if—' She stopped and blushed again.

"'Shall I never be permitted to see you again?' inquired I.

"My look was tender, and was answered by the tenderest glance, with which she replied, 'Perhaps—at some other time—I should be happy to acknowledge my gratitude, but—' She hesitated, curtsied, and departed.

"I returned to the same rocks the ensuing day and saw that she had been there, for I discovered where she was drawn my face on the rock, and erased it with her pencil, and in another place I discovered where she had written some lines of poetry which were almost too much erased to be read. But I found that she was not in any part of the wood at that time.

"A week passed away, all spent in thinking of, and dreaming about, this lovely stranger.

"Again I was passing near the rocks. I heard a scream, and flew to assist the sufferer. I beheld the young lady lying passive in the arms of a man, with her bosom bare and her head leaning on his breast, while he was proceeding to more unwarrantable liberties. I was amazed until I saw that she had fainted and was entirely void of motion. I sprang to the place—. The villain attempted to fly, but I caught him and dragged him back, holding a dirk in my hand which deterred him from resistance.

"The lady had recovered, but screamed again when she beheld Whitford (for such was the name of the ruffian). Irritated to the highest degree, I raised my dirk to plunge in his breast. He trembled, fell on his knees, and begged for his life so piteously that I forbore. But when I beheld the interesting features of the lady, and thought of the crime he had attempted, I was too angry to suffer

[handwritten marginalia: Another captivity / Indian / the story of / previous rescue]

him to depart unpunished. I made the cowardly miscreant strip off his coat while I cut a shrub of brush, and gave him a severe and disgraceful chastisement, and commanded him to let me see him no more.

"I obtained the gratitude of the lady, and conducted her home, and learned that she was Amacette Holbert. She lived with her mother, obscure, and almost unknown. I was the only person that was permitted to visit their hut. Amacette and I were strongly prepossessed in each other's favor from the first time we met, and the acquaintance which had proceeded from the services I had rendered her matured our prepossession into the most unconquerable passion. Her mother gave her consent to render us happy, as soon as I could prepare her a habitation she had formerly held in Amherst.

"To comply with the wishes of Mrs. Holbert, I left Amacette early last spring and went to Amherst. A rumor had spread that the Indians had entered the frontiers of Virginia, and I joined a company of peasants to attack them. They had retreated, and we pursued them for some distance among the mountains, when I, venturing too far from my company on a cloudy day, became bewildered, and never found them again, but fell among a company of Indians and was made a prisoner.

"Those were the Indians from whom you released me.

"After we lost you on the Muskingum, I returned to this place, but sought in vain for Amacette and her mother. A few days since I learned, by some anonymous letters, that Evermont was in town, and that he was the man that had stolen Amacette from her mother by force, and that her mother had grieved herself to death on account of the loss of her daughter. Those letters irritated me, and without knowing that Bridford and Evermont were the same person, I sent the challenge."

After this statement he showed me the letters, and I had no doubt but that they were written by Willford and Emerald L— for the purpose of having me destroyed.

[handwritten marginalia: And more forged letters]

203

I immediately relieved the apprehensions of Carmont by giving him a history of my acquaintance with Amacette and her mother, and informing him of their present situation.

His joy knew no limits. His soul flowed from his eyes, and spoke his thankfulness and rapture. He was extremely anxious to visit Amacette, and parted from me immediately to fly to Hampshire to give joy to her bosom, and to enjoy the sublime transports of reciprocated love.

CHAPTER XX

After this delightful reconciliation I returned to town, with a warmer flow of animation than my spirits had long enjoyed.

I had been a month in Richmond, and became anxious to return to my family, when I now felt that I could taste all the delights they were calculated to inspire. I had several times written to Emerine, and received her answers, but although I had more often written to Zerelda, I had heard nothing from her since we parted. I grew apprehensive and uneasy, but this day I was in a more ecstatic tone of mind than usual, and forgot my fears in the anticipation of future happiness.

On my arrival at my lodging, I broke open a letter f rom Emerine with the expectation of having my joyous feelings exhilarated with the transporting effusions of her heart and pen. I read:

"There is something dreadful in agitation at Engleton's. Zerelda imagines you are killed in a duel, but I have written her the contrary, for the date of your last letter is later than her which contains the information. She is to be forced into a marriage with Barville—I am too distracted to write at the thought—fly to her relief—the enclosed will give you wings."

ZERELDA TO EMERINE

"O my dear sister! I have a tale to tell that will make you shudder! I informed you that my father had recovered and relapsed, and that Willford was often locked in his chamber. These secret conferences are still a portentous mystery, but it is not upon the uncertainty of dark surmises that the fate of Zerelda hangs.

"I was summoned this morning to the chamber of my father; his illness has dangerously increased, and he was fast verging toward dissolution. Her desired me to close the door, and taking my hand, fixed his languid eyes on mine with a gaze of anxious concern, and, uttering a deep, solemn sigh, which appeared to quiver from his soul, observed, 'My dear, precious daughter, I am going to leave you, but before we part, I have one important request—but how shall I divulge it at this melancholy period? It is too much—I will not request it of so dear a child, though it wrings my soul with agony.'

'Dear father, do not suspect my obedience; name your desire, and with my life it shall be performed.'

"He strained me to his bosom in a mournful pause. A burst of anguish gave him utterance, and he proceeded: 'You behold, in your dying father, the most wretched of beings. My days have been spent in accumulating torture for this awful scene, and a life of wretchedness must now be terminated by entailing misery on the darling of my existence, but fate shall perform her dreadful work alone; I cannot make my request.'

'Dear father, I would yield my life a sacrifice to duty. Do not conceal any thing that gives you pain, but let your daughter know, and participate, and comply with your desires—I resign myself to your will.'

'Ah Zerelda! I am in a dreadful dilemma. If I make the request, and you refuse, that instant I breathe my last, in a state of desperation.' A terrible groan rent his soul, and after a few moments of death-like silence, he continued: 'Dearest Zerelda, I can live but a few moments—I must speak the secret of my torture, or die in despair. Oh my daughter! Can you resign your beloved Evermont, and marry Barville?'

"My heart was struck dumb—a quivering tremor ran through my nerves! My blood froze along my veins, and I sank into a state of stupefaction.

"I awoke of reflection, but was in the chamber of Mrs. Willford. My dream had been dismal—the dismal picture still hung before me.

206

THE PRISONERS OF NIAGARA

"To resign Evermont—oh! That I could resign my life! Yes; to ease the pangs of my expiring father, I would open my bosom, with a smile, and see him plunge a poignard to my heart. But to live without the adored soul of my being—to live in the embraces of another—my soul recoiled from the picture. I sank upon a chair. My thought started on every side from the fate that surrounded me. My elbows rested on the table, my head sank on my hand, and I remained in a situation too dreadful for reflection. An open letter lay before me; my eyes caught the following sentence: 'This morning a duel was fought in this place between Mr. Evermont and Mr. Dawson. At the first fire, Mr. Evermont was wounded in the breast, and immediately expired!'

"This intelligence was too shocking for my fortitude. Recollection shrank from the benumbing image—I remember no more.

"The physician was chafing my temples when I awoke. I opened my eyes and exclaimed, 'Is he dead? Or was it a dream?'

'Who, child?' said Mrs. Willford. 'Your father? No, he is in a slumber.'

"Her answer met not the confused rumor of my brain. 'No, he is not dead,' continued I. 'I saw and embraced him. Who said he was shot?'

'Your father shot!' cried Willford. 'Child, you are certainly delirious.'

"O, that I had been delirious! For, at that instant, tormenting memory revived, and I recollected the fatal letter, and pointing to it, exclaimed, 'Who wrote that dreadful—?'

'Lord,' cried Willford, 'the child is thinking of that head-long youth who was killed in Richmond. Is this a time for a girl to be thinking of a giddy young man? Alas! Children have no respect now-a-days!'

"This hypocritical cant only met my indignation, and I retired to my own room, firmly convinced that Evermont was no more, which accounted for his extraordinary silence in not answering my letters. I fell on my bed. O Emerine! Pity me! I have lost the fond, the generous, the inimitable Evermont. I adored him while living as

207

He rushes to her, is accosted by a holdup guy *Stabs him*

the noblest work of nature, and shall ever revere him as the brightest saint in heaven. My soul is sunk into a state of desperate apathy from which it can never revive! O! The expected bliss that was annihilated in one sad moment! Had I been with him, I would have wed him in death! Our hearts should have panted their last throb together, and my soul mingled with his would have flown rejoicing to eternity.

"Despair has rendered me indifferent to life. My mind is irrecoverably sunk in insensibility, and I passively await my destiny—never, never to hope, or smile!

"My father sleeps; when he awakes, I will comply with his request—I will marry Barville. Nothing can add to my wretchedness. I can ease my father's pangs without increasing my own misery.

"Dear Emerine, adieu—your Zerelda is lost. My heart was grafted on a flourishing bough, which fate has plucked up by the roots, and I am left to wither, for the want of vital nourishment."

A dark rumor of apprehensive agony rolled through my mind as the letter fell from my hand. Conflicting emotions stunned me for a moment, but I then suddenly sprang up, as if I could fly to Engleton seat at a single exertion. I saw that my letters had been intercepted, my death fabricated, to force Zerelda into a horrible marriage, and drive me to despair.

I mounted my horse and was immediately on the road to thwart this diabolical scheme of exquisite, unexampled cruelty.

It grew dark, and, as I was passing through a heavy wood, my horse was stopped by a man, who demanded my money.

"I have but little," I replied, and handed him a ten dollar note.

"This will not do," cried he. "Give me more or I will take your life."

I hesitated, for I had no more, and he became furious and presented his pistol at my breast. I was distracted at being interrupted, and knocking his pistol away, gave him a thrust with my dirk. He fell, and his pistol discharged in the air. I dismounted to assist him, and the discharge of the pistol, together with the cry

208

of my servant, brought a peasant from a neighboring hut. Finding the man yet alive, we removed him to the peasant's dwelling. But what was my astonishment when the light enabled me to discover the dark features of the mysterious stranger I had seen in Richmond. I immediately ordered my servant for a surgeon. The stranger opened his eyes, and fixing them on me, exclaimed, "Are thou come to torture me in my dying hour?"

"I have been the unfortunate instrument of your suffering," said I, "but would not intentionally inflict the slightest pain."

"Hah! Was it you that gave the blow?" cried he, in a voice more wild than human. "Then give me your private audience, and I will unfold the curtains of horror."

The peasant withdrew, and the stranger fixing his eyes on me with a terrible gaze, observed, "My day is closed! Evermont, hear, and shudder at my words. You are the woeborn offspring of guilt—the inheritor of unparalleled wretchedness. Frowning fate presided in horrible majesty at your birth, and the moment you opened your eyes, she planted her seal of awful destiny upon you, and with the scowling malignity of eternals, proclaimed in a voice of muttering thunder, 'This shall be a child of mine!'

"Now is the tremendous decree fulfilled. Now the works of horror begin in desperate vengeance! For know young man, and tremble—!"

He fainted with the loss of blood while I remained stunned into stupefaction at his tremendous expressions.

The physician came, and examining the wound, discovered that it was not mortal, but from his great loss of blood, the stranger continued too weak to either speak or think correctly, and I saw no possibility of shortly having my wild waves of feeling allayed by an explanation of his petrifying exclamations.

Zerelda was on the brink of a desperate marriage. A moment's delay might plunge her into that dreary void of apathy where hope has never shed a beam, and no circumstances could arrest my purpose of endeavoring to snatch her from her perilous situation.

From the unfinished declaration of the stranger, I had no doubt but that some agonizing secret was yet to be revealed that would

209

crush me still deeper in despair. I beheld fate, with her frowning brood of horrors, hovering in mysterious vindication around me. Her ghastly, ominous aspect had already frightened my imagination into stupor, but the latent energies of my mind revived from the benumbing shock. Hope arose above the gloomy wreck of ruined prospects, and shed a trembling ray that defied the fury of desperation. And the voice of love, the strongest nature's children ever heard, summoned me to leave the gloomy, eventful stranger, and save the sinking Zerelda.

The physician and peasant promised to bestow on him their utmost attention. I gave them a letter of credit for two hundred dollars on a merchant in Richmond, to be applied to his necessities, and left them, promising to return in the course of two or three weeks.

Engagement

CHAPTER XXI

All was mournfully silent at Engleton's when I arrived. The windows were closed, and no person to be seen. I entered the passage; Emerine appeared from the hall in a countenance of solemn despair. She rushed into my arms. Our embrace was a moment of chilling silence, which first was broken by Emerine.

"Brother, you must not be seen here, Zerelda should not meet you for the world. Fly as you value the lives of your friends. Take this letter; I will meet you in the summer house in an instant."

I obeyed this solemn warning, with the forebodings of death, and when in the summer house, I unfolded the letter with an aching, panting heart.

ZERELDA TO EMERINE

"O Emerine! The deed is done, your letter came too late. My destiny is sealed, and if Evermont lives, he lives to share with his Zerelda a lingering death of despair.

"I complied with my father's request, and he joined my hand to Barville's, to wed him in two weeks after his decease. But a fearful presentiment seized me as I gave consent, and the words quivered on my lips. A keen palpitation panted in my heart. I hastened to my chamber, shuddering at the promise I had made.

"I threw myself on the bed, scarce daring to think of what I had done, but the fatal union was sealed!

"With the belief of Evermont's death, I had lost every blessed prospect in life. No ray of comfort shone through the black clouds of destiny, and a marriage with Barville, by adding to the exquisiteness of my anguish, will shorten its duration.

"I was told that my father was dying; I flew to his bed. He clasped me in his arms, and his departing soul embraced me. My promise had quieted his mind; he fell into a tranquil slumber, and expired in my arms. I sank upon his body as the quivering lamp of life was extinguished, and lay in a state little short of insensibility.

"A dark chasm of feeling ensued, until I was awakened to attend my father to the tomb on the succeeding day.

"It is a solemn scene to behold an only parent consigned to the tomb; the melancholy procession—the dark coffin deposited in the grave—the earth closing over him—O Emerine! I felt—I bled—I fainted!

"It was after I recovered and returned to the house that I read your letter. It has convinced me that I have only passed the prelude of agony, and that the direful catastrophe is to come. I dare not contemplate the past, or the future. O! That Evermont could never have known the promise I have made, and that I had remained deceived of his existence. I might have been happy, had I not been misinformed.

"I dare not see Evermont—I should expire in his embrace. Dare I love him, since I have become the affianced bride of another! Dare I refuse to love him, after so many vows to love him till death! O Emerine! I am sick—I am faint—a cold, damp shivering runs through my veins."

This letter was all that was wanted to rivet my mind to despair. In the first torture of reflection, I thought of seeking an interview with Zerelda, which, from the present exquisiteness of our sensibility, would close our lives in each other's arms, but my mind could yet exert a feeble effort in the cause of virtue and affection, and I banished this idea, and resolved to fly where my presence could never excite the recollection that I was ever dear to her bosom.

O Engleton! What an inestimable treasure have you destroyed. The heart of Zerelda was a heaven of blissful enjoyment, but you have filled it with the corroding poison of woe.

212

I will resign to providence. I will not dare to murmur against the dispensations of eternal wisdom. I have been unprecedented in wickedness, and deserve to be miserable. Zerelda is an innocent sacrifice to the shrine of inordinate ambition. She deserves all the happiness that ever fell to the lot of woman, and I will not augment her sufferings by an interview, which would awaken her generous bosom into a delirium of desire without the possibility of gratification, and leave it to sink into a chaos of despair.

The arrival of Emerine ended my reflections. She trembled as she entered the summer house, and sank upon my bosom. Floods of tears showered from her eyes in eloquent sorrow. A pause of unutterable grief succeeded.

Emerine recovered, and feebly articulated, "William, you are too late! The die of fate is thrown—Zerelda is a bride tomorrow!"

"Tomorrow! O God, tomorrow!"

"Dear brother, endeavor to support the melancholy misfortune. Tomorrow is the day fixed by Engleton on his deathbed, and you must submit. I know not how to offer consolation; my heart sympathizes with you; it bleeds with your pangs. You must not see Zerelda. Fly to your mother—she is weeping for the loss of a daughter, and a son. I love to be with you, but you must not remain here. I trembled lest Zerelda should catch a glimmer of your person or hear of your arrival. She has wept her mind into a tender imbecility, and I fear the consequences would be fatal. Any circumstance which would bring you full image to her imagination would almost shock her into insanity. Go, Evermont, and endeavor to be happy."

I thought of nothing she was saying, and only repeated, "Tomorrow! O, tomorrow!"

Zerelda was discovered entering the garden. Emerine was alarmed, and desired me to conceal myself within a cluster of vines while she conducted her on the other side of the garden, and enjoined me to depart as soon as Zerelda retired.

As she was about to fly, I caught her hand with a frantic grasp, and exclaimed, "Emerine, embrace me once forever."

"Do not distract me. Recall that sickening expression. Whither would you go?"

"Into eternity to wait for Zerelda."

"O! Brother, brother! For God's sake be composed. As you value eternal happiness, do not be rash. I must haste or we are undone. Tarry till I return, I conjure you, by the love of a sister."

She sprang to meet Zerelda, and from my covert I had a full view of that weeping cherub. Her air was solemn and impressive as the movements of a specter. Her countenance had faded into a sickly languor, expressive of the sorrowful diseases of the soul. What a throng of frantic desires throbbed in my bosom as I gazed on her precious form. She passed the summer house with one hand locked in Emerine's, the other pressed on her bosom. My feelings were unutterable—my eyes strained on her solitary features—in the loss of her, time and eternity faded, and a dark wild of overpowering agony lay before me.

I heard her exclaim with tones of tremor, "O Evermont! What will you feel!"

I groaned internally. "My God, what do I feel!" Nature dissolved around my soul and left me in an awful stupor.

She walked beyond my sight, and was again returning to the summer house. Emerine endeavored to draw her to the other side of the garden, but she seemed irresistibly led to the place where I was concealed.

I shuddered as she approached, but what was I when she entered, and sank on a settee almost touching the vines that covered me! O trembling nature! My heart! My heart!

She rested her forehead on the breast of Emerine; a deep groan shook her tender bosom. "O! That I had died in the arms of Evermont!" cried she, in accents shrill and impressive.

"Do not indulge such gloomy reflections," said Emerine.

"My spirit would have clung to his bosom," returned Zerelda, "and kissed his soul as it escaped."

"Merciful heaven support me!" ejaculated my harrowed feelings in my rending, bursting bosom!

214

"O, how I will clasp his soul in eternity," continued Zerelda, clenching her hands in frantic delirium.

"O God! O God!" internally groaned my trembling spirit.

My agonizing bosom was bursting from the feeble hold of reason, and would have risked a "crush of worlds" to have died in her embrace, had not Emerine prevailed on her to leave the summer house.

When she departed, my eyes strained their utmost nerves on her person, as if the moment she disappeared would close them in eternal darkness. My soul hung upon her with an anxious grasp, with a fearful presentiment that her removal from sight would break the bands of being and plunge me into annihilation. The gate closed behind her, and left me to gaze on a desolated universe!

bosom is Holman's favorite word

CHAPTER XXII

Day was closing. The sun was setting in a sea of flaming clouds. I stared at his fiery radiance with a vacant expansion of mind. My soul was a mighty vacuum in which the millions of created worlds were lost beyond the reach of thought.

I tarried for the return of Emerine until the mists of evening were smoking through the garden, and then, thinking myself secure from observation, wandered carelessly among the winding avenues until I came to a new made grave beneath the foliage of a cypress. This is the urn of Engleton—a chilling horror flitted through my mind as I approached it. I gazed a few minutes on the solitary pile, and was turning away. A thicket of hedge opened, and Zerelda appeared. Startled at my unexpected form, she shrank back with astonishment while I stood petrified at what must ensue. Convinced of my reality by a second look, she rushed frantic into my arms with a tremulous shriek, "O Evermont!" and sank upon my bosom without a pulse of life. Distracted with my own feelings—terrified for hers—I seated her on the grass, leaned her head on my lap, and warmed her into life with frenzied kisses. With a groan that made her bosom quiver, she opened her eyes. Their deep blue orbs, lovely in languor, rolled their faded sparkles on mine. Recollection awakened her to her perilous situation, and with the exclamation, "Evermont! O God!" she endeavored to rise, but she was too weak without my assistance, and while I was raising her up, the wild ardor of my fondness overpowered my fainting reason, and I clasped her bosom to mine with the grasp of desperation. The well known throb of her heart panted on mine, and I held her in my arms in a state of feeling that mocked the fear of consequences. Death himself, arrayed in the glittering vengeance of flaming elements,

216

could not have startled me from my purpose, for I longed to strain her into my heart, and end my being in the embrace!

Zerelda's emotions were as violent. Her frame shook with a tremulous quavering—her bosom was in convulsions—her heart beat as if it would burst its narrow bounds and spring into mine with unrestrained embrace. But her woe-enfeebled frame was inadequate to support the feelings and terrors of her dreadful dilemma, and she sank unable to oppose the pressure of my arms.

I closed my lips to hers in a bewildering kiss.

The sacrilegious caress alarmed her into frenzy. "Evermont, desist, or I am undone!" exclaimed she, with a groan. "I am the wife of Barville!"

"Alas! I know—we part forever—but say, O say Zerelda! Am I lost in your bosom?"

"Mighty God! What a question of horror! Evermont, leave me, or drive me distracted!"

"Then I am banished from your heart? Ah, Zerelda!"

"No! Gracious heaven! Nor shall never be," cried she, with a wild energy of look and expression. "I can do no more—come furies and tortures, here I will expire!" She threw herself on my bosom, clung her arms around my neck, and ceased to breathe.

Frantic at what I was doing, I cried in a terrific voice, "Zerelda, arise. I will fly from you—live the wife of Barville—dear, dear Zerelda, recover—God have mercy—angels save her!"

Emerine, who had been seeking me, heard the shrill accents of my exclamations and flew to the grave, exclaiming, "O heaven! Heaven!"

Mrs. Willford had also heard, and was there in an instant. She started with apparent fright, and vociferated, "Lord have mercy upon me! Girl, what is the meaning of this? What will Mr. Barville say when he hears of these proceedings?"

These expressions aroused my passion to triumph over the force of my anguish, and fixing my eyes on Willford with a furious sternness, observed, "What would he say? Or what dare you to say on the subject?"

His blackmail / Pretends to know secret
Valendon
Huron

"I will say that you have reason to tremble at this abominable conduct with the wife of another man."

Zerelda had recovered and was raised up in the arms of Emerine, but this malicious threat made her shudder, and she was again sinking. I enabled Emerine to support her, and with a tone of fearful severity replied to Willford, "Peace, wretch! And as you value the concealment of your villainies, never dare to divulge what has here transpired. Zerelda's innocence is in no danger from the truth, but I know the force of your malignant falsehoods; therefore, on your life, be silent."

"I shall act as duty requires," replied she, with a sneer, "and my silence does not depend on your command."

"Madam, it shall depend on my commands, and shudder to disobey. For by the blood of your butchered offspring, the moment you utter a syllable of what has here taken place, you shall be dragged to the bar of justice to pay the ignominious penalty of your crimes. Vile paragon of infernals! The blood of Alburtus Valendon and his mother is yet unappeased; the fraud of Valendon is known; his will is in being; his heir has an authentic history of your career of criminality; the evidence of Huron is terrible. You see that I know you. Seal up you lips in eternal silence, or the storm shall burst."

Although a part of this statement was surmise, I spake it with a tone of peremptory firmness, and the pallid features and shivering agitation of Willford convinced me she was too much alarmed to brave my denunciations.

Zerelda and Emerine were leaning on each other. I threw my arms around them both with violent embrace, and with the emotions of desperate affection, imprinted a kiss on each of their lips, and sprang through the hedge from their sight.

CHAPTER XXIII

I rambled to the banks of Jackson's River, and throwing myself on a rock, listened with frantic earnestness to the screaming river birds and the wild yelling of owls, which, by fits, reverberated through the darkness from a hundred echoing hills.

Successive volumes of frowning clouds rushed up the west and overran the heavens. Their magazines of fire would burst and stream through the atmosphere in sheets of flame. Rumbling thunder followed them with a deep muttering sound, and all would be silent, threatening blackness. In an instant, the heavens would again burn with a hundred daring torrents of keen, forked blaze, and fiercer peals of conflicting thunder roll in tremendous reverberations over the quaking hills. This awful clash of contending elements long continued to swell its stupendous grandeur on the dark bosom of night, but I still remained unmoved among the wild rocks that hung lowering around the stream. In the morning I wandered again in sight of Engleton seat, and gazed on the mansion that held Zerelda. The curtains of her windows were closely drawn, but fancy rushed into a wild train of bewildered feelings at the thought that that chamber was, at that moment, devoted to the secret anguish of her soul.

I imagined I beheld her, leaning pensive with her elbow on the window, her cold cheek resting on one hand and the other pressed on her aching bosom. The curtain moved. I was startled from my dream and my imagined Zerelda disappeared. I gazed with throbbing anxiety to see the real person of Zerelda, but could not discover even the hand that upheld the curtain. The curtain fell—and all was unintelligible darkness. I continued to gaze till my straining eyeballs sickened, but the adorable Zerelda was invisible.

THE PRISONERS OF NIAGARA

I was strangely inclined to see her again before I yielded her up forever, and this frantic desire at last overcame all power of resistance. It seemed the unconquerable fiat of my destiny, and I desperately determined to see her at the moment she was given to the arms of Barville.

I disguised myself as an Irish soldier, and gained admission among the servants.

The hour of the dreaded ceremony arrived. Zerelda and Emerine were in deep mourning. Zerelda's features had settled into an unmovable paleness, and she appeared more tremulous than she would have if she were going to the flaming stake. When Barville took her hand, she trembled as if falling to the floor.

God of nature! Hast thou made me for this? All creation seemed dissolving round me—life and death, time and eternity, in awful expectation, hung suspended on the termination of the scene! The parson arose, and with a solemn aspect, raised his eyes to heaven. "Eternal justice," exclaimed I, internally, "is this work to receive the benediction of a God?"

He began the ceremony.

My blood stopped—a cold pang froze in my bosom—my heart beat a sullen tremor—sickness seized my soul. The quaver of life was dying. A gleam of reason shot across my mind and I rushed from the rueful scene.

I mounted my horse and rode—I know not whither. I reached the house of a farmer in Augusta. I was seized with a violent fever—three months passed away in a delirium of horrid dreams. At last a skillful physician, aided my the vigor of my constitution, awoke me to misery. It seem that I had only slept for a night, and that yesterday was the marriage of despair. I saw that death would not remove the fearful vision from my sight, and resolved to lose it in the wild clangor of arms. I rewarded the farmer, and left him. I recollected the stranger at Richmond, and concluding his terrifying expressions were the preface of a tale that would probably terminate a hated existence, I immediately hastened thither.

"He is dead," said the peasant.

"Dead!" said I, and the petrifying secret died with him.

220

"He left this letter for you," continued the peasant. I broke it open and read

"Evermont, prepare for unutterable woe, for I am Huron—I am your father!"

His

"O horror! Horror!" I groaned from my fainting soul.

"I was raised in England, in the service of Lord Willford. When *story* his youngest son, Sir William Albertus Valindon, growing tired of England where his fortune would not support his title, came to Baltimore, he brought me with him as the prime minister of his pleasures. He soon became acquainted with Miss Bridford, who, though it was then unknown, had been brought up in New York to the trade of her mother, who had amassed a considerable fortune by prostitution. She was celebrated for her beauty and accomplishments in Baltimore, and procured a crowd of devotees, amongst whom was my master. He engaged me to assist in the prosecution of his intrigues, and so faithful was I in his service that Miss Bridford was pregnant before she yielded to his solicitations. He soon discovered that all her admirers were alike successful, and resolved to abandon her. He married and removed to Shenandoah, but I left his service and continued with Miss Bridford, for she treated the poor father of her unborn babe with more fondness than any of her wealthy suitors. The hour arrived that made me a father—and you—I tremble at the thought, you were the son!

"But to serve the intrigues of Bridford, I yielded up the name in public, and Sir William was believed to be your father. Under this belief he removed Bridford to Shenandoah, and having lost his wife and son, acknowledged you for his child, and when he died, bequeathed you his fortune. This fortune, being extensive, stimulated your ambitious mother to commit a deed too black to name—to attempt the murder of her own child!

"This was done by leaving you near an Indian camp as we removed from Shenandoah to Philadelphia.

"After two years, she removed to Baltimore and began an intrigue with Engleton, whereby she appears to have held him in her power ever since.

221 *His history is revealed*

The money
now a ~~purried~~

"I was pressed on board a British vessel, and never escaped until about twelve months since. When meeting with Bridford, in Richmond by the name of Mrs. Willford, she informed me of your being alive, and that she made the discovery by a mark under your hair. I also discovered that you had been criminally connected with your sister, Armilda. This was dreadful information to a father, which, heightened by the request of your mother that I should murder you for our personal safety, resolved me to abandon her forever. She removed to Bath, and I, disgusted with life, have turned out a robber!

"You are heir to an extensive fortune, but as your mother is the medium through whom you must acquire it, it is useless to know where it is. It would only excite wishes which could receive no gratification. But you are born to grief, which disdains the consolation of fortune. I die—happier by your hand than the executioner's. Weep not that you occasioned my death, for you have saved me from ignominy."

What had I been! But what, o what, tremendous judge! What am I now? A parricide! Awful, awful thought—a parricide!

The pangs of eternal agony rolled in a horrible chaos upon my feelings. I felt the indignation and pronunciations of heaven hovering over my head and involuntarily raised my eyes to behold the coming bolt of lightning descend with the thunder to divine malediction to blast my guilty soul into perdition. A whirlwind of desperation burst in my mind, and hurled the shattered fragments of reflection into terrible consternation. I grasped a pistol with the infernal purpose of ending a dreadful existence! But I was yet incapable of the diabolical deed—I started affrighted at my daring assumption of the sovereignty of omnipotence—the pistol fell—life was struck dumb in awful petrification. My hair stood upright in horror!

CHAPTER XXIV

The army of Lord Cornwallis was besieged at York by the immortal Washington. I rushed with a maniacal transport to that wide theater of death—not with an ardor for martial glory, not with the love of country or enthusiasm of freedom—but with the fury of despair.

The Marquis de La F—, with several distinguished commanders, were ordered to storm an important redoubt from which the British annoyed the Americans. I enrolled myself among the troops of the Marquis; he recognized me, and gave me a place near his person.

We were led to the charge with determined intrepidity, and entered the work with irresistable ardor. The redoubt was defended with resolution and vigor, which rendered the contest extremely violent for a few minutes.

With wild temerity I here sought and expected death. I rushed into the hottest of the engagement; swords and bayonets clanged and blazed around my head, but none entered my heart. *seeks death*

I held a bayonet poised at the side of my valiant commander, who was engaged with other enemies. I rushed to his assistance, and while the soldier was exulting in expectation of his important victory, I laid him bleeding on the earth with my saber. The enemy was overpowered and fled. *kills enemy*

The Marquis embraced me with affection and gratitude, and offered me a commission in his army, but it met no desire of my heart, and I refused.

The siege was prosecuted with vigor.

What as astonishing scene, to a novice in war, is the field of battle. Here is was opened in its most alarming aspect. Day was darkened into night by the thick volumes of smoke which rolled

223

gets 5 people to go w/ him to fight Indians

from beds of burning sulphur exploded from the wide mouths of the cannon. Night was inflamed into dreadful day by the fiery bolts of chain-ball and langrage streaming along the quaking air in an awful tempest. At once, a thousand of those tremendous instruments of death would bound from their hollow dens, and blaze, and burst, and thunder upon the shrinking foes, while a trembling earth, and shaking heavens, and shattered ramparts added to the stupendous clamor and closed the terrific catastrophe in horrible amazement.

The army of Cornwallis surrendered to the united powers of America and France, which terminated the campaign, and the troops were about to retire into winter quarters.

But a state of inactivity was, to me, a state of keen despair. I dared not reflect, and longed to continue in the fiercest engagements where my mind was lost in the loud clangor of arms.

The frontiers of Pennsylvania were still exposed to the savages. Thither I repaired after taking leave of the noble Marquis, who in vain entreated me to accept a commission and remain in the army.

I prevailed on five resolute companions to accompany me in a winter excursion against the Indians.

We passed the headwaters of the Allegheny, and defeated several unsuspecting bands of Indians, and in one of their camps, discovered Carmont a prisoner. He and I rushed to each other's embrace, but it was with the wild solemnity of despair. He told me a mournful tale. He had flown to Hampshire, but Amacette was lost. She had been stolen away, a few days before, by two British soldiers. Her mother was almost distracted—the village was in an uproar. He immediately pursued the rout of the ravishers through the back settlements of Virginia and Pennsylvania, into the Indian territories, and could track them no farther. But after long researches in that wide wilderness west of the Allegheny, he was captivated by Indians. This lamentable misfortune to this precious woman almost overwhelmed the resolution of Carmont. I sympathized with him, for I knew his loss; I felt his anguish! For O! I had fearfully learned to feel the force of such a calamity. But I could give him no consolation but that beyond the stars, where I

224

dared not look myself. "For guilt, a heavy chain/ Still dragged me downward from the skies,/ To darkness, fire and pain."

Carmont expected that Amacette had been conducted to some of the British garrisons on the lakes, and we resoled to disguise ourselves and seek her while a possible glimmer of hope could penetrate through the dark forebodings of our hearts. Our companions were not actuated by the same irresistible impulses; they were not tortured by misfortune until they had nothing to lose. We prevailed upon them to return to their country, and immediately prosecuted our daring enterprise.

Not far from the garrison of Niagara we discovered a small camp of Indian and British soldiers whom we saluted as brothers, and being disguised in their uniform, we were received with the utmost hospitality. We continued with them until the following day, and were about to depart when a shout of salutation was heard at a distance, and a company of Indians approached. They bore a tender American youth in captivity whose pale countenance, though mild and expressive, wore the languid air of grief and anguish, settling in a lifeless apathy. My heart bled for the sorrows of his tender years, but he appeared unconcerned, and indifferent, to everything around him.

The British and Indians all left the camp, except three British soldiers who were to conduct the prisoner to Fort Niagara. We remained, lamenting the pitiable condition of the effeminate prisoner who was scarcely able to move along the frozen wild.

Passing through a close thicket of undergrowth, the vest of the youth was torn open by a brush. One of the soldiers, observing it, exclaimed, "O! Ho! What have we here?" I turned my eyes. He had thrust his hand in the stranger's bosom, who had fallen back in his arms without motion, and with a cry of joyous surprise, burst open his collar, drew the garments aside, and with a shout of exultation displayed the snowy bosom of a woman. A flash of recognition discovered the countenance of Amacette. Murder burst upon my thoughts, but the poignard of Carmont was riving the heart of the soldier. I struck down one of his companions; the other fled.

THE PRISONERS OF NIAGARA

Amacette was recovering. The voice of Carmont was melody to her soul and tuned its dying impulses with life. She clasped him in her arms, and was clasped to his heart.

A full knowledge of our danger would not induce me to interrupt those ecstatic transports, those enraptured embraces, which my soul was never, never to know or hope.

In the effusions of her joy, Amacette gave a short detail of her captivity. She was walking alone on the bank of the Potomac, and was surprised and seized by two soldiers whom she knew to be the companions of Whitford. Resistance and outcries were vain; she was hurried into a boat, and when over the river, she was placed upon a horse and compelled to ride all day and all night through a continued wilderness. Next day they gave her a man's dress and compelled her to put it on, and then conducted her on horseback as before until they were several days journey from any human habitation. One night when they imagined her asleep she overheard them conversing, and learned that they were hired to conduct her to Fort Niagara by the infamous Whitford. But listening a little longer, she heard them mutually resolve to deceive their employer and sacrifice her to their own desires, and then conduct her to Whitford and claim the reward. She shuddered in chilling agitation—but a more important debate ensued. Each soldier contented for preference in villainy; the dispute rose high. Each asserted his right with fearful imprecations, and blows succeeded in a violent contest. Amacette was unobserved, and secretly stole from the combatants, took one of their horses, and fled precipitately.

Next morning she was discovered by a body of Indians and instantly made a prisoner. They were traveling toward Niagara, and bore her with them, so she heard no more of the soldiers. She was never discovered by the Indians to be a woman, and was treated with no species of cruelty. The Indians, after keeping her some months in the woods, had sold her to these three British soldiers who were conducting her to Fort Niagara to exchange with the Americans.

Scarce was the rapturous pair acquainted with each other's suffering and present enjoyment before a loud din of arms, and triumphant yells, burst upon us in terrific thunder. A company of Americans, led by Major Anderville, were flying towards us before a tumultuous crowd of shouting conquerors. Terror ravaged the countenances of Carmont and Amacette, but it was too late to deliberate. We took Amacette between us and joined our retreating brethren who were approaching nearer to the garrison, where they must be inevitably captivated.

Anderville was not fully aware of his danger. I hailed him; he knew my voice and listened to my proposals as the only mode of escaping the surrounding storm.

We retreated to an advantageous wood, where we resolved to make a vigorous stand, and if possible penetrate the confused lines of the assailants. The Indians advanced with hideous clamor, and we attacked them with the fury of despair. They were resolute with the certainty of victory, but our desperate determination at first prevailed. Their center was beaten back, and began to disperse. A second column then formed before us, by the wings on the right and left, and this we also broke, but with a dreadful slaughter. When a fresh party of British rushed at once in our front and rear, awakening hope now perished. Some threw down their arms, while others, who expected no quarter, fought with distracted fury. Both parties were in confusion. Our commander was lost. Carmont and I continued to fight with the fierceness of despair, with Amacette between us. But Carmont was suddenly torn from the side of his love, his life, and hurled wildly into the crowd! A blow struck Amacette down—I saw the angel fall. All the furies of indignation and vengeance arose in my bosom! I rode on a whirlwind of rage—my sword drank the heart's-blood of her murderer. I flew wildly among the enemies—my blows must have been mortal—I saw a glittering battle ax blaze over my head—I remember no more till I awoke in prison.

CHAPTER XXV

Thus, madam, I have transcribed the leading features of my life. The picture is shocking to the eye of sensibility—it exhibits the strongest arguments I have heard or seen in favor of the doctrine of fatality. From the hour of my infancy, I appear to have been an engine, in the hands of a blind destiny, to produce a being unparalleled in vice, a victim of unavoidable misery. And I have often been inclined to murmur against the fiat of heaven as the author of my guilt, but reason dissolves the fallacy; my crimes were my own, perpetrated by my own agency, unprompted by the compulsion of fate, and the heavy hand of avenging justice has visited them with terrible, yet merited, punishment. While groaning under the load of my afflictions, I look back and behold their origin in the abandoned pursuits of my parents, and an unwarrantable indulgence of my own licentious passions, and dare not raise a complaint against the throne of providence.

My nature was organized for a nobler, a happier life, but it was blasted in its bud by an erroneous education.

Let the heedless youth attend to the eventful incident of my tale, and become alarmed by my example, and fly from the fascinating poison of juvenile dissipation. Let it terrify the coquette and the libertine, and all the wild votaries of fashionable vices, from their dangerous and destructive pursuits, to seek the enjoyment of serene and enlivening happiness, which can only be obtained in the practice of active virtue.

My mother and her imitative daughter are yet reveling in the exercise of all the malevolent passions. My father has died in despair, occasioned by the incestuous prostitution of his children, and the parricidal hand of his son.

Dawson is distracted, and his fatherless babe, and widowed Susan, are the inheritors of unavoidable misery.

Carmont is lost, and the dear affectionate Amacette lies bleeding on the field of battle.

Anderville is dead, and Emerine and her mother reserved for the utmost anxiety of grief.

Zerelda, the darling idol of my adoring soul, is torn from my ardent, longing and distracted bosom, and chained to misery and Barville, while I, in her, have lost all that a fond doting heart could desire—all that a warm glowing imagination could paint as lovely or delightful. All this has sprung from the blasting root of juvenile error, my heart wrung in agony in all its writhing shapes, in wasting the energy of its feelings. My mind has become the seat of incessant gloom, and my soul, without an object to endear it to time, is anxiously awaiting the moment when it will stretch the wing for eternity, and fly a broken penitent to the merciful bosom of the God that gave it being.

To you, madam, my heart feels a weight of obligations. I owe you what can never be discharged, and the only attempt I shall ever be able to make will be to acknowledge the unbounded nature of the debt. Although my future prospects are covered with midnight, and all the chords of pleasure are unstrung in my bosom, yet your benevolence has shot a faint ray along the dark horizon, and touched a trembling string to thrill with a soothing vibration. Yes, it is a beamy, pleasurable prospect to behold generosity still showering her blessings on the forlorn dwellings of misery. But am I deemed unworthy to know a resting place for my sensations of gratitude? My heart wanders around for the object of its thankful ejaculations. Gratitude is robbed of half its pleasures when it is inspired by an unknown being; its ardor weakens into volatility for a person unseen, a benefactress unknown. Then, madam, do not leave me in this condition—complete your noble work, let a fervent heart know and venerate its preserver, let it concenter all its energies in a grateful remembrance of its benefactress, and let my soul have at least a name to bear on its prayers to heaven.

* * *

I had been upwards of a week compiling this irregular sketch, during which time I had neither been visited by my mysterious benefactress nor the physician. I feared they had deserted me, but the second night after I had completed my labor, the physician procured an admission by a large bribe. I sealed up the manuscript, which he promised to deliver to my benefactress if practicable, but stated that he had not seen the stranger since she left the prison. He tarried with me a few moments, observing that the utmost caution was necessary, for I was more strictly guarded than any prisoner had ever been before.

When he was gone, I sank on my straw without employment, and consequently without hope. My lamp burned dimly, my mind was vacant, and I sank to sleep. My imagination wandered to the unknown stranger. She appeared before my fancy, the bright vision of divinity, arrayed in the rhapsody of enthusiasm. With the smile of heaven upon her lips she pressed them to mine, while my soul melted in adoring rapture. She clasped me in her arms; her countenance beamed ineffable majesty. The door of the prison burst open, and she bore me in her embrace to the sweetest fields of delightful enjoyment the pencil of fancy ever drew.

The reentrance of the physician broke my transporting vision at the moment when I had thrown my arms around her neck and riveted my lips to hers in an everlasting embrace. It was the first glimmer of delight I had long enjoyed, but now it faded in darkness, and I grasped in vain to hold the heavenly shadow as I awoke. The physician delivered me a packed from the lady and immediately withdrew.

I broke the seal and eagerly hastened to my lamp to read it; the light was dim, and in attempting to trim it, the lamp fell and was shattered to pieces. But my unconquerable anxiety to read the letter was so inordinate that I endeavored to arouse my surly keeper, and prevail on him to furnish me with a light, but he was either absent or asleep, for all my calling had no effect, and my great desires to

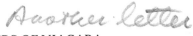

unfold this mysterious personage who haunted my fancy by day and night was compelled to remain ungratified.

Shortly after, the moon gliding from among a confused wild of clouds, I attempted to peruse the paper by the shower of beams that streamed through the window, but I had been there but a moment when a figure gradually arose on the outside of the casement, and, fixing on it a shuddering eye, I beheld the pallid features of Major Anderville. The letter fell from my hand. I shrank from the window and almost fell to the ground. A confused tremor of superstition and astonishment streamed coldly through my nerves—I banished the childish terror, and looking again at the window, the apparition had vanished. I again ventured to the window in shivering trepidation, but the terrific countenance was invisible. I recollected the music, and the majestic apparition that had appeared in the adjoining room, and thinking them over in conjunction with the present circumstance, I was led beyond the pale of mortality and lost in a visionary labyrinth of unknown being. The unaccountable conduct of this mysterious lady, the falling of the lamp at the moment I attempted to read her letter; the ghost of Anderville at the window when the moon would otherwise have afforded me light, all appeared to evince that ruler of superhuman events, forbid the reading of the paper, and operated on my long debilitated mind until I dare not glance my eyes around the room. But reason at last dispelled the illusive shadows, and I again took up the paper and attempted to read. The ghastly visage again glided in the light in the same alarming attitude. It fixed its eyes on me in a pale glare of horror. Its features appeared to dilate into an enormous size, and grin the dread image of death in a gaze of tremendous awe. I flew back in affright.

A confused rumor ran through the garrison. The bells rang violently—the alarm guns fired—a loud uproar of arms and shouts swelled in increasing tumult.

My prison door burst open. The physician rushed in. "We must fly," cried he. "I have horses—here are pistols, follow and defend yourself."

The commandant sprang into the prison at this instant. "You shall die," said the physician, holding a pistol at his breast, "you will betray us."

"I never betrayed a man who justly sought his liberty," replied the commandant. "I am come to fly with you; I will conduct you in safety; the garrison is stormed by the Americans, and there is no time to lose."

"But we fly to America," said the physician. "You will prevent us; move not at the peril of your life. Stranger, he must be confined."

"I am an American prisoner," said the other. "I have assumed this dress to lead you in security."

The physician doubted. I seized the arm of the sham commandant, took the dirk from his bosom, and observed, "You shall not move from my side, and the moment you show the least sign of treachery shall be your last. Doctor, lead the way."

The physician conducted us to a stable where horses were prepared for two, and he saddled another while I kept my arm locked in the stranger's.

The tumult became more alarming. The whole town was one confused uproar. Men, women, and children were flying and screaming in every direction. We hastened to the gate. The sentinels saw the dress of their commandant, and obeyed his orders, and we passed without interruption.

We mounted our horses. The physician conducted us on a trace the lead to the head of the Genesee, and we road all night without a pause. Next day we came to a village of Indians, but the dress of the commandant and physician were a sufficient protection, and they not only permitted us to pass, but when the commandant informed them he was going to command their British brothers in Pennsylvania, they furnished us with fresh horses and provisions. But we feared pursuit from the British garrison, and made no delay for several days and nights.

We were all strangers to each other, and seemed more concerned for arriving at a place of safety than inquiring into private histories, but both the physician and myself were desirious

232

to learn how our companion could assume the dress of the commandant without being discovered.

"Without the least difficulty," said he, after having informed us that his name was Bourbon. "I was taken captive in Virginia, and carried on board the ship in which the commandant sailed to Niagara. He became attached to me, and always kept me as a domestic. When he took command of the garrison, he continued me with him, whereby I was enabled to learn that there were several other American captives there, and several times thought of this plan for relieving them, but was heretofore prevented. But when the alarm was given by the Americans, the commandant was engaged in preparing for his defense, and I was enabled to procure this dress and put my plan in execution, had not this noble physician superceded me."

"Do you know the lady that lived with the commandant?" inquired I.

"I have frequently seen her," said Bourbon, "but she was kept very closely concealed.

"Was she the commandant's mistress?"

"It was so reported," he answered, "but I never saw anything improper in their connection. But she was so much confined that it was impossible, even for the servants, to learn much about her."

"Did she not live with him as a mistress in Halifax?" inquired the physician.

"I presume not," said Bourbon. "She was with him there, but I should imagine from her apparent innocence that there never had been any illicit connection between them."

"Let her conduct be as it will," replied I, "she is a most benevolent being. It is to her unexampled bounty that I owe my existence, and if I was to judge from her celestial air and form, I should almost fancy her to be too pure to be connected with any thing mortal, even in the most exalted ties. But I have a letter she has written, which I never have had a moment's time to peruse. I will now examine its contents, and we may learn something of the enigmatical woman."

He dropped the letter!

I felt for the paper, but it was gone. I had several times taken it out of my pocket, but had returned it again without an opportunity to examine it, and concluded I had unfortunately dropped it while putting it in my pocket. It would be madness to think of returning to search for it—and probably it contained nothing if I could find it. Thus I lost all my anxious hopes of learning the story of that unknown woman, who secret benevolence and affection had filled me with such interest and astonishment.

CHAPTER XXVI

The physician had become acquainted with my name, and inquired into my family. I informed him of the manner in which I had been rescued from the Indians, and he inquired, "What has become of your preserver?"

"I have never known him," I replied. "O, that that dear man had lived! I should have had a friend, a father."

"Blessed heaven!" cried he. "Then you have a friend—you have a father—I am Evermont!"

"You Evermont! My preserver! My father!" cried I, in a tumult of amazement.

"I am Evermont," repeated he, "who bore you from the Indians, gave you to Whitford, and then fell prey to that fate from which he had rescued you, and was torn from his all—his wife—his Amacette."

"Then you are my father," cried I, and fell on his neck in a transport.

After a warm but short embrace, his soul was drawn to its dearer objects. "O, my family!" he cried. "Do you know them? Do they live? My wife—my child?"

"Your wife is living," I replied, "but your daughter—"

"Is dead!" added he. "Hard fated Evermont—"

"She fell by my side," said I, "before the walls of Niagara, but her shade was appeased by the blood of her murderer."

"My precious babe! Ah, my son! I have lived to sorrow. I left my wife with my little Amacette in her arms, and went to hunt game in the surrounding forests. I was surprised and taken by the Indians. As they were carrying me to their camp, a party came in with a little babe, which they were about to destroy. I pled with them to spare its life, and they consented, but only for the purpose

235

of burning it with me the following day. But that night I exerted myself while they slept, and extricated myself from my chains, and escaped, bearing you off in safety. I returned to my house, but it was consumed to ashes, and my wife and child were gone. I feared that they were both destroyed by the Indians, but immediately went in search of them. Whitford was the first man I saw; he knew nothing of them but promised to take care of you until they were found. I left you with him, and renewed my painful, fearful search for all I loved, or prized beyond my life. But the Indians were still lurking in the country, and in a few hours I was surrounded and taken.

"It would be swelling my story beyond the limits of your patience, and living my calamities again, to repeat the particulars of my captivity.

"A thousand times I endeavored to escape, but failed a thousand times. I was carried to Chilicothe—to upper Canada—to lower Canada—to Nova Scotia, from whence I escaped and fled to Halifax, and was pressed on board a British ship of war, where I was kept until I acquired great skill in surgery, and by the recommendation of my captain, I was last fall appointed military surgeon for the garrison of Niagara, where the ship had come to anchor. My ardor to return to my country had continued to increase, but I was compelled to curb it while in the presence of the British, but the first opportunity I obtained was grasped with rapture, and that was when I came to your prison. I shall reach a land that will be free. I have lost my daughter, but she is praying for me in heaven. I have found my son and my wife. I cannot murmur, but rejoice. I will fly to my wife, and proclaim a jubilee of live and felicity."

He embraced me again, and shed the transparent tears of rapture on my cheek. Bourbon was delighted with the joy of his companions; he wept and rejoiced with us with the cordial sympathy of a friend.

I forgot my own solitary situation and enjoyed the present moment, unmingled with the past. My fancy flew to Hampshire to the meeting of Evermont and his wife. Their anticipated transports

236

of love, delight, and wonder filled my imagination, and I had no thought for pain.

We left the Indian camp where this happy discovery had been made, and hastened on our journey toward Pennsylvania. We beheld a large assembly of Indians at a small village on the head branches of the Allegheny, and when we drew near we perceived that they were about to sacrifice a prisoner they had lately taken. It was Dawson, the wretched husband of Susan. My crimes flashed upon my mind, and a torturing pang of conscience rang in my bosom, "This is thy work." The fire was prepared, and they were endeavoring to compel him to sing his death song, but he with a countenance haggard and wild, persisted in a sullen silence, notwithstanding all their efforts to force him to comply with their barbarous customs. We all hastened to the scene to prevent the catastrophe, and Bourbon, as commander of Niagara, proposed to ransom the prisoner, stating that he was anxious to exchange him with the Americans for some they had taken from the British armies. To this the Indians consented, more as a compliment to the commandant than for the sake of the ransom, and by this means the unhappy sufferer regained his liberty.

We conducted him beyond the village as a prisoner, without his knowing his fate was to be less severe with us than if he had remained with the Indians, but we now gave him to understand that we were his friends, and that he was at full liberty to return with us to his country. His transports were so vehement at the unexpected change that he shrieked and fainted away, and it was with considerable difficulty that we revived him.

When he had thoroughly recovered, he cast his eyes upon us in wonder, and now recognized the destroyer of his happiness. I expected to see his soul collected in anger, and his eyes flash the fire of rage, and I trembled at the fear of its effects. But how great was my astonishment when he flew and embraced me with silent rapture. I shuddered with the thought that his mind was deranged, but he recovered from his overpowering emotions, and exclaimed, "Where is my wife? My injured—my adored Susan?"

"Wherefore would you see her?" I replied. "Have you not discarded her?"

"She is innocent," he cried. "You were deceived. It was Emerald L— that you met at Cherry Vale, and not Susan. Here is her letter."

He gave me an anonymous letter, couched in these words:

"Your wife is innocent. You have been deceived by a man who was also the dupe of base artifices. A certain woman, to answer her own purposes, forged a note in the name of Susan Etherford and sent it to Evermont, requesting him to meet her at Cherry Vale late at night. He came, she was veiled, and they passed that, and several succeeding nights together, Evermont believing all the time that he was with your wife, whom he did not know was married, as the first night was the night of your union. This occasioned the mistake in Evermont, and induced him to write in the manner he did at the time he was leaving Richmond. This statement is the truth. Your wife is virtuous; receive her to your favor, and live in unsuspecting happiness."

"After I left you in Bath," said Dawson, "I received that letter, and was at a loss whether to credit it or not until I had shown it to several of my acquaintances who knew the writing of Emerald L— and declared it to be hers, and stated many circumstances of Emerald's attachment to you, and your deserting her, which induced me to give full credit to the letter and fly in search of my wife. I traced her to the frontiers of Virginia, where I was taken prisoner by the Indians, and although I return to Virginia, alas, I know not where I shall find the source of all my sorrow and happiness, who must long before this have been a mother."

I instantly informed him of her situation, and when his transports subsided, I showed him the note I had received.

"It is not the writing of Susan," said he. "It is Emerald's hand." When we compared the two papers together, they were both in one handwriting. "This is sufficient," cried he. "I am again a husband, and transporting thought, a father."

238

THE PRISONERS OF NIAGARA

And now with the impatient ardor, and happy prospects of Evermont and Dawson for an additional stimulus to rapidity, we passed swiftly on our rugged way until we were at Bedford Inn, Pennsylvania.

But the dream of pleasure, which those late events had occasioned, I was here to be awakened into far more powerful emotions. For Bourbon was searching in his pocket for some papers, and among the rest discovered the packet I imagined I had lost in the wilderness.

"This is yours," said he. "It has by some means fallen among my papers, I suppose in the hurry and confusion of our journey."

Enraptured at the unexpected discovery, and eager to gratify an unconquerable curiosity to know my benefactress, I opened the manuscript, and began—it was the writing of Zerelda. I became almost incapable of reading or thinking in a boundless expansion of stupefying thought, but recovering, I perused it with unexampled avidity, but with a tremulous anticipation of horror.

She began at the moment I fled the marriage scene, and proceeded:

"When the parson read the ceremony that was to deprive me of Evermont and happiness, the most alarming images were floating in my imagination. Grief had driven me to the gloomy edge of insanity, and the horrible chimeras of a delirium were tantalizing and tormenting the faint remains of sensibility that yet agitated my bosom. When Barville took my hand, I fancied it was the fiery touch of a dragon whose intention was to drag me down to the unbottomed abyss of everlasting woe. I imagined I beheld the awful gulf, rolling open its flaming jaws in a tremendous chasm to receive me. The terrific scene overcame the enervated powers of my body and mind—I sank affrighted, and fell in the arms of Emerine.

"Recollection never revived, except in the bewildered dreams of a fevered imagination, until five days had passed away. I awoke from a long train of terrifying visions, which yet hung in portentous aspect upon my recoiling memory.

"Emerine was with me, and strove to calm the apparent agitation of my feelings. She assisted me to rise, and led me into the refreshing atmosphere of the garden, and measurably restored my mind to a state of dreary reflection.

"She informed me that after the marriage had been interrupted by my delirium, that Barville had become violently irritated, and resolved to leave the house immediately, and ordered his horses for instant departure. But Mrs. Willford, after a long private conference, prevailed upon him to abandon his design, and it was immediately given out that he had discarded the thought of marrying me, and intended wedding Armilda. This strange unaccountable change was reduced to certainty, and the next day was appointed for the consummation of the nuptials.

"This intelligence awakened a suggestion that by my unpardonable weakness, I had broken my vows to my father, which lacerated my feelings with a new scourge of scorpion reflections that stung my bosom with the dread image of sacrilegious perjury. I leaned on Emerine and wept—but from this painful extremity of agony my sensibility was awakened and driven into a far different channel. Willford met us in the garden, and addressing herself to me, observed, in a tone of imperious severity, 'Well, miss, what have you to allege for your deviation from your father's command? How will you justify your treatment to Mr. Barville?'

'I am not accountable to you for my conduct,' said I, 'and I desire you will give yourself no concern about it.'

'No impudence, miss,' retorted she. 'I will teach you to behave with more respect when in my presence, and let you know you are, and shall be accountable to me for your conduct, so long as you continue in my house.'

'Mrs. Willford,' replied I, 'I wish no altercation with you, and particularly at this period, but you must know, you are not to assume the tone of a mistress, nor exercise an authority which belongs to another.'

'O dear,' cried she, with a tone of satisfaction, 'you will soon know to whom authority belongs. Assume the tone of mistress, indeed. Yes, madam, I am the mistress of all these domains, and if you expect to continue here any longer, you must alter your behavior infinitely for the better, for I shall allow no impertinent flirts about me, I assure you.'

'Madam, you grow arrogant,' replied I. 'Who gave you authority? Who made you mistress of those domains?'

'Your father, child,' answered she, with a smile of contumely. 'He wisely disposed of all he left behind to those who were most affectionate to him while he was living. If you dispute my word, here is his will, duly authenticated.'

She handed it to us in malicious triumph.

We looked and beheld my father's signature, attested by his steward and two clerks, and all his estate bequeathed to Willford, in trust for Armilda, who was acknowledged to be his daughter.

Astonished at such conduct in my father, I exclaimed that it was a forgery.

'We'll see to that,' said Willford contemptuously, 'but since you cannot conduct yourself with propriety in the house of a stranger, you will make use of the earliest opportunity to provide some other lodgings.'

'The house of a stranger,' repeated I with scorn. 'I do not wish to remain a moment where either you or your daughter have the slightest claim, however detestably it has been procured,' and immediately turned away, and walked with Emerine to the summer house where we pondered on these mysterious proceedings of my father.

"From the unlimited influence which Willford possessed over his mind, I doubted not that the will was authentic, but trembled at the belief that Armilda was his daughter. This readily accounted for his anxiety that I should marry Barville, whereby he would secure to me the possession of affluence of which he had deprived me by the disposition of his own fortune.

"This was a melancholy reflection: that I, who had never indulged a thought but tenderness and affection for him, and had resigned myself to misery at his solicitation, should be entirely disinherited, and reduced by him to penury and dependence, and an

241

almost incalculable estate bestowed upon the child of his errors who had never felt the warm delight of one filial feeling.

"It was truly mortifying to behold myself an orphan, a stranger in my father's house, an outcast from the fortune of my ancestors, and at the same time to reflect that this fortune was transferred by a father to my detestable enemies, who would rejoice in being able to triumph over my poverty and supposed degradation. But my anguish for the loss of fortune, and from the insults of Willford and her daughter, was amply counterpoised by my happy deliverance from a dreadful marriage. For I considered myself released from the promise I had made my father since Barville had refused to fulfill the engagement, and that I was now at full liberty to indulge the ardent anxiety of my doting bosom in a union with felicity and Evermont.

"It was true I could bring nothing to the arms of my beloved but my solitary person, and a soul, glowing and expanded, with the ethereal fire and unbounded fondness of a heavenly affection; yet, with only those I knew the noble, the benevolent, the adorable Evermont would be contented, and grant me, naked as I was, a celestial seat in his generous bosom, in which sweet and precious paradise the poor discarded Zerelda would become an heiress to the blest inheritance of blissful embraces.

"Evermont had departed in an overwhelming transport of grief; I knew not whither he might be hurled by the dire tornados of disastrous fate, but so powerful were the rising beams of benighted expectation that every desire seemed practicable, and so strong were the enkindling anxieties of suppressed anticipation that to find you I would have flown over every clime from the burning equinox to the frozen zones.

"Departed hope awakened into living raptures; the morning sun of joy burst over the dark horizon of woe; my heart bounded from the deadly grasp of benumbing sorrow to the happy freedom of enlivening ecstacy; my bosom hurled the fierce tyrant despair from his throne, and swelled into a wide, unconquerable desire for illimitable enjoyment; my soul, shaking off the shackles of a dreadful destiny, rose from beneath an intolerable weight of calamity, caught on fire by the enkindling spirit of Evermont's attachment, and unfolding the pinions of affections, winged from misery to Elysium.

"With this flow of feeling, I returned with Emerine to my room, resolving to leave Engleton seat in the morning, and return to Haylard Village. I met the disgusting Armilda in the passage. She brushed by me with a supercilious smile of envious contumely. I blushed and trembled at the thought that she was my sister.

"Barville was visited by several suspicious characters, with whom he held long and mysterious conferences, but their design was unknown until late in the evening. Emerine, who had been passing through the house, overhead their private discourse, and came running into my room and informed me that Barville was a British officer, and was now appointed commandant of the garrison at Fort Niagara, and intended to set out in the morning to take the command, and that he intended to abandon his marriage with Armilda, and hinted to his companions that he had already triumphed over her virtue. After hearing this conversation, Emerine tarried till the company broke up, and observed Barville steal across the passage and ascend to Armilda's chamber, where he was received by a woman in loose undress. I was alarmed at this intelligence, and shocked at the conduct of Armilda, and exclaimed, "She, my sister! O heaven!", but my mind was too deeply affected with other reflections to give those a serious attention, and I was preparing to go to bed. Emerine had retired to the adjoining chamber when Mrs. Willford's woman came up with a request for me to go to Mrs. Willford, who she said was taken sick in the servant's hall. I followed her without thinking of danger, but when I had stepped out of the house, I was seized by three men, who immediately forced open my mouth with a sharp instrument of iron so that I was incapable of raising the slightest sound, and in that condition I was hurried into a carriage, which drove off with the utmost rapidity.

"At daybreak, I was taken from the carriage and conducted on horseback through an uninhabited country into North Carolina, and there conveyed in a close carriage until they reached the seacoast, where I was put on board a vessel bound for Lake Ontario.

"Barville was at the head of the ruffians by whom I was conveyed, and treated me with some kind of respect and civility, but I found that arguments and entreaties were unavailing, and escape impracticable, and fixed my only hope on that providence who is able to deliver us from the most dark and alarming dangers, where hope starts affrighted, and expectation shudders.

"Barville fell sick, and the vessel arrived at Fort Niagara, before I was tortured with his expected importunities. He still continued unwell, and I endured no persecution except that of being shut up in a narrow room, and visited by no person except a British servant.

"After many endeavors and a seasonable bribe, I had the good fortune to prevail on my youthful keeper to set me at liberty at midnight, when all the house and town was at rest. But my liberty was unavailing, for I was unable to escape to my country. I expected some of the Americans were confined in the prison, and with the hope of relieving their sufferings, and of probably procuring some assistance myself, I obtained the consent of my guard to pay them a visit. But he insisted on my being veiled, and his being permitted to accompany me. The keeper informed me of your miserable condition, and I prevailed upon my guard to conduct me to a baker's, where I procured some food and wine, and by committing a crime I tremble to name, but which I hope was cancelled by the purity of the intention, by forging an order from the commandant, I obtained admission. But how was I shocked and amazed when I beheld my Evermont an inhabitant of that dreary dungeon. My mind was unable for the unexpected discovery; your languid look, your sickly, despairing features, convinced me that your mind was incapable of hearing that your visitor was Zerelda, and I hastened from the prison to indulge the emotions and reflections which this melancholy circumstance excited.

"After I left your prison, I considered the extreme danger of revealing to you my perilous situation. I feared the ardor of your spirits, the debility of your constitution, and the impossibility of

244

your escape, would drive you to desperation. I was alarmed, also, lest Barville should know his fortunate rival was in his power, and when I visited you again, I shrouded myself and disguised my voice so that it would be impossible I should be recognized.

"By the lenity of my attendant I was afterwards enabled to visit you and procure you the medical assistance I have done. How sweet was the hope of recovering you from your sickness and imprisonment! How sacred the tender office of administering to your wants—it was an office that would have delighted angels! O how I longed to rush into your arms, to fold you to my aching bosom, to embrace your pallid cheeks into life. My soul quivered in every pulse of your heart, my breath hung trembling on yours, I would have sat on your bed of straw and rested your fainting head on my bosom; I would have taught the languishing lamp of life to glow with hope, and smiled the balm of consolation into your soul, but stern necessity forbid, and I could only sigh, and long, and pray, for your recovery, your escape, and your embraces.

"I rejoiced in mutual delight with the angels of mercy when it pleased the eternal disposer to shed the blooming blessings of health on the darling cherub, the dear lord of my longing bosom.

"My mind was now exercised in the invention of some plan to divert your attention from your gloomy situation. My first resolve was to arouse your imagination by leading it into the wild fields of superstition, knowing that to an ardent fancy like yours, a few apparent supernatural appearances, although they would not induce a belief in apparitions, yet they would lead you into extensive regions of speculation, and prevent your mind from brooding over its misfortunes, and becoming desperate with the cold languor of torpid woe. For this purpose, I procured a lanthorn which would conceal its light in an instant, and by this means appeared to vanish from your dark prison in a thought, and also raised the music and light which so much alarmed you in the room adjoining your prison.

"But also! Evermont, my destiny is verging to an awful crisis. Barville has recovered, and paid me several visits. He discovered the treachery of my guard, and has dismissed him, and keeps the

key of the prison himself. He has frequently entreated and
threatened, and is so very brutal in his manners, that I dread the
worst. He has given me until tomorrow, and sworn with the most
terrible oaths, that I shall then consent, or be compelled into his
measures. My case is desperate—my room is narrow, my
persecutor exasperated by delay, his servants the absolute
instruments of his will, and escape impracticable if the destined
period arrives; my only hope is in Evermont or death.

"The servant has this moment procured a false key for my door,
and handed me your manuscript. I give him this to be conveyed to
you by our friend the physician. At two o'clock I will again be at
liberty, and will unlock your dungeon, and you must *once more*
bear me home or before another day shall close I shall be no more.
Evermont alone has courage and power to execute this dangerous
enterprise, and in you alone I hope. O Evermont! Remember the
long wilderness of Muskingum! Remember the cliffs of the
Allegheny! Let them inspire your noble intrepidity to save your
Zerelda, and bear her through the dreary desert to the bright fields
of your uninterrupted embraces."

Judge you, to whom nature has imparted the soul of sensibility,
with what sensations I closed this tale. My soul "strays—o'er—the
past,/ In quest of wretchedness, perversely strays,/ And finds all
desert now—" The mysterious vision of my Niagara slumbers,
which had so often wrapped me in the world of wonder, was now
unveiled with a dreadful interpretation—Zerelda relieved from a
tyrannical marriage, robbed of her fortune, driven from her home,
was there plunged into a calamity more terrible, but one which had
enabled her to snatch her Evermont from the grasp of meager
famine and ghastly disease, but only to leave her in the hour of
dread to meet alone the hideous storms of impending horror.

Thought rushed back to my dungeon. I beheld her approach the
door—joy lightened from her countenance with the delightful
anticipation of giving me liberty and love. She opened the
door—she looked within—I was flown—a damp frozen chaos of
"*void and darkness*" fell with shivering tremor on her feelings—a

246

desolated wild of blasted hope stretched throughout the universe before her—despair flashed on her soul, and crushed it to "woe's wide empire," where "Threatening fate wide opens to devour."

"God of eternal justice," I exclaimed, "why am I reserved for this! Why was Zerelda rendered accessible to my affection to be thus torn from me by a fearful doom? Why was she placed within my reach? Why the preserver of my existence? To lose me at the moment she implored and expected my assistance? Why did the lamp fall? Why did Anderville's ghost appear? And why, o my friends, did you give me liberty to plunge me into this dreadful abyss? Fate! Dark monster! This is thy distracting work—blind, tormenting destiny, the deed is thine!"

My friends were alarmed. Evermont caught me by the arm. Bourbon shuddered and left the room.

"But I will again retrace the desert," continued I. "I will scale the walls of Niagara, and blast the wretch that would touch Zerelda."

"My son, you are distracted," cried Evermont. "Is she not the woman you imagined a mistress?"

"A mistress—Zerelda a mistress—she is the breath of angels—I would risk an eternity on the innocence of her smiles."

"Then think of the danger, the impossibility," resumed he.

"Impossibility—and Zerelda in danger—I'd fly through Lybia's fiery wilds—I'd scale the arctic mountains of ice, or rush into the boiling basin of Aetna to save Zerelda, or avenge her death! What are the engines of torture, the apparatus of horror, the yelling legions of death when my life is lost, and love transported to madness? I'll go this instant if then thousand deaths oppose."

"Think of her letter," cried he, "her fate is already decided."

"I will then avenge her death," cried I. "O Zerelda! Bright emanation of divinity! What a lamentable tragedy has been thy life and death! But I will witness the doleful close of thy sorrows! At thy shrine I will receive the ethereal embraces of thy spirit! My tears shall water the grass that shades thy faded eye. "There my soul shall cease its sighing,/ There my last sad groan shall ring." There will I shed this load of clay, an offering on thy urn. Our

Joy! It's Zerelda!

bodies shall embrace in death; the last trump shall awaken them in each other's arms. Zerelda bids me die—"

"Zerelda bids you live!" cried a voice. The door flew open—and—not Bourbon—but o ye heavens! Zerelda! We flew to each other, we pressed our bosoms together, our arms strained around our waists. Enjoyment sank in wonder and delight, but arose in a bright path of undescribable emotion. Silent raptures, spoken with love's blessed eloquence, flowed in a temporary heaven. A soul was leaping, feeling, and enjoying in every pore of our bodies. Of objects besides ourselves, we neither knew, nor thought, nor dreamed—all, all was here, in one exhaustless ebullition of felicity.

It was long before memory knew whether we were in time or eternity; all our powers were drawn into this feast of souls, and wrapped up, and lost in each other.

Zerelda, the best prepared for this entertainment of love, was soonest capable of recollection, and with a look bright in the majesty of smiles, observed, "Will this repay the suspense I have occasioned?"

I caught the last word, ere it left the melting ardor of her lips, with a sweet embrace, and replied, "One moment here cancels the life that's past, but my soul has too much joy for thought," and drew her still closer to my bosom.

"When the alarm was raised in Niagara," continued she, "my former guard opened my door, and procured me the commandant's dress, but would not fly with me. I flew to the prison, and you know the manner of our escape. To have discovered myself at that time would have curtailed the happiness of meeting; in the wilderness, it would have been the same; and once when you slept, my letter fell from your packet, I took it up, and resolved you should know nothing of Zerelda until you were out of danger. The name of Bourbon you know is a part of my true name, in honor to my mother, and the statement I gave of myself was a correct outline of my captivity. But the most powerful motive which urged this concealment was your suspicions of the woman who attended you in prison, and I determined never to be known as Zerelda while the slightest shade of suspicion rested on my character."

"Are not your fears removed by this?" said I, straining her bosom to my heart.

"O yes," cried she, "I will thus hold you in my arms forever."

Evermont and Dawson stood by in wonder and sympathetic delight.

A number of citizens were crowding round the door. I heard the cry of "Tories!" "*Tories*" was repeated in a tumult of voices. The magistrates broke into the room, and ordered us to be seized by the sheriff. We began to expostulate, but were immediately in the custody of the officers. I held my arm around Zerelda, who was trembling with apprehension, and endeavored to prevail on the officers to hear my explanation, but the room soon filled with a mob of citizens, all crying in confusion:

"Drag them to jail!"

"To the gallows!"

"Hang them!"

"Butcher them!"

Zerelda fainted at the alarming sounds. I drew my sword.

"Stand back citizens," cried I, "the peace of this woman shall not be interrupted."

I took her up in my arms, and waving my sword, made a passage into the other room, where I placed her on a bed, and called the landlady to her assistance. I then returned to the officers. Evermont and Dawson were in custody, and the cries of "tory" and "liberty" shouted around them. I raised my sword and commanded silence.

"Citizens of Bedford, hear me!"

"Knock him down!"

"Break his head!"

"A traitor! A traitor!" they all exclaimed in confusion.

At last the magistrates interposed, and procured a moment's silence, and I explained our situation, our captivity, and escape. Murmurs ran through the crowd:

"'Tis false."

"'Tis a mere trick—away with them."

"To prison!"

"To the gallows!"

"Huzza for liberty!"

"You must submit," cried a magistrate. "We will hear you when the tumult subsides."

I laid down my sword observing, "I will go with you to prison, but I will not be fettered."

An officer took my arm and dragged me with the others into the streets. A louder tumult was heard at a distance. The town resounded with uproar. A hundred voices swelled in unintelligible shouts. They approached nearer, but all was clamor and confusion—some were rejoicing, others execrating. When they drew near, a hundred acclamations burst:

"Niagara is taken! Huzza! Huzza! Behold the patriots! The conquerors!"

In an instant, Anderville and Carmont were hoisted on the shoulders of the crowd. They beheld me—the crowd divided before them, and they, accompanied by Amacette, rushed to my embraces. I clasped them all at once, and was wrapped in their salutations, while the uproar was stunned into silent astonishment. I turned my arms to Anderville, to Carmont, to Amacette, and alternately clasped them with a joy indescribable. The first transport subsided. I beheld Evermont and Dawson yet with the officers. I withdrew my arms from Anderville and Carmont, held Amacette with one hand, and took the hand of Evermont with the other, and said, "Amacette, your father!"

"My babe, my Amacette!" exclaimed he, extending his arms, and she sank wondering upon his breast.

"My preserver!" cried Anderville, and ran to embrace Evermont.

A noise in the crowd attracted my eyes. Zerelda was running from the inn. Her majestic form appeared to fly through the air, her drapery flowed in undulations, and her long loose hair floated in streams on the wind. I burst through the parting crowd, my arms extended. She darted to my breast, and exclaimed, "I have you again," and sank out of breath. She recovered. Her eyes were fixed on me. They then wandered around. She saw and was seen by

Amacette—they both uttered an exclamation, and Amacette loosed from her father's arms and flew into Zerelda's which were stretched to receive her. Zerelda beheld Carmont and Anderville and extended a hand to each while Amacette hung on her neck. We separated from the crowd, who became otherwise engaged, and with one of Zerelda's hands pressed in mine, and the other in Anderville's, and Amacette led between her father and her lover, we returned a happy group to the inn, accompanied by Dawson, who was now made acquainted with the circle of friends.

When we were seated, the wonder of each other's existence engrossed our whole attention.

"How is it possible," said I to Amacette, "that you are here? I saw you slain by my side."

"I was only wounded," said she, "and carried with the rest of the prisoners to the door of the dungeon, where the inspector, who was carelessly looking at the wounded, discovered a part of my vest unbuttoned. He immediately ordered me to his house, and I found myself in the power of Whitford. Her ordered his women to clothe me in a female dress, and sent for a surgeon, and this kind man, my father, came to attend on me. He was a father to me, and cured my wound, but when he pronounced me well, Whitford commenced the dreadful intention of his heart. He pled, and threatened, and exerted partial force for two days, but on that memorable night, he resolved that his wishes should no longer be thwarted. He broke into my room at midnight with his servants. I had not undressed, and attempted to spring out of my bed, but he prevented me, and catching me in his arms, threw me back, while his servants confined my arms.

"The alarm guns sounded. A servant rushed to the door: 'Master, master, the garrison is taken.' 'Confusion!' roared he, 'if ten thousand garrisons were taken, I will have my will,' and furiously grasped my bosom while the servants were confining my hands to the posts of the bed. A clattering of arms rang around the door, and he became maniacally desperate on his abominable purpose, and in a moment more—

"But the house was in confusion. My door was assailed, and while Whitford flew to defend it, I had time to loose my hand and adjust my dress. The house shook to its foundation, the door burst with a crash, and Carmont! Carmont entered!"

"O happy entrance!" cried Carmont. "I had been seized in prison while I was asleep. My friend Evermont was raving in a fever and unable to assist me, but while the soldiers were confining my hands, I seized one of their swords and laid one of them bleeding on the floor, but I was overpowered and dragged from the prison.

"They carried me by the house of the inspector, where I heard and recognized the voice of Amacette. I heard her repeat my name, and was dreadfully convinced she was in the power of Whitford. My feelings were awful, but I was not permitted to indulge them, for I was instantly dragged on board a ship, where I found thirty fellow sufferers in chains. The ship set sail, and as soon as we left the shore, our fetters were taken off, and we were put under a close guard. We had been three days under sail when, by a private consultation, we devised a plan for seizing on the crew and obtaining our liberty. At a moment when our guard had carelessly opened our door, we flew to the armory, where, after procuring arms, we left two to guard the door, and the rest of us seized the captain and mate. The crew were in disorder. I held a pistol at the captain's breast, and commanded him to surrender the ship or I would take his life. He immediately submitted, and ordered his men to cease their opposition. We secured the crew, and being now masters, I prevailed upon my comrades to return with me and take the garrison of Niagara by surprise. They had all been prisoners there, and most cruelly treated, and readily consented to take revenge on their enemies.

"We came to anchor before the fort. Late in the night, and leaving five of our company to guard the ship, the remaining twenty six dressed ourselves in the British uniform, deceived the sentinels, and gained admittance into the garrison. But we had scarcely entered before an alarm sounded from the ship. The crew had broken loose, and our five companions came firing to the fort. The gate was not shut, and they rushed in also, but the alarm was instantly sounded throughout the garrison. The utmost expedition was necessary. We divided into two parties, one of which hastened to the prison, while I led the others to the inspectors. A confused band of soldiers and citizens were at the door, but we forced our way through them, and relieved Amacette. We then hastened to meet our brethren at the prison, dispersing on every side the tumultuous throngs of terrified citizens, and met them at the southern gate with the noble Major Anderville at their head. How he came there he can best inform you, and also in what manner we effected our escape."

"How I gained my life," said Anderville, "after it was supposed to be lost, I know not. It is to this generous physician I owe my existence."

"I was examining the dead bodies of the prisoners," said Evermont, "to procure one for purposes in anatomy, and while I was making this search, I heard this officer groan. I immediately selected him and had him conveyed carefully to my house, where I secretly brought him to life, and with proper medical attention restored him to health. It was dangerous to conceal him any longer, and on the night I left Niagara, I procured him a British soldier's uniform, and a passport to make his escape. He has a heart that knows how to be grateful, and his numerous thanks when we parted made me ashamed that I had never done greater services for such men."

"Could a man be otherwise than grateful for his life?" cried Anderville. "When I thus obtained my own liberty, I immediately sought to liberate my friends in prison, but when I came to the window of the dungeon, all was dark within. I heard the keeper's voice, and afraid of being discovered, I removed out of the light of the moon, but when I was about to call, the approach of some person alarmed me away the second time. I waited, and observed some persons going from the prison, and by the light of the moon discovered the dress of the commandant, but he and the others passed hastily out of my sight, and the alarm which had been raised at the other end of town drew near. I rushed to the door of the

Tar & feathered out
and ridden
on a rail.

THE PRISONERS OF NIAGARA

prison; it was open. I entered, and immediately our friends, the
soldiers, reached the door, and thinking me a prisoner, hailed me
with liberty, and asked me if there were no others. I imagined the
commandant had just led some from the prison, and told them there
were prisoners in his house. They followed me there with
acclamations. We were violently opposed by the soldiery around
the door, but forced a passage through, and ransacked the house,
but found no prisoners. We secured the commandant, and,
overpowering his soldiers, hastened to the gate where we expected
our brethren. When they arrived with the inspector, we abandoned a
thought of inflicting further injury on the garrison, for the ship's
crew had arrived, and a firm body of soldiers were composed at the
other end of town, which would have rendered a contest dangerous
and flight probably impossible. We collected all the horses we
could find in the military and private stables, and began our flight
through the wilderness.

"We kept the commandant and inspector silent, and readily
induced the Indians to believe we were British soldiers, marching to
take Pennsylvania. They seemed delighted at the thought, and
informed us our commander and his friends were just before. Those
we expected were some Americans in disguise, and hastened to
overtake them. We followed them to this town and suppose you
must have been the company."

We assured him we were, and also related the manner of our
escape.

"What have you done with the commandant and inspector?"
inquired Evermont.

"Behold them," said Carmont, looking from the window.

Our attention was immediately called to a wild mob of men,
women, and children who were crowding around the commandant
and inspector, whom they had stripped and arrayed in tar and
feathers, and now confining each astride a separate pole, which
they raised as high as their arms could extend, and sounding a
clamor of drums, fifes, and other instruments, marched with them
along the streets of Bedford. It was impossible to refrain from
laughter at the odd group which swelled at every moment. The men

sounded their trumpets and horns, the boys rang the bells, the women beat ladles, kettles, and frying pans, and all throwing their hats and bonnets into the air, raised a thundering shout, "Hurrah! Hurrah!" for the traitors. This ludicrous parade marched up and down the street until they were thoroughly fatigued with their amusement. They then marched their guests to the common prison, where they remained until the proclamation of liberty when they were liberated to live the execration of every true American.

CHAPTER XXVII

Night gave repose to the town. The citizens retired to their houses, and the soldiers who accompanied Anderville and Carmont, after taking an animated farewell of their leaders, dispersed to return to their several homes and families.

Our company of friends were now possessed of happiness too pure to be interrupted by the temporary mirth and confusion of the town, but a shade was thrown over our prospects by a preceding part of Anderville's story.

He stated that he left the army for a few weeks and visited Hayland Village. Emerine was with Zerelda at Engleton seat; he hastened thither, and was informed that both Emerine and Zerelda had departed the preceding night, and no person knew whither they were gone. He inquired for them in vain, returned to Hayland Village, but they were not there. He used the utmost exertions to find them, of which his permission of absence would admit, but to no purpose, and was compelled to return to the army. He was then ordered on a winter expedition against the Indians, and having defeated several parties and pursued them over the Genesee River, he was cut off from the main body of his soldiers by a sudden rise in the waters, and the Indians coming upon him before he could collect his troops into action, he was compelled to fly toward Fort Niagara, where the dreadful disaster took place which has already been related.

The unknown fate of Emerine damped the ardor of our happiness, and we separated to enjoy a night of repose, and hasten early in the morning to our friends in Hampshire.

Soon after I had arisen in the morning, Zerelda met me in the passage with a smile of significant rapture.

256

"I have read your manuscript," said she, laying her hand upon my shoulder, "and find that you have new claims to my affections. Besides, I discover you are almost my relation—you are the heir of my uncle Valindon."

"Valindon," repeated I, "was Valindon your uncle?"

"He married my aunt Emerine Engleton," replied she.

"And who possesses his estate?" inquired I.

"The Willfords," she replied. "It descended to my father on the death of my uncle's family, and was by him transferred to the Willfords in the manner I heretofore related."

"Then, alas, it is gone!" cried I. "I would glory in tearing it from the usurpers and laying it at the feet of the rightful inheritor, but as Willford is the only channel through which my claim can be established, we have nothing to hope, and we must patiently bear the mortification of seeing our vilest enemies feed their voluptuous revels with a fortune unquestionably ours.

"But, my dearest Zerelda, you have read the volumes of my guilt. Dare you trust your heart and happiness to such a child of infamy, such a monster of depravity as I?"

"You have been unfortunate," replied she, "but your birth is an honor to the human name, that such merit, such innate nobility, should arise from so low an origin. O Evermont! I love you more dearly on account of your humble parentage because I love you for yourself.

"Your crimes, had they been intentional, would be awful, but they were committed through mistake, and without the more distant intention, and you have been sincerely afflicted and have sincerely repented for them. I doubt not they are now blotted from the register of heaven, and if God can forgive, shall not frail man? You have lived a life of misery, and it shall now be my only joy to lead you from the past through a futurity of smiles."

The rest of our company assembled, and we sent our for Hampshire immediately.

When we arrived at Haylard Village, Mrs. Haylard was gone to visit the medical springs in Bath, for the late misfortunes in her family had so far preyed upon her delicate state of health as to produce a rapid progress of her debility, but we found Mrs. Holbert, Amacette, and Susan in possession of the mansion, and enjoyed an inexpressible felicity in our meeting. Dawson embraced, and explained the cause of his happiness to his delighted wife. Amacette led her father to the arms of her mother.

After unrestrained joy had given place to the calm of pleasure, we related our various adventures, and were informed of the situation of Mrs. Haylard and Emerine.

Emerine was accused by Mrs. Willford, the morning after Zerelda was forced from Engleton seat, of being accessory to her elopement, and a principal agent in preventing Barville from marrying Armilda. By way of punishment, she locked her up in her room, and when Anderville called to see her, denied that she was there. This was the cause of Anderville's unhappiness in the prison of Niagara when I supposed him dying, and this was the only misfortune that resulted from the violence of Willford, for she perceived in a few days that her proceedings were unwarrantable, and permitted Emerine to return to her mother, with whom she was now going to attend the Bath springs.

These happy consummations of joy to a part, and bright prospects of felicity to the others, made our whole company too enraptured for a thought of unhappiness, and to complete our enjoyments, Evermont sent for a parson immediately, and had the long neglected rite performed in a reunion with his wife.

While our spirits were thus exhilarated, while our present delights and anticipated prospects swelled all our animation to glow and throb around our hearts, and while all the fond desires looked out from the doting bosom on its darling object, Carmont pressed his Amacette to the completion of their wishes. Amacette was warm with anticipations, but the timid fears of virgin delicacy glowed on her cheeks, half willing, half afraid. Zerelda was sitting by her; she united in the request of Carmont, and pressed Amacette to his embraces, and while his warm lip rested on her cheek, she blushed and acknowledged that she was his, and they were that evening united in that delightful union "where soul with soul in mingling rapture blends."

258

In the morning, our attention was turned to our various desires. Dawson and his Susan took their leave in a transport of tears and raptures, and returned to their former dwelling, near Richmond, where they continue to live, forgetful of their misfortune, in a firm union of love and happiness.

Evermont possessed an estate in Amherst, which, though formerly overrun by the Indians, was now adequate to the wants of both himself and Carmont. He resolved immediately to repair and stock it, and whither he removed with his fortunate children in a few weeks, where they still enjoy a competence unknown to want, and a calm of happiness unknown to sorrow.

Anderville, Zerelda, and I parted with them this morning, and hastened to meet our friends in Bath.

***

Our road passed to Bath in sight of Engleton seat. The mansion of her father caught the eye of Zerelda; she looked, and sighed, and burst into tears. I was unable to afford her any consolation, for the image of my prostituted mother, my incestuous sister, my felonious, murdered father, all came upon my mind in a tempest of darkness. I shrank and shuddered. My crimes rolled their blackest features to my mind, and overclouded all the expected bliss of my bosom. Even the anticipated possession of the loveliest woman could give my bosom no relief, nor shed a ray to illumine the heavy gloom that overhung my heart.

Anderville beheld our situation, and strove to arrest the progress of somber reflections by calling our attention to scenes of joy, but our feelings had sunk too deep in the abyss of sorrow to be immediately recalled.

A carriage with splendid equipage drove by us, and on looking within we beheld Willford and Armilda. A hectic of mortification trembled on the cheek of Zerelda, and she instantly became pale and melancholy. I was involuntarily thrown into an attitude of rage and indignation, but it immediately subsided into a torpid anguish. Anderville caught the baleful contagion, and we were all in a state

259

of silent inquietude until we were aroused by the presence of Mrs. Haylard and Emerine.

We were embraced, again and again, with that transporting ardor that flows from feeling bosoms in the highest possible state of astonishment and rapture. Such a scene was too congenial to the wishes of Zerelda and myself not to remove us from every sorrow, and give us every desire, in at least a momentary ecstasy, and we became the children of joy. The blush of delight on the cheeks of Emerine at meeting Anderville discovered that he had a pleasing friend in her bosom, and convinced his penetrating affections that he also might yet be happy.

Mutual explanations of our several sufferings were imparted, and the sorrows of the past gave a sweetening zest to our present felicity. We passed the first hours as joyous as the possession of glowing friends and unmingled affections could render us.

At my earnest request Zerelda produced the transcript of my life, which I had transmitted to her in Niagara, and we read it over, alternately smiling, weeping, and shuddering. They were amazed at the enormity of my crimes, and deeply affected with my anguish and contrition, and united all their efforts to banish their influence from my memory.

"Yours has been an eventful life," said Mrs. Haylard. "Your irregularities in Richmond were numerous, but measurably excusable in themselves from the many circumstances that attended them. Their present apparent enormity is of no greater magnitude, for the blackness with which they appear to be covered not being intentional, cannot be attached to the heart which suggested their commission. You should not allow your mind to brood over them as if committed in their present shape, nor should you lament your unfortunate origin and disgraceful relatives. And as for fortune, it shall be no source of uneasiness. You are heir to my separate property, which is fully competent to the utmost wishes of both you and Zerelda."

With observations like these, and the happiness of all around me, my spirits would awake to pleasing anticipations and participate in the enjoyment of my friends, but grief still held a settled residence in my heart, and frequently made its appearance by an involuntary sigh.

In the evening we visited the watering places, and places of amusement at the springs. We had not long been there before we beheld Armilda and her mother. Armilda was flaunting in the gayest apparel, and almost lost in a profusion of rich, fantastic drapery, and surrounded by a flippant crowd of beaux and coxcombs. We immediately turned in disgust from the sight, and walked to another part of the entertainment. Shortly after I was walking with Zerelda at some distance from our company, and again encountered Armilda and her throng. As they passed us, Armilda made a low, sarcastic curtsey, and turned with a triumphant laugh to her companions. Some of the company inquired who we were and we heard her reply: "A poor foundling boy, and the discarded mistress of a British officer." This was intolerable to the feelings of Zerelda; she almost sank at the sound, but her conscious pride arose above the insults of so insignificant a creature. We saw that they eyes of the whole company were fixed upon us in significant glances, and passed on our way in haste.

Armilda, seeing the tremor of Zerelda, observed, with a tone of contempt, "Poor thing. I pity her. She has seen hard times since she was deserted by her paramour."

"Sure no gentleman would let such a nice morsel suffer," replied one of the men, but as we had walked some distance away, we could not determine which. I entreated Zerelda not to let the sarcasms of such wretches affect her, but her feelings were too delicate for such brutal remarks, and she trembled as I led her to our company, where she now endeavored to compose her countenance, and not permit her friends to discover her weakness, or its cause.

When we returned to our dwelling, Anderville, who had been entreating Emerine for a return of his affection, renewed his solicitations. But the bounding flights of her vivacity were not yet divested of their coy versatility, and she replied to all his tenderness with lively sallies of wit and humor.

He turned to Zerelda, who was sitting near, and observed, "I wish you would instruct your cousin how to yield her heart to an adoring lover!"

"Zerelda has not learned the art herself," replied Emerine, "and I do not wish to exceed her in every folly and weakness."

"Mine is already yielded," replied Zerelda, "and if you wish for true enjoyment, you will also surrender to the solicitations of happiness."

"I will not capitulate at any rate," continued Emerine, "until I see how you succeed after the loss of your liberty."

I withdrew from the room to see a stranger whom the servants informed me was at the door. The stranger gave me a note in these words:

"Follow the bearer—destruction awaits you—fly, or it will be too late."

I told the bearer I would attend him in an instant, and stepped into the room for my hat.

Emerine was still holding out against the joint solicitations of Anderville and Zerelda. As I entered the room she observed to Zerelda, "You have seen and repented the effects of subjugation yourself, and to mitigate your chagrin you wish to see me in the same predicament."

"You are right, Emerine," I replied, "not to acknowledge your love for a man whose head might be taken off by a cannon ball tomorrow."

"Mercy! Brother, what do you mean?" exclaimed Emerine, affrighted.

"Here is a letter," said I. "The spring campaign will commence—"

Emerine apprehended, from my broken expressions, that Anderville was to go immediately to the war, and exclaimed with a tremor of alarm, "So soon! O! This is cruel!" She trembled and looked wishfully at Anderville.

"The out works are demolished," said I, "and if you do not seize the fortress you are no soldier."

"Thus, then, I seize the prize," cried the enraptured Anderville, clasping Emerine to his breast.

"Since you combine force and intrigue," said Emerine, with a blush, "I suppose I must resign, but I will make a refractory subject."

"Ours shall be a warfare of love," replied he, imprinting the bridal kiss on her lips.

Emerine raised her eyes with cheeks of splendid crimson; they were met by Zerelda's. "Aye," said Zerelda, "I thought the acknowledgment of a mutual passion was never to blow the rose on the cheek of Emerine." Emerine more deeply blushed the glow of mingled love and innocence, and withdrawing from Anderville's arms, retired to the window.

I now hastened to the bearer of the note. He conducted me along a secret path into a distant unfrequented wood. The feeble frame of an old man arose from a thicket and advanced, and my guide returned. The old man was masked; he took my arm and led me towards the thicket. I shuddered at the solemnity of his appearance and the mystery of his conduct, but moved almost mechanically along. He turned his eyes, perceived some person at a distance, and disappeared without having spoken a word.

I was amazed at such secrecy, but after waiting a considerable time without seeing him again, I returned to the dwelling. I imagined this ominous circumstance was to terminate in the disclosure of some new crime or source of horror, and trembled with the fearful palpitation of imaginary expected woe.

The company all discovered the dark change in my countenance, and began to make inquiries into the cause. When they heard it, although they were surprised, they endeavored to quiet my tremors with the supposition that the affair could lead to nothing serious.

But their arguments had no effect until Zerelda touched on the sweet, thrilling cord of our mutual affection. She laid her hand on my arm, as I was standing in silent abstraction at the window, and observed, "Is there no method of drawing you from these solitary musings? Has the elixir of love lost its efficacy? Or is it that Zerelda is no longer the object to which your affections center with delight?"

"Why these questions, Zerelda? Do you suppose my mind can lose you for a moment? Or ever cease to dote upon you as the magnet of my soul?"

"Why, then," continued she with a smile, "am I banished, or superceded by my dark rival, sorrow?" saying which, she laid her other hand on my shoulder.

"I am uneasy with myself," I replied, "but still am supremely blessed. Can I look at this face and be unhappy? This blush, this smile, this speaking soul reproves me for my murmurs. He that would call all those inestimable treasures his own, and yet complain, deserves not the sacred blessing."

"They are yours," said she with a smile beaming countenance of blushes and a look that ever makes me the object of her wishes.

Every gloomy foreboding vanished, every deep, imagined grief disappeared, and I beheld nothing in being but her sweet, expressive eye, her glowing cheek, her lovely lips, and that bright realm of lover's fancy, that ermined heaven that sleeps in expectation beneath her bosom's lawn "where they eye has never traveled," but where imagination feasts on raptures most divine. I clasped her to my heart, I pressed her lips, and my soul seemed there to fix its seal as they faintly quivered on mine.

A stranger rushed into the room. I turned my eyes and shrieked, "My God!" and started back in affright. The company were alarmed, but the specter hastening to me exclaimed, "I am not come to terrify, but render you happy. Listen but a moment."

I recovered from the sudden tremor occasioned by the sight of my father, whom I imagined I had slain, but yet trembled as I gazed on his dark and terrible aspect.

"I come," continued he, "to unravel all your life. I was not slain as you were informed, but prevailed upon the peasant to report that I was, that your apprehensions might be no longer tortured with

Unravel all your life

what might be the fate of the robber you supposed to be your father."

"Are you not my father?" exclaimed I.

"Listen to me," cried he. "I was affected with your generosity, and resolved to reward it by restoring you to the fortune of which you were deprived by Willford. For this purpose I disguised myself and got into her family as a servant, by which means I discovered where she concealed her private papers, and about a month since I broke open her desk and took everything that related to you or your estate. I perceived by perusing them that you had lived a life of unnecessary misery.

"Willford discovered that the papers were in my hands and used some endeavors to discover me and get them again, but supposing you were slain, she was not very uneasy until you returned to Bath and she discovered that I was already there. She directly employed an assassin to murder both you and myself, and endeavored to sell the whole Engleton estates. When I discovered her intention, I wrote you the note a few hours since, and intended to explain the whole affair, but I found we were discovered by the servant hired to assassinate us, and immediately retreated. About an hour since, I was approaching your dwelling when I was violently assailed in the dark by a person wrapped in a large cloak, but being prepared for defense, I gave him a wound and he fell. I directly called some assistance and conveyed him to a house, when by the light I discovered no other than Willford dressed in the habit of a man, in which condition she had been waiting for an opportunity to assassinate either you or myself.

"She immediately recovered, and was informed by a surgeon that her wound was mortal. She beheld me and became almost frantic, but when she returned to reason, she had the room cleared of all but myself and acknowledged the whole affair, wrote you a letter, and immediately expired. Her letter will explain the rest. Here are your papers; you will find a miniature of your father and mother in Willford's desk. Adieu. The man who has slain the mother of his children cannot stay to witness a scene of happiness." He darted out of the room and left us in astonishment.

265

I tore open Willford's letter and read:

"Evermont, I have fallen the victim of my own villainy, and have only time to do you that justice I refused you while living. You are the son of Sir William Albertus Valindon and his beloved Emerine."

"Great God! Is it possible?" exclaimed every person present.

My soul swelled into an unknown being at the thought. The letter fell, I raised my eyes and hands and exclaimed, "O heaven! Grant it." Anderville was the most composed. He took up the letter and proceeded.

"It was by my machinations that you were supposed to be mine. I bore a son by Huron, and made Sir William believe he was his father. After the death of your mother, to which I was not an accessory as you have imagined, he trusted you to my care. While he was absent in Baltimore, my son fell sick, and being confident he would die, and unwilling to lose the influence I possessed with Sir William, I circulated a report that it was you that was sick. My son died, but as it was some time since Sir William had seen his son, and the children being both very young, nearly of the same age and somewhat alike, he was easily induced to believe that his William was dead, and you were my son. Still thinking you his natural son, he willed you his estate. It was with the hope of gaining those estates to myself that I prevailed upon Huron to leave you near an Indian camp at a time and place which accords with the manner in which you were found by Evermont. But I had no idea of your existence until some time after you came to Richmond, when I discovered it by the mark of a wound under your hair which you received while an infant.

"This discovery I turned to a villainous purpose, for Engleton, who had obtained your estate, knew that if the heir of Sir William was in being, he would be bereft of all his property. When I informed him of the circumstance, he wished me to conceal it, which, together with the belief that Armilda was his daughter, who is also the child of Huron, enabled me to exercise an absolute sway over his mind, and at last to compel him to bequeath his estate to Armilda. But this he would not do until Zerelda consented to marry Barville, and then only on the condition that I would keep it a secret until the marriage was over. When Barville was about to depart, I thought the promise at an end, and showing him the will, engaged him to marry Armilda, but this intention she thwarted by her own conduct.

"O noble, injured Sir William, I die. Can you pardon a wretch like me? Huron will deliver you a sufficiency of documents to establish that you are the true Sir William Albertus Valindon, the son of a noble father and an angelic mother."

This dying confession unraveled the whole mystery of my existence. My soul, instantly relieved from the heavy weight of a disgraceful origin and a black catalogue of crimes, bounded with a lightness of joy it had never known to meet the transported bosoms of my wondering, enraptured relations, who, with the exulting acclamation of joyous amazement, flew to acknowledge and embrace their long lost cousin Albertus.

"My cousin! My Albertus!" exclaimed Zerelda, with her bosom on mine, her eyes swimming in raptures, and her heart leaping on her lips which were pressed on mine with the sweetest embrace ever tasted by the lips of a human.

My new aunt and cousin, Emerine, clasped me while still in the arms of Zerelda with a joy I never expected to excite or feel. Anderville participated in our happiness, and all the purest springs of delight were opened in our mutual bosoms, and all our mutual emotions were the glowing enthusiasm of unmingled rapture, untouched by the shadow of a pang.

It was long before my bosom was separated from Zerelda's, and when we were apart, Zerelda, like myself, knew not how to contain the floods of new emotion which swelled, sublimed, and overflowed her bliss-expanded soul. Transport reigned triumphant in her bosom, and beamed his divine effulgence on her countenance.

She had never been half so beautiful, and while she flew from me to embrace her aunt, her cousin, and Anderville, her form appeared as airy, ethereal, and majestic as the imagined sylph arrayed in robes of sunshine. Her jetty tresses streamed in the air, her eyes rolled their deep blue orbs in their brightest luster, shedding the divinity of her soul in dewy radiance; her cheeks were lighted by all the mingled smiles of love's rosy glow and the snow of innocence; her lips seemed to melt in fragrance and breathe ambrosial zephyrs to the shrine of love; and her bosom rose in throbbing ardor again its sacred curtain, which waved with the pressure, and O! The bliss fancy beheld within.

When she had embraced all around her, she flew again with an airy bound to my bosom, and clung almost too overjoyed to feel her happiness.

The next day the remains of Mrs. Willford were buried, and Huron disappeared. He flew to the wilds of Kentucky, as I afterward understood, and after becoming a true penitent and useful citizen, was killed in an engagement with the Indians.

Armilda also departed from Bath, inconceivably mortified with the loss of her ill-gotten fortune. She repaired to Richmond and lived for a while on the bounty of Emerald L—, who was deeply interested in retaining her friendship as she was acquainted with her connection with me. But Armilda soon grew tired of a life of dependence, and took up with a British ensign who bore her with him to Quebec, where she is yet living as his mistress. Emerald soon after married a considerable merchant with whom she lives in all the affection and innocence necessary for high life.

***

In the evening we repaired to Engleton seat and took possession of the vacant mansion. I immediately searched for, and found, the portraits of my parents. It was a picture drawn the day of their marriage and exhibited them in their most interesting appearance. I wept as I embraced it at the thought of losing such amiable parents, as they appeared to have been at so early an hour, before my memory had recorded one sweet embrace of my mother, or one kind parental look of my father.

The long contest between Great Britain and America was decided. The surrender of York completely opened the eyes of that blinded and oppressive nation to see the impossibility of enslaving the freeborn spirit of a determined people. The sword of slaughter was suspended. Preparations for peace began. Perseverance and liberty were triumphant. From the echoing cliffs of Erie to the broad St. Mary's the acclamations of "long live liberty and Washington" rode on the thunder of a million huzzas. The unanimous voice of a mighty people shouted a recognition of the rights of man from the bosom of the Atlantic to the boundless wilderness of the west. The star of freedom burst in dazzling majesty above the horizon of despotism, and shed irradiating smiles of liberty on a gazing, wondering world. The fire of independence was enkindled in the capacious bounds of the human bosom, and embryo empires blossomed in the desert.

Anderville received his discharge from the service of a grateful, exulting nation, and nothing now remained to consummate our happiness but the celebration of those rights by which he and I were united to my two charming cousins. The union of our hearts, which the registering angel had long since recorded in the calendar of heaven, was now celebrated in the genuine spirit of happiness, without the dead weight of pageantry or the incumbrance of an unmeaning crowd.

In the evening of that happy day, I assembled all the slaves of the Engleton and Valindon estates, and with the smiling approbation of Zerelda, declared that the *Bill of Rights*, drawn up by the immortal Jefferson and sanctioned by the united wisdom of congress, was a sacred truth, that *all men were born free*, and holding no commission from my Almighty father to enslave a brother, I gave to each the charter of his freedom.

The wild transports of their overflowing joy was a feast for the eyes of angels. It drew tears of rapture from my soul, and all our circle of friends wept with ecstasy. In this I only followed the example of my father, and my ever-memorable guardian, Major Haylard.

Those whom I liberated, I furnished with the means of living comfortably and becoming useful members of the community. To those families I distributed small farms, and accepted them as tenants of the estate, and enabled them to pursue the business of agriculture. Those who had no families still continued at the mansion and served for a reasonable hire.

Mrs. Haylard was anxious to continue at the springs in Bath, and knowing the strong predilection of Zerelda in favor of Haylard Village where she had experienced such strong evidences of my affection, proposed an exchange of the estates, to which all parties readily consented.

When the exchange was made, Emerine observed, "But Sir William, when you and Lady Valindon again teach the grotto to blossom, you need never expect to be rid of my company."

"You will ever be a welcome guest at the village," said I, "and joyfully received by Valindon and his Zerelda, but will never be received by Sir William or Lady Valindon, for no men or women with unmeaning titles, borrowed from our late oppressors, shall ever be the companions of that beloved retreat."

I immediately purchased the Valindon residence in Shenandoah, and ordered it to be fitted up, that with my Zerelda I might spend a part of every year among those scenes of my earliest infancy, which contained the venerable remains of my parents. And Anderville and I erected a mansion on the land where Major Haylard was slain, where Mrs. Haylard had already reared a monument to his memory, at which mansion we all regularly assembled at the anniversary of his death, and enjoyed a solemn delight in commemorating his departure.

After making preparations for these works, Zerelda and I returned to take possession of Haylard Village, accompanied by Anderville and his bride.

Ours was a journey of pleasure, and all the wild, variegated blooms of nature displayed its choicest beauties to charm our delighted senses, ravish our imaginations, and feast our soul with an Eden of delight. The pleasing majesty of the Blue Ridge wrapping its azure summit in the ethereal veil of the heavens, the picturesque imagery of a thousand undulating hills and sparkling streams, together with all the boundless fields of verdure arrayed in the green of May with all the flowery fascinations in the wild luxuriance of primeval beauty blushing on their bosom, could not fail to inspire all the enthusiastic ardor of blissful feelings—the sweet foretaste of anticipated heaven in the bright region of loving souls. But this delightful scenery, warbling with the living symphony of myriad musicians, swelling in varying tones and colors the sweet modulations of native melody on every hill and grove and spray, heightened by the soul of sympathy into reciprocal enjoyment and beautified by the glowing pencil of creative fancy, dipped in the ethereal rainbow beams of love, expanded our transported bosoms beyond the narrow pale of reality, and wafted them to the sylphiad of imagination where visionary bliss blossoms in an unfading spring of wonder and ecstasy.

***

Twelve months after this happy event, Zerelda was with me at the door of the grotto where May had opened her lap of roses and flung her blossoms on every bough. The ethereal was clear, the sun in his highest glory, and all nature in festivity. Zerelda leaned in my arms with her little son of three months old playing and smiling on her bosom, and listened to me with delight while I read a letter from Anderville informing us that Emerine was the mother of a cherub daughter. Zerelda's countenance brightened at the information, and her bosom turned to a sweeter contemplation of her own happiness, while the affection of the wife and the fondness of the mother mingled their loveliest graces in her features. I took the "embryo angel" in my embrace, and while Zerelda fixed on me a look of the most fascinating tenderness, observed, "Sweet babe, in whom thy father hopes to live in future ages, may thy life be free from the misfortunes of thy father and the sorrows of thy mother. But it shall be my care that you shall never be exposed to the temptations of the

271

one or the perils of the other. Thy mind shall be taught the precepts and practice of virtue and tenderness while yet on your mother's breast. And no rude African shall be permitted to instill his uncouth sentiments and contracted principles in your unsuspecting mind. The idea that you are a master shall never stimulate your infant bosom to cruelty or ambition. The excessive fondness of your parents will not be lavished to cherish the principles of capricious self-will and obstinacy, but to inform your heart in all the tender feeling sciences of gentleness and affection. Your mind will never be permitted to run wild in infancy with the hope of its being corrected in maturity, nor shall its native ardor be palled by a too-hasty accumulation of undigested intelligence, nor its genius curbed by being led into a channel variant from its inclinations. A mother's smiles shall lead you into benevolence and love, and a father's unremitting attention shall store your mind with those sciences and principles which will be necessary in the service of your country, which is rapidly ascending to a blazing majesty—a zenith of glory unknown in the annals of nations."

I teased. Zerelda took the child from my arms. It clung to her breast. The lovely burden gave more delightful sensations to her heart, and ineffable sweetness to her countenance. I wrapped my arms more closely around her, strained her with more delight to my bosom, and pressed her cheeks to mine, my lips to hers, with indescribable emotion.

Farewell, ye hated haunts of dissipation—ye billowy wilds of uncurbed passion where mortals, hoping still and still deluded in random search of joy, from wave to wave desponding tumble, and all ye blasting scenes of sensual pastime, a long adieu—here I will rest. In the sweet paradise of social bliss I will repose my soul. This is the magic fountain from whence springs all of good or great—from whence the spirit flows that warms the whole human bosom, and sheds the animating energy throughout universal nature.

FINIS

272

ABOUT THE AUTHOR

Abigail Davis was born in the Catskill Mountains in 1950, graduated from Ithaca College in 1972 and obtained a Master's degree in English and Creative Writing from the University of Minnesota in 1992. Her published work includes a historical novel, *Hanging Katherine Garret: A Novel Based on the 1737 Trial of a Pequot Woman* (Heritage Books, 2003), and more than 200 travel essays, book reviews and interviews; her short stories have appeared in a variety of periodicals and anthologies.

Davis was the first woman pilot hired by Northwest Airlines in 1979. She retired from flying in 1993 as an Airbus A320 captain with more than 18,000 flight hours, 20 trips around the world and seven years of part-time residence in Asia. Twice elected to office in the International Society of Women Airline Pilots, she served as vice president from 1982-84 and president from 1984-86.

Davis is a Ph.D. candidate at the University of Minnesota specializing in early American literature and history; her minor focus is in Literacy and Rhetorical Studies.

Davis divides her time between Minneapolis and her hometown in upstate New York.

Typos

42 or
48 it (5)
69 with (wish)
76 seem (see)
    th (the)
91 then (them)
115 the (to)
126 Repeated line
225 resolved
129 like - life
132 dies (die)
136 sail (assail)
145 alter (altar)
148 ∫ = of
159 read - led
162 might (y)
    fu = (is)

166 pocketbook
168 work ?
171 a = and

193 know (know
197 her (he)

200 writing (sittin
201 a (and?)
223 is

225 resolv
230 packed
    (packe
232 mood
    (rode
264 they (t